Rebecca Winters lives in Salt Lake City, Utah. With canyons and high alpine meadows full of wildflowers, she never runs out of places to explore. They, plus her favourite vacation spots in Europe, often end up as backgrounds for her romance novels—because writing is her passion, along with her family and church. Rebecca loves to hear from readers. If you wish to email her, please visit her website at www.cleanromances.net.

Lynne Marshall used to worry she had a serious problem with daydreaming, and then she discovered she was supposed to write those stories down! A late bloomer, she came to fiction writing after her children were nearly grown. Now she battles the empty nest by writing romantic stories about life, love and happy endings. She's a proud mother and grandmother who loves babies, dogs, books, music and traveling.

Also by Rebecca Winters

Her Magnate's Holiday Proposal

The Billionaire's Club miniseries
Return of Her Italian Duke
Bound to Her Greek Billionaire
Whisked Away by Her Sicilian Boss

Holiday with a Billionaire miniseries
Captivated by the Brooding Billionaire

And look out for the next book
Available June 2018

Also by Lynne Marshall

Her Perfect Proposal
A Doctor for Keeps
The Medic's Homecoming
Courting His Favorite Nurse
Forever a Father
Miracle for the Neurosurgeon
A Mother for His Adopted Son
200 Harley Street: American Surgeon in London
Her Baby's Secret Father
Wedding Date with the Army Doc

Discover more at millsandboon.co.uk

CAPTIVATED BY THE BROODING BILLIONAIRE

REBECCA WINTERS

SOLDIER, HANDYMAN, FAMILY MAN

LYNNE MARSHALL

MILLS & BOON

First Published in Great Britain 2018
by Mills & Boon, an imprint of HarperCollinsPublishers,
1 London Bridge Street, London, SE1 9GF

Captivated by the Brooding Billionaire © 2018 Rebecca Winters
Soldier, Handyman, Family Man © 2018 Janet Maarschalk

ISBN: 978-0-263-26487-6

38-0418

MIX
Paper from
responsible sources
FSC™ C007454

This book is produced from independently certified FSC™
paper to ensure responsible forest management.

For more information visit: www.harpercollins.co.uk/green

Printed and bound in Spain
by CPI, Barcelona

CAPTIVATED BY THE BROODING BILLIONAIRE

REBECCA WINTERS

To my beloved, generous, marvellous parents,
who let their teenage daughter attend school
in Switzerland, where a whole world opened up
to her that she'd never dreamed about or imagined.
To have been born to such wonderful parents
is my greatest blessing.

PROLOGUE

"NIGEL?"

A tap on the opened office door caused Abby Grant to look up from the desk. During this year's summer and fall semesters at San José State University in California, she and Nigel, the visiting professor from Cambridge, England, had offices in the same literature department. They'd fallen in love and often worked side by side in one office or the other while they planned a spring wedding.

"Dr. Belmont is teaching his final class before Christmas break," she said to the thirtyish brunette woman dressed in a suit. Maybe she was a student, but Abby didn't recognize her. "He should be finished at noon. I'm Ms. Grant, one of the teachers in the department. Would you like to leave a message for him with me? I'll make sure he gets it."

"That won't be necessary," the woman said in a British accent as strong as Nigel's. He'd let Abby know right away he spoke an "estuary" dialect. "I'm Lucy Belmont, Nigel's wife. I need to speak to him in person, so I'll wait in here until he returns."

Abby blinked in surprise. "I'm afraid you've come to the wrong place. The Nigel Belmont who's a visiting professor here doesn't have a wife."

A tight smile broke out on Lucy Belmont's face. "Indeed he does and two children. They're expecting a visit from him over Christmas. Here are some pictures taken last spring."

The woman handed a packet to Abby, who opened it and saw Nigel in photo after photo with this woman and two children.

Abby took the packet with shaking hands. Was this some kind of a joke? Could this woman be a sister-in-law or even a sister Abby had never heard of? Or was she a woman who had some pathetic attachment to Nigel? None of this made sense. Abby and Nigel were planning their wedding!

Not wanting to get into anything unpleasant with Lucy until she'd talked to Nigel, Abby got up from the desk. "I had no idea. Of course, you're welcome to stay here. He should be back in about fifteen minutes. If you'll excuse me."

With her heart racing, Abby left the room and hurried down the hallway to the stairs. The lecture theaters were one story below. She slipped inside the room of thirty plus students and sat down at the back while she waited for Nigel to finish up his lecture.

He was popular with the students and looked the part of the jaunty professor in his tweed jacket with his dark blond hair brushed back.

She knew he had spotted her, but he continued talking and finally excused his students so they could enjoy the holiday.

When the last one left the room, Nigel gathered up his briefcase and walked toward her, giving her a quick kiss on her lips. "To what do I owe this unexpected visit from my beautiful fiancée?"

Abby stared hard at him, not wanting to believe what she was thinking. "There's a woman waiting for you in your office who says she's your wife. She introduced herself as Lucy Belmont and showed me pictures of her with you and two children. Please tell me this is a joke." Her throbbing voice reverberated in the room.

Nigel didn't move a muscle, but the light faded from his eyes. The change was enough to tell her the other woman had been speaking the truth. Pain almost incapacitated her. She backed away from him. "So she *is* your wife!"

He shook his head. "Look, Abby. It's a long story. We've been separated close to a year. The divorce will be final soon. You have to listen to me. I would have eventually told you, but—"

"What kind of a man are you?" she broke in on him, destroyed by his admission. "To think we've been together all this time and a whole other part of your life has been a huge secret—"

In a flash, the happy world Abby had inhabited had disintegrated.

You've been in love with a cunning, monstrous, devious cheat!

Abby had often heard the expression about blood draining from a person's face. She knew that was happening to her now and feared she would be sick right in front of him. Besides betraying her and his spouse, how many other women had he deceived? Those poor children.

She took off the engagement ring and flung it at him before dashing out of the room to the hallway. The second she reached the restroom, she retched until nothing more came up.

When she was able to stand without holding on to the sink, she hurried upstairs to her own office for her purse and left the campus. In her pain she needed to talk to the people she trusted and loved. Instead of driving to her apartment near the campus, she headed for her parents' home in San José.

Abby stayed with her parents for several days, after which she talked with Dr. Stewart, the head of her department, about her situation. Once she'd told Dr. Stewart the truth, Abby asked if she could have a leave of absence for the next semester.

To her great relief she was granted a leave and also offered an opportunity to do some research abroad in Europe until the summer. After experiencing a world of pain, nothing could have suited her better than to get away. Best of all, she was assured that Dr. Belmont would no longer be on the staff at San José State and would be teaching at a college back east. She would never have to see him again.

After Christmas, Abby flew to LA for a week's worth of meetings to collaborate with two other women on the project before going overseas. Ginger Lawrence and Zoe

Perkins, who both had similar literature backgrounds from Stanford and UCLA respectively, had also been hired. The three of them, close in age, bonded fast. The thought of going to Europe with the girls gave Abby something to look forward to and the courage to make some changes in her life. So, before returning to San José to pack and leave for Europe with them, Abby decided to get a makeover and visited a beauty salon.

The lady in charge told her to be seated. While Abby waited, she poured through some magazines. In a few minutes one of the hairdressers beckoned her over to the chair. Abby took the magazine with her.

"What can I do for you?"

"I'd like you to cut and style my hair like *this*!" She showed her the picture she liked most. It was a bouncy bob with graduated layers. Each curled layer ending somewhere between the chin and the shoulders. She wanted something in between.

"Are you sure? All this long gold hair cut off?" The hairdresser acted shocked, as if Abby had asked for something sinful. How funny. Why did this woman care what she wanted?

Three weeks ago Abby had cut Nigel Belmont out of her life so fast, he hadn't seen it coming. After Christmas he'd tried to talk to her once on the phone and she'd told him to go to hell in so many words. She'd meant it and it had felt good!

Cutting her hair was her last act to separate herself from any semblance to the old Abby—she'd since vowed never to be duped by a man again.

The woman shook her head, but she did as Abby

asked. An hour later she almost squealed in delight after looking in the mirror. Abby hardly recognized herself. Her apple-green eyes appeared larger and she thought she actually looked her age of twenty-six instead of the tired-looking thirty she'd seemed to be. She'd needed something simple and easy. That was the whole idea!

Abby paid the woman a nice tip. Before leaving the salon, she had to tiptoe over her long locks of silvery-blond hair but did it with no regrets.

CHAPTER ONE

Five months later

WITH HER LAPTOP packed between the sweaters in her suitcase, Abby left the bedsitter in Cologny, Switzerland, where she'd been staying for the last two weeks, and took a taxi to the train station in Geneva, Switzerland.

With her massive research project finished, today marked the first day of her vacation. No longer restricted to suits and dresses, Abby had pulled on her favorite pair of jeans and a crew neck, short sleeve white-on-black print blouse. She had the whole month of June to have fun before returning to San José.

Abby couldn't wait to be with her friends again. They'd Skyped and phoned each other—sent emails—but it would be great to do things together in person.

Once in graduate school she'd become a teaching assistant in the humanities department and had worked hard. Specializing in the romance writers of the early nineteenth century, she'd received her doctorate, after which she'd been given more classes to teach. That's when she'd met Nigel. In hindsight, what a disaster that meeting had turned out to be!

But she'd learned she wasn't the only one who'd been burned in a relationship. One of the girls, Zoe, had just come out of a bitter divorce because her husband had been unfaithful. She'd insisted she would never want anything to do with a man again. Abby didn't need to get inside Zoe's skin to understand how she felt.

The pain of putting your trust in the man you loved only to discover he hadn't loved you or believed in the sanctity of marriage had been too devastating. Abby felt like her heart had been murdered. How could she ever trust anyone again?

As for Ginger, she'd lost her husband recently to cancer and needed to get away from the pain. In a short time the three of them had developed a special camaraderie, and all three of them were ready to play.

Being in an especially good mood, Abby gave the driver a nice tip and walked inside the train station with her suitcase. Since she had fifteen minutes before she needed to board her train, she headed directly for her favorite food kiosk. She'd eaten here every time she'd needed to take the train someplace.

After making her selection of six small quiches, two for herself and two for each her friends, she bought a second-class ticket and boarded the crowded train.

She found a compartment and sat down across from a priest and a couple of teenagers speaking German. They started to listen to rock music, but their earphones didn't block the sound all that much. Abby didn't mind. Not so the priest, who finally got up and left the compartment.

She decided she would wait to eat until she met the girls at the village of St. Saphorin, an hour and a half or so and a quick change of trains away.

The quiet, efficient train ran alongside Lake Geneva, the famous croissant-shaped lake called lac Léman by the locals. Abby settled back, almost preening like a cat in the sun because she was so happy to be free of responsibilities. The train glided from one picturesque village to another in a gentle rhythm.

The surroundings that included the sapphire-blue lake with the snow-crested French Alps in the distance mes-merized her. Before long she had to change trains and it wasn't long after that that St. Saphorin appeared, wedged between the water and terraced rows of vineyards that ran up the steep hillsides.

When the train came to a stop, she reached for her suitcase and left the compartment. Several other pas-sengers had already descended. Finally, she was going to see her friends. Abby was eager to be with them and on vacation.

Yesterday Zoe had flown to Venice, Italy, from Ath-ens, Greece, to meet up with Ginger who'd been doing research in Italy. The two of them had boarded the night train to Switzerland. They'd planned to get off in Montreux to pick up the rental car and drive the few ki-lometers to St. Saphorin.

Relieved to be here, Abby walked around to the front of the station. There was no sign of the girls yet. She sat down and took in the sight of the Jura Mountains in the distance while she waited. After twenty minutes, she phoned Ginger and had to leave a message. Then she called Zoe, who answered.

"Abby? Are you in St. Saphorin?"

"Yes. Where are you?"

"The rental car we were promised isn't ready yet. Too many tourists were booked. Ginger is dealing with them now. It may be a while, so I phoned the château where we'll be staying. Someone will come for you soon. I gave them a description of you. Just stay put. We can't wait to see you!"

"Same here," Abby said before hanging up.

Someone was coming to get her, but it could be a while. She reached for a quiche and savored every bite. In the distance, she took in the vision of gray stone walls and steep inclines covered by the famous Lavaux vine-yards of the region. They were riddled with hiking trails, a sport the Swiss adored. So, did Abby. She loved the yellowish colors of the homes spotting the landscape.

How lucky she and the girls were to be the recipients of their boss's largesse! Magda Collier, one of the most acclaimed female film directors in Hollywood had hired the three of them to do research for a movie being pro-duced by a revered mogul friend of hers.

After the New Year, Magda had brought Abby and the girls together in Los Angeles for a week with some writers who were working on an important script. She wanted to create a historically authentic film that accen-tuated the positive aspects of the colorful life of Lord Byron, the famous British romantic poet and satirist.

They'd been thrilled about the project and had be-come friends.

Magda had assigned each of them a different area in Europe to do research, and Abby had been sent to Switzerland. Now, because of their "great work"—Magda's words after they'd turned in their information—she'd delighted them with a reward. It turned out to be a vacation at a château and vineyard called the Clos de la Floraison on the shores of Lake Geneva. Nothing could have pleased them more.

Magda explained she had a permanent arrangement with the old owner of the vineyard. From time to time she used it for herself and guests to enjoy. They could stay there while they did all the touring they wanted around the region.

Since the three of them had to return to their teaching assignments for the upcoming fall semester, they planned to take advantage of this time together and sightsee to their hearts' content.

As they had another month before going back to the US, Abby was also hoping to find evidence of a poem that Lord Byron had been rumored to write called *Labyrinths*, or some such title, while he'd been in Switzerland. But it was a work that had never seen the light of day and many experts dismissed it as sheer fiction. But Abby hadn't given up on the possibility of finding out the truth, if it existed.

Recently a fragment of a memoir by Claire Clairmont, who'd traveled in Switzerland with Byron, had been found in a branch of New York public library. It had shed new light on Lord Byron and Shelley. What Abby would give to unearth a find equally sensational, but no amount of digging had been successful so far.

While Abby sat there beneath a sunny sky, wondering where else she and the girls might look while they were here for the month, she noticed a vintage black Renault drive up and park.

Out stepped a tall man, maybe early thirties, who stood fit and lean. With his overly long black wavy hair, he epitomized her idea of the quintessential drop-dead sensational male. She didn't know such a person existed.

Only a Frenchman had that appeal, the kind she'd conjured in her mind and fantasized about from time to time growing up. He had an expression much like the one she'd seen on the French actor Charles Boyer who had played the lead in a famous old film classic *The Garden of Allah*.

Abby had been a teenager when she'd first watched it and had fallen in love with the actor. He played the part of a monk who ran away from a monastery in North Africa and fell in love with an Englishwoman. They went out in the desert together, but he carried a terrible secret.

At times his sadness combined with his male beauty was almost painful to watch. Abby had watched it over and over again. His performance had seemed so real that she always been haunted by him and had decided there was no Frenchman alive more captivating.

Until now.

Abby couldn't take her eyes off the stranger, something that had never happened to her before, not with Nigel or the boyfriend she'd loved earlier in her life. There was a brooding aura about him that caught at her emotions though she fought not to be attracted.

Who was he? Where had such a man come from?

Abby felt as if he was burdened by a great weight. It was there in the way he carried himself. The lines radiating from his eyes and around his mouth spelled pain. His work clothes, a white shirt with the sleeves shoved up to the elbows and dark trousers, told her he'd stopped whatever he'd been doing to get in his car and drive here.

This was the magnificent someone who'd come for her?

His bronzed complexion, close to a teak color, overlay chiseled features. The man worked in the sun. Beneath black brows his midnight-black eyes met hers and roved over her with an intensity that sent a ripple of sensation through her. She trembled for no good reason, something she couldn't prevent.

There was an unrehearsed sensuality about the way his hard mouth smiled almost derisively, as if he knew she'd shivered slightly and found it amusing. Even though he'd caught her staring, she refused to avert her eyes. Her pulse raced as he approached her.

"Mademoiselle Grant?"

Those two words, spoken in a deep seductive voice, curled their way through to her insides. She heard no trace of the singsong French spoken in this part of Switzerland. He was a Frenchman down to every atom of his hard-muscled body.

"Yes. You must be from La Floraison."

He nodded. "I was told to look for a woman with golden hair." His excellent, heavily accented English came as a shock.

"You have the advantage. They didn't tell me your name."

"Raoul Decorvet."

"I thought Magda's friend was a great deal older."

"He was. Sadly, Auguste died a month ago at the age of eighty."

"Oh, no—" she cried. "We didn't know. Magda didn't tell us."

"You weren't supposed to know."

Abby shook her head. "I don't understand."

"I'm here negotiating the sale of this property business for the former owner. Auguste had a bad heart so he never knew how long he had to live. The vineyard managers, Louis and Gabrielle, have said that you and your friends are welcome to stay here for the month. I was on hand when Gabrielle received a distress call from your friends. She was busy so I offered my help."

"Thank you, but this isn't right. We don't want to put anyone out."

Again, she felt his penetrating gaze wander over her, missing nothing before it rested on her hair. "It's no imposition. If you'll get in the car, I'll explain while I drive you to the château."

His potent male charisma made her so aware of him, it was hard to act natural. She felt nervous. After her experience with Nigel, Abby was almost frightened by her visceral response to this total stranger who blew away every man she'd ever known. He reached for her suitcase and helped her into the front passenger seat before putting it in the back.

After he'd started the car, she said, "I'm sorry you had to come for me. I could have waited until my friends showed up. Providing taxi service is hardly the work of a busy Realtor."

"Pas de problème."

Abby was sure that wasn't true, but Raoul Decorvet had a certain air of authority. She didn't want to argue with him since he'd put himself out on her behalf, so she kept quiet while he started the car. They headed toward the road and wound around the village toward the hillside. En route she detected a flowery scent.

"What is that fragrance I can smell in the air?"

"La Floraison is greeting you."

She studied his striking profile. "What do you mean?"

"The flowers of the grape vines open in June. This is the reason why Magda wanted you to come now. For the next fifteen days, they'll emit their intoxicating perfume while they undergo automatic pollination. Their dual reproductive organs, mostly female among the male, ensure the future of the species." Their glances fused. "Nature's way is remarkable, *n'est-ce pas*?"

For some reason the subject of their conversation sounded personal, especially the way he said it in that deep, silky voice. It brought heat to Abby's cheeks. "Have you found a buyer yet?" she asked in order to change the subject, hoping to break his spell over her.

"Oui. It's already done. The new owner will take possession at the end of June."

"Please don't tell me you put it off for the benefit of me and my friends."

"For your information, it's to honor the commitment Auguste made. While you're here, Gabrielle will take care of you. You'll be staying in the unattached farmhouse next to the château and should be comfortable there."

"I'm sure it will be wonderful." Magda had seen to that, but the appearance of this fascinating Frenchman had knocked the foundations out from under her.

Before long the château came into view. Abby marveled at the gray stone structure. It reminded her of a small fortress and caught at her imagination. In former times it would have been a commanding landmark.

He drove them along rows of lush vineyards in full flower and past a thriving vegetable garden until they arrived at a charming farmhouse with a mansard roof.

"There's Gabrielle now. It's getting late in the day. She'll make something for you to eat if you're hungry."

"No, no. I'll wait for my friends."

Abby spotted the wiry, middle-aged woman wearing a straw hat with a broad rim, who came around the side of the farmhouse. She was dressed in slacks and a tunic.

"Bonjour!"

The woman's warm smile made Abby feel welcome. She got out of the car, liking her already. *"Bonjour, Madame."*

"Soyez la bienvenue!"

"Merci. Thank you."

"I see Raoul found you." The Swiss people impressed her with their ability to speak good English. "My husband is up in the higher vineyard and I was doing some pruning. When your friends called about their difficulty, Raoul volunteered to take our car and go for you."

"I'm very grateful to both of you."

"I understand they should be here soon. Come inside

with me." She reached for Abby's suitcase. "We have five bedrooms with en suite bathrooms. Since you are the first one to arrive, you may have your pick."

"This is exciting. I've been looking forward to this vacation for a long time."

Abby turned to Raoul. He was too gorgeous and too intriguing. She should be relieved to say goodbye to him, yet deep down she would rather have stayed outside to talk to him, which was crazy. He had the power to sweep any woman away, especially Abby. She couldn't believe her feelings were so strong, not when she'd promised herself never to get seriously involved with any man for the rest of her life.

"Thank you for picking me up."

His brooding dark eyes narrowed on her features. Again, she sensed he was in some kind of turmoil. She could feel it. "Don't forget this." He handed her the purse she'd left in the car.

What on earth was wrong with her? In his company she'd forgotten all about it and had left it lying on the seat. The slight contact of skin against skin sent another shiver through her body. *"À bientôt, mademoiselle."*

She knew that phrase well enough. It meant "see you soon." To read any real meaning into it meant she was a fool. But he *had* called her *mademoiselle*. Maybe he'd noticed she wore no rings. For that matter she hadn't seen a wedding ring on his finger either, but that didn't necessarily mean he wasn't married.

Abby turned and followed Gabrielle inside the house, but her mind was filled with unanswered questions about him. Why would a French Realtor be doing business here?

Maybe he lived on the French side of Lac Léman and was authorized to operate in both countries. In that case he wouldn't be staying at the château. If he had a car, where was it? She wondered if he'd be leaving soon. The manager would know the answers, but if Abby were to ask her anything, it would suggest she was interested.

Don't do this, Abby. Don't be a fool.

Gabrielle led her through the beamed common rooms. She found the restored nineteenth-century farmhouse warm and inviting. They went upstairs to the bedrooms. Each had a mini fridge filled with drinks, and every room had a basket filled with fruit and Swiss chocolate.

Abby chose a room that looked out over the vineyard to the west. She could see the estate workers. One of them was probably Louis. Of course there was no sign of Raoul.

"If you need anything, pick up the bedside phone and ring the château. I'll answer. Your friends know to come straight to the farmhouse. Your breakfast will be laid out at seven every morning in the dining room."

Abby turned to Gabrielle. "Everything is perfect. Will it be all right to open the window? I love the fragrance coming from the vineyard."

"Of course."

"Thank you."

"De rien. À tout à l'heure, mademoiselle."

CHAPTER TWO

AFTER GABRIELLE LEFT, Abby undid the lever and pushed the window open. The smell was divine. She unpacked her suitcase. With that done she put her purse and laptop on a round table in the corner around which several upholstered chairs had been arranged.

The bathroom contained every amenity. Once she'd refreshed herself and put on her frosted tangerine-colored lipstick, she went downstairs and walked outside.

There was no point in lying to herself. While Abby waited for the girls, she felt compelled to see Raoul again and couldn't understand it. What was it about him? How could he create all these feelings and yearnings roiling inside of her in one short meeting?

Again, she had to question her sanity after what she'd experienced with Nigel. But she'd never felt like this with him. Not even close. Their attraction had grown over time with mutual interests.

Nothing could match this violent explosion of feelings that had made her heart trip over itself from the moment Raoul got out of the old Renault and walked toward her. The Frenchman had caused her to forget the lesson she'd thought she'd learned following Nigel's treachery.

Something was definitely wrong with her. It scared her that she was so drawn to him. Afraid of her feelings, Abby ran back toward the farmhouse and waited in front to watch for her friends.

She checked her watch. Since boarding the train, time had gotten away from her. It said 5:00 p.m. Concerned at this point, she pulled out her cell to call them. But just then she saw a dark red car pull up. She put the phone away and ran toward them.

"You're here at last!"

Her friends got out and both hugged Abby. Zoe smiled at her. "You look great!"

"So you do you guys."

"Sorry we're so late, but nothing's perfect."

"It doesn't matter. I'm thankful we're all here in one piece."

"Obviously you were picked up at the station."

An image of Raoul flashed through her mind, causing her body to melt like butter in the sun. "Their Realtor picked me up."

Ginger eyed her. "What Realtor is that?"

"Why don't we drive to the cheese fondue restaurant Magda told us about and I'll tell you everything. But first let's get you settled."

When the girls heard the news about Auguste, they would feel as sad as she had. Abby decided that it would be better to prolong their happiness by eating first. "Sounds great."

The three of them hugged again. She helped carry

their things inside and led them up the stairs. "You have your choice of four rooms."

Zoe entered a room with an antique armoire and declared it her home away from home. Her dark blond hair worn in a windblown style had new highlights streaked by the sun while she'd been in Greece. With her azure blue eyes she was a knockout.

Abby's friends were both attractive. Ginger's gray eyes combined with her cap of black curls made her look French. She could be taken for a movie star. They inspected the other three rooms and she chose one that looked out on the lake. After opening her window, Ginger turned to them.

"I'm starving, you guys. We had to wait forever for the car. I say we unpack later and go eat!"

"You won't get an argument out of me." Abby ran to her bedroom for her purse and hurried outside with the girls.

Since Ginger had done the negotiating, she was the designated driver. That was fine with Abby who kept her eyes glued for any sign of Raoul, but he didn't make an appearance. She should be thankful, not crushed that she might never see him again.

Determined to put him out of her mind, she sat back, resigned to enjoy the bucolic scenery. But that was easier said than done. Raoul's image wouldn't leave her mind.

Zoe served as navigator and pulled the directions Magda had given them out of her purse. "We have to drive to the small village of Chexbres, which according to Magda is seven hundred feet above the lake. We should pass through the most important Swiss wine region. Apparently their main product is a table grape wine."

"The Swiss call it *chasselas*," Abby added her two cents. She loved the sound of the word. "I've learned a lot about it while I've been working here."

They drove higher, gasping over the landscape. "You guys—" Ginger cried out. "Look at those rows of grape vines going up that steep hill! It's amazing!"

"That's why they have to be terraced," Abby explained. "Sometimes they use pulleys and have to be irrigated because the Rhône valley can get warm and dry here."

Zoe had opened her window. "I love this climate. Smell that air. Delicious."

Her comment reminded Abby of those moments with Raoul when he'd told her about the fragrance from the flowers at La Floraison. Nature truly was remarkable to have created a man like him, but she kept that memory to herself.

They continued to drive until they reached the town of Chexbres with its magnificent view. "There it is! The Lion d'Or." Ginger pulled over to the curb near the restaurant and they went inside for a feast of cheese fondue eaten with French bread.

Their hunger was at a pitch and they ate every morsel of bread accompanied by goblets of *chasselas*.

"Before we plan what we're going to do tomorrow, tell us about this Realtor who picked you up. You've been kind of quiet about that."

Abby looked at Zoe. The time had come. "I have

something important to tell you guys. It came as a shock to me."

"What?" Ginger asked.

"Magda's friend Auguste, the owner of the château, died last month."

Both girls fell back into their seats. "What?"

"I think the man who came to get me must be a Realtor because he's been here selling the estate. His name is Raoul Decorvet. We've been allowed to stay on until the end of June when the new owner takes possession. It's Magda's wish."

Ginger frowned. "You're kidding! She never said anything. We can't go on living here now. It wouldn't be right." Zoe shook her head in agreement.

Abby knew that would be the girls' reaction. "I feel the same way. Since we're in Europe, where would you guys like to go? I need to conserve my funds, but I've been budgeting in my mind. I believe I have enough money to spend two weeks here. What about you two?"

They both figured two weeks would be all they could afford.

"Any ideas where you'd like to go?"

Zoe took a deep breath. "If I had the chance, I'd fly back to Greece in a minute."

That didn't surprise Abby. Their divorced friend hadn't said anything, but Abby sensed there was a man involved. "What part exactly?"

"Patras. I didn't get to spend nearly enough time in that area."

"Maybe we could take a small tour of some of the Greek Islands too. What do you think, Ginger?"

"Not that I wouldn't love to travel there, but to be honest, I'd rather go back to Italy. There's so much to see and it's so glorious. I couldn't get enough of it." By the tone in her voice, Abby wondered if Ginger had also experienced some kind of romantic interest.

As for Abby, she'd met a mysterious Frenchman earlier today, but it was best she never saw him again. "Where do you want to visit in Italy, Ginger?"

"Venice. It's the most romantic city on earth."

Well, well. Their friend *did* have a reason to want to go back. Abby was sure of it.

"I have an idea. If we pool our resources, we can afford a two-week vacation. Maybe we could drive to Venice tomorrow and spend a few days there before visiting Rome. From there we'll fly to Patras and tour around that area for a week before we go back to California. What do you think?"

Ginger looked at Zoe before she said, "What do *you* want to do, Abby?"

She wanted to stay longer and see if she could find that rumored poem, but it probably didn't exist. "I've been living in Switzerland since January and am ready for a new adventure." Which was true.

"Not even one guy has caught your eye who wants you to hang around?"

Zoe had just given herself away.

Abby shook her head. "I'm not ready to meet a man."

Ginger's eyebrows shot up. "You will be when the right one comes along."

Someone out of this world *had* come along earlier today, but she needed to run from him and keep running. "Let's change the subject. Are you guys on board with our plans?"

"According to Magda, we have to visit the Maison Cailler Chocolate Factory in Broc," Zoe interjected. "She has already paid for us to take the tour. Why don't we at least do that tomorrow to make her happy?"

Abby eyed them both. "I toured that plant in March. It's really worth the time. While you do that, I'd like to do a little more research on Byron while we're in St. Saphorin.

"Maybe you guys should drop me off at the local library in the village. That's one place I haven't visited. Then I'll walk back to the farmhouse and wait for you. If you two leave in the morning, you'll be back by afternoon and we can leave for Italy." Magda was funding their rental car.

They agreed it was a great idea and drove back to the château. If Raoul Decorvet was still around in the morning, Abby didn't plan to be here. She would be insane to hope they might see each other again. She had the fear that getting involved with a man who made her feel this besotted without even knowing him could destroy her.

After a shower and shave, Raoul Capet Regnac Decorvet, the elder son of the duke of the Vosne-Romanée region in the Burgundy department of France, concluded his business with the new owner of La Floraison.

Once Raoul had assured him he'd be back at the end of June to tie up any loose ends, he hung up the phone and ate the breakfast Gabrielle had brought to his room in the château. He drank more coffee and made half a dozen calls to members of his staff while he looked down from the upstairs window that faced the courtyard.

The three women had left early in their rental car and hadn't returned. He knew from Gabrielle they hadn't checked out. To his shock, Mademoiselle Grant hadn't left his thoughts all night. He was overwhelmed by unfamiliar feelings for her that made him desperate to see her again. It astounded him he should have these desires when he'd only spent a few minutes with her. Nothing like this had ever happened to him in his life.

Raoul had of course enjoyed relationships with women from time to time growing up. It had been his destiny to marry the woman his father had demanded he marry, but he had felt nothing like this. Two years ago his wife and baby had tragically died in a car accident. Since then he'd been a slave to work.

When he came to Switzerland on business, he'd never dreamed he'd meet a woman who seemed to have invaded his mind, his psyche, his body the way she'd done yesterday. He couldn't explain it, but her effect on him had brought him alive.

His senses were involved from the moment he'd seen her sitting on the bench at the train station seemingly happy on her own. She'd made a breathtaking picture.

The sun's rays had turned her hair to liquid gold. Instead of wearing sunglasses like the typical tourist, she'd been drinking in the landscape and had that look of a young woman on the brink of life.

He could feel her reacting to everything she saw. It made him breathless with excitement to observe her. She'd been in sync with his emotions when she'd wanted to know about that fragrance in the air. That aspect of her had fascinated him on a level that went deep beneath the surface.

There was a quality of innocence that appealed to him too. A gift like that wasn't present in the women who inhabited his world and certainly not within the confines of his own family. If innocence had been there once upon a time, their lifestyle and entitlements had robbed them of such an enticing virtue.

Why did he have to discover it now, with this woman who would be returning to the States shortly? She could never mean anything to him. Yet she already did mean something to him in a way that was so profound he couldn't let it go.

Lines darkened his Gallic features. They would never cross paths again unless he made it happen. The longer he sat there, the stronger his resolve grew to see her again. He needed to explore these powerful feelings or lose his mind.

While he contemplated an idea that had been percolating in his brain all through the night, his cell rang. It was his private secretary getting back to him. He picked up.

"Félix?"

"You were right. Jules didn't think it was time yet, but he checked and said black rot *has* shown up in the *terroir* to the north."

"I knew it," Raoul murmured. "The weather has been warmer than usual. Even though I'll be home tomorrow, tell him to get started on the fungicide immediately. By now the infection is releasing spores."

"I'll get right on it."

"Don't let him put up an argument. The spray will stop this infection prior to the bloom period. Last year the spore production didn't happen this soon. I've told Jules all along this has to be checked every year due to weather changes. We may have to add an additional fungicide application after blooming occurs. Tell him I'll talk to him tomorrow."

Raoul hung up in time to see Mademoiselle Grant come walking up the drive. His pulse raced to realize she wasn't with her friends. He watched her pause at the vegetable garden to inspect some of the plants. She'd dressed in jeans and a short-sleeved green top, darker than her amazing eyes. On her feet she wore shoes for hiking.

He reached for his phone and keys, then left the room in jeans and a T-shirt to catch up with her before she disappeared. On his way out the door, he told Gabrielle he would inspect the château's powerboat to make sure it was in good shape for the new owner.

By the time he reached the outside, he glimpsed the younger woman walking along one of the vineyard paths beyond the vegetable garden. He strode toward her, admiring her shapely body as she paused to lean over and smell the flowers.

She must have sensed him coming and turned in his direction. Her gaze wandered over him as if she were startled to see him. "Hello. I had no idea you were still on the property. I guess I assumed you had real estate business elsewhere."

"I've only been here a few days. Tomorrow I'll be leaving for home."

"Does that mean you have a wife waiting for you?"

"No. I was married—" He hesitated, somehow knowing that he could confide in this beautiful stranger. "Tragically my wife and our baby died in a car crash two years ago. Angélique was coming home from her parents' château five kilometers away and was involved in an accident. The other driver was to blame."

Abby's eyes closed tightly. "I can't even imagine it." The brooding pain he exuded was no longer a mystery.

"Neither could I at the time, but it's in the past. What about your plans?"

"My friends and I will be leaving soon too. This morning they drove me into the village, then they went to tour the chocolate factory in Broc. I've already seen it and wanted to do some research. I expect they'll be back any minute now so I decided to stay out here and wait for them."

He frowned. "I thought I'd made it clear you're welcome to stay at La Floraison through the end of June."

"You did, but we talked about it and just don't feel it's right."

Raoul sucked in his breath. He knew she'd felt that way the moment he'd given her the news about Auguste. On reflection, he found it unusual that these women chose not to take advantage of the situation. Again, he found himself admiring her. "Does that mean you're flying back to the States?"

"Not yet. We're going to gallivant for two weeks in Italy and Greece. Then we'll go home."

"Not France?" He didn't want her to leave.

"I'd go there in a shot, but the girls have been doing

research in Italy and Greece since January. It's hard for them to leave, so they want to go back one last time now that they have the chance."

"What about you?"

"I've been working here in Switzerland."

He needed to know a lot more about her. "You've been here all this time?"

"Yes, but now I'm anxious for a change."

"Mademoiselle Grant," he began, "I have to take the château's boat out for a run on the lake to make sure it's in top order before I report to Louis. How would you like to go with me so we can continue our conversation? I'll drive us to the dock in their car."

"I'd better not. I can't swim."

Raoul could feel her pushing away from him, but in his gut he knew she wanted to go with him. There'd been an instant attraction between them.

"That's what life preservers are for. Can you imagine an accident happening in this giant bathtub of a lake? You can't even hear a lapping wave on the shore."

"You mean you think it's too placid?"

"Let's just say I can only take the peaceful ambience in doses."

"Our boss has led such a hectic life in Los Angeles, I can understand why she loves to come here every year to regenerate. She's a very generous woman to have offered us this vacation."

"I agree. Why don't you risk it and come with me? *I* can swim."

She looked hesitant. "I'd better not. I don't want to miss my friends."

Whatever was going on in her mind, he wasn't going to let her get away with it. "You have a phone."

"I know, but—"

"We wouldn't be gone long. I only need enough time to check out the engine and would like the company."

He heard her take a deep breath. "All right."

The chemistry between them was alive. She couldn't fight it any more than he could. If she'd said no, he would have been forced to come up with another ploy to spend time with her.

They started walking toward the Renault. He helped her into the car and drove them to the pier. The cabin cruiser was a few years old, but looked to be in good shape. Raoul walked along the dock and guided her into the boat. The first thing he did was hand her a life jacket.

"Thank you. What about you?"

Was she worried about him? He liked the idea of that. "If I need to, I'll grab one."

Raoul would have loved to help her put it on, but worried he wouldn't be able to restrain himself, he jumped back out to untie the ropes, then climbed in to start the engine. Once he'd backed out at a no-wake speed, he took off. Being with this woman was like a breath of fresh air.

She didn't have an agenda that prompted her to ask a lot of questions. He decided she was at peace with herself and seemed to enjoy the world around her. Raoul believed she was the kind of woman you could be with and not have to make conversation if you didn't want to.

"Why don't you sit opposite me?"

She sank down and glanced in the direction of the

sailboats. "There's no wind. How sad they have to rely on motors."

Her comment was the same one he'd reflected on while being here. "Where have you been living in Switzerland?"

Abby eyed him curiously. "All over. Grindelwald, Lauterbrunnen, Mürren, Interlaken, Lake Thun, the Reichenbach and Staubbach Falls, Montreux, Geneva, Cologny."

"Why?"

"I guess you wouldn't know why our boss gave us this vacation."

"I only recall that she's a movie director in your country who was friends with Auguste."

"That's right. Magda is working on her most important film to date. It's a new look at the life of George Gordon Noel Byron, the Sixth Baron Byron, known as Lord Byron. She needs new eyes for fresh research to make the script authentic. The girls and I were picked to help because we teach college students about the romance writers of the early nineteenth century."

Abby Grant was an expert on Lord Byron?

The coincidence of meeting her at all, let alone here in St. Saphorin, where Auguste had made his find years ago, blew Raoul away. Excitement filled his body.

He shut off the engine so they could really talk. "You're all university professors?" He was still incredulous.

"Not tenured yet, but one day. Our goal has been to help supplement the script with new facts and a different look. There's been so much material written about

Byron, but Magda has been hoping for something more. So have I."

"In what sense?"

"I'd hoped to come across a poem he was supposed to have written while he was in Switzerland. The girls dropped me off at the village library this morning so I could do a little investigating, but nothing came of it so I walked back here. Of course no one in the last one hundred and ninety years has ever pretended to find it, so maybe it doesn't exist."

This woman was not only intelligent, she had an enquiring mind that made her a very exciting person. Raoul's heart pounded like a war drum. "Did it have a title?"

"Yes. Something like *Labyrinths*, but there was another part to it. I don't know exactly."

"'Labyrinths of Lavaux'." Raoul could tell her it did exist and where to find it! Chills ran up and down his spine.

"For the last five months we've been doing research in the different parts of Europe where Byron traveled. Magda's goal is to illuminate Byron's virtues and leave the negatives alone."

"Now I understand," he murmured. "You've been following his travels here with Shelley and Mary Godwin that put the Swiss Riviera on the map."

A quiet smile curved the corners of her delectable mouth. "I can see you're well-informed. Do you want to know something funny he wrote in his journal? When he left the mountains and returned to Lac Léman he said,

'The wild part of our tour is finished…my journal must be as flat as my journey.'"

Raoul was impressed with her knowledge, but his thoughts were racing. "He could have been reading our minds right now."

"Exactly. Too much peace and tranquility needs some stirring up. Byron saw nature as a companion to humanity. Certainly natural beauty was often preferable to human evil and the problems attendant upon civilization, but Byron also recognized nature's dangerous and harsh elements.

"Have you ever read 'The Prisoner of Chillon'? It connects nature to freedom, while at the same time showing nature's potentially deadly aspects in the harsh waves that seem to threaten to flood the dungeon during a storm and—" But she suddenly stopped speaking.

"Please go on," he urged her.

"Sorry. I forgot I wasn't teaching a class. Though I'm ready to move on with the girls tomorrow, I'll never be sorry I was sent here to work. I've always had a special love for that poem."

"We're looking at the Château de Chillon right now." The lake steamer had pulled up to its dock.

She nodded. "It's a magnificent château. I've been through it half a dozen times, but after seeing the dungeon where the Swiss patriot Bonivard was imprisoned, I've been haunted by Byron's words."

"Can you quote any of it?"

Her eyes lit up. "Would you believe I memorized all 392 lines in high school for a contest?"

There was fire in her. He sat back against the side of the boat. "Did you win?"

"Would it sound like bragging if I said yes?"

She was getting to him in ways he would never have imagined. "I bet you could still recite it."

Abby shook her head. "That was too long ago."

He leaned forward. "I know I read it in my teens with my grandfather who loved Byron's works, but I would be hopeless to recall it. Come on. Give me a taste of it. We're right here where he was inspired. Enchant me."

She cocked her blond head. "Maybe some of the first part."

"I'm waiting." *Mon Dieu*—he was far too attracted to her for only having known her such a short time. Whatever was happening to him had come like a bolt out of the blue and wasn't about to go away.

Once she started to recite, the emotion she conveyed filled him with a myriad of disquieting sensations.

"My hair is grey, but not with years,
    Nor grew it white
    In a single night,
As men's have grown from sudden fears:
My limbs are bowed, though not with toil,
    But rusted with a vile repose,
For they have been a dungeon's spoil,
    And mine has been the fate of those
To whom the goodly earth and air
Are bann'd, and barr'd—forbidden fare;
But this was for my father's faith
I suffered chains and courted death;

That father perish'd at the stake
For tenets he would not forsake;
And for the same his lineal race
In darkness found a dwelling-place;
We were seven—who now are one"

The last two lines she'd recited brought back remembered pain. He could have rewritten them. 'In darkness found a dwelling place. We were three—who now are one.'

As he sat there staring at Abby, he suffered guilt for finding himself so intensely attracted to her. It seemed a betrayal to Angélique's memory. It wasn't this woman's fault—nor her desirability nor the recitation that had reached his soul, reminding him of the tragedy. He felt Abby had gone to another place too.

"Byron was a great poet," Raoul said in a voice that sounded thick to his own ears. "Thank you for bringing his words to life for a few minutes so eloquently."

She shifted in place while she looked at the château in the distance. "It hurts to know how men have been persecuted. Byron had many problems, physical and otherwise. I believe his suffering came through in that poem." Raoul felt she'd suffered too and wanted to know how.

"There's no doubt of it. No wonder you were chosen to help on the film."

She smiled. "I love what I do."

He stared hard at her. "Do you love it enough to come to France for a few days?"

A stillness washed over her. "What did you say?"

"I asked if you would like to spend some time with

me at my home in Burgundy. You said your life needed a little stirring up. Your friends are welcome too."

His question seemed to have shaken her. It took her a long time before she said, "You're only saying this because you think the news about Auguste has ruined everything for us."

"Not at all. You're not the type of person to fall apart because of a change in plans. I'm quite sure your friends aren't either. That isn't the reason I've invited you."

He wanted to tell her about "Labyrinths of Lavaux" but wanted to approach her slowly. Maybe asking her to lunch would help her stay with him long enough to entertain the possibility that he was telling her the truth about his uncle's find.

She shook her head. "I don't understand."

"There's something I'd like to show you because I know you would be one person who would appreciate it. If you'll come to lunch with me, I'll give you details."

He sensed she'd try to put him off again, but after this talk on the lake, he was driven by an idea that refused to let go of him.

"If you say no after our lunch, then I'll take you back to the château and that will be the end of it."

Without waiting for a response, he started the engine. "Louis will be happy to know this speedboat seems to be in fine working order, but I'll open up the throttle to be certain."

CHAPTER THREE

ABBY STARED AT this striking man wearing a white T-shirt and jeans. If he were featured on a billboard, the sight of him alone in whatever he wore would be worth millions for the advertisers. She found him more fantastic than any fantasy of her imagination.

"You're not a Realtor are you?"

In a few minutes, he'd pulled into the slip and turned off the engine, but the blood was still pounding in her ears. "I'm afraid that's an assumption you made."

"But you let me keep thinking it."

He slanted her one of those seductive glances he probably wasn't even aware of. "Forgive me?"

With a look like that, she could forgive him anything and probably a lot more. That's what frightened her.

"I don't know," she finally answered him. It depends on what you do when you're not picking up strange females, at a lonely train station, no less," she went on. "In the middle of the week. In a car that looks like the one De Gaulle rode in on Bastille Day after World War II."

His quick smile took her breath.

She removed the life jacket and climbed out on her

own beyond his reach. Abby felt his gaze on her and knew he was still waiting for her answer. To give in to her desire and accept his invitation would be heaven. But at what cost later on, when he no longer wanted her? After she'd sold her soul, she would never be the same again and would never be able to pick up the pieces.

"Who are you?" she blurted in panic. "*What* are you?"

"Would it help if I told you I'm a vintner?"

"From Burgundy…" She hadn't seen that coming, but she should have. Chalk it up to her being turned inside out by his male magnetism. "The clues were there. Not every Realtor knows the intimate goings-on during the pollination season at La Floraison."

"I left out one detail in my résumé. Auguste Decorvet was a distant relative of mine. The Decorvet family has many offshoots, none of them into the selling of real estate. Years ago, one of them came to Switzerland to buy a vineyard, and to get away from the dark internal fighting and struggles between family members who all wanted to be in charge."

She smiled. "I'm afraid that's true of some dynastic-minded families."

"But not yours?"

"No. My parents are quite easygoing. If I do things they don't like, they show it by being disappointed. I don't like to disappoint them."

"You're lucky to have grown up in such a household." The tone in his voice led her to believe he hadn't exaggerated his family's infighting, which probably contributed to that brooding countenance. "While we eat, you can ask me all the questions you want. But I need to know what kind of a meal will give me the answer I'm looking for from you."

"I'm afraid it's not the white fish entrées they sell along the lake."

"You really do need a change of scene."

As they walked to the car, she knew what her friends would say if she said he'd invited them to come to France for a few days. Abby had only spent a few hours with him so far.

You didn't just go off with a virtual stranger who was a vintner, even if it sounded exciting. Even if he had a legitimate familial tie with the former owner of this vineyard. Even if he had something important he wanted to show her.

But was it really so wrong if she wanted to throw caution aside and enjoy an adventure with him for as long as it lasted? To know what it would be like to lie in his arms and forget the world? Heaven help her that she was even entertaining the idea.

"I… I don't know how soon my friends will be back," her voice faltered. "If we eat in the village, they might be able to join us, depending on their timing."

"Maybe they've returned. Let's drive back to the château and check first."

When they couldn't see the red car, he drove them to a sidewalk café. They served the most divine lunch of *escalope de veau* she'd ever tasted served with peas that had to be fresh from the garden. Halfway through her *galette framboise* dessert, she put her fork down because his black eyes were studying her.

"Why are you smiling?"

"It's a pleasure to watch a woman eat a meal with enjoyment."

"I'm afraid it's not ladylike."

"According to whom?"

She didn't have to think about that one. "Other women."

"Then they're envious of your figure. If I'm being transparent, I can't help it. I'm a man."

Yes. He was a man like no other and she was growing more enamored of him by the second.

"All right. I'm waiting to hear the real reason you've invited us to come to France."

"Let me tell you a story first."

Abby. You're an idiot to sit here and listen to this any longer. This had to stop before he realized she was crazy about him.

"Raoul? Thank you for the delicious lunch. Now I think you'd better drive me back to the château." She got up from the table, but he still sat there.

"You want to leave before you're told where 'Labyrinths of Lavaux' can be found?"

With that question, she wheeled around.

"*That's* the information you wanted to tell and show me?"

"I can tell you're surprised," he came back with enviable calm. "Only Lord Byron himself. It's about the vineyards at La Floraison. When my relative Auguste Decorvet first moved into the château fifty years ago, he found it written in a notebook tucked in some *terroir* maps in the library. Perhaps Byron had stayed at the château when he was passing through years earlier."

What?

"Auguste didn't know what to think. Knowing my grandfather's English is excellent and that he has a love for Byron's works—especially those written during his Greek period—he sent the notebook to him."

Abby stood there in shock and clung to the chair back. "Your grandfather has it?"

"That's right. He thinks it's the real thing. Apparently, Byron was intrigued with the vine terracing system of the steep terrain that he called labyrinths. It's yet another example of what you were saying about the beauty, yet the harshness of nature."

Unable to stand any longer, Abby sank back down on the chair. "So he's never shown it to an expert to be authenticated?"

"No. If it was authentic, then he wanted to hold on to it and not let it be turned over to the world. I've read it. The piece only covers two notebook pages. He signed it Byron in that unmistakable, flamboyant style.

"With Auguste gone, no one knows my grandfather has possession of it except my grandmother, me and now you. If you'd come to France with me, he'd be honored if you would look at it and give him your expert opinion."

Abby had already made up her mind to go to France with him for a day or two. But if he was being serious about this and the poem was authentic, then this would be the most exciting event ever to happen to her.

While she was sitting there in a daze, Ginger texted that they were back. Abby let her know she'd be there in a few minutes and put the phone in her purse.

"My friends ate in Broc. I told Ginger I'd join them

shortly." He wanted a yes or no answer. "If you're telling me the truth, of course I'm tempted to meet with your grandfather and see it for myself, but—"

"But you're not sure you believe me," he broke in on her with a frankness that took her breath. He put some bills on the table and got to his feet.

She looked up at him. "After you drive us back to the farmhouse, I'll talk to my friends."

Raoul came around to help her up from the chair. She was already too sensually aware of him before she felt his hands on her shoulders. For a moment she wished he'd have pulled her into his arms. Now her legs had become traitors as he walked her out to the car.

She knew the girls had their hearts set on returning to Greece and Italy. They wouldn't want to go to France and would laugh at her for being so gullible. She knew they'd question her sanity if she took Raoul up on his invitation.

Her thoughts were more than prophetic when a half hour later, after she'd introduced them to Raoul in the courtyard, they went upstairs to her bedroom. She told them everything, including the fact that he was a widower who'd lost his child too.

Zoe eyed her with compassion. "I understand the attraction. He's gorgeous and has a male virulence no woman could be immune to. But maybe he's a little too clever. Once you told him about the supposed missing work of Lord Byron and mentioned the name *Labyrinths*, it wouldn't have been that difficult for him to fill in the word *Lavaux*, right?"

"I was thinking the same thing," Ginger murmured.

"What I don't understand is why he feels he has to bribe you. A man as attractive as he is could get his way with a woman anytime without using subterfuge to entice her. He must want you to go with him very badly."

Not as badly as I want to go.

"That's what I'm thinking," Zoe concluded. "I don't think I could do it, but I guess it all depends on how much he means to you already."

Abby averted her eyes. "You guys would be shocked if you knew the intensity of my feelings."

"If they're that strong, then all I can say is, don't let him hurt you like Nigel did."

Heat filled Abby's cheeks. "That's my dilemma, Ginger. I don't want to get involved with him, yet I'm so drawn to him, I can hardly bear the thought of never seeing him again."

"Then it sounds like you've made up your mind to go with him."

"I don't know. I believe he's telling the truth, and he has invited you guys to come too. We could all take a look at it."

"If it exists," Ginger interjected. "But let's face it. You want to be with him, whether he has something to show you or not, right?"

"Yes," she whispered, "but I need more time to think about it. Why don't you two take off for Italy so I don't hold you up. I'm going to have another talk with Raoul this afternoon. If I decide it's not worth the risk, I'll fly from Geneva to Venice and meet you there tomorrow. How does that sound?"

Zoe smiled. "Whatever you decide, we're behind you."

"Just be careful," Ginger cautioned before they all hugged.

Since they'd already packed the night before, there was nothing to do but walk them out to the rental car. "We'll phone each other every day."

"Absolument," Abby assured them with one of the French words she loved and waved them off. Then she walked back in the farmhouse to phone Raoul from her bedroom phone. Her heart beat so hard in her throat she could hardly ask Gabrielle to put her through to him.

"Abby—" came his deep voice. "I was wondering if I'd hear back from you. What's the verdict?"

Maybe she'd regret this, but she couldn't stop herself. She longed to be with him and nothing else mattered. "The girls have already left for Italy."

"Which means they don't believe what I told you."

She gripped the phone tighter. "They want me to make up my own mind."

"And have you?"

"Yes. The likening of the vineyards to labyrinths sounded...Byronic. Not every charlatan is that clever."

There was silence on the other end for a few seconds. "How soon can you be ready to travel and finding out if that label fits me?"

"I'm ready now. If I come with you, it will only be for an overnight. Once I've seen the notebook, I'll be leaving for Italy."

"I admire you for being more open-minded than your friends."

Or so much more foolish.

"I'll pick you up outside in five minutes."

"In what?"

"It won't be the Renault."

"I'm sure Gabrielle and Louis will be relieved. So will I. I wasn't sure it was going to make it back from the village."

Abby hung up on his chuckle and hurried to call Gabrielle to thank her for everything. Once that was done, she reached for her suitcase and walked down the stairs, wondering what on earth had come over her. How could she be this excited when she might be welcoming a heartache that could mean her ruination? But somehow it didn't matter.

When she opened the doors, Abby didn't know what she expected. But it wasn't the metallic blue Maserati GranTurismo convertible sitting in the courtyard with the top down.

A car like that cost close to two hundred thousand dollars. Her gaze met Raoul's. "Where did this come from?"

"I parked it around the other side of the château." He reached for her suitcase and put it in the backseat. "I like the sun and the wind, but I'll raise the top if you prefer."

"No, please—I love a convertible!"

A heart-stopping white smile broke out on his tanned face. "A woman who doesn't mind getting her hair mussed."

"Give it time."

Little did she know when she'd had her hair cut that she'd be thankful for the short style while he drove her to France. She felt his eyes on her legs as he helped her into the passenger side. Abby was glad she was wearing jeans.

Every look, every slight touch made her come alive. When he got behind the wheel, he angled a piercing glance at her. "We'll be home in three hours. Fasten your seat belt."

Abby's misgivings about getting in over her head intensified as they wound around to the E23. It was too late to back out now. For a little while neither of them talked as they headed in a northwestern direction toward France. He drove with the expertise of a race car driver.

They stopped at the border for a cola and some madeleines. She could have brushed her hair, but didn't see the point since they'd be off again in a few minutes.

He ate a couple of the cookies. "These are some of my favorites."

"I like them too. Would you tell me where we're going exactly in Burgundy?"

"To my home outside the village of Vosne-Romanée. It's near the city of Dijon. The Regnac Capet Decorvet Domaine was founded in 1475 by my family twenty generations ago."

"How wonderful to have a family history that dates back so far." This man had an amazing heritage. But he also had a heartache no one could forget or totally recover from.

"When my great-grandfather died, my grandfather became the head of the corporation. He's still alive, but because of their old age and maladies, he and my grandmother keep to their own suite in the château with nurses and a health care giver taking care of them.

"My father, Étienne, the eldest child, was made the head, but unfortunately he's been stricken with an aggressive form of arthritis and is in a wheelchair. My mother, Hélène-Claire, and a health care giver look after him. Because of his condition, he made me the head of the corporation a year ago.

"But my uncles Pierre and Lucien, and my aunts Mireille and Abeline, along with their spouses and children, have been upset about my ascension and have a great deal to say about every move I make."

"Why is that?"

"As I told you earlier, everyone in the family wants to be in charge."

"But that doesn't make sense."

"You're right, so don't even try."

There had to be more to it than that. "It sounds like the Decorvet dynasty has been prolific," she observed. "That *is* a lot of family. Do they all live close by?"

"For those not living in the château, they're too close."

"Which king was it who complained to his minister that he had no friends, and the minister said, 'Of course not. You're the king!'?"

"Where did you acquire such wisdom?" he murmured, but she heard him.

"Do you have siblings?"

"Two. My sister, Josette, is married to Paul. They have a three-year-old boy Maurice, and are expecting their second child. My brother, Jean-Marc, is still single and works in the exporting office for our corporation with Uncle Pierre. Everyone is involved in some way in the family business, thus the friction."

Abby remembered his telling her about the relative that left for Switzerland because of the dark side of his family's relationships. The one who'd found the supposed notebook with Byron's writing. Friction was no doubt the polite description of what went on within the Decorvet inner circle.

"As I see it, your family can't help but have difficult moments. It's natural because they work in the same business." She shook her head. "That would never work for my family.

"Tell me about yours."

"I have aunts and uncles on both sides," Abby informed him, "but they don't work with my dad. He runs an insurance agency and my mom works for a hospital in medical records. My brother, Steve, just finished law school and my older sister, Nadine, is pregnant with her third child.

"I have four cousins and everyone is a free thinker. Thank goodness there aren't any secrets to be kept under lock and key, like a secret recipe for the wine *you* produce. No one would be able to keep quiet." Low laughter rumbled out of Raoul.

"What kind of wine do you make?"

"The only grape we grow is the pinot noir. Nothing but *grand cru*."

"What does that mean?"

"That it's superior quality. The earth here has an exceptional purity."

"Why?"

"Because it's made up of red-brown clay and large bits of limestone. The soil drains so well that the flavors are kept concentrated and powerful. It's known that this area's soil takes our crop to a new extreme of depth and concentration, producing a one-of-a-kind wine."

Abby heard pride in his voice. "How much does your wine cost?"

"I'm afraid the bottles are priced at extravagant levels. Depending on weather conditions, we sell three hundred thousand bottles yearly from seven different *terroirs*."

She finished her drink. "Is that a lot?"

"Not really."

His answer proved she knew nothing about his work, but she was fascinated by everything she'd learned so far. "I've only been told a little about the *chalessas* grape variety that grows around Lac Léman."

One dark brow lifted. "Then you know more than most tourists. And I've told you more than most people will ever know about my family, so we don't have to talk about it again."

She knew he meant it. Then his half smile appeared and her heart jumped.

They drove back to the motorway. Now that they were on French soil, the signs and architecture were different. When they reached Dijon, she exclaimed over the fabulous *toits bourguignons*. Raoul explained that their polychrome roofs were made of tiles glazed in green, yellow, black and terracotta. They'd been arranged in geometric patterns. Abby took pictures with her phone.

Before long Raoul gave her a tour as they followed the sign for Vosne-Romanée, teaching her about the area and its wonders with every kilometer. They drove past many lush *terroirs* of vineyards growing on the limestone slopes of the Côte d'Or escarpment.

"It's evident Gauguin never traveled here, Raoul. He would have had a field day painting the landscape of Vosne-Romanée—the different *terroirs*, hedges, trees and gardens all arranged like a great patchwork in his unmistakable style. I have to tell you I'm entranced."

"So am I by every word that comes out of your mouth."

Like an underwater geyser, his comment sent steaming heat through her body. Abby could feel his magic getting to her. It frightened her that she was so susceptible to him. Too much longer in his company and she'd never want to leave. He'd had such a cataclysmic effect on her, how would she be able to bear it if it turned out his feelings for her blew hot, then cold because she could never take the place of his beloved wife?

Eventually they came to a tall ornate grillwork gate. At the top it said, Regnac-Capet Decorvet Domaine. But her attention was caught by the coat of arms beneath the words.

Her gaze flew to his. "Was this a royal property at one time?"

He took his time before he said, "My ancestor was a duke from the House of Burgundy."

Bits and pieces of unassociated information flew at her while she started piecing them together. Talk about a patchwork. But this one added up to a canvas so extraordinary, she started trembling and couldn't speak for a minute. Yesterday when he'd appeared like a Gallic prince out of one of her dreams, she'd known something in her world had changed.

"You're a duke, aren't you?"

CHAPTER FOUR

"THE OBSOLETE TITLE belongs to my grandfather."

"But when he and your father die, you'll inherit it."

"It won't mean a thing."

"Except in your family's mind, I'd wager."

Good heavens. Raoul wasn't just the head of a famous Burgundian family. He was a titled aristocrat, too removed from ordinary life for her to imagine being any part of it. And two years ago he'd lost his wife and child. It was only natural that he had a man's appetites and needs and had found himself attracted to Abby on his trip. It didn't mean anything.

But he wasn't your typical male. A brief relationship was all that could come of their being together. She'd have tonight with him, but tomorrow she would leave and fly to Italy while she still had the strength to tear herself away.

He pressed a remote on his keys and the doors swung open. They passed through and continued along a drive lined with trees and velvety green lawns. But when he turned to the right, she gasped, not prepared for what awaited her.

Set among the foliage lay an enormous ochre-toned château. The sides with their turrets bookended a middle section where there was one of those geometric patterns of tiles on the roofs covering the three stories of mullioned glass windows.

This was the ancestral home of the Frenchman who'd climbed out of the old Renault at the train station yesterday? It was no longer a mystery why he hadn't come for one pitiful stranded tourist in his Maserati. Unpeeling his many layers needed to happen in increments.

"I'll give you the grand tour of the whole estate by car first, then I'll feed you." He kept on driving. In the distance she saw a helicopter on a landing pad. The ancient and the modern, side by side.

They continued along a private road behind the château where there was a miniature structure built along the same lines as the château with a pond in front.

Beyond it were many outbuildings and vineyards in the distance where the estate employees processed and stored the wine. There had to be hundreds of workers to keep it all going. "This is like a town within a town that has grown from the Middle Ages. My parents' home in San José was built twenty-five years ago. We thought *it* was old."

"America is a young country."

"Have you been there?"

"Several times."

Of course he had.

He followed the road around, making a loop. "You see those vines to the south? They're young, under twenty-five years old. We don't include them in our *premier cru* bottling."

"Why not?"

"Because it takes the vines that long to express the greatness of the *terroir* where they are planted. My grandfather taught me that the young vines remain young vines, however fine the grapes they produce. To quote him, 'They're like you gifted teenagers.'"

"Your grandfather sounds kind." The warmth in his voice revealed his affection for him.

"I plan on your meeting him and my grandmother. Your sense of humor and your knowledge of Lord Byron will appeal to him."

"Why does he love Byron's writing so much?"

"My grandfather had a dog he named Vercingetorix in honor of the most notable Gallic warrior who fought against Caesar. After his dog died, he happened to come across Lord Byron's, 'Epitaph to a Dog,' and he wept. That started his love for the poet. He read everything."

Abby nodded. "Like 'The Prisoner of Chillon,' that's another piece that touches your heart. Byron had been devoted to his dog, not caring it had rabies. He nursed it without worrying about infection."

"My grandfather used to add his own words, 'All the virtues of man without his vices.'"

At this point she was positive she would wake up at any moment to discover Raoul was not only bigger than life, he was a figment of her imagination. He drove them back toward the château, but he stopped in front of what he called the *petit château* by the pond.

"I'm sure you need to freshen up. Let's go inside and

I'll show you to your apartment while you're here. This is used when we have important guests who must stay overnight. The *grand château* is a relic, too museum-like and formal to enjoy. One day soon I'll take you on a tour of it, but I guarantee you'll much prefer staying here in privacy and modernized comfort."

There wouldn't be another day after tomorrow with him. She was leaving as soon as he let her take a look at the notebook, *if* there was such a thing. To stay any longer would be a mistake she would never recover from. Her mind could tell her she'd come with him to see if this work really was Byron's. But her heart had a mind of its own where the man himself was concerned.

The apartment turned out to be a home within a home, lavish enough for a queen with every accoutrement imaginable, including a kitchen with anything she'd want to eat or drink. Raoul carried in her suitcase and set it down on the exquisite parquet flooring. They exchanged cell phone numbers.

"I'll be back for you in an hour and we'll go out for dinner." He disappeared behind the French doors too fast for her to say goodbye.

The conversation with Ginger rang in her ears. *What I don't understand is why he feels he has to bribe you. A man as attractive as he is could get his way with a woman anytime without using subterfuge to entice her. He must want you to go with him very badly.*

What was the truth? Did he want to be with Abby beyond logic or reason? That's the way she felt about him, but she couldn't honestly answer her own question. She didn't *want* to answer it because if the truth didn't match the man she thought he was, she knew it would devastate her to the point she'd never get over it.

After he left, she unpacked her suitcase. The task only took a few minutes. She showered and put on a *café-au-lait*-colored sundress with a short-sleeved white jacket. Once she'd brushed her hair and put on lipstick, she went back outside full of nervous energy while she waited for Raoul's call and drank in her lush green surroundings.

With rose bushes in bloom and lily pads decorating the picturesque pond, she felt like she'd walked into a Monet painting. Her mind kept going over the things he'd told her about his family. He had responsibilities she couldn't imagine. As she leaned over to smell one of the brilliant pink roses, she saw a figure.

Coming from the direction of the *grand château* she watched a man stride toward her dressed in a pullover and trousers. He had a certain look that reminded her of Raoul. They seemed close in age, but he wasn't quite as tall.

"Eh, bien." His dark brown eyes played over her with what she felt was an interest a little too familiar. *"Puis-je vous aider?"*

"Pardon me?" She pretended not to understand him. She understood that much French, but she didn't want to get into a conversation with Raoul's brother.

"Ah. *Americaine.* I thought my eyes were deceiving me when I stepped out of the château and saw a beautiful woman standing there. Where did *you* come from?" His French accent wasn't as pronounced as Raoul's. Because this must be Raoul's brother, she needed to be careful what she said.

"I'm a tourist from California."

He continued to appraise her with an undoubtedly practiced smile that would work on most women. Jean-Marc had his own brand of charm. "I spent time there when I was in the States. What part?"

"San José."

"I'm afraid I only made it to the Napa Valley. May I know your name, *mademoiselle*?"

"Abby Grant."

He put his hands on his hips. "You must be here with a buyer. I wasn't aware we were expecting one this late in the day. If you'll allow me, I'd be happy to show you around while you're being kept waiting."

The man didn't waste time. He was a huge flirt. "That's very nice of you, but I don't even know your name."

A shocked laugh burst out of him. "Jean-Marc Decorvet."

"Ah." She smiled. "When Raoul arrives in a minute, I'll tell him I met his brother."

In an instant, the mention of his sibling wiped the smile from his good-looking face. Judging by that unhappy reaction, Raoul hadn't exaggerated about the dynamics in his family. "How do you know him?" It might have been a normal question, except that he sounded upset. Maybe that wasn't the word, exactly. She didn't understand.

"We met while I was on vacation."

He acted stunned. "Where?"

It wasn't his business, but she didn't want to offend Raoul's brother. "Switzerland." As politely as possible she said, "It's very nice to meet you. Maybe we'll see each other again."

On that note Abby continued to walk toward the vineyards in the distance. She felt his eyes on her back, but never turned around.

Please call me soon, Raoul.

After Raoul had left Abby, he'd driven by the main *domaine* office on the estate to check in with Félix. His dependable forty-year-old secretary hadn't left for home yet. He looked pleased to see Raoul. "I'm glad you're back."

"I'm sure your wife is too."

He smiled. "You were gone five days too long. When you're away, it gets like a madhouse around here."

"That's why I leave everything in your capable hands. How did it go with Jules?"

"He assured me he took care of the spraying."

"Bon."

"Solange de la Croix Godard has come by every day expecting to see you back. She hopes you haven't forgotten the Regional Wine Association Dinner tomorrow night."

"No."

But Raoul had never made plans to take her. She could hope, but that was a fiction she and her parents had dreamed up. Since his trip to St. Saphorin, he had other plans.

Meeting Abby had changed his world. Yesterday he'd experienced a *coup de foudre*. Raoul had never given any credence to two people falling in love at first sight, but there was no other explanation for what had happened to them. It surpassed any reservations he might have had thanks to his guilt about Angélique.

She'd felt it too, otherwise she wouldn't have come with him even though she'd tried to fight it. He needed and wanted her in his life no matter what.

"Anything else, Félix?"

His secretary started to say something, then changed his mind. Raoul didn't need to know the reason why. "What did my brother do now?"

"It's what your uncle Pierre mentioned to me. I don't know how important it is."

"If that were true, you wouldn't have that frustrated look on your face."

"I understand Jean-Marc tried to handle a possible new client from Denmark while you were gone, but he quoted a lower price to seal the deal without checking with Pierre until it was too late."

That sounded like Jean-Marc. His unhappy twenty-nine-year-old brother was only a year younger than Raoul, and had always resented the fact that Raoul would have first claim to the title once their grandfather and father passed away. Things had gotten worse since their father had chosen Raoul to take over the company a year ago—another nail in the coffin. Jean-Marc had always made everything into a competition—work, sports, women. The situation wasn't going to improve anytime soon.

Raoul needed to talk to their autocratic father. If Jean-Marc were to be given total control over some aspect of the business, it might help him feel more important.

"Thanks for telling me. I'll speak with Pierre. Anything else?"

"Yes. The funeral of André Laroche. I was informed it's set for tomorrow at twelve at the church."

One of their best employees had suffered a fatal heart attack. "I'll be attending as no doubt will some of the members of the family."

"Shall I arrange to get flowers sent?"

"I've already taken care of it, Félix."

He nodded. "Was your trip to Switzerland successful?"

"Very." Raoul was elated that Abby had come to Burgundy with him and was staying in the *petit château* a short distance away. Tomorrow he'd show her the piece written by Byron and get that out of the way. Then they'd take advantage of the time to love each other. He was living for that.

"Go on home to your wife and take the day off tomorrow. You deserve it."

Félix blinked, which wasn't surprising. Raoul had never been in love until now. The feelings he was experiencing now defied description and his secretary sensed it.

Raoul left the *domaine* headquarters for home. Since the deaths of his wife and child, he'd moved out of the *grand château* to a small, vacant cottage on the property he'd had renovated to suit him. He liked the distance it gave him from the family. It had allowed him to grieve in private for losing his daughter and for not loving his wife the way he should have.

From the day he'd married her, his emotions had been

raw with regret for their marriage, which should never have taken place. It had torn him apart. Yet the guilt he'd always felt because he'd never wanted Angélique, hadn't stopped him from bringing Abby here now. It seemed a betrayal, but he couldn't suppress his desire to be with her as he hurried to the cottage to shower and change for dinner.

Of course word had gotten out that he was back. While he was dressing in a silky sport shirt and trousers, he had four phone calls. One from his parents, one from his sister, plus two others from his Aunt Abeline and her son, Gilles. He knew exactly what the latter two wanted. This was one time he decided to have it out with his cousin.

"Bonsoir, Gilles."

"Sorry to bother you when you just got back, but Maman wants to know what's happened to the Floraison property."

Abeline wasn't the only one interested. Gilles, divorced and low on funds, wanted it for himself. Once he got it, he'd sell it and gamble away the money. "I'm afraid it's been sold."

"What? When she hears that, she won't stand for it."

Gilles was as transparent as glass. "She'll have to."

"Then she'll get an attorney and fight you."

"It won't matter. The attorney of record followed Auguste's will to the letter. No member of the Decorvet family can be the new buyer. I only went to Switzerland to arrange for a few of Auguste's things to be shipped back to the estate. Tell her that when you talk to her.

Since I'm in a hurry, it will save my having to call her back. *Au revoir, Gilles.*"

The calls to his parents and Josette could wait. Since he'd become a widower, the one thing on their minds was to force him into a marriage with Solange. With the help of her father, they all assumed it was a *fait accompli* in the making. How little they knew what went on inside Raoul...

Without hesitation, he rang Abby who answered on the second ring. "Raoul?"

"Sorry I've been longer than an hour."

"It's all right. I realize you've come home to business."

"I'm through dealing with the emergencies. If you're ready, I'll pick you up in front of your accommodations."

"Not there—I took a walk past some of the vineyards beyond the pond while I was waiting. I'm starting back now and will watch for you on the main drive."

"I'll find you. What kind of dinner are you in the mood for?"

"Surprise me with the type of local food you enjoy."

He'd never met a woman with a nature like hers. Abby was charming, educated, bright, funny and so damn attractive. But she was planning to fly to Italy after she'd seen the notebook.

The thought of her going anywhere was anathema to him. But he needed to be careful. He knew she didn't trust him completely yet. The sooner she saw what she'd come to see, the sooner he could carry out his plans for them to explore what could be between them.

After hanging up, he left the cottage and walked

around the back to get in his ten-year-old black Jaguar. He preferred to take the convertible on trips, but used his older car around the village for business.

When he caught up to her, Abby had walked quite a distance on her long, slender legs. Though the sky had clouded over, she stood out from her surroundings. Raoul's gaze took in the sheen of her silky blond hair, which the breeze had disheveled. His eyes couldn't help but follow her womanly shape clothed in a sundress that looked made for her.

He slowed down when he reached her. At first she stared at the car without recognition. "Have you changed your mind about dinner?"

Then her eyes, green and alive, met his. In that moment he knew she was excited to see him.

"Oh—it's *you*!" She hurried around and got in the car, bringing the scent of her strawberry shampoo fragrance with her. "I didn't know you had another car. I love the British pronunciation of this one. Jag-u-*ar*. You must think I'm crazy. I don't know why I like the sounds of certain words. It's a quirk of mine."

Raoul didn't think she was crazy. "I like your quirks." He turned the car around and they drove out of the estate beyond the gate to the road that would take them into the village. It was then he heard a sigh from her that sounded troubled. "What's wrong?"

"Not wrong, but there's something I should tell you."

He knew it. The last twenty-four hours had been too good to be true. "I presume you had a phone call from your friends. They think I've preyed on you and now you believe it."

"That's not it," she muttered.

He pulled over to the side of the road. "Can you look me in the eye and tell me you never once wondered if I'd been lying to you?"

She moistened her lips nervously. "No. I believed you."

"Then let's start again. Something's bothering you. Have you decided you don't want to stay here after all?"

Her head turned in his direction. "Anyone who didn't want to stay here would have to be comatose."

"But?"

"While I was walking by the pond, I met your brother."

A grimace marred his features. That was all he had to hear to understand.

"He said he thought I'd come to the estate with a buyer and offered to show me around while I waited. I thanked him, but told him I was waiting for you. His shocked reaction surprised me."

Abby's instincts were right on. His brother wouldn't have believed Raoul had invited a woman to come to the estate for personal reasons. He knew Raoul had been in mourning since the funeral.

Jean-Marc would be inordinately curious over what was going on. It was only natural that his brother would have taken one look at Abby and decided to make her his next conquest.

"What did you tell him?"

"I gave him my name and told him I was a tourist from California. He wanted to know how we met.

I told him it was in Switzerland, but of course I didn't say anything else."

"I hope he didn't make you uncomfortable."

"No." She was searching for the right words. "He just seemed…caught off guard and curious."

"That's his nature." But the knowledge that Raoul had invited Abby here was one bombshell his brother wouldn't have seen coming in a million years. Like the rest of the family, Jean-Marc always wanted to know Raoul's personal business and tried to anticipate his next move. His grandparents were the exception.

"Is he older or younger than you?"

Raoul wanted to get off the subject. "He's twenty-nine, younger than me by a year."

"Almost like twins."

"Not quite." Jean-Marc and Gilles were the ones who resembled each other in certain behaviors. "Let's just say we have a difficult history and let it go at that." He gripped the wheel tighter and drove back on to the road.

"Where are you taking us?"

Raoul gave her another sideward glance. "Any place to get away from the claustrophobic world I live in."

"I guess you can get claustrophobic in a château the size of yours, or a one room dwelling, depending on the company."

Abby was incredibly easy to talk to.

The Petite Auberge Blanche served a good meal he thought she'd like. He pulled into the parking and escorted her inside the busy establishment, cupping her elbow. The owner knew him from boyhood.

His eyes rounded in surprise because Raoul hadn't

brought in a woman since long before his wife's death. The older man, all smiles, showed them to a table outside on the terrace where a group was playing the kind of soft rock music that catered to tourists. Some were dancing. He sent a waiter over to take their orders and serve them the house wine.

Since touching her, Raoul needed more physical contact. "Would you like to dance?"

"I'm not very good at it."

He was getting used to her refusing him, but it wasn't going to work. "At least in this case you don't need a life preserver. Just hold on to me."

CHAPTER FIVE

SOMEHOW RAOUL GOT his way with Abby because she'd fallen headlong in love with him. There was no way to avoid what was right in front of her. When she felt his arms go around her, all coherent thought ceased.

Though she needed to fight her attraction to him, when he pulled her against him, she enjoyed it too much. She stood five-seven in her low wedges and felt made for him as he moved her around the floor with his face resting in her hair.

No man could equal Raoul in looks or demeanor. Though his expensive charcoal silk shirt and black trousers distinguished him from the other males in the restaurant, it was the very essence of him that caused every female to follow him with their eyes.

His solid, powerful legs brushed against hers, sending curls of desire through her body. That's when the alarm bells went off. She didn't dare let this go on for fear everyone in the room could see they needed more privacy.

"The waiter has brought out our food, Raoul," she whispered. "We'd better go back to the table before it gets cold."

His hands tightened on her upper arms before he relinquished his hold on her, as if he didn't want to let her go. She hadn't wanted this to stop either.

He walked her back to the table laden with their meal: escargot, baked duck in honey, skewered pork tenderloin marinated in red pesto with sweet chorizo, creamy risotto and apple tart for dessert.

"Are you trying to fatten me up?" she teased later to keep things on a lighter note. The band had taken a break that stopped any dancing for a little while.

His gaze narrowed on her features. "If it keeps you happy."

She paused before taking another sip of wine. "You think I'm not?"

"I know you're waiting to see that notebook. We'll visit my grandparents tomorrow. In the meantime, I'd like to show you a part of the château that might interest you."

That probably meant they'd be together alone. Abby put the goblet down with a trembling hand. "I'd like that."

His touch was electric as he walked her back to the car.

Raoul didn't speak while they drove to the estate and passed through the gate. Instead of parking in front of the *petit château*, he took another route that circled around the *grand château*. They wound up at a back entrance.

"I've brought you to my office, one of two places on the estate where I have completely privacy. The other is the cottage where I live." He helped her out of the car.

"You don't stay in the château?"

"Not anymore. After the funeral, I needed to live strictly alone."

"I can understand that," she whispered. He and his wife must have had a great love. At times the memories had to torture him.

He opened the door and let them inside. "This room was once known as *le Salon de Dionysos*, the Greek god of wine. For a hundred years it was used during the yearly *vendange*, what you would call the grape harvest. But last year I claimed it for my *Saint des Saints*."

"What does that mean?"

"I believe you refer to it as your inner sanctum."

Abby liked the sound of it in French. After he turned on a few lights, she started to walk around the huge vaulted room. She was speechless. It had been modernized to create a state-of-the-art office with comfortable furniture.

But everywhere she looked on the walls and ceilings were colorful scenes of the famous god riding on the back of a panther or walking through a pine forest with an ivy wreath on his curly head. In another section Dionysus was being pulled in a chariot by a pair of beasts.

She rolled her eyes at him. "This room is so spectacular I don't see how you get any work done. When you were a little boy, you must have been in heaven running around in here. I don't have to see the rest of the château to know it has to be one of Burgundy's treasures."

He'd been checking information on his computer. "A costly one. Last year France's grape harvest was among the smallest in thirty years, down ten percent from the year before."

She frowned. "That has to be troubling news to every vintner."

"Especially for those who haven't modernized. For the last ten years I've been navigating through the high-tech investments necessary to keep this place going. When I lift my eyes, the decor in here keeps me grounded to my roots and reminds me of what is important."

"Taking care of your family means you carry a heavy weight on your shoulders." Plus the terrible personal tragedy that had to have been so devastating for him.

"I'm not complaining. I simply want us to understand each other better."

So did Abby who didn't know nearly enough about him. She walked over to one of the upholstered chairs near the massive fireplace and sat down.

Raoul's black eyes gleamed in the soft light as he moved toward her and perched on the end of the couch next to her. "I realize you don't trust me yet."

"We hardly know each other."

"I'm afraid I've expected too much from you."

For him to admit to any vulnerability came as a complete surprise. "Now I'm going to ask *you* what's wrong."

He made a strange sound in his throat. "I shouldn't have brought you to the estate."

Her breath caught. "Because there's no notebook after all?"

In the next instant Raoul's hand shot out to cover hers. "You know there is," his voice grated. "And you *know* that's not what I meant!" A tiny nerve throbbed at the corner of his compelling mouth.

"I'm sorry I said that."

"You had every right. Would it shock you if I told you I wanted to bring you back with me from the moment I saw you sitting on the bench at the train station? But life on the estate is like living in a fish bowl. I would spare you that if I could."

"Well, that can be easily remedied," she said to hide the sudden stab of pain she knew he hadn't inflicted on purpose. "I'll stay at a hotel in the village tonight and leave for Venice tomorrow as planned."

"Without seeing the poem you came to look at?"

"Raoul—you're confusing me. Do I seem that emotionally fragile to you?"

He removed his hand and shook his dark, handsome head. "Of course not. But there's an untouched purity about you I can't put into words."

"Pure—that's the way you see me?"

"You're the most real woman I've ever met. No pretense or affectation. I don't want that unique quality of yours to be blighted because of your relationship with me."

"Spoken like a vintner," she said to lighten his mood, but it didn't work. "We don't have a relationship, Raoul."

"But we could have one," he fired back. "I've told you about Angélique and the baby, but you haven't shared a word about yourself. Is that because there's someone else waiting for you when you return to the States? A man who wouldn't like it to know you were here with me?"

She lifted her eyes. "No. No one."

He raked a hand through his black hair. "Even if there isn't, there have to have been many men who wanted a relationship with you."

"Many?" She shook her head. "I've known two men whom I thought I could marry."

"Why didn't either of them work out?"

"When I was twenty and an undergraduate, I met a guy called Jim while on vacation in Carmel. He was a fun and easy-going cowboy from Nevada who lived on a cattle ranch. I eventually met his family and spent some time with him there. But hard as I tried, I couldn't see myself adapting to the life he adored. It was obvious I didn't love him enough."

Raoul cocked his dark head. "You were young."

"True. Four years later I met Nigel, a visiting professor from Cambridge, England. We worked together for two semesters. I fell in love with his accent first."

Raoul smiled. "One of your quirks."

"Yes, then I fell for him. He was brilliant and fascinating and wanted to marry me. Right before Christmas break we were planning a spring wedding. While he was teaching a class, a woman came in to his office. She claimed to be his wife and showed me pictures of the two of them with their children.

"Needless to say, I told him I never wanted to see him again. You don't need to know how ugly it was. But after that experience, I don't want to be hurt again like that. Not ever."

"I'm sorry you've been through that kind of pain," he murmured in a voice filled with a compassion she felt through to her insides. "Is that how you ended up in Switzerland?"

She looked up and searched Raoul's eyes. "When I went to the head of the department and asked for a leave of absence, he told me I could do some research for Magda until the summer, and that brought me to Switzerland."

"*Dieu merci* it did. But after what you've been through, I'm surprised you agreed to drive here with me."

"Frankly, so am I, even with the prize you dangled in front of me."

"That prize does exist, but whether it's authentic will be for you to decide."

Abby eyed him seriously. "Assuming you've told me the truth about your life so far, what was it about your wife that made you want to marry her? Why did it work for you?"

He took time answering. "Angélique de Dampierre was attractive and born into an aristocratic Burgundian wine family. Our family had known hers all our lives, but I didn't begin spending time with her until three years ago. That was at the time when my father's arthritis was advancing.

"One evening after a party where the Dampierre family was in attendance, he took me aside. In private he told me he was stepping down as the head of the estate and would be making me the head. I knew he'd been cultivating me for that position from the cradle. What I didn't know was that he expected me to marry Angélique."

Abby sat there in stunned disbelief. "Are you saying you entered into an arranged marriage?"

Raoul nodded. "He and René Dampierre had talked it over years earlier. The union of our two families would ensure stability and bring financial security for years to come. But my father said I had to be married first and Angélique, with her aristocratic background, would make the perfect vintner's wife."

"That sounds so feudal."

"If you knew my father, nothing would surprise you. Once in a while the ruthless side comes out in him, making him a formidable opponent. I had no plan to marry anyone at the time and told him he should make Jean-Marc the heir. We had some violent quarrels and I threatened to leave the estate and move to Paris.

"In fact I was in the process of packing my bags when my mother got hold of me and posed an argument that forced me to listen. The doctor had told her my father didn't have more than a year to live. She couldn't abide anyone else in our difficult family taking over once he was gone. She said it had to be me in charge or the Decorvet estate would fall into ruin.

"My mother is a shrewd woman with a will of iron. She comes from an old aristocratic wine family too. She understands what it takes to keep the family on top. I knew deep down as I listened to her that she was speaking the truth. Once my father passed away, there would be chaos. My grandfather couldn't possibly run things, and he'd die watching his fifty years of unceasing work as the patriarch fall apart."

"So you married Angélique," Abby whispered.

There was a silence before he said, "It didn't go well."

"Did she know how you felt?"

"I'm sure she did."

"But she married you anyway because she wanted to be your wife."

At least he didn't try to say that she was following orders too. No doubt Angélique had been in love with him for years.

"My father got what he wanted, and then miraculously didn't die. He's still alive trying to run things even though he put me in charge. I wouldn't put it past him to have bribed the doctor to lie about his condition in order to get his way."

"I can't comprehend a parent doing that."

"What saved any of this for me was the birth of our little girl Nicolette. She was two and half months at the time of the crash."

A groan came out of Abby. She wished she hadn't asked him about his marriage. She knew he would always be in pain over that. "I'm so sorry for your loss." Raoul hadn't been married to Angélique very long. Even if it hadn't been the ideal marriage or anything close, how could one get over losing both of them in such a horrid way?

What kind of a dream world had Abby been living in to drive here with this fabulous, enigmatic, important man in order to see something possibly written by Lord Byron? What was she hoping for now? That Raoul would fall desperately in love with her? That she'd live happily ever after with a man this tormented by family problems and tragedy?

Abby should never have mentioned his wife. She looked around the room that shouted as nothing else could how foreign his world and aristocratic background was to hers. She could never be his *raison d'être*. Abby needed to leave for Italy tomorrow, no matter what.

Unable to sit there any longer, she stood up. "Thank you for dinner and the opportunity to see the Salon de Dionysos. I feel very privileged that you would allow me a glimpse inside your *Saint des Saints*." She'd tried to pronounce it correctly. "But it's getting late and I'm positive you're tired after our long drive today. I'd better go back to my room."

Lines darkened his striking features. "Now that I've been honest with you, why do I get the feeling you're running away from me already?"

He could see through her with those piercing black eyes. She started to tremble. "Because I'm questioning my own judgment. Since we arrived at the estate, nothing feels right."

"That's because what we felt for each other when we first met was like a clap of thunder out of a blue sky. I was reminded of a line in 'The Young Fools' by Verlaine."

"What line was that?" She'd enjoyed much of the French poet's translated work.

"Suddenly a white nape flashed beneath the branches, and this sight was a delicate feast for a young fool's heart."

"Raoul—" Where had he pulled that from? He never ceased to amaze her.

"The reverberations have been growing stronger with

every passing minute, so don't deny it." He got up from the couch and reached for her with his strong hands. Their mouths were only centimeters apart.

"I don't deny it, but I'm not looking for any kind of complication. I never want to go through the pain of betrayal again."

She heard his sharp intake of breath. "I'm positive my father lied to me to get his own way. You think I don't understand betrayal?"

Abby shook her head, not immune to the tortured tone in his voice. "I don't know what to think," she cried.

"Then don't," he said before covering her mouth with a kiss so hungry and full of desire that she moaned. Finding herself immersed in sensations her body had never known before, she slid her hands up the silk covering his chest and wrapped her arms around his neck.

As Abby began kissing him back, she was overwhelmed by her need for him and what he was doing to her. She couldn't get close enough to him. The thought of his stopping was agony.

He rubbed her back and hips, molding her to him. "*Mon Dieu*, you have no idea what you do to me," he whispered against her lips. "To think I almost put off going to Switzerland until the end of the month."

"I shouldn't have come with you. My friends warned me, but I couldn't help myself. Verlaine was right about young fools."

"But he got it right." Raoul shook her gently. "Now that you're here, I'll take you to my grandparents' apartment in the morning. Come on. Much as I'd like to keep you in here all night, I'll drive you back to the *petit château*."

He kept hold of her hand during the quick trip. When he pulled up in front, he took her to the door and unlocked it for her.

"Good night, Abby. I don't dare kiss you again or I'll never leave your apartment. Do you hear what I'm saying?" he ground out with a fierceness that shook her before he disappeared.

Abby awakened early the next morning after a restless night. Today was the day she was going to see something that might be a fantastic new discovery to delight the literary world. But in truth she was still reeling from being in Raoul's arms last night while he'd kissed her senseless.

Everything she'd promised herself not to do, she'd done, like falling in love with him. In his office, he'd pulled her against him and she'd gone willingly, clinging to his tall, hard-muscled body. When he'd picked her up at the train station, she'd known deep down in her bones that she'd wanted to become a part of this man, to merge with him.

Though Ginger and Zoe had told her she'd be taking a risk to go with him, she couldn't help how she was feeling right now. By tonight she would have flown to Venice—far away from his fish bowl—but for the rest of today, she would be with Raoul and it was all she could ask of life.

She debated what to wear to meet his grandparents and finally chose a summery, leaf-green blouse and a green-on-white print skirt. Abby wanted to make a good impression on the relatives he loved.

Her heart jumped when she heard his knock on the entrance door. She hurried across the salon to open it.

To her surprise he wore a dressy black suit with a white shirt and monogrammed tie. Talk about a ducal presence. She couldn't put the image out of her mind. He smelled divine, having just come from the shower, but didn't try to kiss her. His striking looks caused her to stare.

"Raoul—I didn't realize I should get more dressed up."

His gaze traveled over her features. "You look perfect. Shall we go? I'm anxious to be rid of the charlatan image you have of me."

She swallowed hard. "I should never have said it."

One black brow quirked. "If I'd been in your shoes, I'd have said something much worse. Shall we go?"

"Yes."

He closed the door. They walked to his car and he drove to the château, taking them to the south entrance. "My grandparents live in a suite on the second floor. We won't stay long because they tire easily."

They passed one of the security guards at the door and climbed the marble staircase to the next level. He opened one of the tall paneled double doors and ushered her inside to the main sitting room. A brunette care giver came to greet him.

"Lisette? I'd like you to meet my friend Abby Grant from the United States." He turned to Abby. "Lisette takes care of my grandparents like they were her own parents. She's been with them for two years and we're very lucky to have her."

Abby gave the woman a warm smile. "It's so nice to meet you."

"They're very excited to know Raoul has brought such an important guest. I've taken them into the dining room."

He put a hand on the back of Abby's waist and guided her through another set of French doors to the dining room where his grandparents were waiting for them.

"I bought the latest wheeled chairs that can be used as beds if necessary, so they can be comfortable when there are visitors. Lisette takes impeccable care of them."

"I can see that." Abby could feel his love for them.

The windows looked out on the grounds. Breakfast had been laid out on the round table. There were flowers everywhere.

"What a beautiful room."

"It's their favorite place," Raoul murmured.

"Mon enfant." His silver-haired grandmother lifted her frail arms to him.

His gray-haired grandfather had a harder time and only mouthed his name. He made a hand motion so Raoul would give him a hug.

"Céline and Honoré, I want you to meet the woman I told you about when I called you from Switzerland." Before they'd driven away from the vineyard, he'd let them know he'd fallen in love with her. "This is Abby Grant, the distinguished literature *professeur* from San José, California.

"It's a shame Auguste never got to meet her. She's a

kindred spirit, Papi. Because the two of you share a love for Lord Byron's poetry. I wanted her to see the notebook Auguste sent to you."

"It's right here," his grandmother spoke up. "Lisette brought it from the study."

"Why don't you sit by my grandfather, Abby? I'll hand it to you."

After she did his bidding, he reached for it and put the thin, seven-by-three-inch pale blue notebook in her hands.

Her fingers trembled. She looked at his grandfather. "You have no idea what this moment means to me."

"Go ahead and open it," Raoul urged her.

Abby carefully lifted the cover and began studying it. The poem had been written in pencil. "Labyrinths of Lavaux." There it was, just as Raoul had said. She couldn't stop the gasps that kept coming as she read through to the second page, marveling over the poet's thoughts. Like Raoul had told her, it was a short piece, but brilliant. Byron's authentic signature made it priceless.

When she looked up at Raoul, she could hardly make out his features for the tears. "You have a priceless treasure here." She turned to smile at his grandfather. "I'm holding an important part of history in my hand. It's a great honor to be allowed to see this. I can't thank you enough for the privilege."

Honoré nodded with a smile.

Raoul patted the old man's thin shoulder. "Well, Papi, after all these years, you've finally been told by an expert on Lord Byron that this is the treasure you'd always believed it to be."

His grandfather crooked his finger at Abby who gave his hand a squeeze. "I've never been so thrilled, monsieur. This piece on the vineyards must have special significance for you since you ran your own vineyard for fifty years."

The old man nodded.

"Raoul also told me about your dog Vercingetorix. Like you, I found Byron's 'Epitaph to a Dog' very touching. I also loved 'The Prisoner of Chillon.' Do you know Raoul and I took a boat ride on the lake right by the château? That's when he told me about your love for Byron. I also learned how much he loves his grandparents."

Honoré's eyes misted over and he had enough strength to smile and press her hand harder.

Raoul leaned down. "Come around and meet my mamie." Abby moved and sat down next to his grandmother.

"This is an exciting moment for my husband and me. I want you to know our Raoul had his favorite books too." The older woman's soft brown eyes still twinkled. She looked at her husband. "Honoré? What one did he love the most?"

He didn't answer. "My husband has a hard time talking now."

"That's all right," Abby assured her.

She called to Lisette. "Will you find *Blondine*? It's in with the old books in the case in the study."

"Bien sûr." While Lisette rushed off, the four of them ate breakfast. Raoul's grandmother only ate a portion of a croissant Abby handed to her. His poor grandfather

had to sip a fortified drink through a bent straw. Raoul held it for him.

Lisette came back in the room holding a little tattered storybook. His grandmother took it. "Our Raoul probably hasn't seen this since he was four years old." She had difficulty opening the cover. "Look here. You printed your name the best you could, Raoul. The *u* is upside down." She laughed.

Raoul took the book and showed it to Abby. She looked at it for a minute. Emotions had almost caused her throat to close. His grandmother must have seen how overcome she was. "If you want to keep the book, it's yours, Abby."

"Are you sure?"

She nodded. "Raoul will translate it for you."

"Then I'd love it, Madame," she said in a tremulous voice.

"Call me Céline."

"Thank you, Céline."

Abby listened while Raoul gave them some news about the estate they might enjoy hearing. "Now I can tell you're getting tired, so Abby and I are going to leave. I'm hoping to fit in a drive to Cluny so she can see it."

His grandmother looked at Abby. "The power of the monastery once extended to over ten thousand monks. I was just a girl when I first visited the huge church there, and it made a massive impression on me."

"I'll let you know what I think after we get back, Céline."

"We'll come visit again later, Mamie. Stay well. Love you."

After he hugged them, Abby got up and kissed them on both cheeks. "I'll treasure this book," she whispered to Céline. They said goodbye to Lisette and left the château.

"Your grandparents are very dear," she told him as they walked out to the car.

When he helped her inside, he didn't start it right away. "I don't think I would have made it through this life without them. Do you know when I saw you at the train station, I was reminded of that old French fairy tale you're holding. My grandmother used to read it to me as a child. Have you heard the story of *Blondine*?"

"No."

"'There was a king called Benin. He was good and all the world loved him; he was just, and the wicked feared him. His wife, the Queen Doucette, was also good and much beloved. This happy pair had a daughter called the Princess Blondine, because of her superb golden hair, and she was as amiable and charming as her father the king, and her mother the queen.'

"I loved the beginning of that story, especially the drawings, because their family looked and sounded so happy. I begged my grandmother to read the beginning over and over again. It made me want to crawl inside the pages where I could be that happy too."

Tears stung Abby's eyelids. "Raoul—was your childhood that unhappy?"

"Let's just say it left a lot to be desired. The rest of the fairy tale isn't important. But the picture of Blondine looking so happy stayed with me. That was the look I saw in you that first day, an intangible quality impossible to describe. It's certainly one reason why I was drawn to you."

Listening to Raoul, Abby gained an insight into why he'd told her he didn't want their relationship to cause her pain. His desire to protect her from his difficult family made the kind of sense that helped her to feel closer to him. Combined with his recent loss, it made his desire to crawl into the pages of the fairy tale that much more poignant.

"I had no idea that's what you were thinking about when you got out of that old black car. Thank you for bringing me here to meet your grandparents. I loved seeing Byron's work in his own handwriting. It was a moment I'll never forget. Please know your grandfather's secret is safe with me."

"You're not going to tell your coworkers?"

"Much as I would love to claim I'd come across something of great worth from Byron, in this case it's not my secret to give away, not even to my friends. You told me your grandfather has kept this quiet all these years. It's his secret to keep.

"To be honest, it means much more to me to meet the two people who've had such a great impact on your life."

"As long as you don't think I'm the con artist *par excellence*, I'll sleep better tonight."

"Raoul—" She leaned across the seat and kissed his cheek. "Thank you for today, for everything. I'll cherish these moments and this book forever."

He cupped her face in his hands. "I've done my part, but we haven't talked about your flight to Venice. Have you booked it yet?"

She fought to stifle the pounding of her heart. "No. I didn't know how long we'd be with your grandparents." The thought of leaving him was too painful to consider.

"In that case, would you be willing to attend a funeral service with me first? It starts at noon. I'd rather not go alone. We'll deal with your flight after."

She couldn't think about leaving right now. "*That's* why you're dressed in black!"

"Yes. It's for one of the estate employees."

Maybe heaven had heard her because she'd been given a reprieve. "After what you've done for me, how could I turn you down?" she answered without hesitation. Besides wanting to be with him, she knew any funeral would be painful for him to get through. If it helped him to be with her, it was the least she could do when he'd given her a gift beyond price.

He kissed her hungrily. "Do you have something black you can wear?"

Abby nodded. "One all-purpose black dress in my small, pitiful wardrobe."

"Then I'll drive you to your apartment and wait while you change."

She slid back to the passenger side, dying inside because he'd been the one to ask her if she'd booked her flight to Italy yet. He'd brought the subject up first. Did it mean he was prepared to let her go? It hit her hard that leaving him was the last thing she wanted to do. Abby was in terrible trouble.

CHAPTER SIX

WHILE RAOUL SAT in his car in front of Abby's apartment, his cell phone rang. His brows furrowed to discover it was his brother. He picked up.

"Jean-Marc?"

"Rumors are that you haven't phoned Solange about tonight's dinner since you got back from Switzerland!" he blurted without preamble.

Raoul's hand tightened around his phone. "Now that you've gotten that off your chest, did you see the text I sent you earlier?"

"I haven't checked my messages."

"Then you need to. Since I'm busy, you and Josette will have to take the parents to the Laroche funeral at the church today. It starts at noon, so plan ahead to make certain father's wheelchair is put close to the front before the priest begins the service. The flowers have been taken care of. *À bientôt.*"

In a few minutes Abby emerged from the *petit château.* At her appearance he drew in a deep breath. The female lines and curves of her figure were made for the simple short-sleeved black dress that fell to her knee. In the darkest room, her hair and eyes would gleam gold and green fire.

He got out to help her into the car. If he didn't suppress the urge to devour her mouth, they would never make it to the funeral. In moments, they headed for the local church.

"Who is the person who passed away?"

"André Laroche. He's been our director of viticulture for sixty years and died at eighty-three. He left a widow, three children and four grandchildren."

"How hard for them. What did he do exactly? That's a long time to carry out one job."

"He managed multiple *terroirs*, a difficult task."

"It's a coveted position, right?"

Raoul nodded.

"I presume there are many others who would like to step into his shoes."

"You have no idea."

"Then you're going to miss him terribly."

Abby had amazing insight *and* compassion. "His sons have helped him, but he's virtually irreplaceable. Still, he has one grandson with a feel for the *terroirs*. Working with his grandfather has helped him to understand climate, soil type and geomorphology. Not everyone is gifted with that sensibility. I have great hopes for him and am grooming him to take over."

"Did André know you wanted his grandson to replace him one day?"

"I assured him of it last month after he'd been put on bed rest for failing kidneys. His heart attack happened after that."

"Oh, the poor thing. But to give him that news was a great compliment and must have thrilled him. You helped him die a happy man."

"You think?"

"I know."

Raoul swallowed hard and clung to her hand. Before long the church came into sight. Already a large crowd had gathered. He found a spot and parked the car. "Stay by me today."

She darted him a puzzled glance. "Where else would I go?"

"One of the relatives might try to take you aside."

"Don't worry," she murmured, giving his hand a reassuring squeeze.

"We'll go in now and pay our respects to his family before the funeral starts."

She held on to his arm as they lined up behind the people and waited their turn to enter the nave. If this hadn't been such a solemn occasion, he would have laughed to see the way every eye in this closed, provincial group of mourners stared at him and Abby.

He saw shock and disbelief in every expression. Angélique had been his *duchesse*-to-be, revered in their elite community. To see him bring another woman to an occasion not meant for outsiders represented something close to blasphemy in their minds. But if he had his way, they were going to have to get used to it.

Raoul walked Abby down the aisle to the front of the chapel, which was filled with flowers. One huge wreath of white roses and lilies with the Decorvet *domaine* banner dominated.

The Laroche family were seated near the draped coffin. Raoul approached André's widow. "Madame Laroche, may I introduce Mademoiselle Grant, visiting from the US? On behalf of the family, I want to tell you how much we'll miss André. He's irreplaceable."

When Abby shook her hand, the other woman broke down. Raoul moved down the line taking Abby with him. He introduced her to each member of the Laroche family. Raoul kept her planted at his side.

Once he'd greeted all of them, he escorted Abby down a side aisle. A fourth of the way, they came to the row where his own family was seated. His graying father sat in the wheelchair on the outside and shot him a black glance of disapproval.

He stopped in front of him. "Papa? Maman? May I present Mademoiselle Grant from San José, California."

His father made no sign of acknowledgment, but his mother said, *"Mademoiselle."*

"It's very nice to meet you," Abby responded.

Next to Raoul's mother sat Josette and her husband, who only nodded. His brother's and sister's judgmental expressions mirrored his parents'.

"Don't forget the dinner tonight," his father half growled at him before they moved on.

Raoul ignored the comment. He was glad he'd brought Abby with him. Now everyone had seen her with him at the same time and they couldn't say a word. He drew her closer and kept walking to the rear where he found them space in the last pew.

Abby sat without moving throughout the service and prayers. Being close to the exit, they were able to leave as soon as the priest gave the final blessing and the pall-bearers carried the coffin out to the hearse.

He walked her toward the car. "You can breathe now," he said once they'd gotten inside and had driven away.

"You're not going to the cemetery?"

"No. You and I have provided more than enough interest by being at the funeral. I'll pay my own respects to André when I visit his grave site tomorrow. When I asked you if you'd like to come to France to see Byron's poem, I know you weren't expecting to attend a funeral too."

"Please don't apologize. This is part of who you are."

Again, he reached for her hand. "Is that so?"

"Yes, and you were right about one thing. After we passed your family along the aisle, I found out what it's like to be a fish in a goldfish bowl. What did your father say to you?"

"I have to attend a dinner tonight in Dijon…and I want you to go with me. Tomorrow we'll worry about your flight plans. How do you feel about that?"

She hesitated for a moment. "Is this dinner very important?"

"Not particularly, except that I have to make a few remarks."

"After what you've done for me, of course I'll come."

The blood pounded in his ears. She didn't want to leave him. *He knew it.*

Raoul parked in front of her apartment, determined to grab at happiness for another twenty-four hours. "Do you have something formal to wear for evening?"

"I'm afraid this black dress is it. Why?"

"Since this is the Regional Wine Association Dinner, I thought you might like to visit some of the shops and find something different to wear."

"You don't think black will be appropriate?"

"That question isn't worth answering. But you've already worn it to the funeral and would probably enjoy something different."

"If I had any spending money, there's nothing I'd love more than to buy a new outfit, but my budget won't allow it. When I first flew over, I brought some dressier clothes for the colder weather, but two weeks ago I shipped a lot of them home and kept the black dress to see me through."

"Naturally I intend to buy something that pleases you."

"That's very generous of you. Under the circumstances I'll pick out something to suit the evening."

Afraid he was dreaming, he turned to her. "Hurry inside and get what you need, then we'll drive to Dijon. I'll show you around and then stop to buy you an outfit you can wear right out of the store."

"I'd better bring my black high heel sandals with me."

Unable to hold back another second, he kissed her thoroughly before she left the car. But he was haunted by one question. Did he have the right to love her heart and soul when he hadn't been the kind of husband Angélique had wanted and needed?

Throughout his marriage and after, he'd suffered remorse for not being able to love her. If it was a flaw in him, he hadn't been able to overcome it, even though she'd been the mother of their precious baby.

Could he finally forget the past and embrace the glorious life he wanted with Abby? He could deal with his family's censure, but there was one thing he couldn't endure. That would be to let her get on a plane and fly away. He couldn't let it happen.

* * *

Abby had never had so much fun in her life as they spent the rest of the afternoon meandering through the city filled with medieval and renaissance architecture. They would eat a meat pastry here, and a piece of fruit there. Raoul would tease her with a chocolate truffle, then kiss her while they walked on hand in hand.

At five they went to a shop called Clarisse. Abby was afraid to look at the prices. When she found the stunning cherry-red crew neck sheath, she loved it on sight. It had three-quarter sleeves and large colorful flowers on the lower half of the skirt and sleeves. After putting it on with her black heels, she emerged from the dressing room to show Raoul.

The way his black eyes played over her, Abby felt herself to turn to flame. "That's the one."

More than ever she knew this dinner meant something of importance, and she was glad she would be wearing a dress he liked. She gathered her other clothes and they went out to the car.

"Where is the dinner being held?"

"Over at the five-star Grand Hôtel la Cloche. It's been classified as an historic monument overlooking the capital of Burgundy."

In a few minutes, he pointed out the nearby famous Place Darcy. They drove to the private parking before walking inside the hotel to the sumptuous hall with flower-laden banquet tables. At the front of the hall she spotted a rostrum.

Two of the forty or so men and women assembled turned out to be his uncles. Everyone looked elegantly dressed. No wonder Raoul had offered to buy her something special to wear. The seated guests nodded to Raoul while they stared at Abby in what she could only describe as astonishment. After attending the funeral, she ought to be used to it.

"It's already full," she whispered. "Are we late?"

He put his arm around her waist. "It doesn't matter. Now we won't have to wait so long for me to get my part over with. Our place is up in front at the head table."

In seconds, she found herself seated in the middle on Raoul's left. The food had been served and people were starting to drink their wine. He introduced her to a distinguished middle-aged man with a trace of silver in his dark hair on her left. The man couldn't take his eyes off her, but she knew instantly it wasn't because he found her attractive.

"Mademoiselle Grant? I'd like you to meet Monsieur Raimund Godard, owner of the prestigious Pascal Godard Domaine here in Burgundy," Raoul spoke in English. "And on his left, his daughter Solange."

Abby smiled. "How do you do, Monsieur, Mademoiselle?" She assumed his daughter wasn't married since Raoul hadn't attached a different last name to her.

"Mademoiselle Grant," the man murmured.

The other woman leaned forward to see around her father. Abby had heard the expression "staring daggers" at someone. She now saw it for herself. Solange de la Croix Godard, a real beauty with copper-red hair sweeping her shoulders, came close to impaling Abby with the dark brown eyes she'd inherited from her father.

By now Raoul had gotten involved in a conversation with an older man seated on his right. Abby ate in silence until another man, seated at the end of the table, walked up to the rostrum. He tapped his wineglass with a fork to get everyone's attention and introduced himself. After a welcoming speech in French, he asked Raoul to come up.

"I won't be long," he whispered against her ear before he made his way to the podium. She was still reacting to the contact when he started speaking. Throughout the five-minute speech she didn't understand, she sensed Solange's eyes on her, but Abby refused to let her know she was aware of her.

There was a burst of applause before Raoul returned to the table. Two other men gave speeches and dessert was served. Raoul put an arm around the back of her chair. "If you're ready, we'll leave now."

That was fine with Abby, who didn't like being the center of attention. He held her chair while she got up, and then the two of them left the banquet hall, aware every eye had followed them out of the room.

"There. That wasn't so bad."

She gave an ironic chuckle, but didn't say anything as he helped her into the car. When he got behind the wheel, Abby turned to him. "What was your speech about? You got a resounding ovation."

"Remember when I told you that France's grape harvest was among the smallest in thirty years, down ten percent from the year before?" She nodded. "I passed on some thoughts my grandfather and I discussed recently. It's still too early to draw a conclusion about the quality of the wine this year. In truth, the future weather conditions haven't been predicted by the experts to be all that bad even if the quantity of the wine will be economically tight.

"That's why it's advisable for some vineyards that have a system of reserves to hold back selling a part of the production year to year. That practice serves as insurance to help ride out those times when there is a poor grape harvest."

"That's what you've been doing on your estate?"

"And will continue to do. My grandfather and I are in lockstep on that score, even if some of the family have a hard time wanting to conserve," he emphasized.

"I'm sure that's why you're in charge."

"Many of my family members would like to replace me if it weren't Decorvet tradition that the eldest son becomes head of the estate if the present owner dies or is unable to function."

"What about the eldest female if she's the oldest sibling?"

"Not in my archaic family, even if she's the most qualified."

"That leaves your sister out. How does she feel about it?"

"I'll leave that to your imagination."

"For what it's worth, I think your family is lucky with you at the helm. Thanks to you they still have their legacy and have survived, even after passing through such a terrible harvest."

He flicked her a burning glance. "I can't wait to get you home."

The impact of those words sent a thrill through her body. "Raoul—the daughter of the man I sat next to tonight, Solange, kept staring at me with hostile eyes. I'm not making it up."

"I know you're not."

Abby struggled to find the right words. "I can only assume she wished she'd been with you tonight."

They left the hotel for home. "One of these days she'll find the right man."

But Solange wanted Raoul.

"What's going on in your mind?"

"Nothing specific." Which wasn't true.

"That's the first lie you've told me. Tell me what's bothering you.

"Was it accidental that we sat right next to the Godard family?"

"No. The Wine Association plans these regional dinners and they always place the head *domaine* owners at the same table. It's a tradition I'd love to see abolished, but it's not my decision."

Abby noticed they were headed back to the estate. "Solange's father gave off an unsettling aura of hostility too."

"He's hoping I'll propose to her. There's nothing he'd rather see than a marriage between his *domaine* and ours. I knew which way the wind was blowing a year ago. That's why he brought her to the dinner tonight. When you and I sat down at the table, he came close to having a coronary."

"Good heavens—" she cried. "Does everyone have an agenda?"

"Not my grandparents. After we reach the cottage, I'll explain my reasons."

Her breath caught. "Do you think that's a good idea?"

His face closed up. "The entire region is aware that there's a new woman in my life. An American woman no less, one who knows nothing about vineyards and doesn't speak French except for a few words like *absolument*, *chasselas* and *Saint des Saints*."

She lowered her head.

"Now that I've gotten my duties out of the way, I'm planning to concentrate on you. You're the only thing of real importance to me. I don't want to waste a moment of our precious time together."

"But to go to your private home—"

"Abby—it must have occurred to you by now that I don't want you to leave." He reached for her hand and kissed the palm. The gesture melted her to the core.

"Surely you realize I'm asking you to spend the night with me. I've wanted you from the very first moment we met." *I've wanted you too, Raoul.* "I need to feel you in my arms and hold you. But if you don't feel that way about me, then I don't want you to be uncomfortable. All you have to do is tell me."

Abby was listening. He was the most honorable man she'd ever known. The way his marriage had ended so cruelly had left him grief stricken and she understood his needs.

She had needs too. Abby knew deep in her soul that Raoul would always be the great love of her life. If she gave in to her desires for a night of temporary rapture, it would ruin her for other men. To go back to California and pine for Raoul for the rest of her life was unthinkable. She couldn't put herself through that kind of hell.

Don't let it go any further, Abby.

She didn't dare bring that unending pain on herself. It was going to be like a death to fly to Venice tomorrow, but she knew it was what she had to do for self-preservation.

"I think you'd better drive me to the guest apartment."

Without his saying a word, he drove her to the *petit château*. He helped her with her things and walked her to her apartment where he set everything down. His dark eyes narrowed on her mouth. She could almost feel him kissing her.

"Go ahead and make plane arrangements. I'll call you in the morning. Depending on the time of your flight, I'll pick you up for breakfast in the morning and drive you to the airport."

"Wait—" she cried because he'd pivoted too fast and was already walking away.

He looked over his shoulder. "That wouldn't be a good idea."

When she couldn't hear his car, she shut the door, devastated by what had just happened. She waited there for at least five minutes, hoping he'd come back and beg her to reconsider. But it was evident it wasn't going to happen. If he'd really wanted to be with her tonight, he would have found a way.

She hurried in the bedroom to call the girls. Though it was late, she had to talk to them. She phoned Zoe first and got her voice mail. Too frustrated to leave a message, she called Ginger.

"Abby? Hey—what are you doing phoning this late?"

"I'm sorry, but I'm flying to Venice tomorrow and will try to plan a flight that fits in with yours and Zoe's schedule."

"You're not staying in Burgundy?"

A shuddering sigh escaped. "No."

"So the 'come and see my notebook' thing turned out not to be for real."

She gripped her phone so tightly, she could have crushed it. "Actually there was a notebook with a poem, but it wasn't an authentic signature of Byron's." In this instance, she had to lie after promising Raoul she'd let the find stay a secret.

"But he really had something to show you?"

"Yes. I met his grandparents and they showed it to me."

"Then he was on the level."

"Yes."

"You sound odd. Are you okay? What's going on with you two?"

"It's been a very full day with a funeral and a dinner. He's a very important man." But tonight he hadn't pressured her to stay with him and it hurt like crazy.

"Don't let me keep you up any longer. Shall I come early or late? You'd better check with Zoe."

"She's not here."

"What do you mean?"

"Zoe decided to fly to Greece early, so I took her to the airport today and now I have the car. Tomorrow is Sunday and I'm going to Burano Island for a couple of days. I've already paid for travel and the hotel room for two nights on a special deal. Why don't you check flights for Tuesday and I'll meet you whenever you say?"

Another two days with Raoul. Abby could hardly breathe.

"That sounds fine. I'll call you Tuesday and we'll plan from there."

"Perfect."

CHAPTER SEVEN

AT SIX-THIRTY SUNDAY MORNING, Raoul's phone awakened him. He worried it might be Abby and checked the caller ID. One look and he knew his father was summoning him, but he ignored it.

Last night he'd worked for a half hour sending instructions to Félix, then he'd stretched out on the couch in his office. It had taken all the self-control he could muster to leave Abby alone.

The phone rang again. Raoul got to his feet and clicked it on. *"Bonjour, Papa. Ça va bien?"*

"You and I need to talk." His father never changed.

"Whatever it is, let's do it on the phone now. I have other business in a little while." Like driving Abby to the airport.

"You're talking about that American woman staying at the *petit château* who is out for all she can get. Jean-Marc told me you met her in St. Saphorin. Whatever possessed you to bring her here?"

"With the property sold, she and her friends didn't feel right about staying on the vineyard for their vacation. I invited them to come here for a few days."

"But only one arrived with you. How dare you take her to the funeral! It shocked everyone to see you with someone else so soon after Angélique's death."

So soon? After two years? Raoul had to count to ten.

"I heard you took her to the banquet last night. Solange expected you to take her."

"I'm not interested in Solange and never will be. Abby has never been to France and I wanted to be a good host."

"She's not one of us," his father muttered angrily. "It would never do for you to form an attachment. You must see that! I want you to get rid of her."

Raoul grimaced because part of what his father said kept his guilt alive. "Was there something important about vineyard business you needed to discuss with me?"

"How soon is she leaving?"

"I have no idea." That much was the truth at least.

"You can't allow this to go on. Your mother and sister won't stand for it and I forbid it! The whole family is in an uproar. Pierre rang me when he got home from the banquet, demanding to know how she managed to be at the head table. If you don't cut her loose, I'll cut you out of the family business."

It didn't surprise him that his father would go that far. Again, Raoul chose to ignore it. "How are you feeling today?"

"How do you think?

"I've made arrangements for Dr. Filbert to be by later to check on you and the grandparents. He'll give me an update on your condition."

"The only thing I want you to do is make sure she's gone by tonight."

Click.

He didn't like that his father was in pain and suffered, but since the crash, Raoul hadn't let anyone dictate what he'd do with his life. After setting the electronic lock, he drove back to the cottage for a shower and shave. Then he made the phone call to Abby, prepared to tell her he didn't want her to leave.

"Raoul," she answered on the second ring. "I'm glad you called. There's been a change in plans with my friends. I won't be able to meet up with Ginger until Tuesday, but I'll book my flight for tomorrow around noon."

"If she's not going to be there until Tuesday, then you and I should make the most of the time."

"I… I'm afraid it's just prolonging the inevitable," her voice faltered.

"I never want you to leave, so don't pretend otherwise." When his heart rate slowed down he said, "If you're ready, I'll come by for you now, and take you to breakfast. I don't know about you, but I'm hungry."

"All right." Her quiet response was all he needed to hear.

After hanging up, he hardly remembered getting in the Maserati to drive to her apartment. She was out in front when he drove up. Those jewel-green eyes were the first thing he saw. Raoul sensed Abby was anxious, but she looked a vision in jeans and the same white-on-black print top she'd been wearing the day they met.

"Bonjour, ma belle."

"Good morning," came her slightly breathless greeting. While her glazed eyes played over him, a little vein throbbed at the base of her throat.

"I thought about you all night." Heat swept into her cheeks. He walked her to the car, holding on to her arm. "Are you hungry?"

"I think by now you know you don't ever have to ask me that question."

He gave her a kiss on the cheek after helping her into the passenger seat. "I'm hoping you'll enjoy La Mère Valois. It serves a simple breakfast eaten by the locals. Homemade country-style bread fresh from the oven and hot coffee."

"Mmm. A totally French breakfast."

"*Oui.* They have yogurt and fresh fruit if you ask for it."

"I'll have what you have."

"I'm warning you now I follow a Spartan diet in the morning."

Five minutes later he'd taken her inside the little bistro and had shown her how to dip her bread into the coffee and eat it. She followed his lead and probably disliked it, but she pretended to enjoy it.

"You're sure you don't want anything else?"

Her eyes flashed. "Positive. As long as I'm in France you know…"

Abby's spirit of adventure prompted her to try anything. She had many qualities he was crazy about. "I'll feed you properly after we reach Cluny."

When they'd finished eating, he walked her out to

the car and helped her in. "We're supposed to get a fair amount of sun today." He'd left the top down.

"Is Cluny far?"

"Sixty miles. Long enough for you to tell me what's going on with your friends."

"Zoe decided to leave for Greece early, and Ginger has already made plans away from Venice for a few days."

"Does that upset you?"

"You don't really expect me to answer that question."

"We're together for a while longer. I can't ask for more than that right now."

She looked around. "The scent of the flowers is heavenly here, Raoul."

"Pollination is going on everywhere."

"You tried to embarrass me once, but you won't succeed again."

"I have to make one stop at the cemetery, then we'll leave for Cluny."

Elation to be with Abby filled his system as he drove beyond the church to the place where André had been buried. Floral arrangements still decorated the grave site. Two figures were huddled there. Raoul stopped the car. "I won't be long."

Abby watched him walk over to the man and woman and kiss them on both cheeks. He must have wanted to be alone with them.

She reached into her purse and pulled out the little storybook his grandmother had given her. There was something touching about seeing Raoul's name printed by him at such a young age.

It thrilled her that his grandmother had kept his favorite book all these years. No doubt she'd realized early on how much Raoul needed to be with them. She wiped her eyes when she realized he hadn't had that same relationship with his own parents.

She'd been broken up after the visit to his grandparents and had needed a good cry. Their sweetness explained more than anything else why he adored them. The love between the three of them and the way he cared for them was moving beyond words.

Abby understood a few of the French words as she turned the scant pages. The artist had created a dreamy rendition of Blondine. In the story, she wore her golden hair long, like Abby had done before getting hers cut. But whatever likeness Raoul saw between Blondine and Abby had to exist in his mind because they were nothing alike. The idea that Abby was dreamy-looking would never have occurred to her.

She held the book and reflected on the talk with Ginger last night. While she thought about the way everything had changed since they'd all met in Switzerland, Raoul returned to the car. He eyed the book.

"My grandmother would never have given it to you if she didn't know you'd appreciate it."

Abby took a shuddering breath. "How much do they know about us?" she asked before putting it away.

"I rang them from Switzerland before we left La Floraison and told them I'd met a woman who had already changed my life."

Raoul, her heart cried. So *that* was the reason she'd given the book to Abby. She couldn't believe he'd shared something so personal with them before bringing her to France. "They…were wonderful and accepting in a way I can't describe."

"That's who they are. Looking at them yesterday made me realize their time is short."

She put the book back in her purse. Abby had yet to contact her own parents and tell them she wasn't with the girls, that she'd driven to France with a stranger and was out of her mind in love.

"I take it you were speaking to some of André's relatives."

"His grandson and wife. He fears he doesn't have what it takes to fill his grandfather's shoes. I've said what I can to reassure him."

"Wait and see. Knowing how you feel about him will go a long way to helping him, Raoul."

"One can hope."

"You have a way with people or they wouldn't revere you so highly. Once in a while you should accept a compliment. Or doesn't mine count?"

"More than you know. But as you've discovered, I've brought you to a hornet's nest."

"Except you can't say that about your grandparents. They adore you and I can see why they mean so much to you. But it hurts me for your sake that you and your parents don't have the same relationship."

"*Papa* wants things from me I can no longer give him."

"Like what?"

"He's expecting me to marry Solange."

"But that doesn't make sense."

"I know, but you try telling my father."

"Has he ever been happy?" she asked.

"Yes. When I married Angélique."

"So Solange is second best."

"He believes she will fill the role adequately."

Abby shook her head. "I'll never understand that kind of thinking."

"I didn't understand it from the cradle."

They left the cemetery behind. Once out on the open road they passed one charming village after another. Abby loved the scented breeze that ruffled their hair. With a disheveled look, Raoul was almost too breathtaking.

But this wasn't like the carefree drive they'd taken from Switzerland to Burgundy. Her whole body and soul ached for the love of this unique man who exuded a melancholy brought on by many things.

When they reached Cluny, they parked and walked around the monastery where there were crowds of tourists. Raoul wasn't in a mood to talk except to make a few comments about its history. For once he didn't reach for her hand. Not only the physical, but the mental separation was killing her. She took a few pictures of Raoul along with the abbey, then put her phone away.

"Are you ready to go back?"

She nodded and they walked to his car. Once he'd helped her inside, he asked her where she would like to eat. "Can we do what we did at the border? Buy some picnic food and eat it in the car on the way home?"

Without saying a word, he drove to an *épicerie* where they bought a small feast of finger foods and drinks. Then they were off again. The silence tore her apart. By the time they returned to the estate and he parked in front of the *petit château*, she was worried about him but didn't know how to help him.

For once he didn't get out of the car. He didn't plan to walk her to the door.

"Raoul? Would you come in with me?"

His eyes were slits when he looked at her. "I think not, and you know why."

"Please. I know something has been bothering you, but we can't talk about it out here where people will see us."

After a long wait he unbent enough to get out of the car. He followed her in and shut the apartment door.

"Why don't you freshen up in the guest bathroom before we talk?"

While he did her bidding, she visited her own en suite bathroom and returned to the salon. He was already back and on the phone. The grimace on his face was chilling. A minute later he hung up. Their gazes collided.

"Is everything all right?"

"No. Pierre has had another blowup over a bad decision Jean-Marc made with a client about lowering prices. It's the second time he's done it. Pierre's gone to my father about it and there's going to be hell to pay."

"Do you need to be there?"

"Yes. I'll tell my father what I think should be done, but he'll fight me on it like he always does."

"I thought you were the head of the *domaine*."

"He may be living inside a crippled, arthritic body, but there's nothing wrong with his mind. My father's a raging anachronism, still believing in the divine right of dukes. He resents his disability."

"So he takes it out on you. What was his excuse before he was afflicted?"

Raoul rubbed the back of his neck. She doubted he'd ever been asked that question before. "That my grandfather was still looked to as the true head."

"And now it's the way everyone looks to you." They stared at each other. "You rarely talk about your mother."

"She's lives for my father and what he decides. If she's ever defied him, I don't remember it. I'm sure she loves me and my siblings in her own way, but it has always been clear our father came first with her. I learned early that trying to appeal to her for something that went against my father's wishes fell on deaf ears."

On that note he started for the door. "We'll have to talk later. I don't know how long this will take, but I'll call you."

She followed him. "I'll find a way to stay busy."

He left without kissing her. Since leaving the cemetery his behavior had changed. For the time being she was helpless to do anything about it.

Raoul left her apartment and drove to the château. His parents' suite was on the second floor in the opposite wing from his grandparents.

"Maman." He kissed her cheek after entering their salon.

"Now that you've come, I'll be in the garden."

Maman was too thin, but with her strawberry blond hair and fine features, she was still attractive. He watched her leave the room like the good wife his father had trained her to be. Jean-Marc stood near the fireplace with a foul expression on his face.

Their uncle Pierre, filled with resentment to have to be in this situation at all, sat in a chair across from their father whose wheelchair had been rolled in. He couldn't manage it alone. Josette and Paul sat on the couch.

Raoul lounged against the wall and looked at his father. "What is it you want to say?"

"Jean-Marc has undermined Pierre twice on prices to foreign buyers."

"Because they're too high!" his brother argued. In principle he was right, but the Vosne-Romanée wine region would always demand the highest prices.

"Did you hear that?" his father almost shouted. "This can't go on. I won't allow it. You said you had an idea."

His father wouldn't be happy, but Raoul had to try for all their sakes. "Forget what's happened in the past. Jean-Marc has always been very good with people. He knows how to handle them. If you want my opinion, he should be working where he can do the most good."

With that remark, surprise broke out on his brother's face.

"Go on," his father barked.

"Pierre and Grégoire see eye to eye. Why not let father and son work together from now on? I'd like to pull Jean-Marc from the exporting department and give him a new position that's been needed for a long time."

"What do you mean?" His father always seemed to growl.

"For want of a better word, let him be the concierge of the estate with an office in the main building of the *domaine*. We've never had an official one, but I believe it's time to make some important changes. We need someone to meet and greet, to act as a liaison for all the different aspects of the business."

"That's part of your job as CEO," he fired at Raoul.

"When you can find me." He shook his head. "I have other concerns to do with our investments that require my full attention these days. Jean-Marc and I learned the business from you. No one knows more about our history than he does. He'd be our most valuable asset."

For once his father didn't have a comeback.

"I recommend that he and Grégoire start their new jobs today. Then everyone should be happy. Now you'll all have to excuse me."

"Where are you going?"

He glanced at his brother-in-law. "I was hoping to have a business conference with Paul. Are you free now?"

Paul eyed him in surprise. "Of course."

"Good. Then I'll leave it to you to sort everything else out, Papa."

"I want an answer to a question before you go. How soon will the American be leaving?"

His father couldn't resist. "You asked me that before. Remember she and her friends were cheated out of their vacation in Switzerland because Auguste's estate had to be sold. She's still not through sightseeing." How he enjoyed saying that. *"À bientôt."*

He left the room with Paul and they drove away from the château.

Abby had no idea how long Raoul would be. Since she had the afternoon ahead of her, she decided to go for a walk through the vineyards.

The sky had darkened by the time she stepped outside moments later. Not used to the climate yet, she couldn't tell if it might rain later. Maybe she wouldn't be able to explore for as long, but it didn't matter. She started out on the main road, then took a different road to the left. The workers were already out. Some waved to her and she waved back.

Every so often she passed little huts or shacks. There were a couple of men in pants and work shirts talking outside the third one. They eyed her with unmistakable male interest.

"Eh, bien. Mademoiselle Grant."

"Oh—Jean-Marc!"

He turned to the other man who seemed close to his age. "Gilles? This is the *Americaine* I was telling you about who's visiting the *domaine*."

The other guy flashed her a smile. "You're the one from California." He spoke with a heavy French accent. "I saw you with Raoul at the dinner last night."

She nodded. "He thought I'd enjoy seeing what goes on in the world of a vintner."

His eyes squinted at her. "How do you like it so far?"

"I'm still trying to take it all in."

Gilles smiled. "I'd be happy to show you more after work."

With that comment, Jean-Marc moved closer to her. "I'm free now and will do the honors. We'll talk later, Gilles. *À bientôt.*"

Abby hadn't expected to run into Jean-Marc. "I don't want to interrupt your work."

His beguiling smile was reminiscent of Raoul's. "I've just been made the new concierge for the estate. Since this *is* my work now, visitors are our first priority."

"Well, thank you."

So their father *had* listened to Raoul and now his brother had been given a position of importance. His compassion, even in the midst of turmoil, made Abby love him all the more.

"It's going to rain soon. I'll accompany you to the main *domaine* building. In my private office you'll see some ancient maps of our ducal land dating from the fifteenth century."

Abby assumed it might have been an office Raoul had used and had just relinquished in order to keep the peace.

"I'm a history buff and would love to see those."

His dark brows lifted. "What do you do when you're not traveling?"

"I'm a teacher of early nineteenth-century romance poets and writers at San José State University. My classes start again in the fall."

They started walking back to the main road. He cocked his head. "Even if you are on vacation, there must be a man in your life." Her heart jumped. *Only one.* "Is he anxiously awaiting your return?"

"Why do you ask?"

"Because if there is no one, I would like very much to get to know you better while you're here. Not long ago Raoul buried his heart with his wife and daughter. What you wouldn't know is that Solange de la Croix Godard, the woman you would have met at the dinner, is waiting for him to come out of his mourning period so they can be married."

Abby was aghast that Jean-Marc would warn her off his own brother that way when he knew nothing about their relationship. "I heard about their deaths" was all she said in a quiet tone.

They came to the *domaine*'s headquarters where half a dozen cars were parked. He took her inside, introducing her to several people working in the different offices, among them Félix Moirot, Raoul's sandy haired private secretary.

"Come with me." Jean-Marc showed her inside a huge office that was more like a museum. The maps and charts of the estate with its hectares of vines on every wall, all under glass, fascinated her. "You start in that corner. By the time you've made a tour of the whole room, you'll have seen the entire Decorvet chronological history."

"I've never seen anything like this!"

"I'm not surprised Raoul hasn't shown it to you. He has too many calls on his time."

"I'm sure that's true," she murmured.

The less they talked about him the better. "Do you mind if I study these for a little while?"

"Be my guest."

He stayed at the desk to make phone calls, leaving her to examine the earliest wall hanging. It was a charter with the ducal insignia of a lion, just like the one on the gate at the entrance to the estate. The handmade drawing showed two *terroirs*, intricate and incredible.

The rain pounded on the roof as she moved around the room, examining each step of history. Abby marveled at the artwork. The wording of the earlier drawings was done in old French. But her heart was heavy. Raoul had said he didn't want their relationship blighted by his complicated family. Jean-Marc had done a good job of putting a damper on this day.

He eventually walked over to her. His dark eyes were smiling. "I never saw anyone take this kind of time to look at everything." It sounded like a genuine compliment He was quite attractive in his own way. Abby felt sorry for him. To live in Raoul's unmatchable shadow wouldn't have been easy.

"Only a few people in the world have a heritage like yours. It's wonderful and different from anything I've ever known. I'm grateful you've let me browse to my heart's content."

"Grateful enough to let me take you for an early dinner? The rain has stopped and I need to eat."

It was getting late. Already ten to five. Abby had to do some quick thinking. She hadn't heard from Raoul, and she was hungry too. Why not agree with him so he wouldn't know his remarks had gotten under her skin?

"I'd enjoy that as long as it's close to the estate and doesn't keep you from your work too long."

He shook his head. "Entertaining a guest is part of the job, especially one as attractive as you."

Oh, dear. "Thank you. You make a great tour director." The remark was meant to put him off any ideas he had.

He led her out of the office to a silver Mercedes and unlocked it with a remote. The parking area still had puddles from the rain. She hurried to get in before he could help her, already fearing this wasn't a good idea.

To her relief he drove them to a small bistro in the village called Le Petit Pinot Noir. She pronounced the name out loud, loving the sound of it. When he asked her why she chuckled at the sight of it, she said, "I think it's a very clever name."

Again, she got out before he could come around and went into the restaurant first. Jean-Marc found a table by the window and gave their order to the waitress. "I've ordered us *boeuf bourguignon*, a regional favorite."

"That sounds good."

He ordered a bottle of red wine and poured some for her. "Try this, then later tonight I'll take you to our wine cellars where you can taste our superior *cru*."

"I did have some at the dinner last night. I'm no connoisseur, but it was like velvet."

"But they didn't serve you from a fifteen-year-old bottle. *That's* an experience." His eyes traveled over her while he drank his wine. She hadn't changed her mind about him. He was a flirt. She would simply have to see this through.

Within minutes the waitress arrived with their meal. The meat had been cooked in wine with baby onions and mushrooms. What made the difference in the flavor were the little bits of bacon. "This is delicious."

"I thought you'd like it."

When she lifted her head to smile, a gasp escaped her lips and every thought went out of her head. Raoul, dressed in a polo shirt and chinos, had just entered the bistro with another man who was dark-blond and looked to be in his mid-thirties. Then she remembered seeing him at the funeral. It was Paul. He'd been the one sitting next to Raoul's sister.

Raoul's black gaze surveyed the room, looking for a free table when he zeroed in on Abby. Lines darkened his features to see that she was with his brother. He walked over to them without hesitation and drew up two chairs.

"So this is where you are. Mind if we join you?" he asked, staring directly at her.

CHAPTER EIGHT

ABBY WAS SO happy to see him she blurted, "I'm glad you've come!"

The waitress came over and took their orders.

"Abby? You met our brother-in-law, Paul Ridoux, at the funeral. He's married to Josette."

"Hello again."

"Have you enjoyed your day so far?" Raoul inquired as if they were the only ones at the table.

"Very much because I've learned a lot. While I was out walking in the vineyard, I met your cousin Gilles and your brother. He took me to the *domaine* office so I could see all the maps. I'm afraid I studied them too long."

"You liked the display?" His eyes seemed to pierce hers.

"Who wouldn't? But a lot of the script was in Old French. I would imagine that would take a long time to learn."

"Not if the interest is there."

What did he mean by that? "Do you know this bistro has the funniest name? The Petit Pinot Noir has a ring to it that makes me laugh."

"I can't figure out why," Jean-Marc interjected.

But Raoul could. Suddenly she saw amusement light up his eyes, melting the frost.

Had he been upset because she'd come with his brother? Raoul had given her a look she never wanted to see again. When she got him alone, she'd explain the circumstances.

Soon their meal arrived and the waitress brought two more wineglasses. Raoul reached for the bottle and filled three of the goblets. The other one was Abby's, but she'd barely touched hers.

"Let's drink in celebration. The *domaine* has a new concierge in Jean-Marc, and Paul has just accepted the management of our European investment accounts." When their father died, Raoul would make Josette the head of the company. "My workload has just been cut in half and no one could be happier than I am. Next week we'll fly to Paris, Paul, and I'll introduce you to the groups I've been working with."

"I'll look forward to that."

Abby rarely drank alcohol, but this was one time she felt she needed it and picked up her glass to sip some. After they ate, Raoul was the first to break up their meal. He put some bills on the table that covered everyone's food and got to his feet.

"We've all got more work to do before this day is out. Since I have to run Paul back to the château, I'll take you with us, Abby."

Thank heaven he'd said that.

He looked at his brother. "That'll free you to meet the Spanish *ambassadeur* from Madrid. Félix just informed me that he and his entourage will be arriving within ten minutes. I have no doubts you'll have them eating out of your hand." He eyed Abby. "Shall we go?"

She stood up. "Thank you so much for the tour, Jean-Marc. It's been one of the highlights of my trip here. And this is a charming little bistro."

"*À tout moment,*" he said through wooden lips.

Abby didn't know what that meant. But she did know that the advent of Raoul coming into the restaurant had changed Jean-Marc's mood and she couldn't have been more grateful to leave.

When they walked out to the Jaguar, Paul climbed in back and Raoul helped her in the front passenger seat. On the short drive back to the estate, she turned to him. "I've never heard the expression *à tout moment.*"

"My brother meant that he would be glad to do it for you anytime."

"Oh. Thanks for telling me." She looked over her shoulder at Paul. "I understand you and your wife have one child and another one on the way."

He nodded. "Maurice is three and waiting for a brother."

"How exciting! When's the due date?"

"Two months."

"Have you thought of a name yet?"

"No. We're still arguing over it."

She smiled, but talk of babies was no doubt painful to Raoul. If he married again and had a child, would it help fill the hole in his heart? Every day he had to live with the loss of his little girl.

Before long they arrived at the estate. Raoul stopped

at the *petit château* and let her out. "I'll call you in a few minutes."

She nodded. "It was nice talking with you Paul." Abby got out of the car and hurried inside her apartment, wishing Raoul didn't have to leave.

Much as Raoul wanted to follow her, he had to drop Paul off first.

His brother-in-law leaned forward. "She's one beautiful woman. Nice."

"I agree. If we hadn't happened to stop in there, Jean-Marc would have forgotten all about the appointment with the Spanish contingent."

Except that it wasn't an accident. Raoul had seen Jean-Marc's car. He was curious why he'd gone there to eat so late on his first day as concierge. It wasn't his kind of place. Seeing Abby at the table explained everything.

Raoul wound around to the east entrance. Paul got out. "I can't thank you enough for giving me the new job. I know Josette complained to your father."

"That's not the reason, Paul. Since my trip to Switzerland, I've been thinking about several changes to relieve me of so much work. Your head for finance makes you the ideal choice to work with the Paris group. You'll be a great asset."

"Thanks for the confidence, Raoul."

They shook hands. After he walked away, Raoul headed back to Abby's apartment. He phoned her from the car to let her know he was out in front. She didn't know it yet, but he had plans for the two of them.

She came out the entrance a minute later and hurried to the car. After she got inside she said, "I hope you don't thin—"

"I don't think anything," he cut her off. "Jean-Marc has always had a roving eye."

"Still, you looked upset when you first walked into the bistro, and I couldn't explain. The thing is, I didn't know what to do when Jean-Marc saw me out in the vineyard and told me he would show me the office. I didn't want to be rude to him."

"Rudeness isn't in your nature. What you saw was a man who experienced a temporary fit of jealousy when he saw you having dinner with another man, even if he happened to be his own brother."

His admission thrilled her. "Thanks to you he's very happy about his new position."

"I'm glad to hear it."

"Your brother-in-law must be happy too."

"I believe he is. Before I let Paul out, you should know he said you're beautiful. In private he said he could understand Jean-Marc's interest. The whole estate is talking about you."

"What an exaggeration."

"You think? Paul and I had to stop by the *domaine* office. Every male there mentioned he'd gone off with the stunning blonde *Americaine*. Gilles happened to be there and was upset because he'd planned to ask you out for dinner after work, but Jean-Marc got there first."

"I'd rather not talk about that. Where are we going?"

"Where we won't be disturbed."

Her breath caught as he drove them along several roads that wound deep into the vineyard. Raoul had told her before that there were only two places where they could be together in private. Since he wasn't taking her to his office at the château, there was only one other spot she could think of.

When they came to a low-lying ridge, she saw a charming cottage straight out of a Grimm's fairy tale. Raoul hadn't exaggerated about where he lived. From the massive Decorvet château to this isolated hideaway?

As they drew closer she noticed his Maserati parked around the side. He pulled to a stop in front and turned off the engine.

"I wish you hadn't brought me here." Her desire to be alone with him was like a flash fire. She no longer felt she had the strength to keep him at a distance. If she went inside with him, she'd become the wanton who lived only for him.

"I want to discuss something important with you. Surely you're not afraid of me. Have I ever taken advantage of you?"

"You don't have to," she admitted. Abby despised her own weakness.

"Since providence has given us until tomorrow before you have to leave, it seems fate has chosen the moment to be now."

"What moment?"

"I'm afraid you don't know what you awakened when you were willing to come to Burgundy with me. You're familiar with the saying, 'who rides the tiger'?"

"Of course."

"Then you understand my meaning."

He was being cryptic. But before she could ask for an

explanation, Raoul helped her out of the car and walked her inside.

After turning on a lamp, he showed her around the modernized, comfortable-looking interior. The small cottage contained a living room and a kitchen off to the side. There were two bedrooms and a bathroom.

But all Abby could see were the small framed pictures on his bedroom dresser. One showed his lovely wife holding the baby. The rest were photos of his little daughter, Nicolette. Jean-Marc's words pressed in on her.

Not long ago Raoul buried his heart with his wife and daughter.

He handed her one so she could see it up close. "Oh, Raoul—she's adorable and had your black hair."

"She had colic and cried a lot in the beginning. I walked the floor with her many a night."

Tears filled her eyes. "I can only imagine your pain."

"It never leaves, but the initial, excruciating pain has gone. Now it's more a case of what happens when I see any young child My mind immediately imagines my little daughter at that age, probably following Maurice around."

"I'm sure I would do the same thing for the rest of my life."

She put the picture back and left the bedroom. He followed her into the living and grasped her around the waist from behind, burying his face in her hair.

"I've learned to live with it." But had he? "What I'm waiting to hear is your impression of my private *Saint des Saints*."

She turned in his arms. "It's cozy and warm. You'd

never know that the most famous vintner in all Burgundy hides out in here instead of the château you call a relic."

His white smile turned her heart over in the semi-darkness of the room. "Do you like it enough to stay here with me tonight? Now that I have you to myself, I have no cares."

"I thought you brought me here to talk."

"Later."

He pressed a hungry kiss to her mouth, tasting it over and over again. This was what she'd been aching for all day. Too soon they were both breathless. Raoul was the most beautiful, virile man she'd ever seen in her life. In her heart she knew his first wife had to have felt the same way about him.

Had they made love before their marriage? No woman could ever be immune to him, and he would have felt some attraction to Angélique or he couldn't have married her.

Did she dare dream that Raoul would ask Abby to marry him? She didn't have to hear Jean-Marc's warning again that Raoul had buried his heart at the funeral. If he'd been letting her know marriage to Raoul wasn't in Abby's destiny, he'd done a good job. She tore her lips from his.

"Raoul—we shouldn't be doing this. I'll be leaving in a few days."

He shook his head. "I can't let you go. Let me love you, *mon amour*. While we were in Switzerland, my soul was struck by what we French call the *coup de foudre*. Love at first sight. It makes no sense, but there's no other explanation to account for my feelings since I met you. Don't be nervous."

"But I am," she confessed in a tremulous voice.

"Why? I know you want this too."

"I do. More than anything I've ever wanted in my life, but we're not thinking clearly. There are too many reasons why we mustn't."

He crushed her against him. "Name one that matters."

"How do we know this *coup de foudre* won't happen to you again?"

"You mean to *us*! No, *mon amour*, you and I have experienced something that only happens once in a lifetime."

"But your family needs more time."

Raoul released her enough to look at her with a puzzled expression. "What's going on with you? My family has nothing to do with my personal life."

"Oh, yes, it does."

Lines marred his striking features. "Be honest with me, Abby. What are you really saying?"

She couldn't avoid this. "I don't want an affair with you!"

Raoul's black eyes pierced hers like lasers. His hands gripped her shoulders. "That's what you think I want?"

She averted her eyes. "I don't know anymore. I could never be intimate with you and then just fly away as if it never happened. That's why I'd like you to take me back to the apartment now."

"Are you saying this because Nigel is still in your heart and that's what you can't get over?"

"No—" she cried softly. "All feeling for him was burned out of me the second I saw pictures of his children and realized his wife was telling the truth. I honestly haven't thought about him since."

"Even so, being intimate takes time to get over and it hasn't been that long since you broke it off with him."

She eased away from Raoul. "You don't understand. I never went to bed with him. We were going to go away over Christmas to be together for the first time. Thank providence his wife came to the office that day and opened my eyes."

"Are you saying you've never made love?" Raoul sounded incredulous.

"That's right."

"Not even with the other man?"

"I couldn't until I knew my heart. That moment never came." She folded her arms to her waist. "Does that shock you?"

"Yes."

"It wasn't because I was afraid of intimacy. But I didn't think it fair to sleep with him before telling him I couldn't marry him. I did love him, but not enough. However, the same can't be said about you and Angélique."

His black brows knit together. "What are you talking about? I told you my marriage lacked the passion of a real marriage. We slept together in order to have a baby. But after Nicolette was born, I didn't touch my wife again."

She moaned. "But Jean-Marc said—"

"I can just imagine what my brother said," he cut her off. "But he didn't live with me and Angélique behind closed doors. I'd like you to tell me what Jean-Marc said."

"He said several things, among them that Solange was waiting until your pain lifted."

His head reared. "You and I have already had this

conversation. She'll have to wait forever. As for Nicolette, she definitely took a part of my heart with her. And I *was* grief stricken, but it was because I could never love Angélique the way a husband should love his wife. I'll pay a price for that to the end of my days. I'm not an honorable man, Abby."

A bleak expression had broken out on his handsome face, filling her with turmoil.

"Raoul—surely you don't mean that! You *can't* mean it. When you gave in to your mother and father's wishes to marry her, Angélique knew you weren't in love with her. But she married you anyway."

He shook his head. "But it was wrong."

"How can you say that? You gave her a beautiful life, and you had a baby who turned out to be a great blessing. Nicolette brought both of you joy. For you to go on punishing yourself makes no sense. You were forced into that marriage because of a lie. Now you're free to marry the woman you love."

His pain-filled eyes searched hers. "Are you telling me you could marry me, knowing my history at this point?"

"But we're not talking about me."

"Now you're deliberately misunderstanding me." He grasped her upper arms. His black gaze burned with an inner fire she could feel. "I want to marry you, Abby Grant. Tonight if we could. I want it more than anything I've ever wanted in my whole life."

She gasped.

"What else could all this be about?" He shook her gently. "Losing my family within seconds of the crash has taught me one important lesson. We don't know how much time we have before life strikes a blow. The idea of meeting you and not being able to love you forever is anathema to me. Are you listening to me?"

It was a good thing he was holding on to her, or she would have fainted on the spot. "You couldn't want me for your wife, Raoul. I'm afraid I'd be an embarrassment to you."

"*Embarrassment*—don't you have that turned around? Be honest. In your wildest dreams you couldn't have imagined a man like me coming into your life."

"That's because you had a special destiny decreed generations ago. All that you are, your identity, everything is tied up here in Burgundy."

"But my curse is that I have good and bad baggage. The question is, why would a brilliant American college professor who has lived by the Pacific Ocean all her life want to leave family and country for an entrenched French vintner?"

"Raoul. Listen to me, please. I'm afraid I couldn't measure up to you."

"That argument doesn't hold water and you know it," he bit out. "It's because you're afraid to take a chance on me. Admit it—" His voice throbbed.

"Don't you ever say that!" she cried. "You're the most wonderful man I've ever known. You wouldn't have had to tell me about the poem for me to come with you. Aren't you convinced yet that I'd give anything to lie in your arms and never have to leave? From the beginning, I wasn't able to hide my feelings from you. Only love could have made me drive to France with you in the first place."

"Then will you marry me right away? We'll say our vows at the deputy mayor's office in Dijon. He was a judge and is a good friend of mine with the power to waive the banns requirement." He leaned closer and pressed a kiss to her lips to stifle any other words. "A civil marriage is mandatory before we could be married in church."

Abby couldn't keep up with him. "Stop! You're going too fast. I have to think about it before I can say yes."

She felt his hard body shudder in response. "While you do that, you're in too much danger from me here, so I'm going to take you back to the apartment."

"But where will you be?"

"In my office doing a ton of work that has backed up. When I pick you up in the morning, I'll expect an answer from you."

Before she knew it, he'd driven her back to the *petit château*. After an intense kiss at the entrance to her apartment, he eased away. *"Dors bien, ma belle."*

She watched him drive away in the night. Abby held on to the door handle, shaking because his words had taken hold inside her.

He wanted to marry her. He'd already talked about a date...

With her mind reeling, Abby went inside her apartment and curled up on the bed, throwing a duvet over her.

Raoul's first marriage had been forced on him. It wasn't because of a great love. He'd admitted how painful it had been. But the fact that he felt so undeserving of a woman's love was much more painful to her.

Once again she could imagine what her friends would

say. *You can't marry a man this soon. You've been swept away on a riptide.*

But Abby was so desperately in love with him, she couldn't imagine life without him. Yet she'd never felt so conflicted in her life.

Turning to the two people whose advice she treasured most in life, she phoned home. To her relief her mother answered. It had to be late afternoon.

"Abby, darling—I'm so glad you called. We haven't heard from you since your vacation started."

"I know. I'm sorry, but so much has happened, I hardly to know where to begin. Is Dad home yet?"

"No. He has a meeting and will be late."

"Tell him I love him. Mom? I need to talk to you. Is this a good time?"

"What do you think."

"Will you play King Solomon for a few minutes?"

There was a long pause. "That's the most serious question you ever asked me."

"That's because it is." In a shaky voice Abby said, "I've met the great love of my life. He has asked me to marry him right away. There's no way to describe him."

"Try."

For the next half hour Abby poured out her soul to her. When she'd finished talking, she wiped her eyes and waited for her mother to say something. "Mom?"

"King Solomon would tell you to wait and give it time. But I'm your mother and I'm convinced you're too in love to take anyone's advice. You said you have to be married in a civil ceremony first. So why don't you do it without telling anyone?

"I'm sure your father would tell you the same thing. While you go through the waiting period so you can be married in the church, you'll know if you've made a mistake. Then you can tell the whole world, or not."

Abby let out the breath she'd been holding. "Thank you, Mom. That's what I was praying to hear. It won't be a mistake! I'm sending you some pictures of him and the estate on my phone right now."

Again, Abby waited to hear her mother's response. Finally, she said, "He's the most gorgeous man I ever laid eyes on."

"Mom—"

"I may be your mother, but I'm not blind. Please don't tell your father what I said."

Abby chuckled. "It'll be our secret. Have you scrolled to the picture of the château yet?"

"Oh, my heavens!"

"That's what I said."

"Your father's not going to believe it."

"I'm afraid Dad's not going to approve of doing anything too soon."

"You're right. He won't be happy."

"Maybe you shouldn't say anything to Steve or Nadine yet."

"Don't worry. I'll keep this under wraps until we hear from you again. All we want is your happiness, darling."

"I love you, Mom. More than you know. I promise to call soon."

Abby got ready for bed, but she barely slept waiting for morning to come.

CHAPTER NINE

WHEN MORNING CAME, Raoul texted Abby that he was driving over to the apartment. By the time he arrived in front, his nerves were so shot he was trembling and felt ill. If she told him she couldn't marry him...

Abby opened her door to him, wearing a creamy linen blouse with a wrap-around khaki skirt. He walked her inside and reached for her, kissing her so soundly they were both weaving by the time he allowed her to breathe. "Did you get any sleep?"

She avoided his eyes, terrifying him. "No. I talked to my mother last night. Dad wasn't home. I told her everything."

His insides froze. "Abby?"

"She said if it's going to be a mistake, it would be better we have a civil ceremony first. Then no one will have to know."

Raoul could hardly breathe. "Is that how you feel? That it will be a mistake?"

"Not if we set some parameters. How do you feel about a working wife?"

With that one question, his taut hard body relaxed.

She lifted her green eyes to his, revealing a shine that almost blinded him.

"You realize I'll have to find a teaching position somewhere around here, and I'll have to go to school to learn French."

"Abby—" he whispered her name again, and started to reach for her.

"And one more thing. I want a baby with you so badly I expect to get pregnant ASAP. If that happens, we'll work out everything else."

In the next breath he cupped her face in his hands. "You just gave me the answer I've been dying for. All my adult life I wondered when or if the right woman would come along. When I found you sitting on the train station bench, my heart almost failed me. Somehow I knew my search was over."

"So did I. It was a feeling that grew stronger with every passing minute," she murmured against his lips, hugging the life out of him. "I love you so terribly."

"Je t'aime, mon amour."

Raoul began kissing her with abandon. The freedom to love her had caused him to forget everything else. His hunger had taken over and he couldn't get enough of her. He buried his face in her neck.

"Our wedding day can't come fast enough, but I agree with your mother. I don't want anyone to know we got married until after the fact. By the time my family comes to grips with it, they'll be ready to see us married in the church. But I'm going to have a devil of a time pretending that nothing is going on when all I want to do is steal you away for weeks on end. Come on. We have work to do."

"Where are we going?"

"To my office. I'll have our breakfast brought in from the château kitchen. While we eat, we'll start to make arrangements. The first thing we have to do is meet with Boris Rochefort, our attorney in Dijon who's licensed to practice law both here and in the States. He'll issue us affidavits of law and marital status. I'll also need a copy of Angélique's death certificate. Next we'll go to Dr. Filbert's office for our medical exams."

"Ooh. I forgot about that. Can you trust these men not to tell anyone about us?"

"If they want to keep their jobs." She laughed. "Before we leave, you need to send for a certified birth certificate."

She leaned over to kiss him again. "I brought one with my passport, just in case of some emergency. Who would have thought I was going to need it to get married to the most marvelous man on earth?"

He gathered her in his arms. "You've made me so happy, I'm never going to let you out of my sight."

"Promise? Oh, Raoul." She wrapped her arms around his neck, but he was too hungry for her and knew this couldn't go on if they were going to make the appointments he'd set up for them.

After they left her apartment and ate breakfast in his office, they drove to Dijon in the Maserati. Once they'd gone through the motions to receive the various certificates, Raoul took her to the city hall where he introduced

Abby to Deputy Mayor Judge Tibault. His friend would marry them and waive the banns. Because of his packed schedule, the soonest their wedding could take place was nine o'clock on Thursday morning, three days away.

By evening they dined at the Coin Caché. He reached across the small round table for her hand. "I brought you here to eat their two specialties: eggs in red wine, and Paris-Brest."

"What is that?"

"One of my favorite desserts. It was named for a bicycle race between those two cities."

She smiled. "Now I understand."

"It's a wheel-shaped pastry, made with a praline-flavored filling."

"Umm. That sounds delicious. When I cook for you, I'm afraid I won't be making anything so exotic."

"You like to cook?"

"I love it when I have the time. I'll fix you some American dishes I know you'll like."

"Abby—" Emotion made his throat swell. Instead of talking, he kissed the palm of her hands before letting it go.

"I'm so excited to become your wife, Raoul. Everything that other wives have been doing since time immemorial, I'll be able to do for you. For the next three days I don't think I'll be able to sleep."

"Don't plan on getting any after we're married."

She answered back with fire in those gorgeous green eyes. "I was going to tell you the same thing."

"Chérie—I know you don't want me spending money

on you, but since your family isn't here, will you at least let me buy you a dress to wear on Thursday?"

"Yes." Her answer surprised and pleased him. "I've seen a few bridal shops while we've been going in and out of buildings. Will you have time tomorrow to drive me there?"

"What do *you* think. Speaking of driving, we need to talk about a car for you."

"I left my old Honda at home in my parents' garage." Abby finished the last of her pastry. "When we get back to my apartment, I'll call my folks when we can talk to dad. I'll add that they can keep the car. They'll want to talk to you."

"I'm looking forward to telling them that they've raised the loveliest woman on both sides of the Atlantic."

"I love you," she whispered.

"I need to take you home where we can be alone. When are you going to tell your friends about us?"

She gave him an impish smile. "After the deed is done."

Raoul burst into laughter, loving this woman beyond anything he thought possible. On the way home he clung to her hand. It was still hard to believe she'd agreed to spend the rest of her life with him. That's what he told her parents when they called them later that night on her phone.

To Raoul's surprise her father was friendly and made him laugh. "I've never been able to afford the Decorvet Pinot Noir. It's too high-end for anyone I know. My daughter has come a long way," he teased, emphasizing the *long*.

Raoul said, "I'll send you a case."

"If you're trying to win my approval, that's the way to do it. But seriously, our daughter has never sounded happier in her life."

"You have our blessing." This from her mother.

"Thank you. Later on, we'd like to have a church wedding where you and your family can come," Raoul interjected. "It will be my pleasure to fly you over and back."

"We'll look forward to that. Be sure to send pictures as soon as you're married in Dijon."

"It'll be the first thing we do, Mom," Abby spoke up. "Give my love to everyone."

When they hung up, he wrapped her in his arms. "They're incredibly nice for two parents who couldn't possibly think this will work. The first thing I'm going to do tomorrow is send a shipment of wine to them."

"They'll love it. *I* love it. They're already so impressed with you, and I'm so madly in love with you it's pathetic, even if your phone is ringing."

Raoul pulled it out of his pocket. "It's my father."

"Go ahead and get it."

He kissed her thoroughly. "This is for business. I'll call you in the morning and we'll make our plans."

She walked him to the door. "I'll be counting the hours."

After he walked out to the car, Abby shut the door. There couldn't be a happier woman in all France tonight. She hurried into the bedroom and got ready for bed. Knowing she wouldn't be able to go to sleep yet, she reached for her laptop as she got under the sheets.

The first thing she did was write a lengthy letter to the head of the literature department at San José State to let them know she was getting married and wouldn't be returning in the fall. She would hand write an official letter of resignation later, but they needed to know her plans immediately.

Before she'd met Raoul, she couldn't have imagined this scenario, not when she'd worked so long and hard for that position. But the world had changed on its axis when Raoul had come into her life. To think it hadn't even been a whole week!

With her missive sent, she got busy on another project. It had been a long time since she'd gone shopping for clothes, let alone a wedding dress. For the next hour she looked at everything under the sun. By the time she was ready to shut her computer off, she knew exactly the style and color she wanted. She'd pick up some other items too, including a few nightgowns.

Abby got out of bed long enough to put the laptop back on the table and turn off the overhead light. Only a few more days and she'd be going to bed with Raoul every night. She climbed under the covers, imagining he was with her.

The next morning she got up to shower and wash her hair. Since she would be picking out her wedding outfit, she wore her sundress with the jacket to look a little more dressed up. More new clothes were needed, but she'd worry about that later.

Her phone didn't ring until eight-thirty. She hoped everything was all right and picked up after the first ring. "Raoul?"

"Forgive me for not calling sooner. I'm afraid our plans are going to have to change today." Disappointment swamped her. "I'll explain later, but I'm going to be tied up with business until the afternoon, so I've instructed a maid from the château kitchen to bring you breakfast.

"She should be there any minute. Anything else you want to eat, you'll find in your kitchen. Feel free to explore the property or do whatever you want. I can't give you a definite time when I'll be back, but I promise to call and keep you informed." He sounded rushed.

"You always do. Is everything okay?"

"It will be when I put out this latest fire."

This was his life and she'd better get used to it. "Good luck, my love."

No sooner had she hung up than the maid knocked on the door. Abby thanked her and walked into the sitting room with the delicious-looking meal. Once she'd eaten her fill, she walked back to her computer while she waited for Raoul.

At noon he returned to the apartment. He swept her in his arms. "What have you been doing?"

"Last night I sent in my resignation to the department. While I was waiting for you to come just now, I received an answer from Dr. Thurman. I'll show it to you later."

He walked her out to the car and they took off. "Did he say he'd make you a full *professeur* to keep you on?"

She smiled. "It wouldn't have mattered if he'd offered me the moon. You have no idea how much I love you." After kissing him again she said, "I wrote to Magda. If she hadn't chosen me to help on that script, I would never have ended up in Switzerland and met you. To think if the girls and I had arrived a day later..."

"I don't want to think about it, Abby. It was meant to be. Do you know what kind of a dress you want to buy for our wedding?"

"Yes! I saw exactly what I wanted online last night. If you'll drive us to the Grace Loves Lace shop, that should be the only place we have to go. I hope you won't mind staying in the car. I don't want you to see it until Thursday."

He found it on the address locater. "After it's put in a bag, I'll come in long enough to pay for it."

"I'll need some shoes too, and some lingerie. I can get everything there at the same time. I promise I won't take a long time."

One thing he knew about Abby. She wasn't one to play games and always kept her promises. After he dropped her off in front, he parked and made arrangements for their honeymoon. He had a surprise for her.

Before long she waved to him from the entrance. He went inside to pay the clerk. After helping her out to the car with her garment bag and packages, he took her to dinner at a sidewalk café.

"You look happy." In truth she was radiant.

"I am, but I'm wondering how I'm going to make it through to Thursday. I wish we were married right now."

He'd been thinking that for days now and took her back to the car. Before starting the engine, Raoul took a deep breath. "I have a lot of work to do, which will help me stay away from you tomorrow. As for tonight, it's getting late. I'm going to take you back to the apartment and we won't be seeing each other again until Thursday morning."

She chuckled. "I didn't know you were so old-fashioned about not seeing the bride before the wedding."

"Surely you realize I have to let you go right now because I don't trust myself to be around you any longer. At 6:30 a.m. Thursday, my assistant, Félix, will come for you in his car."

"I don't understand."

"Gossip will follow that you're moving out of the apartment for good. Which you are. He'll load your luggage and everything you've bought. Be sure to wear something to suggest you're dressed to travel. He'll drive you to the helipad beyond the château and my pilot will fly you to a hotel in Dijon where I'll be waiting."

"So this is it?" The disappointment in her eyes made him want to drive into the night with her and never return.

"It would be a mistake to touch you again once we get back to the estate. Just remember that the next time we do this, you'll be my wife." On that fierce note he leaned toward her and kissed her fully, losing himself in the love this magnificent woman miraculously returned.

Raoul saw Abby to the door of her apartment with her things, but he didn't reach for her. She trembled uncontrollably when she heard him drive away.

Everything had to be kept secret. It seemed wrong, but her mother thought it was best and she had to trust Raoul that this was the only way for them. As soon as they were married, they'd go immediately to the château and announce it to his family in his grandparents' suite.

Trying to throw off her worry, she took out her dress and opened the other bags. She wished her friends were here to see the knee-length white lace dress and celebrate with her.

Abby hadn't planned to tell them until after the wedding, but she was too excited to hold back. Since it was late, she texted both of them and to let them know what was going on before she went to bed.

When morning came she still hadn't heard back from them. Afraid that Raoul might send a maid with her breakfast, she repacked everything and put it out of sight. Since she couldn't stand to be alone with her thoughts any longer, she looked up some addresses in Dijon, then phoned for a taxi.

After it arrived, she asked the driver to take her to the jewelry store address on her list. It was very small and they spoke English. For the next hour she looked at all the men's wedding bands. "Do you have any special, unique kinds of bands?"

The jeweler brought out another tray. When she saw the yellow gold one with a small cluster of round purple jewels in the center, she knew she'd found what she wanted. "This looks like it was made for a vintner."

"Indeed it was." The jeweler looked pleased. "I've been wondering when someone would buy it."

She smiled. "I think it's been waiting for me. What's the price?"

When he told her, she blinked. It would take all the money she'd planned to spend on her vacation, but she decided it didn't matter because she only intended to be married once. She could never do enough for Raoul to show him how much she loved him.

"Will you engrave something for me on the inside?"

"Bien sûr." He handed her a pad and pencil.

Abby printed the words for *my beloved* in French and the date of the wedding.

Mon bien-aimé, le 9 juin.

"It won't be ready for a couple of hours."

"Then I'll be back." She paid him with her credit card and left to get lunch at a café she'd seen around the corner on her way here. Once she'd given her order, her phone rang. Her pulse raced, thinking it was Raoul. But when she pulled it out of her purse, she saw the caller ID and answered.

"Zoe?"

"So you're really going to do it!" she blurted first thing.

"Yes."

"Without giving me or Ginger a chance to be there?"

"We'll get married again in church in front of all our family and friends, but we have to be married civilly first." She gripped the phone tighter. "Do you think I'm crazy?"

"Yes, but I can tell you're so in love with him you can't help yourself. Just remember that Ginger and I will be thinking of you tomorrow, even though you won't be thinking about us. Now I've got to run to catch the ferry. God bless. May you have joy, Abby."

Joy was the right word.

Abby ate her pasta salad and then did some window shopping until it was time to pick up the ring. When she walked into the shop, he had it waiting for her.

"Do you want this gift wrapped?"

"No." She inspected the inscription. "This is perfect. Thank you. Just put it in the little box."

"Très bien."

With it tucked safely in her purse, she started to leave, then went back to the counter. "Do you have any pins for a woman to wear on a suit jacket or dress? Maybe something with flowers?"

He frowned. "What do you mean exactly?"

"Well, I'm getting married in the morning to an important vintner in the region, and I'd like to have a gift to give my fiancé's mother. Nothing extravagant, but something meaningful that says I love her wonderful son."

"Let me think. I'll have to go in back where I keep my special collections." He came out a minute later and laid a little one-inch gold pin on the velvet. It was a vine with enamel purple grapes and one enameled white flower at the top.

Abby shook her head. "I can't believe you have something like this."

"Burgundy is famous for its vineyards."

"It's exactly what I was hoping to find. How much is it?"

"Consider it a wedding present from my shop. I hope you'll come in again."

"Of course I will! I can't thank you enough. Will you please gift wrap it for me?"

She was so thrilled with her purchases, she couldn't stand still. As soon as he handed it to her, she put it in her purse and hurried outside to a *tête de taxi*. When she said the Decorvet Domaine, the driver nodded and they took off for Vosne-Romanée.

En route she received a text from Ginger.

I was right. He did get to your romantic soul. Forget everything I ever said. I couldn't be happier for you.

Tears stung Abby's eyes to have her friends' blessings.

When the driver reached the gate, he made a phone call and the doors swung open to let them through. She gave him directions to the *petit château* and paid him before getting out of the taxi.

For the rest of the day she did work on the internet. First she looked up the University of Burgundy located in Dijon and discovered that the humanities and sciences were well represented on the main campus with law, medicine and literature in separate buildings. She didn't know if she could ever get a teaching position there, but it wouldn't hurt to inquire.

Then she looked up where to get French lessons. Abby could go many directions, but thought it might work to hire a private tutor. She found the names of three qualified instructors and phoned them for more information.

After saying she would get back to them, she fixed herself some food from the kitchen and then sat down to watch TV. But she could hardly concentrate while waiting for Raoul to get in touch with her. She knew he wouldn't be coming over, but when it got to be nine o'clock, it surprised her that there'd been no phone call.

It wasn't until she climbed in bed and set her alarm for six a.m. that she received the long-awaited text.

Tomorrow every dream of mine is going to come true.

She sent a text back.

Get a good sleep, beloved. You're going to be loved the way no one has ever been loved before.

After putting the phone on the side table, she buried her face in the pillow, whispering his name.

Raoul waited near the landing pad at the Dijon-Bourgogne Airport in the Maserati. He rechecked his watch. Five after seven. The helicopter should be here by now. *Mon Dieu…* if anything unforeseen happened to her at this point, he wouldn't want to go on living.

He was ready to contact his pilot when he saw the helicopter approach. The second it set down, he got out of the car and hurried toward the door even though the rotors were still going. His pilot opened it and there stood Abby who cried out his name and climbed right out into his arms.

"*Dieu merci* you're here." He covered her face with kisses. "Another minute and I would have lost my mind."

"You're not the only one." She kissed him with enough passion to rock him back on his heels.

"Let's get you in the car with all your things and I'll drive us to the hotel near the city hall where you can change."

With the help of his trusted pilot, they stowed all of her things. Raoul waved him off and got in behind the wheel. He shot her a piercing glance. "Are you ready?"

She reached for his hand and squeezed her answer hard.

Once they reached the hotel parking, they took only the things she'd need for the ceremony and hurried inside. Everything else would stay locked in the car.

He'd gotten them a room on the second floor near the elevator where they'd both change. Raoul had ordered breakfast. They ate quickly. As soon as she disappeared into the bathroom with her garment bag, he put on his white dress shirt and formal gray suit.

Then he waited with pounding heart for her to emerge. When she walked out a few minutes later, he couldn't catch his breath. Her dress, made of the finest white Chantilly lace, covered her from her neck to her wrists, and followed her curving shape to her knees. On her feet were matching lace high heels.

"Abby—" His voice shook.

He took one white rose from the white rose bouquet he'd had made up for her and tucked it behind her ear.

Abby's green eyes roved over him hungrily, feeding his desire. "I'm the luckiest woman in the whole world."

Raoul handed her the bouquet of roses and her purse. "Let's go get married."

A taxi waited for them out in front of the hotel and drove them to the entrance of the city hall. As he helped her out to the pavement, a volley of whistles sounded. She literally stopped traffic as they walked up the steps into the building.

He cupped her elbow and walked to the room where Deputy Mayor Judge Tibault was waiting for them. The older man couldn't take his eyes off Abby. After introducing them to the two witnesses who'd been brought in from the other room, he winked at her. "No wonder Raoul wanted the banns waived. If I were thirty years younger…"

Abby blushed and clung to Raoul.

"If you're ready, then stand in front of my desk and hold hands."

She put her bouquet on a chair, then placed her right hand in his.

"Abby Cederlof Grant and Raoul Capet Regnac Decorvet, do you both come together of your own free will in the prefecture of Dijon on this ninth day of June to be united in marriage?"

"Yes," they said in unison.

"Raoul? Do you take Abby to be your wife?"

"I do"

"Do you promise to love, honor, cherish and protect her, through the good and the bad, forsaking all others and holding only unto her?"

"I do"

"Abby? Do you take Raoul to be your husband?"

"I do," sounded her tremulous voice.

"Do you promise to love, honor, cherish and protect him, through the good and the bad, forsaking all others and holding only unto him?"

"Yes," she said emotionally.

"Abby? Hold out your left hand. Raoul? Repeat after

me. Abby Grant, I take thee to be my wife, to have and to hold, in sickness and in health, for richer or for poorer, and I promise my love to you. With this ring I thee wed."

After saying the words, Raoul pulled the diamond ring from his pocket and slid it on to her ring finger. Her eyes took in the three-carat diamond solitaire before she lifted moist eyes to him. They burned with love.

"Abby? Do you have a ring for him?"

"Yes."

Her answer came as a complete surprise.

"Raoul? Extend your left hand."

He did his bidding.

"Abby? Repeat after me. I take Raoul Decorvet to be my husband, to have and to hold, in sickness and in health, for richer or for poorer, and I promise my love to you. With this ring I thee wed."

He looked down as she put it on his ring finger. A gasp escaped his lips. The design of the purple gem stones resembling a cluster of pinot noir grapes set in gold shook him to the very core of his body. Was this what she'd been doing when he'd found out she'd left the estate yesterday in a taxi?

"Just as two very different threads woven in opposite directions can form a beautiful tapestry, so can your two lives merge together to form a very beautiful marriage. To make it work will take love.

"Love should be the core. Love is the reason you are here. But it also will take trust—to know in your hearts you want the best for each other. It will take dedication—to stay open to one another; to learn and to grow together even when this is not always so easy to do.

"It will take faith to be willing to go forward to tomorrow, never really knowing what tomorrow will bring. In addition, it will take commitment to hold true to the journey you both now pledge to share together.

"In so much as the two of you have agreed to live together in matrimony and have promised your love for each other by these vows, I now declare you to be husband and wife. Congratulations. You may kiss your bride."

"Darling," she cried as he covered her mouth with his own. All the love he could ever hope for or imagine was surrendered to him in a kiss that went on forever.

He rocked her body in his arms, never wanting to let her go. But when he opened his eyes, he realized that the deputy mayor, who had a broad smile on his face, was waiting for them to join the world once more.

Raoul looked down at her. "Madame Decorvet. Do you have any idea what it means to call you Madame Decorvet? I think we need to get a room of our own."

"Just as soon as you both sign the marriage certificate."

His bride blushed again before they wrote their signatures. Raoul asked Tibault to take some pictures of them with his phone. With that done, they shook the older man's hand, then Raoul swept his bride out of the room and the building to their same taxi. The driver knew ahead of time where to take them.

Once in the backseat, Raoul pulled her onto his lap, ignoring the flowers and kissed her passionately until they arrived at the hotel. When they got out and reached their room, he carried her over the threshold and followed her down onto the bed.

"I can't begin to express all the feelings exploding inside me, Abby. All I know is, I adore you, *mon épouse*. It's killing me that we have to drive back to the château right now. Once we make our announcement to the family, then we'll drive to the cottage and forget the world."

She caressed the side of his jaw with her hand. "I know how important this is, especially for your grandparents' sake. They love you so much and are waiting. And I haven't forgotten we were seen by officials who will tell the press. The news of our marriage will be all over French TV by tonight. We *have* to tell your family immediately.

"I did some research about you. You're one of the most important men in France." Her eyes misted over again. "It's an honor to be your wife. I'm still having a hard time believing that this is really happening."

"You're going to know it all right, once I get you home and in my arms. I may never let you go. This ring I'm wearing... No man was ever given a greater treasure."

"There's an inscription."

Excited, he removed it and read it aloud.

After giving her another deep kiss, he rolled away and got to his feet. "The sooner we leave, the sooner our new life will begin."

Still wearing their wedding clothes, they gathered up their few things and took everything to the car. As they left the city and headed for home, he reached for her hand. "For the first time in my life, I'm seeing my world in Technicolor. It's all because of you."

CHAPTER TEN

"THAT'S EXACTLY HOW it feels," Abby exclaimed. "While you're driving, I'm going to phone my parents. Can I use yours? I'll send the photos at the same time."

Raoul handed it to her.

"First I'm going to take a picture of this gorgeous diamond ring you gave me. I love a solitaire more than anything. How did you know?"

"It has a pureness and reminds me of you."

Everything he said touched her heart.

By the time she got off the phone, they'd reached the estate and Raoul drove them to the south entrance of the château. Suddenly the gravity of their announcement and what it would mean to his family took hold of her. When he turned off the engine and helped her out of the car, she hugged him hard.

"Don't be afraid. We'll just have to give them time. Remember part of our vows? It will take faith to be willing to go forward to tomorrow, never really knowing what tomorrow will bring."

"I know." She pressed a kiss to his lips. "I have faith in you."

He checked his watch. "We have ten minutes before everyone will congregate. Let's go greet my grandparents first."

With his arm around her waist, he ushered her inside and up the stairs to the second floor. After a knock, he opened the double doors. Lisette had wheeled his grandparents into the main salon. She congratulated them first.

"Ah—" his grandmother cried when she saw them. "That lace is breathtaking. How beautiful you look, Abby!"

"Thank you. It's because I'm so happy to be married to your grandson. Doesn't he look handsome in his gray suit?"

His grandfather smiled and nodded.

"Papi? Mamie? May I present my wife, the joy of my life. Look what she gave me." He walked over to the old man so he could examine the ring.

Abby hurried to his grandmother and gave her a kiss on both cheeks. They both marveled over the dazzling diamond.

She grasped Abby's hand. "I've never seen him this happy."

"That's what my parents said about me when we sent pictures to them a little while ago. We're going to have a wedding picture made up for you."

"We would love it. Abby—don't let what anyone says or does disturb you," she whispered.

"I won't," she whispered back. "We know you and your husband approve of our marriage. That means the world to us."

"This is a difficult family."

"I think all families are, a little."

She stared at Abby. "I can see you are the right one for him."

"I'm glad if you think so."

"I'll pray for you."

Her words stayed with Abby as they heard voices in the entry. Raoul reached her side and put his arm around her shoulders. Soon the family entered the salon. She counted at least twenty-five members. She recognized Jean-Marc, Gilles, Paul and Raoul's father, who sat in his wheelchair, but not anyone else.

The shock on each face told a story Abby would never forget. Raoul's arm tightened. "Thank you all for dropping everything to come here today. I wanted you to know that Abby Grant, the light of my life, became my wife this morning at the *mairie* in Dijon by Deputy Mayor Tibault. We'll be married at the church in Dijon in a few weeks."

Before he could say another word, she heard a cry and the pregnant brunette woman standing next to Paul left the suite. That had to be Josette.

Her husband walked over to Abby and Raoul. "Welcome to the family." He kissed her on both cheeks. After giving Raoul a hug, he hurried after his wife.

In the next breath Raoul's father, with a scowl on his face, barked to Jean-Marc to wheel him out of the room. The lovely older woman who'd been standing next to him—the thin one with the reddish-blond hair who had to be Raoul's mother—seemed to pale. She looked conflicted before following her husband out of the salon.

"Just a minute, darling," Abby said to Raoul. Then she ran after his mother and caught up with her in the entry hall. "I wanted to give you this." She put the tiny wrapped gift in her hand. "I love Raoul desperately and want us to be friends."

His mother looked utterly bewildered before Abby ran back to Raoul, passing his two aunts and their families who were walking out.

It was like watching dominos fall one by one.

"Congratulations," said one of the men who resembled Raoul's father. "I hope you'll be happy."

"Thank you, Oncle Pierre."

The other older man who stood next to Pierre nodded to Raoul. "I must say I'm surprised you didn't pick a woman of our own nationality, but I wish you both well."

"*Merci, Oncle Lucien.* That means a lot. To be honest, love picked me," he said, kissing Abby's cheek.

Gilles frowned at Raoul. He said something in French Abby didn't understand and strode out of the salon behind his father.

Abby felt like she'd been watching a bizarre play, not believing that anyone could sketch characters as unbelievable as these real people. Did inheriting a title truly do this kind of damage?

When his aunt left the room, Raoul pulled Abby into his arms and held her for a long time. She wanted to tell him they should leave here and never come back. No one deserved this kind of treatment.

There were so many things she wanted to say to him, but she knew she couldn't. This was his life. He'd been totally honest about it. She'd just pledged to love and support him.

Learn and grow together even when this is not always so easy to do.

Those words were part of the vows she'd taken just hours ago. She *had* to honor them, but she knew it was going to be the hardest test she would ever have to pass in this life.

The sadness in his grandparents' eyes since the rest of the family had come into the salon haunted her. Raoul had clung to them all these years for a reason. Well now he had Abby too! She would be his rock.

When Raoul let her go, she walked over to his grandfather and gave him a hug. "Now that we'll be living in the cottage, we'll come to visit you every day. Raoul needs your help and your wisdom," she murmured near his ear.

She felt him reach for her hand and squeeze it hard, but she knew he was getting tired. So was his grandmother.

Raoul blew both of them a kiss, then grasped her hand and they left the suite for the car. Neither of them spoke as he started the engine and drove to the cottage. When they arrived, he sat there without moving. "I knew it would be bad, but I can see I should never have subjected you to this."

"But you're too honorable to behave in any other way."

"Why did you run after my mother?"

"To give her a little gift for having the most fabulous son on earth."

"Abby—"

"Tell me something. Why did your sister walk out like that? What's the real reason?"

"Father should have made her the head of the *domaine*. She's as capable of managing it as I am. When Angélique and the baby died, she didn't think I'd get married again. With no child to come after me, it would mean their son, Maurice, would be the next one in line. Seeing me married again, she's afraid we'll have a baby and that will be the end of any hope she has. Paul's promotion still won't bring her what she'd hoped for."

"But she's your sister."

"And we love each other. We've shared good times too, but you have to understand that my father's decision to name me has hurt her and my aunts who are equally capable of running the estate. He sees running the grape business as men's work."

Raoul turned a solemn face to her. "This is nothing against you personally, Abby. My mother would have stayed to welcome you if my father hadn't forced Jean-Marc to wheel him out. She's never had the courage to stand up to him when something important mattered to her."

"We're all too human at times. What did Gilles say to you? Did he hurt you?"

"No. He said I was a damn lucky man."

After a dark sound escaped his lips, he helped her from the car. To her surprise he carried her over the threshold. Once inside, they clung to each other.

"Darling? Please don't suffer for my sake. We're home in our happy refuge. This is our *Saint des Saints*.

Nothing can touch us here. We have each other. What else do we need? Are you listening to me? You're my everything, Raoul. I ache to love you. Let me show you what you mean to me."

"Abby—" He kissed her mouth. She tasted the salt from his tears. "This was no way to start out our marriage."

"Your grandmother said she'd pray for us."

A sad chuckle escaped. "That sounds like Mamie."

"Guess what? You and I promised to love and cherish each other through the good and the bad. Since we've gotten the bad out of the way really fast, how about you help me out of this dress *toot sweet*?" It was the word for fast in French.

The reaction she'd hoped for came out of Raoul who let out a deep belly laugh. "I think you meant *tout de suite*."

"Yes. I love the sound of it."

"I love you, *ma femme*. I love every particle of you." He carried her into the bedroom and put her down gently before unfastening the button at the back of her neck. "Get ready to be loved," he warned her.

"I was ready when you brought me to the cottage for the first time, remember?" She undid his tie. "If you want to know a secret, I've been waiting for the *dénouement* since the moment you got out of that old black car how many eons ago?"

He grinned and flung his suit jacket on the chair. "Something tells me my new bride has been studying her French."

"It's a beautiful language." She started unbuttoning his shirt. "Almost as beautiful as you."

"You think a man is beautiful?"

"Not until I met you."

Raoul helped her off with her dress and put the divine white lace concoction on top of his jacket. His eyes burned like black fire as he drew her onto the bed and a husband's desire took over, making her thankful she'd been born a woman.

Three days and nights of nonstop loving had made a new man out of Raoul. They'd wanted for nothing. Before the wedding, he'd had the cottage stocked with everything they'd need so nothing could disturb them. Their world was so perfect he refused to let anything or one intrude on their happiness.

Abby was not only his wife, she was his generous lover who poured out her heart and soul to him while they worshipped each other with their bodies. Hers was glorious. He loved her with a passion that scared him whenever he thought of losing her.

Monday morning he awakened early with a desire so intense for her, he rolled her closer while she was still asleep and started kissing her. Her lovely legs twined with his. She made little sounds until her eyes opened. Her seductive smile set him on fire.

She rubbed his jaw, which needed a shave. "I thought I wore you out in the middle of the night. What are you doing awake again?"

"As if you didn't know, *mon amour*."

Her voice caught. "Do you think all newlyweds feel the way we do?"

"Only if they're in love the way we are, which is rare. I've been lying here trying not to think how I would ever handle losing you."

"Raoul—" She leaned over him with a little frown. "What a thing to be thinking!"

"I can't help it. Don't you know you're my heart?"

"If I got started on how much I love you, I'd never stop." She kissed him with a hunger that sent a thrill though him. Two hours later they surfaced long enough for her to escape his arms and get out of bed.

He reached out to trap her hand. "Where do you think you're going?" he asked in a gravelly voice. "I didn't give you permission."

"To shower and fix your breakfast."

"I'd rather you stayed right here. I want to discuss something with you."

"Well, in that case." Abby crawled back in next to him. "Is it serious?"

He kissed her hungrily. "I want to take you on a honeymoon."

"Raoul—that's what I felt we were on when you brought me to Burgundy."

He smoothed the hair from her brow. "I mean a real one."

"Do you have a spot in mind? I read some statistics that showed most French people preferred to vacation in France."

"It's true a lot of them like to camp. But I'd love to spend time on a beach with you."

"Then let's do it when you can get away. I know this isn't the best time."

"How do you know that?"

"I heard you tell Paul you were taking him to Paris sometime this week."

"So I did."

"How long would you be gone?"

"I'll leave in the morning and be away until the next night, but I don't want to leave you. Marrying you has put everything else out of my head."

"While you're gone, I'll start my French lessons. I already have several tutors lined up. When you return, we'll plan a trip after you've looked at your schedule. Living in this cottage with you is the only honeymoon I could ever want."

"I'm thinking the Cinque Terre on the Italian Riviera. You'll be enraptured with the landscape."

"I don't know of it."

"That makes it even better." He kissed her throat. "I want to shower with you and then I'll help you fix breakfast."

She flashed him that come-hither look. He didn't know if she did it on purpose, but it didn't matter because it worked.

"You know I'm learning to like what you eat in the morning? Bread dunked in coffee. It's so easy and non-fattening. It won't do for your wife to put on weight. All I need to hear someone say is 'There goes that plump *Americaine*, waddling her way through the Decorvet vineyard.'"

Raoul burst into laughter. It reverberated throughout

the cottage. He'd give her the moon if he could. "After we eat, let's drive into Dijon and buy you a car. You can always use one of mine, but I'm sure you'd like your own. What kind would suit you?"

"Something that's economical and will always start."

He chuckled. "That can be arranged. You're too easy to please."

She slid her arms around his neck beneath the spray of water. "If you don't know it by now, all I want is you." The new ways she showed him proof of her love told him without words this marriage would last forever.

Once they'd dressed and eaten, Raoul left the cottage a new man as they walked out to the Maserati. With his delectable wife clinging to him, the sunny day added a punctuation mark to his mood of euphoria.

By dinnertime she'd decided on a Peugeot 308 in dark blue, but it wouldn't be ready until he returned from Paris.

"Tonight I'd like to take you dancing." He drove them to a popular restaurant/discotheque, but after a few dances he wanted to take her home. "I need to be alone with you as much as possible before I have to leave in the morning."

"I'm so glad you said that," she whispered against his neck.

They couldn't get back to the cottage fast enough. When his alarm went off at six the next morning, they both groaned. Loving her half the night had only made him hungrier for more.

He leaned over her. "I have to meet Paul at the helipad in twenty minutes. Take care and don't let anything happen to you while I'm gone."

"Call me. I won't be able to breathe again until you're back safely."

Abby slept in late. After getting up, she ate some fruit and bread, then started cleaning. Raoul would have sent a maid, but she wanted to keep house for him. She put in a wash and by midafternoon she'd showered and dressed in jeans and a blouse.

He'd given her keys to both cars. She could take either one if she wanted to go out. While she was debating whether to take a drive around the region to get more acquainted with it, she heard a knock on the door. Maybe he'd sent one of the maids after all.

When she opened the door, she received the shock of her life. Josette and their mother stood on the porch. They'd known Raoul had left for Paris with Paul and that she was alone.

"Will you forgive us for coming without phoning you first?" This from his mother who spoke excellent English. "I was afraid you might hang up, and you would have had every right. We haven't even been formally introduced yet. I'm Hélène-Claire. This is my daughter, Josette."

Abby never dreamed she'd see them on the doorstep, not after what happened last Thursday in the grandparents' salon. Even more astounding was that she was wearing the pin Abby had given her. She wore it on the lapel of her pale blue cotton suit. It had to be some kind of a miracle.

"Please come in." She was thankful she'd done the housework. If they'd come a couple of hours sooner and seen the mess… Wait till she told Raoul. "Sit down, won't you?"

"If we're disturbing you, we won't stay."

"But you're not," Abby assured them. "Can I get you coffee or tea?"

Both of them shook their heads. "Nothing thank you."

Josette looked pale and nervous. "The way I treated you and my brother on your wedding day was so inexcusable I know neither of you will ever be able to forgive me. But I had to come and tell you how sorry I am."

"It's all right, Josette. I know our marriage came as a huge shock to everyone. Most of all to me!" The two of them looked surprised. "Raoul and I met under the most unusual circumstances. He was very honest with me about the loss of his wife and baby. I could tell how he'd suffered."

Their eyes filled with tears.

Thrilled that they were listening, Abby broke down and explained everything to them. "My friends were worried about my coming to France with him, but I couldn't not come b-because I'd fallen in love with him that fast," her voice faltered, "and he with me.

"I've cared deeply for two men in my life before Raoul, but I could never see myself married to them. But then I met Raoul and realized he was the one I'd been waiting for. We've come from opposite ends of the world, opposite lifestyles, but we love each other."

"I could tell that," Hélène-Claire murmured. "I saw the way the two of you looked at each other. For the first time in his life, my son looked completely happy and my mother-in-law agrees with me. His marriage to Angélique—"

"I know about that," Abby interrupted. "Nothing else needs to be said. But I know he'll never get over losing his little girl."

"You're very sweet. Raoul couldn't help but fall in love with you." She touched the pin. "This gift you gave me was unexpected for many reasons. It touched my heart."

"I wanted you to have something meaningful. You raised a son who has made me so happy I can't begin to describe how I feel about him. I plan to be the best wife I can be, but I'm going to need help from all of you. My parents are behind our marriage a hundred percent, but what do I, an American literature teacher, know about the family Raoul was born into?"

"I'll help you."

"Thank you, Josette. Raoul loves you and your boy very much. When I met Paul the other day, he let me know how excited he is about the baby that's coming. He was so nice to me."

"Much nicer than I was," she murmured. "He told me my brother deserved a woman like you. Now that we've talked, I couldn't agree with him more."

"Thank you."

"Will you let us make it up to you for the way we treated you?"

"You don't have to do anything. All Raoul would love is to hear what you've just told me."

"We intend to do that," his mother asserted. "What

I'd like to do is host a party to welcome you into the family. My husband—"

"Raoul has explained many things to me," she broke in once again. "He suffers a lot of pain."

"Yes, but he needs to demonstrate his love for Raoul, which of course he has always felt. I'm ashamed for his actions as well as the way my two sisters-in-law walked out of the salon. Here's what I'd like to do. Raoul and Paul will be back Wednesday evening. We'll have a family dinner in our suite on the *terrasse*."

Abby got excited. "Let's make it a surprise. Can Maurice come? I want to meet my new nephew."

Josette broke into a genuine smile. "He'd love to be a part of things because he adores my brother."

"Who doesn't?" Abby quipped. "Will the grandparents be able to come?"

"If it's too much for them, we'll visit them after we've eaten dinner."

"And Jean-Marc?"

Josette's brows lifted. "If he can get over his jealousy."

"What do you mean?"

"Our cousin Gilles and my younger brother have a crush on you at the moment."

"Tell Jean-Marc that I found him very charming. If I hadn't met Raoul first…"

At that comment both women laughed. Josette nodded. "I *will* tell him."

Hélène-Claire rose to her feet. "We've kept you long enough. We'll set a time when we know Raoul and Paul will be back from Paris."

"Wonderful!" Nothing sounded more perfect to Abby, who was overjoyed that the two women in Raoul's life had come around to make peace at last. "Let's exchange phone numbers to stay in touch."

When they'd done that, she walked them out to the porch. As soon as they'd driven away, she went inside and checked out some Dijon toy stores. When she found a couple of addresses on the internet, she grabbed her purse and drove the Jaguar into town. What a fantastic car, once she got the hang of it!

Within an hour, she'd purchased a darling musical box called Les Papoum, and a kaleidoscope with a circus motif. You twisted both ends to make different colors. Those gifts would be fun for Maurice.

Raoul phoned just before she went to bed. "I miss you so much I've been no good to Paul today."

"I don't believe it."

"Tell me about your day."

If he only knew. "I slept in, cleaned and drove around in the Jaguar. I promise it's still in one piece, but you'll have to adjust the seat."

His laughter sounded over the line. "I'm going to work all night so we can get home earlier tomorrow."

"What do you want to do when you get here?" she teased. Inside she was struggling to hang on to her secret.

"If you have to ask me that question, then I've been doing something wrong."

Had she said something that worried him? "Darling, I was just checking to make sure you're not tired of me yet."

"Do you honestly think that could ever happen?"

He *was* upset.

"Next time you fly anywhere, I'll go with you, but I can't promise to behave and you'll wish you'd left me behind."

She'd hoped to wring a chuckle from him at least. No such luck.

"I'm never leaving you again." His voice sounded savage. "I'll phone you in the morning. Miss me, *mon amour*."

"Raoul?"

But he'd hung up. What on earth was wrong?

Their conversation had left her restless and she didn't sleep well. At eight the next morning he phoned her again. She picked up immediately. *"Bonjour, mon mari."* She'd been practicing how to say *my husband*.

"Have you started your tutoring lessons already? Is that where you went in the car yesterday?"

What? "Actually I went shopping."

"I see."

She frowned. "I've been waiting for your call."

"We'll be back at three."

"I'll drive to the helipad and wait for you."

"You don't have to do that."

"What if I want to? I love you."

"I love you too."

Again he hung up, leaving her worried and dissatisfied. Abby flung herself out of bed. Thank heaven he'd be home soon so she could find out what was going on with him.

For the next few hours she sent emails to relatives

and friends in and out of the department letting them know that she'd gotten married and where she could be reached. She received a heartfelt congratulations from Magda.

Josette called her later and asked if she wanted to go shopping with her in Dijon while Maurice was napping. Abby had jumped at the chance to get acquainted with Raoul's sister, who bought a becoming aqua maternity dress for the party.

Abby found a green-beaded ruched knee-length sheath dress. Josette assured her Raoul's eyes would pop out when he saw her in it. The dinner was scheduled for six o'clock.

After their return, she put the dress in the closet and drove the Jaguar to the helipad, wearing her jeans and blouse. Raoul had said three, but it was three-fifteen when she heard the sound of the rotors. Soon the helicopter came into view. Her heart thudded as she watched it set down. Out came Paul with a suitcase. Raoul followed with his.

She left the car and ran to hug him. If something was still bothering him, he didn't let it show as he crushed her against him and swung her around. The intensity of his kiss melted her insides before he swept her toward the car. He helped her in the passenger seat and got in the driver's seat out of habit. Paul sat in back.

Abby turned to her brother-in-law. "Did business go well?"

"I never realized how much I didn't know."

"He's going to do great work for us," Raoul commented. He dropped him off at the château, then drove them to the cottage. Her husband was still in an odd mood.

"Before we go inside, I want to know what's wrong. You haven't been yourself since we talked on the phone last night."

He shut off the engine and turned toward her. "The truth?"

"Always."

"I should never have left you this soon after our wedding. When you told me you'd taken a drive and had gone shopping, I knew you couldn't bear to be here alone. You seemed a little evasive. I was angry with myself and I'm afraid I let it show."

"All is forgiven." She might have known that he'd sensed she'd been keeping something from him. Raoul wasn't a man you could toy with, not when it came to his deepest emotions. "I *was* being evasive, but for the best of reasons. At six this evening, all will be revealed. Can you trust me until then?"

"You know I trust you with my life," his voice grated.

With those words she jumped out of the car and hurried inside first. When he followed her through the door, he had to run to catch up with her. She reached the bedroom first. "I thought you'd never get here."

"Mignonne—" He caught her to him. The moment their mouths fused in need, the world reeled. His loving took her to such a divine place, she almost forgot about the party.

"Darling? What time is it?"

"Ten to six."

"Uh-oh. We have to get ready."

"For what?"

"You'll find out. Put on something semi-dressy. I'll shower first." She dashed away before he could pull her back. They were going to be late.

At ten after six she walked in the living room where he was waiting for her. As Josette had predicted, his black eyes glittered with desire as he studied every curving inch of her. "I approve of your shopping spree."

"Good. I like your black silky shirt. You're impossibly handsome, you know. So handsome, I'd like to lock myself up in a tower with you."

She thought he sounded a little out of breath. "Where are we going?"

"To the château."

He looked taken aback. "I don't understand."

"You will. In fact you're going to have to show me where to go. We were due at your parents' suite ten minutes ago."

Raoul shook his head. "Don't tease me about this."

"I'm not, my darling." She grabbed the sack with the presents. "We need to hurry."

Abby started for the car first and got in without his help. He was totally quiet as he drove them to another entrance to the château she hadn't seen before. This time he opened the car door for her. Before he let her go, he ran his hands over her hips and back. "You're so beautiful, it hurts."

She kissed his lips before hurrying inside with him. He led her up the stairs to the second floor. When they came to the entrance, the doors had been opened. Abby hooked her arm through his and they walked inside.

The first person they saw was an adorable brunette boy who came running toward Raoul, calling out something like "Rool." Abby loved the little guy already. Her husband picked him up in his arms.

Maurice asked him something in French. "What he did say, Rool?"

Raoul's laughter delighted her. "He wanted to know if I bought him a present while I was in Paris. I can't believe it, but I forgot to get him anything on this trip."

"No, you didn't." She lifted the sack. "These are for him."

His black eyes stared at her in shock.

"Go on. Give them to him."

He carried Maurice to the couch in the salon and reached inside the bag to hand him his presents. Josette and Paul came in to see what was going on. A smile lit up their faces to watch as their boy tore off the wrapping paper and examined his new toys.

Raoul grabbed Abby around the waist, propelled by emotions erupting inside of him. He stared at his sister. "You look lovely tonight."

"Don't they both?" Paul had his arm around her shoulders. "Our wives went on a shopping spree while we were away. I have a feeling we're in for it when we have to travel on business."

Abby shook her head. "*Mon mari* won't be leaving town any time soon, so you don't need to worry."

Josette smiled. "Maman has dinner waiting for us on the *terrasse*."

Once again Raoul stared at Abby. She grasped his hand. "Come on."

Paul swept Maurice into his arms, toys and all, and they walked through the suite to the *terrasse* that overlooked a fabulous rose garden. Abby heard one of those male whistles and looked to the side. Jean-Marc stood there with his arms folded, wearing a grin.

"Congratulations on your marriage." He walked toward her and kissed her on both cheeks. "I should have been the one who went to Switzerland." Then he faced his brother and gave him a hug that brought tears to her eyes.

Over their shoulders she saw his mother wheel their father over to them. She wore a filmy yellow dress. On the shoulder, she was wearing the pin. Abby could hardly breathe.

"We're so happy for the two you." She approached Raoul who wrapped his arms around her. As they clung, his father eyed Abby. "My son is a very fortunate man. If you'd lean over, I'd like to give you a kiss and welcome you to the family."

Abby's heart was full to overflowing as she did his bidding. They kissed on both cheeks. He was probably in pain to put forth that much exertion. But the fact that he made the effort meant the world to her.

Raoul watched the two of them as if he couldn't believe what he was seeing. His father finally looked at her husband. Abby saw love in those dark eyes before he held up his hands. The sight of father and son embracing would be etched in her mind and heart forever.

Paul had put Maurice in a high chair. He kept tapping his kaleidoscope against the tray. Abby hurried around and sat down to talk to him. "Will you let me show you?"

Of course, he didn't understand her. She put it to her eye, then urged him to do the same.

Josette said something to him in French and suddenly Abby could tell he was seeing the designs inside.

"I'm starting French lessons and can't wait until I can talk to him."

"He'll love it, but I'm afraid I'm going to have to put him to bed in a minute."

"Thank you for letting him stay up."

Raoul sat down next to Abby and put his hand on her thigh beneath the table. Heat rushed to her face. She couldn't look at him as everyone gathered and their meal was served.

His mother looked at Abby. "This is such a special occasion, I cooked dinner myself. This was always Raoul's favorite. Rack of lamb and mint from our garden. Before we eat, I'd like to make a toast to our son and his bride." She lifted her glass. "To new beginnings."

Abby knew they were drinking the most treasured pinot noir from their vaunted wine cellar. After she swallowed a healthy amount, Jean-Marc raised his glass. "Here's to the fresh California breeze that has blown through the vineyard."

"Amen," Paul chimed in.

"That was very poetic for you," Josette teased her younger brother and held up her glass. "To a new friend I like very much."

Their father kept his hand around his glass, but Abby knew he was going to say something. "This is good. To my family."

Raoul had to be overcome. She waited while he

cleared his throat. Then he stood up with his glass. "As you all can see, with Abby in my life… I've been reborn." He kept swallowing. "Thank you," he whispered.

Please, please, let this last, Abby prayed while they ate together, amused by Maurice's antics.

Toward the end of the meal his mother stood up. "We'll have dessert with the grandparents now. It's your favorite, Raoul, my *crème brûlée*."

Raoul clung to Abby's hand. She knew he was still in disbelief that any of this was happening. She could hardly believe it herself. They moved as a group to the other end of the second floor and gathered around the salon with the grandparents.

"This is divine, Hélène-Claire. I want the recipes for everything you've made tonight. A wife wants to be everything to her husband, but there's no way she can compete with his mother's cooking."

Raoul's grandmother nodded. "You are very wise for one so young."

Josette broke in on them. "I've got to get Maurice to bed." She eyed Abby. "We'll talk soon."

"Please."

"It's time for us to leave too." Raoul got up to kiss his grandparents and parents.

Abby turned to everyone. "This has been one of the most wonderful evenings of my life."

His mother followed them to the entrance of the suite. "We'll do it again with the entire family after your church wedding. Let us know when you want to plan it."

"Merci, Maman."

He whisked Abby down the hall to the other end of

the château where the car was parked outside. Silence reigned during the drive back to the cottage. She found herself savoring this night. When he took her inside their house, she grasped both his hands and kissed them.

"Your heart has to be so full. After we get in bed, I'll tell you what happened after you left for Paris. I thought it was a miracle. Tonight, I know it was. I really like your family. All of them. Because they love you, they're trying to like me. I can't ask for more than that as long as you love me."

"Jean-Marc said it best. You *are* the fresh breeze blowing through the vineyard, casting a spell on everyone, including your husband who adores you." He picked her up and carried her into the bedroom. "Get ready to be loved tonight like you've never been loved before."

EPILOGUE

FAR INTO THE night Raoul came awake and reached for Abby. Since their marriage four months ago he still awoke with anxiety at times, in case this was all a dream and she wasn't really there.

"Mon amour," he whispered, rubbing her arm gently until she turned to him.

"Raoul—" His loving wife gave him a kiss of such desire, he was breathless as they lost themselves in each other for the next few hours. He'd never dreamed marriage could be like this. He hadn't thought it possible. "No man could be as happy as I am."

"I hope that's true," she spoke against his lips. "But to make certain of it, I have a gift for you I know you're going to love."

"Is that so?"

"Yes."

"Are you going to give it to me now?"

"Not quite yet."

He raised up on one elbow. "That's not fair."

"I know, but I love teasing you."

Raoul kissed her throat. "Give me a hint. Is it expensive?"

"I don't know yet."

"What do you mean?"

"We'll have to wait and see after it arrives."

"Did you buy it in Dijon?"

"No. It's coming from an entirely different place."

"Abby—" He rolled her on top of him. "You're being very playful tonight. What's going on?"

She covered his face with kisses. "It just so happens that no woman could be as happy as I am tonight. After my French tutoring session in town this morning, I made one more stop before coming home and found out I'm *enceinte*. Did I pronounce it right?"

"You're *what*?"

"I thought that might get your attention. Dr. Filbert says we won't be able to tell the sex of our *bébé* for a little while longer, but we're definitely expecting. I was going to tell you in the morning, but since you woke me up now, I decided I couldn't keep it a secret any longer."

She felt him tremble with excitement. He rolled her carefully on to her side. After feeling her stomach, he leaned down and kissed the place where it was growing. When he lifted his head to kiss her, he tasted the salt from her tears.

"Isn't it wonderful, Raoul? You're going to be able to raise your second child and you'll be the most wonderful father in the world."

Tears sprang to his eyes. He embraced her gently. "I was just going to say what a beautiful mother you're going to make. I'm the luckiest husband alive."

"I only have one request. I would like you to choose the name if we have a boy. But if it's a girl, I want to call her Blondine. Won't it be thrilling for her to read the storybook her *papa* loved?"

"Abby—"

* * * * *

SOLDIER, HANDYMAN, FAMILY MAN

LYNNE MARSHALL

To our true heroes
who risk their lives for their country,
their cities, their neighborhoods,
their friends and their families,
and who often pay a personal price.
You have my deepest respect.

Chapter One

The attractive brunette juggling a cardboard box and a plastic trash bag filled with who knew what needed help. Mark Delaney had first noticed her yesterday when her bobbing ponytail had proved to be very distracting. Now, seeing disaster about to happen, he sprang from the ladder, where he painted the underside of The Drumcliffe Hotel roof trim, nearly rolling an ankle. Then he jogged across the street attempting to hide the limp.

"Need help?"

"Oh." She tossed him a flustered glance, the box precariously slipping from her grasp. "Yes, please."

He rushed in and grabbed it, surprised how light it was.

"My favorite English tea set's in there." She used her head to signal the delicate nature of the contents. "Should've thought this through more." She stopped, took a breath and made an obligatory smile. "I'm Laurel Prescott, by the way, and you are?"

"Mark Delaney." With his free hand, he gestured across the street. "My family owns The Drumcliffe."

Her honey-brown brows, a few shades lighter than her hair, lifted. "Ah, so we're neighbors."

He deposited the box on the porch as she came up beside him, then noticed the eyes that were light hazel and shaped like large almonds. He liked that. "Guess so. When are you planning to open the B&B?"

Another inhale, this one deeper. "Good question. My goal is next week, but there are so many last-minute things I need to do, and of course hadn't even thought of." She shook her head rapidly. "Don't know what I was thinking doing this final move the week school started." She hoisted the trash bag over her shoulder. Something clanked inside. "Oh, yes, I do—I'd finally have a few hours to myself!"

He couldn't help but laugh with her even if it was over impending hysteria. "Anything else you need carried in?"

Her downright attractive eyes sparkled, signaling he may as well have been sent from heaven. Which felt good for a change.

"Are you sure you have the time? I mean it's obvious you're in the middle of painting."

He glanced down at his black T-shirt and jeans, both splattered with the eggshell paint his mother had meticulously picked for the trim. "I was ready for a break anyway." Then he looked across the road where he'd left the lid off the paint can. "Just give me a second, okay?"

"Of course!" She continued up the steps to the grand Queen Anne–styled Victorian house, which had been sitting empty, according to his mother, for ages. Some nice old couple used to live there when he was a kid, right up to the time he'd left home. He remembered once having the best apple pie he'd ever eaten in that kitchen.

He crossed the street heading back to the hotel. For the last several months, he'd seen crews inside and out bringing the gem back to its original beauty and then some. By the extensive upgrades, he knew his mother had been right about the old home being turned into a bed-and-breakfast. The workers had finished a few weeks back, making the steeply pitched roof with the dominant front gable and oddly shaped porch look picture-book perfect. Once a blah blue with ho-hum white trim, chipped and peeling from years of neglect, now the house was sage green with cream trim and forest green detailing between the cornices, and Mark had to admit it looked classy. Like her. That had been his first impression of his new neighbor last week when she'd stopped by to check on the finishing touches.

The lady was way out of his league, so today, when she was dressed in work clothes—faded straight-legged jeans with slip-in rubber-soled shoes, and a stretched-out polo shirt that'd seen better days—it made him smile. She fit right in with his style. And for the second day in a row she'd worn a ponytail. Not that he was keeping tabs or anything, but man, the ponytail was distracting.

Mark replaced the lid on the paint can.

"Little early for a break isn't it?" Padraig Delaney chided his middle grandson, while he had no doubt just finished a Monday morning round at the city course judging by his loud patterned golf slacks and a salmon-colored shirt. His daily routine at eighty-five kept his craggy face tanned and his blue eyes bright, not to mention the notorious toothy grin pasted in place. Which he was currently flashing since noticing where Mark had come from and the lady across the street waiting for him.

Mark smiled at his grandda with the Guinness-soaked voice and tendency toward magical thinking. They had an understanding since both had known how it felt to be young, far away from home, frightened and lonely—though one in peacetime and the other, well, in that hot mess known as the Middle East. Yet that was their unspoken bond, and nothing would break it.

Everyone knew Padraig Delaney's history. As a young Irish immigrant in the 1950s, he'd been brought over to work the new and lush golf courses along the central California coast. Cheap labor for sure, but he'd also had the foresight to scrimp and save money and buy the small patch of land in Sandpiper Beach. As his jobs and responsibility advanced, he saved more and worked like the devil to build the humble hotel back in the late sixties and early seventies. If it weren't for that hardworking dreamer's spirit, who knew what the Delaney clan would be up to now? So he'd cut him some slack over playing golf every morning. The man had earned it.

As Mark always did, he also tolerated the supernosy man's inclinations. "I'll get 'er done. All of it. By the end of the day. Have a good game?"

"Every game's a good game, Marky my boy, 'cuz I'm alive."

Mark had heard a similar statement from his grandfather at some point every single day since he'd returned from Afghanistan last year. He understood it was a less-than-subtle message, but most of the time he couldn't relate to it. Though today, glancing across the street to the lady with the ponytail, his personal outlook struck him as somewhat optimistic. "That it is, Grandda. That it is." He stood, ready to set off again for the B&B and the woman who needed some serious help.

"Fraternizing with the competition are ye?" Ah, he wasn't going to let this slip by.

Mark laughed, knowing Grandda was making a joke. His mother was the one and *only* person in the family fretting about the B&B opening. Padraig Delaney understood different types stayed at a place like that than their modestly priced hotel. The B&B wasn't about competition, it was about revitalizing the town, which would be good for everyone. "Just helping out a neighbor."

"A mighty attractive neighbor I might add." The old man winked.

Mark returned a let's-not-go-there stare, though Grandda already had.

"Have you thought more about taking over the hotel?" So he'd gotten Mark's hint and changed the subject.

"You know I'm not ready to do that." He placed the paint can next to the hotel wall, then folded the ladder and put that next to it. "Besides, Mom and Dad really don't want to retire yet." At least he hoped so.

"Could fool me, the way they talk about it mornin' till night. Besides, you're the only one who loves this hotel the same way I do."

Mark couldn't deny that he was the logical person to pick up where his parents left off, if they retired like they kept threatening to. With Daniel being a doctor with his own practice and Conor a deputy sheriff for the county with plans for advancement, neither brother showed the slightest interest in running the place. But since being honorably discharged from the army last year, he'd wanted nothing to do with responsibility. For now, being a handyman every morning and surfing every afternoon was about all he thought he could handle. Still he did have a vision for The Drumcliffe, which he'd talked to his parents about under the condition that they would give him time, and postpone any immediate plans to retire. If Grandda caught on, he might insist Mark take on more responsibility right away. But he flat out wasn't ready. Yet.

Mark kept his head down, rather than pursue the pointed conversation about the future of the family hotel. Grandda cleared his throat in resignation, but Mark knew there would be future dialogue on the subject. The man would probably hound him until he gave in. It might even be for his own good.

"Well, I'm off, then." Padraig set out heading up Main Street for his daily visit with the other local business owners, using an ancient wood putter as a cane. "Remember the selkie, lad," he said, not bothering to look back for Mark's reaction, knowing it would be annoyed.

Would the old man ever let go of the notion Mark and his brothers had saved a selkie the day they'd gone deep-sea fishing together? First off, it wasn't a selkie, it was a *seal* that was being hunted by a pod of orca. Foolish or not, the brothers had used the fishing boat to interfere with the obvious training session for a young orca on how to catch a snack. Turns out they'd distracted the pod just long enough for the seal to escape. Their biggest mistake, after risking getting their boat flipped by ticked-off orcas, was repeating the story during the Sunday night family dinner in the pub. You'd have thought they'd saved the king of the little people judging by their grandfather's reaction. *The seal was a selkie,* he'd said.

The selkie now owes each of you a favor. As if he knew the selkie rulebook backward and forward.

Ever since, Padraig Delaney, a wise and intelligent man on many other levels, but obviously not this one, insisted each brother would find true love.

Right. And there's always a pot of gold at the end of a rainbow. Anyone ever find it?

His oldest brother, Daniel, hadn't helped Grandda's notion a bit when he'd hired Keela and, after a few months, started dating her. Now they were newly married with a baby on the way, and calling that proof, Grandda had doubled down on his woo-woo predictions. Especially after he'd had a Guinness or two. He'd gaze over his glass and give Mark, the middle brother, and Conor, the baby, meaningful glances meant to convey they'd be next. What a load of malarkey.

"Remember the selkie, my ass," Mark mumbled, watching the old man stride up the street without a care. What had made him bring *that* up again, anyway?

Because their new neighbor was a knockout, that's why. Mark smiled to himself. So Grandda had noticed, too.

And with that undeniable thought, he grinned and cleaned his hands with the rag hanging on the ladder and headed back across the way, even though she wasn't likely to give him the time of day after he'd finished helping her. He was still just a fix-it guy.

Laurel walked back to her car and secretly watched Mark reseal a paint can when an old gentleman approached him.

Here she was, thirty-five, a widow second-guessing her every move. Being the mother of a teenage boy dealing with grief and anger on top of the usual teen angst, and twin four-year-olds just beginning their journey with school, only added to the doubt. Buying the old house with one of Alan's generous insurance policies had been a risk, for sure, but it had also been her way of beginning again. Lord knew she needed a fresh start. They all did. The last five years had been hijacked by Alan's cancer, then remissions, praying the worst had been over, followed by the nightmare two years later of those demon cells' return. If anyone deserved a do-over it was the Prescott family. Though Alan never got the luxury of a second chance.

She swallowed a hard and familiar lump. Life had been difficult without him the past two years, and may have kicked the wind out of her, but now she wanted to move on. What choice did she have, really?

She retrieved a few small items from the trunk of the car and subtly watched on the periphery, the conversation going on across the street at the hotel between the old golfer and Mark, her disturbingly attractive neighbor. The fact she'd noticed him was progress, wasn't it? He was good-looking. There, she'd admitted it. But so what?

Before the move, she'd been walking around in a trance, dealing with the lowest rung on the Maslow hierarchy of needs—excluding sex, of course. That rarely entered her mind, except on those nights when she missed Alan's touch so badly she cried. All she wanted to do was build a new life for her family, to keep them safe and fed, healthy, while wondering if this B&B had been the best idea she'd ever had or the craziest.

Regardless, she owned the Queen Anne–styled house in Sandpiper Beach and planned to become a small businesswoman. A full-time job outside the home would provide a paycheck, but it would also keep her away from the ones she wanted to look after. This solution, buying and running a B&B, was the next best way she knew how to provide for her kids.

She glanced across the street. Why was that man so distracting? She had a world of other things to think about, didn't need a single distraction, yet there he was, tall, dark hair, intense blue eyes, totally Irish American. Younger than her.

She walked back to the house, trying not to look over her shoulder. What could be the harm in allowing a tiny, secret attraction for someone who lived across the street? Could she go so far as labeling it a crush, or merely an interest? Whichever, she'd felt something the very first time she'd spotted him. Why now? Could it be a signal that, after two years of living in limbo, she was finally ready to move on with life?

Maybe.

A half hour later, after passing each other with arms loaded on trips back and forth to the house, with nothing more than glances and respectful smiles, Mark carried the last of Laurel's boxes up the porch steps.

The grand entrance and main sitting room were detailed and updated with fresh paint, crown molding, a traditional fireplace, ornate mantel and rich wood balustrades lining the otherwise modest staircase. But the impressive dining room with its long and grand oak table, antique print wallpaper and classic crystal chandelier was clearly the focal point. Visitors were going to love this old house.

"Looks great," was all he said.

"Thank you," she said with an earnest gaze. "I'm petrified. After all the money I've sunk into it, what if it's a big bomb?"

"Have you done this before?" He also wondered if she was married, which bothered him. Why should he care?

"Never." Something close to panic flashed in her eyes, but she recovered quickly. "Can I get you some lemonade? It's the least I can do for all your help." *Maybe she's divorced.*

He wasn't the type to stick around and chat. In fact, he'd kept mostly to himself in the year since he'd been back from Afghanistan, skipping socializing outside of his family, but something nudged him to accept her offer. "Sounds good. Thanks."

He followed her into the modest-sized kitchen for a house this big, and took in the view from the updated double-paned back window. The beach and ocean weren't far off, and he assumed most of the guest rooms would have views of the same. "I wouldn't worry too much about bombing out. Unless you overprice the rooms."

"I've done my homework on pricing," she said, opening the double-wide stainless steel refrigerator and grabbing a pitcher of lemonade. He also noticed she'd gone the modern route with the appliances and the long marble-covered island. Seemed like an efficiency decision, if she planned the usual serving of breakfast for her guests. "I'm right in the middle of the current going rate. Except for the honeymoon suite, of course." She gave a flirty wistful glance. "It's beautiful and well worth the price."

He didn't get what the deal was with rooms that were supposed to enhance romance—seemed to him you either had it or you didn't—but figured Laurel was depending on other people who did. Whereas The Drumcliffe appealed more to families and seniors on budgets. So he was content to leave the "lover's weekend packages" for her B&B. More power to her. Though Mom adamantly voiced the need for their hotel to have broader appeal, and she'd been on a quest to start wedding packages maximizing the gorgeous view and their large lawn area right along the ocean. An idea popped into his head: Why not turn the biggest room with the best view at the hotel into a honeymoon suite? Maybe he could get some ideas for decorating from Laurel. Of course, that would only mean more on his ever-growing to-do list. Which reminded him he was supposed to start building an arbor today, and a gazebo after that.

She handed him a dainty hand-painted glass of lemonade. So instead of gulping like he'd intended from thirst, he took only a sip of the fresh lemon and hint-of-mint liquid. "This tastes great."

"Thanks. I made it myself using the Meyer lemons from the side yard."

"Really good." The yard, he'd noticed, needed some serious trimming and weeding. But she'd probably already made plans with a gardener for that, so he didn't offer his services. Why would he? Besides, he had enough going on with the hotel.

He sensed she had all kinds of extra-special tricks up her sleeve where the B&B was concerned, like this homemade lemonade, and figured her guests would return because of those extra-special touches. That was if they found the house in the first place. "You have plans for a grand opening or something?"

She took a drink, her lashes fluttering. "I plan to run some ads and have an open house."

"That's a good idea."

She looked gratefully at him. "I grew up in Pismo Beach, so I know we have a long season. Does it ever get really dead around here?"

"I've only been back the past year, so I'm not a great resource. I'll check with my parents, if you'd like."

"Oh, sorry, I just assumed you—"

"—I was in the service for ten years. My parents run the hotel. I'm still getting used to being back." Would that matter to her, that he wasn't the guy in charge? Again, he chided, why should he care?

He'd left home at twenty-one an accomplished surfer, surf bum as Grandda often teased. Then he'd come back after a few tours in the Middle East, mostly Afghanistan, but also in Iraq, someone he didn't recognize anymore. He'd dealt with his mood swings in his own way, spending the last year withdrawn, just trying to get his bearings in the real world again, while working on the hotel. And surfing. It had all been part of his healing journey, as the VA therapist had suggested. That was the reason he and his brothers had been fishing the day of the "selkie" incident. A bonding trip, they'd called it. But in truth, Daniel and Conor were worried about him and had wanted to help him over the slump he'd slipped into. Some trip that'd turned out to be. He still wasn't 100 percent past PTSD. Still had occasional nightmares, hated being in big crowds, but he was on the road back to being a combination of the guy he used to be and the man he'd become. Less outgoing, more inclined to think things through before acting. Less lighthearted, grimmer. Someone he'd have to get used to. Maybe all thirty-one-year-olds went through the same thing?

Laurel studied him, those caramel eyes subtly moving around his face, her mind probably wondering what his story was. Well, she wasn't the only one with questions. "What brought you here?"

"Oh." Obviously unprepared for him to turn the tables. "I missed the beach. After college I got married and moved inland to Paso Robles to raise my family. Then I lost my husband a couple years ago."

"I'm sorry." And he meant it, even though he could only imagine how horrible it would be to lose someone you loved.

She quietly inhaled, then took another sip of lemonade. "Yeah. It's been rough."

That was something he could relate to, the rough part. He wasn't good at this sort of thing, sympathy or empathy or whatever it was called, but he honestly felt bad for her. She had a lot going on, and a big project like opening a B&B all alone was probably as stressful as it got for a person. There went that nudging sensation again. "If you need any help, I'm around." *What happened to being too busy?*

"Thank you." She looked sincere and grateful. "I'll definitely take you up on that offer."

Good. A decisive and wise woman. But, out of character, he'd just opened a door he wasn't sure that (a) he had time for or (b) he wanted to go through. Yet. She might be single, but she had a family, for crying out loud.

Her appreciative eyes suddenly widened. She frantically looked at her wrist. "Oh, no! It's time to pick up the girls." She grabbed her purse and rushed for the door. "It's their first day at school. Kindergarten! I can't be late."

He followed, then noticed she had to work extra hard to get the front door locked. "I'll come back later and have a look at that lock, if you want."

She flashed another earnest gaze, this one accompanied with a pretty smile, which caught him off guard. "That'd be great!"

Then off she ran for her white minivan, where identical car seats were installed in the back—such a total mom.

Man, he must be completely out of his antisocial mind, because somehow, he found the whole entrepreneur—and multitasking-mother bit—sexy as hell. And that was way off course for his current game plan—keeping a low profile and figuring out where he fit in life…or even if he wanted to.

Laurel kept to the speed limit, but barely, trying desperately to get the image of Mark Delaney out of her head. Did he have any idea how gorgeous he was? Dark brown hair combed straight back from his forehead and just long enough to curl under his ears, clear blue eyes, a two-day growth of beard with the hint of red in the sideburn whiskers. His black T-shirt stretched across a broad chest and shoulders, with a peekaboo tear along his sleek abs, and arms that qualified for a construction worker calendar. His faded black jeans had matching tears at the knees from hard work, not superficial fashion, and fit his slim hips and long legs like he'd been born in them. Damn he was hot! Whether he realized it or not was the question. He certainly didn't act "all that." In fact, there was something dark and tender about him that put her at ease. And that ease put her on edge.

Laurel glanced at her face in the rearview mirror, horror soon overtaking her. She'd been looking like that? Her hair in a messy ponytail, not a stitch of makeup. Not even lip gloss. The man probably thought of her as a poor, struggling aunt.

She slammed on the brakes, nearly missing a red light. *Woman, get a hold of yourself! You're thirty-five, obviously older than him, and not to mention the mother of three. It doesn't matter how you look, he's not interested.* Still, there was much to appreciate about Mark Delaney, and she wasn't blind—or dead—in that department. Yet. Sometimes she thought she might be, so he was a pleasant surprise, after all she'd been through. She tugged the elastic out of her hair and let it fall to her shoulders.

Pulling into the parking lot, she prayed she hadn't cut it too close and that her kids wouldn't be the last ones there. They'd dealt with enough abandonment issues losing their father two years ago, and having to live as if the hospital was their second home for a year before that. Now was their time to get back to living a regular life, and nothing would get in Laurel's way of giving that to her kids. A quick thought of her fourteen-year-old son, Peter, made her chest pinch, but now wasn't the time to go there. She had to pick up her girls.

She parked and jogged into the kindergarten classroom. Gracie and Claire were happily playing puzzles with the little girl they'd met on Welcome to Kindergarten night, who wore a cast. *Anna was it?*

"Can Anna come home with us? Her mom's late, too." Claire, the oldest by twelve minutes, and clearly the bossiest, spoke first.

"I don't think the school lets kids go home with just anyone." Laurel used her diplomatic-mother voice.

"Stranger danger!" Gracie piped up.

"We're not strangers," Claire corrected, as she always did with Gracie. "Remember, we played together before." She used her middle finger to slide her pink glasses up her tiny nose.

"I pre-member. Do you, Annie?"

"It's Anna." Claire the clarifier simply couldn't help herself. "And *re*-member."

During Alan's long remission from the first bout of leukemia, and nearly a decade since Peter had been born, no one had been more shocked to discover she was pregnant with twins than Laurel. But life had always been crazy that way.

When Alan relapsed with a vengeance when the girls were a year old, everyone had been so distracted that Gracie's chronic ear problems had gotten way out of hand before Laurel had taken her to the pediatrician. She'd been walking around with fluid in her inner ears, which had affected her hearing. It was like listening to people speak underwater and had slowed her speech, while Claire seemed to have been born chatting, and now speaking for and chronically correcting her twin. Since having tubes inserted, Gracie's hearing had improved, but she still often got words wrong. Claire never let her forget it, either.

"Oh, there you are, Anna." A breathless voice with a distinct accent spoke from behind. "Sorry I'm late, sweetness."

"That's okay, Mom, these are my friends."

The woman introduced herself to Laurel as Keela. "Thank you for staying with Anna. I don't want to be accused of running on Irish time, but we had a walk-in at the clinic and it threw things sideways."

Delighted by Keela's Irish accent, Laurel grinned. In the week she'd been in town, she'd already heard about the Delaney Physical Medicine Clinic from one of the women at the local farmers' market, who'd told her, after chatting and discovering Laurel's B&B was right across Main Street from The Drumcliffe, about Daniel's recent marriage to an "Irish girl." Small town. News traveled fast.

"I just got here myself. Honestly, I don't think the girls missed us a bit."

"Probably right."

"We should set up a playdate some afternoon," Laurel suggested, keeping in mind Keela worked full-time.

"T'would be *grand*. Maybe a Saturday would be best."

Ms. Juanita, the young teacher not much taller than her students, wandered over. "Are we all ready now?" she asked diplomatically, dropping the major hint it was past time to leave. So they did. But not before exchanging phone numbers.

As promised, later that afternoon after he'd finished painting the trim and had gotten a good start on the arbor, Mark headed back over to Laurel's B&B with his toolbox in hand. He planned to fix her lock. One of the benefits of being raised around a hotel was learning to be a jack-of-all-trades. *Otherwise we'd go bankrupt*, as his father used to say when he and his brothers griped about spending their Saturday afternoons working around the hotel. It'd always been extra torture when the surf was up and he'd been itching to hit those waves.

Laurel was in the front yard, and two young girls in matching striped leggings and navy blue tops sat on the porch steps, though one wore glasses. Looking stressed, Laurel faced off with a scrawny kid by the yard gate who was somewhere in the early teen stage and who hadn't yet grown into his nose. He wore cargo shorts and an oversize, ancient-looking T-shirt with a picture of Bart Simpson on the front. Shaggy dark brown waves in an obvious growing-out stage consumed his ears and partially covered his eyes. He leaned forward, confronting her, his mouth tight and chin jutted out.

Mark thought about turning around, leaving them to their personal business, but their heated interchange, and the fact her hair was down and blowing with the breeze, prodded him to keep going. Maybe she could use some backup.

"Peter, I've got too much on my plate right now."

"I'm sick of having to drag those pests around." His voice warbled between boy and man, cracking over *those pests*.

"We're not pests!" The little one with glasses sounded indignant.

"Not pets!" the thinner of the two incorrectly echoed, garnering a confused glance from her twin.

"I need you to watch the girls while I do some errands. Is that too much to ask?"

"I'm sick of being their babysitter."

The fair-haired girls looked like twins. Identical twins, but with the help of one wearing glasses and one being slightly smaller, to tell them apart. The glasses girl took it upon herself to move in on the ongoing argument. "Sing with us, Peter. Please?" A future peace activist, no doubt.

"Pleee-sio?" Little Miss Echo being creative?

Without waiting, they started singing "Where Is Thumbkin" using their fingers and acting out the verses, oblivious, while Laurel and Peter continued to square off.

"You know it'll take me twice as long if I bring them."

"Don't care."

What should he do now? Just walk right up and pretend he didn't have a clue they were fighting? He slowed down. That seemed lame.

"Okay, I'm not asking, I'm *telling* you to stay here."

"I need time by myself!" Peter pounded his fist on his chest while his voice cracked again. "You're the one who told me to get out and explore the neighborhood! Meet kids my age."

Ten feet away from the picket fence and gate, Mark stopped. If anyone could understand the need to be by himself, Mark could. Hell, he'd been the king of withdrawal when he'd first come home. The girls continued singing and gesturing—*"Where is pointer, where is pointer...?"*

"I need your help." Laurel wouldn't back down.

"I'm leaving!"

Mark figured it must be damn hard to lose a father when a boy needed him most, but it still bothered him the kid was taking his anger out on his mother. He decided to step in, offer Laurel some support. "Is this a bad time?"

"Oh, Mark." Laurel looked flustered and frustrated, her cheeks flushed. Those soft hazel-brown eyes from earlier now dark and tense. Edging toward the street side of the gate, Peter stepped backward, gearing up for his escape.

"How are you today, sir?" the twins sang louder.

Mark stepped closer, giving Peter a forced but friendly smile, hoping to keep him from taking off. "I'm Mark. Nice to meet you."

In response, he received a death glare. It was clear the kid was furious, not just about Mark butting in, or his mother demanding he pull his share of responsibility, but about life in general. About how sucky it must be when a dad dies.

Unaware, the girls kept singing their nursery rhyme. *"Run away. Run away."* Their way of coping with stress?

Still glowering, Peter spoke verse three. *"Where is tall man?"* He added the middle-finger gesture for the sake of his mother and Mark, made sure they both saw it clearly, then took off running, flip-flops flapping, down the street toward the beach.

"Peter!" Laurel yelled, anger flashing in those eyes.

He thought about running after Peter and straightening him out, but stopped the urge. It wasn't his place.

It took guts, or total desperation, to flip off a complete stranger in front of his mother, he'd give Peter that. He didn't envy Laurel's having to deal with that on top of opening the B&B. Guests didn't go to places like this to hear family arguments. Yet Laurel was a widow with three kids to take care of, and the proprietor of an about-to-open business. After he fixed her lock, he'd steer clear.

Laurel called after Peter again. When Peter didn't stop or turn around, she dug fingers into her hair, obviously torn about whether to run after him or let him go. The girls had stopped singing, now zeroing in on their mother and gathering close to her. She put a hand on both of them, giving a motherly rub and pat, which immediately eased the tension in their sparrow-sized shoulders. Then she steered them back toward the porch.

Looking downcast, but not defeated, Laurel glanced back at Mark. "Welcome to my world."

Chapter Two

Ten minutes later, Mark kept to himself as he tested the key that Laurel had given him in the stubborn front door lock. The scene with Peter had been unpleasant to say the least, and he'd had to bite his tongue to keep from butting in and telling the kid what he thought. Really thought—*listen, punk, you don't talk to your mother like that. Ever!* But it wasn't his place, and keeping it real, he'd heard a similar warning—without the punk part—from his father a long time ago. Disrespecting parents must be some teen rite of passage. From the way Laurel had mostly kept her cool, she'd probably been down that road with Peter before.

While he fiddled with the lock, Laurel went about distracting the little ones with a snack and a promise to watch one afternoon kid's show. He was pretty sure "yay" meant they'd accepted her deal.

A minute later, he'd squirted powdered graphite into

the keyhole, moved the key in and out a few times, then retested the sticky mechanism. The lock opened and closed just fine. For good measure, he repeated the process on the bolt lock, since her guests would most likely be using their keys after hours, and Laurel might appreciate their not waking her up to get in.

Before The Drumcliffe had switched to card keys, he and his brothers had become experts with fixing sticky locks. They'd learned the hard way that vegetable oil and WD-40 helped for the short term, but eventually made the problem worse. Then they'd discovered graphite, the non-gummy way to fix a lock.

On his knees with the door open, Mark surreptitiously watched Laurel wander his way, carrying a small plate of cookies. She sat on the nearest rocker in the row along the porch, stretching out her sleek legs, then offering him the plate.

"Do you barter?" she toyed, waiting for him to catch on.

"Work for chocolate chip cookies? You bet." He took one and popped it whole into his mouth. *Holy melting deliciousness*, it was good. "Pretty sure I got the better deal, too." He should've waited until he'd finished chewing and swallowing. He probably still had chocolate teeth.

She laughed gently. At least he'd done that for her. Made her smile. And a nice one it was, too, wide, straight and lighting up her eyes.

"You know he's grieving, right?" she said, growing serious, her eyes seeking his, needing him to understand why her kid had shot off his mouth earlier.

"I figured something was going on. I get the impression a lady like you wouldn't put up with that behavior otherwise."

She put her head against the back of the rocker, nibbling on a cookie. "He blames me for everything. Sometimes I think he even blames me for his father getting cancer."

"From what I recall, being a teenager is hard enough. Losing a parent on top of it, well, that's got to bite. Hard."

"He was only twelve when Alan died, but for so many years before that, Alan's being ill was the focal point of our family. He missed out on a lot of things other kids his age took for granted. And the insecurity of it all, that I know firsthand. Must have been devastating for him, because it nearly killed me."

Moved by her opening up so easily, Mark sat on his heels, wanting to give back, to make this an interchange somehow, but he was out of practice. "He's, what, fourteen now?"

She gave a thoughtful nod without looking at him, taking another small bite of cookie. "Who invented adolescent angst, anyway?"

Mark made one quick laugh. "He probably doesn't know how to move on. Maybe he's in a rut and needs a nudge or something." This conversation had edged into familiar personal territory. He could say the same thing about himself—not sure how to move on, feeling in a rut—but for the sake of Laurel he focused on her problem and her son.

"We've tried therapy. He went to a teen grief group for a while. Then he stopped. I couldn't bring myself to force him to go." She glanced at Mark for understanding. He assented. "I think he's afraid of his feelings. He's hurt so much for so long, he can't imagine going over everything again, examining the pain of losing his dad." She sighed. "I don't know." Now she looked at him, really looked at him, her eyes searching his, waking up some dark and forgotten place. Did she sense his pain? "And you probably never thought you'd get sucked into my family problems when you offered to help fix my locks today, did you?"

He pushed out a smile, just for her, because he figured she could use a friendly face right about now. Sticking to the superficial, rather than let himself *feel* something, he concentrated on how her hair looked resting on her shoulders. "It's okay. Every family has issues."

She lifted her brows, in a prove-it kind of way, but soon exchanged that for a quizzical expression. "I have no idea why I'm telling you my life story." She leveled him with a stare. "Just strike that part, okay?"

"No worries. You feel like talking, go right ahead." A long moment followed where they quietly assessed each other, and she must have decided she'd spilled her guts enough for the day. She took another bite of her cookie, which, for some crazy reason, looked sexier than it should. He couldn't take the intimacy of watching her mouth, or sharing concerns and feelings, especially if she expected him to open up about himself or his family in return. So he deliberately changed the topic. "And if you give me another cookie, I'll throw in checking all the guest room locks."

As though relieved, she smiled, pushing the plate toward him. "It's a deal."

As he went through the rest of the house, he noticed all six of the guest rooms were on the second floor. Laurel and the kids must have taken up residence on the first floor, in the back part of the house.

Out of the blue he wondered what she'd look like with that top layer of stress erased from her pretty face. And then he stopped himself from going a single thought further. What was the point? She had her hands full, and the last thing he needed was to pursue a woman with kids.

He grabbed his small workbag, went downstairs and found Laurel in the kitchen slicing apples and carrots. He stopped for a second to enjoy the view.

"I'm all done here." He set the small bottle of graphite on the long central island. "If you have any more problems with locks, just use this."

She stopped slicing. "Thanks so much."

In rushed the twins. "We're hungry," Claire, the spokesperson, said.

"Yeah, my tummy's qweezin'," said Gracie.

She tossed them both a piece of carrot and apple. Surprisingly, they accepted her offer and scuttled off for the backyard like contented bunnies. Intuition must be part of the job description for a mom. Another thing about her that impressed him.

"You may be wondering about Gracie's speech."

"She does have an interesting way of saying things."

Laurel sighed as she leaned forward, elbows and forearms resting on the kitchen island countertop. The pose shouldn't be appealing, but it was. "During Alan's illness, I was so caught up in his needs, I didn't realize that Gracie's unusual speech was a sign she had fluid in her ears. I thought it was baby talk. It wasn't until after Alan died I snapped out of my trance and took them both to the pediatrician. Gracie needed tubes in her ears, and Claire flunked her three-year-old vision test. I didn't have a clue about either of them."

She looked defeated, and it bothered him. "You had a lot on your plate. The main thing, nothing was life-threatening and you fixed the problem." *Listen to me,*

Mr. Logical. He stepped closer to her end of the island. "Maybe quit being so hard on yourself?"

She blinked and sighed. "I might have to hire you as a life coach."

"Ha! First you'd have to find *me* one."

"And what's your story?" Her inquisitive stare nearly pushed him off balance.

"Ten years in the army. Tours in Iraq and Afghanistan. Need I say more?"

She looked horrified at first. That was the only way Mark could explain her expression, then it changed.

They gazed at each other, her manner seeming sympathetic, understanding. Mark was almost positive she thought the same thing—they were two people who'd come through tough times humbled and haggard. He'd worked out a drill to deal with his, but had she?

Mark's usual routine was to work all morning and through the early afternoon, then grab his board and head down to the beach to catch a few waves. What used to be his passion had now become his solace, better than a doctor's prescription or a cold beer. Funny how time changed things like that—passion to solace. He figured the PTSD had a lot to do with needing to be alone, at sea, man against nature, at least once a day. Plus, other than the noisy seagulls, it was amazingly quiet out there, and was the perfect place to shut down all the clatter in his life. Whatever it was, surfing was still a lifeline for him and he needed it. Especially today.

She wiped the counter with a sponge, and he was ready to leave, but something made him stop. It was like his body had quit listening to his brain. Don't get involved. "Just call if you need anything, okay?" Now his mouth had gone rogue. Seeing a notepad on the adjacent counter, he scribbled out his cell phone number, then left.

"You might be sorry!" she teasingly called after him.

He already was. Why walk in on someone else's life as a fix-it guy, when he'd yet to fix his own mess? He really didn't need the frustration.

But when he hit the street, he grinned. Like an idiot. Because he'd just given a woman his phone number for the first time since getting discharged from the service.

A half hour later, dressed in red board shorts and an old stretched-out, holey T-shirt, with surfboard under his arm, Mark strode toward the beach where the sun cast a golden orange tint on the ocean. Being the middle Delaney brother, he'd opted out of the role of peacekeeper by default early on. Instead, he'd elected to become an attention-getting surfer. It'd paid off in spades, too. Popularity. Girlfriends. Respect.

He'd intended to sign up for the army right after high school, but his father and mother had convinced him to try the local community college first. He did, without an inkling of what he wanted to major in, for two years, but didn't get a degree because the classes he took didn't add up to one major's requirements. Then that faraway Middle East war got personal. A good friend since grammar school had been killed in Iraq. It might not have been logical thinking, but after that he felt called to serve, so, without his parents' blessings, he'd enlisted. After voting in a presidential election for the first time, signing up for the army had been his next major life decision. And he was still re-adjusting to civilian life.

A predictable afternoon breeze had kicked up and the water was choppy, but he smiled at the swelling of sets forming in the distance. A few of the usual guys in wet suits were out there, most of them half his age. They'd probably been there all day. One with long sun-bleached hair caught the next wave, road the crest, then wiped out.

Halfway down the beach, he passed a group of loud teenagers talking trash to someone. He turned his head to check things out. Five guys ranging from tall and buff to short and heavy, wearing board shorts and brand-name skateboarder T-shirts, were getting their jollies by bullying someone much smaller. He looked closer, saw the shaggy brown hair, the nose he was still grow-ing into and that oversize T-shirt with Bart Simpson on the front. It was Peter with a frown cast in iron on his face, staring at his flip-flops. Obviously hating every second, he let the jerks taunt and tease him, but what choice did he have, one against five?

Mark dropped his board and headed their way. "Hey, Peter, I was lookin' for you, man! It's time for your surfing lesson."

Peter looked up, surprised. So did the other kids.

He walked right up to the group as if everything was A-OK, but making eye contact with the leader let him know he understood what was going on and it was ending right now.

One perk—or pain, depending on what kind of mood he was in—of being Sandpiper's very own surfing champion was the whole town knew him. His first-place regional championship trophy and a larger-than-life pic-ture of him at eighteen with awful peroxided hair, at the height of his competition days, were on display at the local high school. He'd been the captain of the Sand-piper High surf team—hell, he'd been the guy to orga-nize the team—and had led them to regional victories for two years. Then he'd moved on to statewide and a few national competitions where more was at risk, but with respectable success. From the reaction of these losers and tough-guy wannabes, even they knew who he was. Or used to be.

"We wus just horsin' around with the new kid."

"Didn't know he knew you." The tallest nudged Peter toward Mark.

"Yeah, I'm mentoring Peter. He's a natural. See you *boys* around," he said, making sure the kids understood he'd be watching them, and escorted Peter toward his board. So much for not getting involved.

"Want to tell me what was going on?" he asked when they'd retrieved the board and, out of earshot, were heading toward the ocean.

"I was just sitting on the beach, reading a book on my phone and they came out of nowhere. Started giving me a hard time. Bully a-holes."

"Punks are always gonna be punks."

"Nah. They think I'm a nerd because I'm different. I'm skinny and I've got a big nose." His anger radiated toward Mark, making the ocean air seem thicker. They walked on.

Mark also understood, since talking to Laurel, that Peter was still grieving and working through the stress of losing his father, which also made him an easy mark. For some reason, jerks had special radar for vulnerable kids. "Hey, first off, they should talk, if that's the reason. Did you look at them? Listen, it could be something as dumb as the fact you're the new kid and they know you don't have any friends yet to stick up for you, which will change soon enough."

"And I keep getting stuck watching my sisters. It's not exactly cool to hang out with four-year-olds."

So that was why he'd put up such a fight earlier with Laurel. Mark figured it was worth mentioning to her. In the meantime, he'd practice treating the boy like a young friend.

"Yeah, but I bet girls love that, in an 'aw' kind of way."

Peter screwed up his face, like Mark had said the dumbest thing in the world.

"What's with the Bart shirt, man? He back in style?"

"It was my dad's." Peter looked at his chest as if reconsidering the meaning.

What was he supposed to say to that? The kid still missed his father. They continued on, quiet for another few moments, watching the waves as they strolled.

"Well, now that I've announced you're my student, I guess we better get started. Take Bart off. You got trunks under those cargos?"

Peter nodded.

"Wearin' sunscreen?"

He nodded again, but Mark suspected it was a fib, so he grabbed the small bottle from his back pocket. They both put it on.

"Let's hit the waves."

Whether it was because Peter was shaken up from what had just transpired and was grateful, or the kid had always secretly wanted to learn to surf, Mark hadn't a clue, but highly out of character, from what Mark had witnessed of Peter so far, he did what he was told. And gladly!

After the initial "how to" lesson, and a discussion of strength and balance exercises Peter needed to do to get into shape for surfing, Mark used the time waiting for waves, both sitting on the board, to get to know a little about Peter. "Where'd you go to school last year?"

"Paso Robles Middle School."

"What's your favorite subject?"

"Art, I guess."

"Are you good at it?"

"Kind of."

"Have a girlfriend?"

He got a killer "as if" glare for that.

"Who's your best friend?"

Peter stared down at the board, silent.

"No friend?"

"My dad was sick all the time, okay?"

Mark didn't react to the kid spitting the words at him. He could only imagine how hard it would be to maintain a friendship when his world was wrapped tight with worry and a fatally sick father. Or maybe parents were hesitant to let their sons sleep over at Peter's house, like cancer was contagious or something. Who knew. "Must've been hard."

"I hated it. I mean I loved him, but everything was so crappy all the time."

Now they were getting somewhere. Peter's guard was coming down. "I hear ya. Must have been a bitch."

"They made me go to some stupid group. We were all a bunch of losers."

"You mean you'd all lost someone you loved?" He needed to reframe it for Peter—something Mark himself had learned when he went into group therapy—because he couldn't let Peter get away with the negative opinion of himself and other grievers, or anyone in therapy.

The kid's mouth was tight, in a straight line, and he looked on the verge of crying.

"This anger you're feeling all the time is real. It's part of grieving. When we lose someone we love, we grieve for them. Sometimes it makes us angry as hell."

"How do you know?" He spit out the words, challenging Mark.

"I lost more military buddies than I care to count in Iraq and Afghanistan. I know what I'm talking about." His grief had been the single hardest part of coming back to Sandpiper Beach, because he no longer had the distraction of fighting a war. He was faced head-on with all the loss and horrifying memories. They'd crashed against him every single day and knocked him down. Made him want to either strike out or withdraw, so he chose to pull back, lie low, until he felt fit enough for society again. When it came to anger, he knew what he was talking about. Yet dealing with Peter, he already felt in over his head.

He saw a flicker of something in Peter's gaze—maybe understanding, or firsthand experience grappling with fury. He'd also become more attentive.

"It's hard, man," Mark said. "Really hard. I get it."

"I'm never gonna stop being mad. I hate death!"

The statement made him think about Laurel and all she'd had to face alone. They had that in common. Since they'd met that morning, she'd popped into his head a dozen times, which worried him. He remembered how she didn't smile easily—but when she did, wow—and how cautious she seemed with him, insecure. Then the next thing he knew, she was spilling her life story over chocolate chip cookies.

Though she looked way too young to be a mother of a fourteen-year-old, she was still bound to be a bit older than Mark. Why was he even thinking this stuff? He wasn't going to get involved.

He liked her hopeful attitude, trusted her instincts about the B&B and decided she was nothing short of an inspiration the way she refused to let loss and grief—

being a widow, a single mother of three kids and over-loaded with responsibility—drag her down. Not to mention how tough it must be dealing with a hurting and grieving teen like Peter.

Ah, hell, he already was involved. The kid was still staring at him.

"You have a right to your anger, but your mom isn't the one who deserves it." Mark glanced up to see a perfect-sized swell for a newcomer. He jumped off the board, leaving Peter on his own. "Okay, catch this one. Paddle. Paddle. Paddle!"

And Peter paddled as if his life depended on it. Mark bodysurfed alongside him, keeping up as best he could as Peter first attempted a time or two to stand, then finally got up on one knee, stood for the blink of an eye, then fell off. When he resurfaced, Mark met him with a smile and praise.

"Hey, that was the best you've done yet!"

Surprisingly, considering the topic they'd just been tossing around, Peter smiled, too. "I'm starting to get the hang of it."

"Then you'll just have to keep taking lessons until you've got it."

"Can we catch one more?"

"That's the spirit."

An hour and a half later, the wind picked up and Peter was visibly chilled—his skin was pink-and-white blotchy to prove it—yet he didn't complain, just kept trying to stand up on the surfboard. He'd come close a couple of times, but never quite pulled everything together. Still he never gave up. Mark discovered he liked something about Peter—he wasn't a quitter.

"Lie down and I'll push you in," Mark said, treading water beside Peter and the surfboard.

For the second time that day, Peter didn't argue.

As he swam closer to shore, with the help of a wave pushing them the rest of the way, Mark wanted to ask a favor of Peter while he still had him on his turf. "When we get back, tell your mom you're sorry. She loves you, and it's got to hurt when you treat her like that."

Peter's lips curled inward as he put on his flip-flops and covered up with his father's Bart Simpson T-shirt. "Okay," he mumbled, reluctantly.

At 5:55 p.m., they walked back to where Main Street curved into the cul-de-sac, the B&B on one side, The Drumcliffe hotel on the other. Like Grandda always said, they really did own a little piece of heaven. "Good first lesson. I'll see you tomorrow at four for the next, okay?"

Peter nodded, seriously tired, but still interested.

"And start those exercises I showed you."

"Okay. My legs are kind of sore, though."

Mark grinned, leaving the kid at his front gate. "Get used to it. Later, man."

Peter smiled. "Later."

"I've been worried sick about you!" Laurel said from the porch.

"I was surfing with Mark." He rushed by her and toward the house like he hung out with Mark all the time.

"Mark?" He turned, and there was a near-shocked expression on her face. "Thank you."

"No problem."

Maybe Peter was saving the apology for dinner.

Tuesday, when Mark delivered Peter back to the B&B after his second surf lesson, Laurel was waiting.

"Will you join us for dinner?"

Did he want to do that? After spending his morning

finishing up painting the hotel trim, then working more on building the arbor, truth was, this was the most appealing offer he'd had all day. "Sure, what time?"

"Forty-five minutes?"

"Sounds good. Thanks." His spirits lifted by the invitation, Mark was struck that Laurel was the first woman he'd been drawn to since coming home to Sandpiper Beach.

A widow with three kids. Seriously, Delaney?

"One time I was on a fwing an—an a pider came an—an—an, I queemed!" Gracie said an hour later, as the girls took Mark on a tour of their living quarters. She must have felt obligated to entertain him while Laurel put the finishing touches on their meal. The unusual speech pattern was sweet, and knowing the history of her ear problems from Laurel yesterday—thinking she'd fallen down on the Mom-job—made him feel protective of both girls. And Laurel. He couldn't forget Peter, either. He wasn't sure what to make of that protective feeling, but he wouldn't deny it. Though it did make him uneasy.

"I fell off a swing once." Claire jumped in with a long and drawn-out story about exactly how her accident happened, the injuries she'd obtained, how her mother had cleaned her up, and on and on and on, while they walked down the hall toward their family room. Since he was the guest, for the sake of the little girls, he did his best to appear fascinated.

During the never-ending story, he also managed to assess the Prescott family living situation. The kitchen and in-dining breakfast area, downstairs bathroom and apparent three bedrooms with a medium-sized study, which they'd turned into their family room, was the

section of the grand old home where they lived. About
the size of a medium apartment. Unlike the foyer, the
front sitting room and the dining room, or the six upstairs bedrooms, it was furnished with modern, wear-
and-tear-styled furniture, which made sense with the
kids. Laurel Prescott knew how to be practical.

"And this is my mommy's room," Claire said. "She
has her own bathroom, but we all have to share that
one." She first gestured to the largest of the three bedrooms, probably once meant for the staff when the house
was built. Or an in-law suite? He glimpsed a humble
room with a comfortable-looking bed with tall bedposts
reminding him of her flair for antiques, and immediately felt like he'd invaded her privacy. Would she want
him gawking at her room? Then Claire pointed across
the hall to the main bathroom, and he was grateful for
the distraction. The main bathroom was spacious and
still had, what looked like, original tile in small white
hexagon shapes. The pedestal sink and bear-claw tub
also looked original, though the shower curtain encir-
cling it was covered with colorful safari animals. Yeah,
he bet Peter liked that, all right.

"We share, but Petie gwipes," Gracie added.

"That's Petie's room," Claire continued by pointing
to a closed door toward the end of the hall.

Since he'd arrived ten minutes ago, he hadn't seen
"Petie," but Mark had new understanding for why the
kid shut himself off.

The girls saved what they felt was the best for last.
Their room. Pink! White! Blindingly so. Frilly little
girl stuff throughout. Putting him completely out of
his comfort zone.

"Dinner's ready," Laurel called out. Thank God!

"Come on, awah-bubby! Dinner," Gracie said, taking off first.

"She means *everybody*," Claire quietly clarified, then made a beeline for their family dining room in the kitchen alcove.

Mark made a point to knock twice on Peter's closed door. "Dinner's ready." Just in case he hadn't heard his mother's announcement. Then he followed the girls.

Laurel looked great in tan capris and a pale blue tunic top, which brought out her hazel eyes. Maybe the touch of eye makeup she'd put on helped with that, too. Had she done that for him? He smiled, glad he'd combed his hair and dressed a little nicer than usual, wearing one of his best T-shirts, then waited for her to sit first. She looked a little nervous, so he didn't linger on her eyes, instead casting his gaze down to her sandals and noticing her tangerine-colored polish. Yeah, definitely in over his head. He never should have accepted her invitation.

Peter clumped down the hall, his feet seeming far too large for those skinny legs. Before he sat, he acknowledged Mark with a nod and partial smile. Then Claire insisted on saying a quick grace.

"I should say it. I'm Gwacie!"

"I said it first," and out went Claire's tongue.

"Now, girls."

Like so many family dinners at his own house, soon the plates were passed and the chaos began.

Mark wasn't used to being around kids, especially the chatty Claire and her little echo Gracie. He figured Laurel rarely got a quiet moment with them in the house. At least Peter's mood had lightened some since yesterday. His second lesson had gone about the same as the first, but Mark made sure he understood that everything worth learning took time.

Peter let his mom know she'd made his favorite—turkey meat loaf. Mark could tell by Laurel's surprised and pleased expression a compliment from the kid wasn't routine. She'd rounded out the meal with small baked potatoes, with several choices for toppings, and fresh green beans that smelled great thanks to lemon slices and a large sprig of rosemary cooked with them.

Conversation around the table had more to do with bargaining over how much each twin had to eat in order to call it dinner, and whether or not Peter had homework and had he done it yet, than getting-to-know-the-neighbor gab.

It brought back a slew of memories for Mark, of him and his brothers when they were young kids, squirming and trying to behave. And later when they'd all become touchy teens, ready to pounce on each other at the drop of one wrong word, or unwanted glance.

Other than Mark occasionally catching Laurel's gaze, and a special zing that took him by surprise whenever he did, they weren't able to communicate much at all. He was okay with that, since his goal was to keep the distance.

"So tell us about your surfing lessons, Peter," Laurel asked.

The kid said just enough words to qualify for an answer, then shoved more meat into his mouth. He seemed to have a healthy appetite, and Mark assumed it was from the beating he'd taken in the ocean that afternoon.

"Have you been doing those exercises I told you about?"

"Some." More eating, this time potato. "I'm gonna do more later."

"After your homework, right?" Laurel added between bites.

"Can we be excused?" the twins said in unison.

Laurel made a big deal out of checking their plates to make sure they'd eaten enough. "One more bite each."

They both crammed another tiny bite into their mouths, washed it down with the last of their milk and rushed off for the family room.

Peter had to be asked to clear the table, but he didn't protest too loudly, which surprised Mark. Maybe he wasn't such a problem all the time after all. Or maybe that was Peter on good behavior because of Mark being there.

Mark wanted to help, too, but Laurel wouldn't let him. "I'll clean up later. While the girls watch their TV show and Peter finishes his homework, I thought we could have some coffee or whatever you'd like to drink in the front sitting room."

An invitation for time alone? No matter how complicated the Prescott family's situation was, Mark couldn't resist the chance to get to know Laurel a little better. "Sure. Coffee's fine."

"I'll meet you in there," she said.

So he meandered into the front of the house. Rather than sit on the pillowed-out and overstuffed couch, or the matching ornate curved armchair beside it, he chose the classic paisley upholstered straight-backed chair across from the sofa, and waited for Laurel.

After looking around the room, he glanced out the front window toward the decidedly vintage-styled Drumcliffe and smiled, a few more ideas for perking up the place popping into his head. He also thought about Laurel and how having a brooding teen must stress her out, especially while juggling the twins and the hundreds of duties of the B&B. And the place wasn't even open yet. And once it was, would it even support them? He wouldn't suppose her situation, but figured there was probably life insurance meeting some of their needs.

He wondered what profession her deceased husband was in.

Then stopped himself. Enough already.

She brought coffee on a tray, like they did in old movies, and he got a kick out of all the effort she'd gone to for him. But this was a B&B, and she was the proprietor. Of course she'd do this for the guests. In fact, she was probably practicing on him. That was all.

He poured cream into his coffee and soon enjoyed the hint of vanilla and cinnamon. If this was only practice, he was happy to be her guinea pig, because it made their sitting alone together in a fancy room feel less intimate.

"I wanted to personally thank you for your help these last two days. Peter told me what happened at the beach yesterday."

"No big deal. Those kids were up to no good."

"It *was* a big deal. Who knows what would've happened if you hadn't shown up."

"Well, I did, and Peter got some surfing lessons out of it."

"I hope he keeps it up."

"He says he wants to."

She went quiet for a moment. "I never thought he'd get bullied simply for being the new kid in town."

"In a perfect world, it shouldn't make any difference, but…"

She primly sipped her coffee from a pink patterned cup that probably came from England. The one inside the box he'd first carried yesterday?

He didn't want to, but couldn't help noticing her

mouth, how the top lip was slightly plumper than the bottom. Rather than get caught staring again, he took in how tonight her hair was tamed with a conservative hair band, and how she looked like a proper bed-and-breakfast owner. Then he glanced down at her bright tangerine toenails, enjoying the contradiction.

She caught him staring, too, and he didn't even try to look away. Why pretend when he liked what he saw? So he smiled, and judging by the twitch at one corner of her mouth, she didn't mind.

"So what are you going to call this place?"

"The Prescott Bed-and-Breakfast. I've got a sign, just haven't put it up yet."

"I can do it."

"Would you?"

On impulse, he decided he might just help out from time to time. She was a widow with three kids and needed all the help she could get. Not because he found her attractive, and she interested him, and he felt good around her. But as backup. Only to help her out, as a handyman, because she could use it. That was the main reason.

Right. And Grandda didn't believe in selkies.

"Sure. The sooner you start to advertise the better."

"Tomorrow, then?"

He refilled his coffee. "Absolutely."

For now, he'd buy the little white lie about helping her out because she needed it. Otherwise he might get uptight about making another excuse to see her tomorrow, and he didn't want to be tense when having her all to himself in the sitting room right now felt so right.

Laurel sipped coffee and watched Mark's big hands as he grappled with the teapot made for ladies. She hid her smile behind the antique china cup. He'd obviously ogled her pedicure, and she wondered if there was anything else he might like about her. It had been a long time since she'd seen appreciative gazes from a man, and, being honest, she'd missed it.

Was that why she kept asking him to come back?

Or was it because, beyond his all-man appearance, he was nice? He'd intervened on her son's behalf. He was a man and her boy needed male mentoring? Lord only knew she was out of her depth on that one. She hadn't a clue that Peter, gangly and new in town, would be the subject of teasing. From what Peter had said, the teasing had been heading in a much more serious direction when Mark showed up.

What kind of mother was she? One who seriously needed to make time to read some books on parenting teens. Maybe if he was more confident, hadn't been devastated by losing his father…

Her mind drifted back to the present. Instead of required reading, she was sitting in the parlor with a man who emitted more sex appeal than the last three seasons of bachelors combined. Did he have a clue?

Yesterday he'd hinted at needing a life coach as much as she did, so that was something they had in common. With his time in the Middle East, and her husband's losing battle with cancer, they'd both been through hell. There was one other, more positive thing they had in common, too: they'd both been raised in a small beach town.

She could hear him swallow. Deep in thought, it'd grown too quiet. "So tell me about the history of The Drumcliffe."

An easy subject to tackle, he did so with ease, giving her the story from all the way back when his grandfather came from Ireland. As he spoke, she enjoyed the sparkle in his blue eyes, darkened by the parlor lighting, and how tiny the teacup looked in his hands. His lower lip curled out the tiniest bit, and she wondered how it would feel to kiss him.

What? She took another sip of her coffee. Maybe she *was* ready to…

Oh, the mere thought made her stomach knot and a hope chest of guilt crash over her shoulders. But there he was, sharing his family's story, natural as could be, smiling with pride. What could be wrong with a little longing?

She took another sip, admiring every aspect of Mark Delaney. She'd caught him checking her out earlier, and knew how that felt. Good, by the way. Now the tables were turned, but she didn't want to give the wrong impression, and the last thing she needed was to get caught. Taking yet another sip of her cooling coffee, she wondered how long she could hide behind her teacup before being obvious.

Chapter Three

"Hey, Peter, give me a hand," Mark said that Wednesday afternoon, as he prepared to sink the white posts for the brand-spanking-new Prescott Bed-and-Breakfast sign.

The teen sat on the front porch playing a handheld video game and didn't bother to look up.

So he made his loud tooth whistle. "Dude!"

Finally, Peter's head bobbed up.

"Come help." It wasn't a question.

"I don't know how."

"So you'll learn."

Reluctantly, Peter put down his device and padded in his flip-flops across the grass toward Mark. "Like I said, I don't know how to do this stuff, and we're supposed to have another surf lesson."

"We'll make up for that tomorrow." He watched the kid hide his disappointment. "I promise."

That got a better response.

"Okay, here's what we're going to do."

Over the next hour Mark showed Peter how to dig a hole, set an anchor, use an electric drill—which he especially liked—place washers and install a nut. Peter had obviously never so much as hammered a nail, but the how-to approach seemed to capture his interest enough. At least he tried.

"See that pile of wood over there?" Mark pointed to the grassy yard across the road, between the hotel and the beach.

"Yeah?"

"That's going to be a gazebo, and I want you to help me build it this weekend."

"Me!" The kid's voice cracked and his eyes nearly bugged out.

"Yeah, you need experience hammering nails, and I can teach you how to use more power tools, a cross-cut saw, table and band saw, you name it. What do you say?"

"Why?"

"Because knowing how to do a few useful things will build your confidence." Which he needed. *And will come in handy for your mother, too.* "Like learning how to surf."

"What if I don't want to?"

"Surf?"

"No. Help."

Not an option. Think fast. "Think of it this way. Our hotel is right on Main Street, the biggest road that leads straight to the beach." He glanced up the road lined with palm and fruitless olive trees, small local businesses, storefronts and, in the distance on a hill, the local high school. "All the girls come this way to the beach, and they'll see you building stuff. They'll notice you. Might open some doors."

Peter stood staring across the street at the pile of wood, then glanced up toward what passed as the town center, small as it was.

"It's better than babysitting your sisters, isn't it?" Mark noticed the click in his expression from on-the-fence to makes-perfect-sense. Whether it was the girls or not dealing with his sisters, Mark had sold him on the proposition, and though the last thing he needed was a novice assistant, he wanted to help the kid. Maybe he'd find out something new about himself, feel better and, like he'd said, be more confident. Or, he could smash his finger with a hammer, get the mother of all splinters and never want to go near wood again. It was a gamble, but worth the risk.

A half hour later, after a few finishing touches on the posts, and with plans to meet Saturday morning to begin building, they'd hung the B&B sign.

"It's beautiful!" Laurel called from the porch, her eyes bright with excitement. It was obvious she'd made a conscious effort not to hover over her son while he helped Mark, but from a safe distance she'd followed the whole process. "I've got to take a picture." She whipped out her phone and rushed down the yard toward them.

"You get in it, and I'll take the picture," Mark offered.

"Oh." Her hand flew to her hair. "I wasn't planning on—"

"You look fine. I'll get a few shots and you can choose the best one, then put it on Facebook."

"I'm not crazy about social media."

"But you've got to create a buzz."

"You've got a point." She glanced at her son. "Peter,

you worked so hard on this, come be in the picture with me?" she said with pride.

"Ah, Mom." He obviously didn't want anything to do with smiling for a camera, but he hadn't wanted to help sink the posts, either, and there they were.

"We want to!" Claire came rushing through the screen door and down the porch steps wearing plastic play heels, clicking all the way, Gracie hot on her tail clack, clack, clacking. Laurel split them up, putting one on each side of the sign.

After some arm-twisting, Mark managed to get a picture of the entire family, with a good portion of the beautiful house behind them. He had to admit, Laurel's smile was captivating, and he thought about secretly sending a copy of one shot in particular to his email. It was of her alone, of course, looking proud, maybe a little nervous but alluring, as she often did. Her understated confidence was just one of the things he liked about her.

"This is the best picture. Agree?"

She shrugged, but he could tell she liked it, too. *Yeah, that one, definitely that one.* "Should I post it?"

"Sure."

It was time to face the fact. His grandfather had a word for it—*smitten.* Mark would never use that term, but he needed to admit he dug her. Yup. There. He'd finally allowed himself to think it. He liked her, and not just in a pure neighborly sort of way. Ready or not. Maybe he'd blame it on the tangerine pedicure.

"There you go." He handed her the phone. "Anything you want to say with the picture?"

"Oh, sure." Her thumbs flew over the phone, and Mark took the opportunity to watch her up close. Yeah, as bad of an idea as it was, he liked her all right.

* * *

Laurel finally realized, with Mark's hinting, she was behind in the social media game. Instead of going all ditzy over an appealing man like she'd been doing since he'd helped her that first day, she needed to hunker down and finalize her plan for opening the B&B. Sure, she'd given it a lot of thought before she'd bought the place, but making the move and starting the kids in new schools all at the same time had taken her eye off the prize.

She had catching up to do and plans to firm up. Ads to run in the tricounty local papers, visits to make to the chamber of commerce.

What about a mock run? She could invite three local travel agents to spend the night as a sort of rehearsal, maybe get some good endorsements in the process. Her head spun with new ideas, thanks to Mark's gentle nudging, and she needed to get back on her game, instead of ogling her sexy neighbor. Pronto.

On Thursday afternoon, Peter finally stood on his own for a short ride during their surfing lesson, and the kid beamed all the way on the walk home. On the porch, Laurel lifted a brow when her son gave her a hug on his way into the house. Progress.

"He had a good day at the beach," Mark said. "I'll let him tell you about it."

She lifted her shoulders as if she'd just seen magic. "That's great." Her earnest glance kept him from rushing off, that and how her hair lifted with the afternoon breeze.

She ventured down the stairs—he couldn't take his eyes off her—and met him at the gate. "Can I borrow you tomorrow night?"

The request put all kinds of thoughts in his head.

"I'm putting together a few appetizers I plan to serve in the evenings along with wine for the guests." With her head tipped, she hopefully glanced up. "I need a taster."

Looking bashful, like a young girl, she'd used words like borrow and taste, and had thrown him. "Me?" His delayed response. "I should put you in touch with Rita, our restaurant chef. Get her opinion. Or my mom, she'd be great for this."

"But I want you." Her fingers lightly grazed his forearm.

Want me? When was the last time he'd heard a woman say that? "What time?" he said, far too aware of her touch.

"Seven. Be sure to save up your appetite." Her sweet smile, and twinkling eyes made the hair on his neck salute.

Liking the way she'd made him feel, he let go a slow smile, and they spent a long moment looking in each other's eyes. "See you then."

Friday evening, after a long day of construction work on the early stages of the gazebo, and yet another surfing lesson with Peter, Mark took extra time to clean up good. He'd shaved off his usual two-day growth, even slapped on for the first time the woodsy aftershave his mother had given him last Christmas. *Sniff, sniff.* Too much? He stepped out of the bathroom.

Conor sprawled on the couch in the sitting room of their shared hotel suite watching the local news. Yup, they were two grown men still living at home. Well, at the family hotel, anyway. It used to be even more cramped when Daniel lived there, too, while starting up his physical medicine clinic. No wonder Grandda was hell-bent they'd each be finding the love of their life soon, just to get them out of the fold. *Remember the selkie!* The phrase was beginning to sound like a T-shirt slogan.

Daniel had met and married Keela, so chalk one up for Grandda. Conor had a good excuse for still living at home, though. He was saving all his money for the down payment on a house he'd wanted since he was a kid. The Beacham house was abandoned, forgotten and falling apart, and sat hauntingly along the cliffs on the outskirts of town. Whereas Mark still lived here because he had nowhere else to go while getting back on his feet.

The family offer was clearly on the table—take over the hotel—but he still wasn't sure if he wanted the responsibility of running the entire family business. His parents thought he could do it, but what if he failed, ruining decades of their hard work? Three generations could go down the drain. It occurred to him, while he was so bent on helping Peter develop some confidence, maybe he should start working on himself, too.

"Man, you smell like you mean business," Conor said the minute Mark stepped out of the bathroom, naked except for the towel around his waist.

"Good or bad?"

"If I say I like it, will you think less of me?" The tallest though youngest of the three brothers, Conor, who looked more like a professional athlete than a sheriff, grinned.

Mark smirked. "Can I borrow a shirt?"

"Okay, now I'm curious." Conor muted the TV. "What's up?"

"Just helping out the lady across the street."

"You mean the good-looking brunette?"

Mark stopped riffling through Conor's abundant collection of shirts.

"Think I hadn't noticed?"

He met his brother's knowing gaze for the first time.

"And she's got three kids."

Mark opted to pass over that reminder, for another fact. "I figure she's around thirty-five."

"A cougar," Conor teased. "All *riight*."

"Her? Hardly. Besides that's only four years' difference. We're just feeling each other out." He did his best to sound nonchalant, though inwardly grimacing over his word choice.

Conor's brows shot up. "Sounds promising."

Mark gave an ironic laugh and chose a smoky-blue button-down shirt from his brother's closet, then tried it on. "What about this one?"

Conor went overboard standing, assessing, rubbing his chin with his fingers while walking around him. "It brings out your eyes," he said doing an obvious imitation of the male fashion consultant from that runway reality show.

Mark unwrapped the bath towel, twirled it tight, then snapped it at his brother.

Jumping aside, Conor grinned. "I dare you to show up like that," he said, making note of Mark being completely naked from the waist down. "Make one helluva first-date impression."

Laurel fed her kids an early dinner and set the girls up playing Candy Land and building a new Legos kit. Peter was always happy to be left alone, especially after another surfing lesson from Mark. She liked how Mark had made the effort to get Peter engaged in the B&B

sign hanging yesterday, too. Once again reinforcing the boy really needed a man's influence.

She finished making half a dozen different appetizers, hoping Mark would help her decide the top three for the B&B opening. She uncorked the red wine—a silky mixture of three different grapes—to let it breathe and next opened an unoaked white, pushing it into the ice bucket to keep the crisp wine chilled. Then she went to the dining room and carefully laid classic china plates and linen napkins on the antique oak buffet.

Why were her fingers trembling? Was she that nervous about the mock run she'd planned for next week, and opening the B&B for business after that? Or did the tall and intriguing Mark Delaney with great abs have something to do with her jitters?

No-brainer.

The doorbell rang and she rushed to answer it, and what was on the other side nearly took her breath away. She'd already made the mistake of noticing Mark's sexy mouth, so now as it stretched slowly into a relaxed smile, she couldn't avoid the gorgeous spectacle. Because he'd shaved, and there was nothing like a man's smooth face to make a woman want to run her hand along his jaw. Her eyes widened and she looked away…to his eyes.

Beneath his brows, those deep-set blue eyes stood out like they never had before. Maybe it was the time of day, or the shirt—which was a definite good choice.

"Hi," he said. "Too early?"

Scrambling to cover how flustered he'd suddenly made her feel, she swallowed and forced a welcoming grin. "No. Not at all." She invited him in, noticing a catchy masculine fragrance, and liked it, then started immediately toward the back of the house. "I've got the appetizers lined up in the kitchen. Just gotta move them to the dining room, where they'll actually be if I ever get guests."

"You mean when. *When* you get guests."

"Oh, right. Positive thinking." Why did sensing him right behind her make her edgy? Was it the fact he smelled so great? Or looked so handsome, in a natural all-guy kind of way. He was younger than her—she couldn't forget that little zinger.

"Whatever's easiest for you," he said, watching her oddly, like he'd totally caught on how he made her feel.

Could he tell? "Well, the ambiance is nicer in there."

Without being asked, he stepped up and carried two of the platters to the dining room. "Wow, these look great."

"Thanks." She brought two others, then they made one final trip together for the last two platters and the wine. *Focus on why you invited him, not how great he looks. Or smells.* "I plan on rotating the appetizers for those who stay more than one night."

"Makes sense." He stopped, his hands on his hips in a total guy way. "So you want to pretend I'm a guest?" A mischievous smile creased those inviting lips, and she went all skittish again. It'd been far too long since she'd been in the company of an attractive man. Since Alan's death, she'd never even missed it until she'd noticed Mark Delaney across the street five days ago. A quick pang of sadness and loss settled in her chest. Reminding her of what she'd been through and how much she'd lost. She took a breath. All she had to do was focus on Mark's pretending to be a guest.

"Oh, well, okay." She gestured for him to sit.

"Wait," he said. "Have you taken a picture and uploaded it to your social media pages?"

Why hadn't she thought of that? Because she'd been too distracted by him. "No. Another great idea." She went back into the kitchen to retrieve her cell phone, then snapped a couple of pictures and got Mark's approval for the best one to share. The one with the two wine bottles in the background. He took her phone and used his thumbs superfast, then showed her what he'd written.

Appetizers at five. Join us? Prescott B&B, Sandpiper Beach. Opening soon.

"You've got a real knack for this sort of thing."

"Mom needed some help getting The Drumcliffe online. I had to take a crash course on the whole social media thing. Even figured out how to upload a virtual tour on our website."

"Impressive. You're a natural."

"We could do one for the B&B, too," he said.

"I'd love it!"

He smiled like he was as excited for her opening as she was, which touched her. She gestured for him to sit again. "I plan to show every guest around when they check in. Mind if I practice my talk on you?"

"Not at all."

"Oh, and don't wait for me, start eating."

He sat and looked at everything, but did wait while she recited a little welcome speech she'd worked up, feeling more like a child in school instead of a thirty-five-year-old woman. As she did, she poured him a small glass of each wine. To help him decide, she placed before him the cheese platter with honey, fig spread and assorted nuts. On the second plate was crostini with three different homemade toppings to choose from—guacamole, mashed minted peas and salsa. The third item was pinwheels made from feta and cream cheese with dried cranberries in flour tortillas, then came the stuffed mushrooms, and finally the sweet-and-sour meatballs on one plate and tiny crab cakes on another. She'd labeled each plate since her guests would self-serve at their leisure between 5:00 and 6:00 p.m. each evening.

"Wow," was all Mark said, but looking deep in thought.

"Be honest, okay? Rate them favorite to least."

"Aren't you going to join me?"

She sat next to him, poured herself a small glass of red wine and spread some Brie with honey and fig on a cracker. "Sure. It's no fun to eat alone." Though occasionally she longed for the luxury of eating by herself, without a single kid needing her attention.

"Don't I know that." He appeared to be having trouble choosing which appetizer to have first.

Did he eat alone a lot? Could a person be lonely living and working at a family hotel like The Drum-cliffe? She'd assumed otherwise, but his reply had told her different.

"Damn, I feel like I've died and gone to mini-buffet heaven," he said, smiling as he popped a meatball into his mouth. "Oh, that's good."

"Have as much of everything as you want." His general reaction to her efforts and to her invitation warmed her on the inside in a way she hadn't felt in two years.

Then she realized how much she'd missed being around a man, and Mark Delaney was the reason. Just as quickly, that pang of fear returned.

Mark had eaten until he was full, enjoying every bite. Having a glass of wine, something he didn't do very often, had also mellowed him out. He wondered why The Drumcliffe didn't do something similar as a perk for their guests. They put carafes of coffee out every morning in the lobby, so why not add something like this in the evening? It wouldn't need to be as special as this, but something. Maybe Grandda could offer house wine and draft beer in the pub for their guests for a couple of hours each evening, too. Guests only, though, or the locals would flood the pub if word got out. The flowing ideas were all food for thought, along with Laurel's amazing appetizers.

She looked great, too. Her hair was down, and she'd put on lipstick. For him? Could a woman like her be the least bit interested in a guy like him? A handyman working for his parents? *Don't flatter yourself, buddy.* This was nothing more than practice for future guests. Of course she'd dress up. He tried to convince himself he played zero part in the reason she looked so nice right then, but part of him—a long-forgotten part—wanted to think she might be attracted to him, too. He hoped so, anyway.

What was it about Laurel that made him wish things could be different, and want things again?

She wore a yellow summer sweater set with a knee-length, straight khaki skirt, affording him the best view of her legs yet. Narrow ankles, nice calves, smooth-looking skin. And thanks to her choice in sandals, he got another glimpse of those tangerine-colored toenails. He liked everything he saw, and most of all was glad he was here with her.

He took another drink of the wine, she'd done the same, and their gazes overlapped midsip, causing a tiny pop of adrenalin in his chest. Her hazel-brown eyes were warm and rich like the silky taste of the three-grape blended red, and they watched him thoughtfully.

Hopefully she wasn't a mind reader, because he was still all kinds of messed up from his stint in the military. Part of him wanted to slide right into something nice with her, another part unsure and reluctant to try. But staring into those gorgeous eyes, he wanted to.

"Hey, can I have a meatball?" Peter appeared, hair disheveled like he'd just woken up.

"Of course." Laurel quickly snapped out of their invigorating staring contest, which disappointed Mark, even though he understood she couldn't continue making doe eyes at him in front of her son.

"Can we have some?"

"Can we have some?"

The twins had arrived. Laurel handed them each a cranberry and cream cheese pinwheel.

The boy wolfed down the last three meatballs before hitting the guacamole and toast.

He seemed in a good enough mood, so on a whim, Mark decided to take advantage of the situation.

"Peter, will you watch the girls for a little while so your mother and I can take a walk on the beach?"

Midchew, Peter looked confused, probably wondering why Mark would want to hang out with his mother.

"Play game-ios with us?" Gracie pleaded.

Peter screwed up his face. "I'll watch TV with you, but I get to choose," he bargained. "And I'm taking the guacamole with me." He gathered up the plate, and without giving a definitive answer, walked down the hall with his sisters.

"I guess that's a yes," Laurel said, looking happy.

As they started out the door, Laurel called back into the house. "Be good. I'll be back in a while."

"Okay," Peter called out, apparently unfazed by his

involuntary assignment. At least he was inside. Nobody from school would see him.

"Okay!" Claire.

"Oh. Kay!" Gracie.

They stepped off the porch into cool night air and a clear sky, a bit too early for most of the stars to show.

"Since you've started giving Peter surfing lessons, he seems a little happier. Doesn't brood as much. Well, maybe *happy* isn't the right word for it, but...*calmer*? Anyway, I've noticed he's not giving me as much attitude as usual."

"Seriously?"

"Yes, and I have to thank you for that."

He wasn't at all sure he deserved the credit, but he liked the expression on her face as they headed for the beach, so he smiled back. Maybe he was a good influence.

"Definite progress. He doesn't resent every single thing I say to him, only a few." She laughed and took off her sandals to walk barefoot in the still-warm sand. "He's lightened up with his sisters, too."

Mark kept quiet, enjoying her carefree conversation. If she wanted to attribute the kid's attitude adjustment to him, fine, but the only payment he needed was seeing the lack of stress on her beautiful face.

And yes, he'd just secretly admitted he thought she was beautiful.

If he continued to keep connecting with Peter, maybe he'd earn the kid's trust. Did he want the responsibility of that, though? Mark let go of the uncertain thought, focusing instead on Laurel and her shapely legs walking ahead of him toward the waves. In the moment, attraction overruled concern. He lengthened his stride and caught up.

"We're not in a hurry, are we?" he asked.

"Oh. No. I'm so used to rushing through everything, I guess I've forgotten how to relax."

Crazy thought, but he wanted to teach her how. Maybe it would help him remember, too. He took her hand, which she didn't fight, and set a slower pace. "Take a deep breath. Enjoy yourself for a change." Her thin fingers were cool, though her palm felt warm against his, and it was great to hold a woman's hand again.

She did as he suggested, slowing down to a stroll, inhaling the ocean air, then a few steps later she looked at him with a questioning gaze. "Is that how I come off? Uptight all the time?"

She hadn't said it defensively, or as a challenge, just a query, so he gave her his honest opinion. "You've got a lot of responsibilities, and let's just say, sometimes I can tell you're struggling."

She went silent as they walked past the lifeguard station, toward a long stretch of beach. A minute later she squeezed his hand. "I've probably taken on more than I should've, but we needed a new start." She checked him out, as though wondering if it was okay to talk about her past. He sent an encouraging glance. "It was so sad at our old house, all the memories, the gaping hole Alan had left by dying. He'd written me a note telling me to do something special with his second life insurance policy. It took close to two years to decide, but I finally did. Now, most days I think I'm crazy."

"I think it's great you bought that place. The house is gorgeous." *So are you.* "Everything you've done is amazing." He stopped to look at her before saying his next thought. "I know how it is to focus so hard on something that all the rest fades away. As a person who may have forgotten how to enjoy myself, too, I'm just saying."

"Takes one to know one?"

He smiled and nodded, enjoying how the moonlight sparkled in her eyes. How she suddenly looked impish.

She pushed him with both palms, then took off running for the damp sand, heading toward the ocean. "First one in wins!" She hiked up her skirt to her thighs so she could run faster. He definitely liked that.

Momentarily stunned by her sudden change, Mark stood still, then quickly responded to her challenge and ran after her.

She squealed when her feet hit the cold water. "I win!"

"That's just a toe dip. You said first one *in*." He rushed beside her, not giving a damn that his jeans were sopping wet up to his knees, and his cross-trainers pooled with water, and swooped her up into his arms, then pretended to throw her into the next wave.

She screamed and stiffened, then laughed, but screamed again as he pretended to hoist her into the waves, counting one, two, three! She buried her face on his shoulder, and he liked having her there, in his arms, laughing.

A fast-moving, receding wave pulled at the backs of his knees, and he lost his footing as the sand quickly got sucked from under his feet, nearly dropping her. Staggering back to a wide stance, refusing to let her go, he nearly recovered until a second wave rolled in, hitting faster and harder, and higher up. Drenching both of them. His jeans were sopping and heavy, now. And they didn't stand a chance. Down the two of them went into the cold pool of swirling ocean. He yelled and she screamed.

"I'm sorry!" he called, worried what she'd think of him, assuming she was ticked off. But she laughed hysterically, and once he helped her stand, she splashed him, then ran back to the wet sand and took off farther down the beach. What could he do but follow? Though running in drenched denim and soggy shoes was a definite challenge. Not to mention the chaffing.

"What'll the kids think when I come home like this?" she called over her shoulder.

"That you had some fun?"

Finally, he caught up. They were both out of breath, but she was still smiling, and he realized how much he liked Peter's mom. In fact, as he wrapped his arms around her and they smiled at each other up close—she cold and shivering—he understood exactly how much he liked her, enough to want to kiss her.

It'd been a long time since he'd been in a good enough place to even think about kissing a woman. He hadn't felt this drawn to someone since before his last deployment, two years ago.

But Mark and Laurel were just getting to know each other. If he followed through on this crazy whim and kissed her, wouldn't it mess up the friendly-neighbor bit? With three kids, she needed a helping hand more than a boyfriend.

From the shift in her playful expression to serious, he sensed she'd figured out exactly what'd just been going on in his mind. Yeah, he still wanted to kiss her. And where he'd hesitated, with a lift of her chin she seemed to dare him.

So he kissed her, cold, salty and wet, discovering soft, warm and inviting lips. That her pouty upper lip did indeed feel as good as it looked. The cautious kiss didn't take long, but it planted a warm, glad feeling in the center of his chest. Though Laurel gave a modest look when it ended, like they'd just broken a rule or something, she took his hand as they walked back to her house.

He liked holding her hand even more now, and wished he'd kissed her the way he'd really wanted.

When they got to her gate, sopping wet from the waist down, Mark opted not to go in. "You can tell them I dared you to go swimming."

"I was going to tell them I had to save you from a shark."

"Good one."

She looked relaxed all right, and playful, and he wondered what she'd be like, just the two of them in that big old house now that they'd broken the ice.

"Got anything for me to do tomorrow?"

She took her time answering, letting her gaze travel around him, a different kind of look in her eyes. Flirty. "Oh, I'm sure I'll come up with something." Then she turned and headed for her porch. "Before or after your project with Peter?" she said at the door.

"After."

"I'll make lunch."

"You don't have to do that."

"I want to."

"Okay, then, good."

"Good," she said, sounding sassy.

If he wasn't mistaken she'd just flat out flirted with him. He liked that. A lot. So he smiled to himself. As he walked back to his room, shoes squeaking, rubbing his heels, his cold, water-laden jeans dragging on the asphalt, and scraping the insides of his thighs, even with beach sand finding its way into strange places, he kept grinning. Tonight, spending one-on-one time with Laurel had been great, and with plans to see her again, tomorrow was already looking up.

Chapter Four

Saturday, after five long hours of manual labor with Mark as the foreman and Peter the journeyman apprentice, they'd managed good headway with the gazebo frame. Peter had learned how to use several new-to-him power tools, including table and band saws, plus, from the way he grinned every time he used it, his personal favorite, the nail gun.

Laurel made an appearance around 12:30 p.m. to remind them that lunch would be served at one. They worked across the street on the cul-de-sac yard abutting the side of The Drumcliffe. The rolling green lawn extended toward the beach, and was the perfect spot for the gazebo. She showed up wearing brown leggings, displaying her nice curves, and a sleeveless top, loose, but sexy, giving him a glimpse of her light olive skin and thin arms. Best of all, her hair was in a ponytail again. Mark was surprised how much he looked forward to lunch, too, so he rushed things along on the building front. They sunk the posts, braced the beams, even adding some windows in record time. In other words, they were more than ready for lunch when, a half hour later, Laurel called from her curb. What a spread she'd made, too. The kitchen island was covered in do-it-yourself sandwich fixings. Assorted meats and cheeses, three different breads, everything from lettuce to tomatoes and pickles.

"You may want to try that before you use it," Laurel said, pointing out a small bowl of something that looked like he'd want to spread it on bread. It sat next to the standard mayo and mustard jars.

Mark hadn't washed his hands yet, and Laurel dipped her index finger into the "secret sauce" and came at him.

"Taste this. Let me know what you think."

He stared for an instant at her proffered finger. A dozen inappropriate thoughts crossed his mind. Did she know what she was doing to him? Innocently, she waited for his tongue to appear, then served the tip of her finger, covered in spread, for his tasting pleasure. He went for it, savoring every sensation as it came along. Warm skin, spicy spread.

It happened so fast, he was stunned by how sexy licking her finger could be. He'd also made the mistake of looking her in the eyes when he did. Oh, yeah, this was more than tasting the spread, this was a continuation of that kiss they'd shared and took it to a whole new level. A dozen more thoughts blasted through his mind, causing his skin to heat up, and since they were in front of her kids, all crowding around the island to make their own versions of lunch, he fought off the urge to grab and kiss her.

She'd seen it, too. His flash of desire. Because she'd been watching. Teasing? Had she done that on purpose, that uber-sexy taste-my-finger bit?

The moment stretched on, and he realized she waited for his reaction, preferably something verbal, and definitely from above the belt.

"Wow," he said. "What'd you put in there?"

She dipped her head sideways, wearing a sweet, yet smug expression. "That's my little secret. Trust me." Oh, he wanted to. "Spread that on your bread and it'll make any meat pop."

Did she just say that? Right in front of the kids? He hadn't been this turned on discussing sandwiches since, well, *ever*.

"Definitely going to use that." He pointed at the innocent little bowl sitting on the counter, then went to wash his hands, thinking cold, cold water over the head would be more appropriate.

After lunch at the B&B, where his turkey definitely popped between the sheets—uh, he meant bread—Laurel, as promised, had found something for Mark to do.

She got out her laptop, opened it on the counter and, while the twins carried the dishes and utensils to the sink and she cleaned up, she had Peter display the big surprise.

A website for the B&B. She'd taken his advice, and that fact touched him nearly as much as tasting her finger.

"I uploaded a website for the Prescott B&B," Peter said. "It's just a basic theme, but Mom helped me pick some pictures and, well, what do you think?"

Besides the fact it was awfully late to just be doing this? "This is great." Mark was truly impressed, and glad to get his mind off Laurel and how she made him feel. "It doesn't look like you need my help with *any-thing*."

"Wasn't it your idea to include virtual tours?" Laurel reminded, from the sink area.

"Oh, yeah. This is the perfect place to post them."

"That's why I need your help." And there he was staring into those amazing eyes again. "You're the guy with the fancy-schmancy seven plus smartphone."

"Ah, right." So she'd wound him tight around her finger for a reason. But he preferred to think she'd been flat out flirting with him.

For the next hour, he and Laurel toured each of the six guest rooms using his phone video camera to film a slow 360-degree turn. They had to reshoot a couple of them because Mark had bumped into something by accident, or his hand wasn't steady enough. How could he be steady in bedroom after bedroom, with Laurel standing close enough to breathe on his neck?

After, he took a picture of each room from the best angle to post under the ROOMS heading on the website. Next, he went out front and filmed a walk up to the wraparound porch and entrance into the house. He got the bright idea to walk slowly up the inside stairwell to the second-floor landing, too. She'd done such a beautiful job of arranging the antique furniture there. The sitting area seemed to invite guests to try out the chairs and love seats, to linger and enjoy reading a book from the well-stocked built-in bookcases. She must have spent a lot of time in used bookstores to find most of the leather-bound classics, though she also had a wide assortment of current paperbacks. When all the filming was done, he sent the videos to Peter to upload on the new website.

These were the only moments he had alone with Laurel, and it was strictly business. Sure, they'd accidentally bumped into each other while filming several times, followed by exaggerated "excuse mes" and "no problems," but that wasn't the quality time he'd been hoping for. Just her and him, alone, in her pretty house. Maybe another day.

He still enjoyed himself, because it was time spent with Laurel. What had gotten into him? He was still fighting the idea of taking over the hotel. Why the sudden desire to get involved? With a woman who came complete with a family, no less.

After Peter completed the website, Laurel, the twins and Mark watched Peter as he clicked the various pages, conducted each virtual room tour and signed up for the Prescott B&B newsletter. They all cheered and high-fived like they'd invented a rocket set for outer space.

"Time for cookies!" Laurel announced. The twins jumped up and down, and Mark smiled.

While Peter chowed down several cookies, Mark went through the website again, comparing it with The Drumcliffe Hotel's online presence.

"Your online reservation link isn't hooked up with anything," Mark noted.

"What do you mean?" Laurel looked concerned, maybe uptight?

"To other programs that give you more visibility. But we can fix that. Let me give my dad a call." As predicted, Sean promptly picked up. "Dad, can you come across the street for a minute? We need your help." Mark liked how "we" sounded, like he belonged somewhere besides with his family.

In the time it took Mark to eat a cookie, his father's shadow loomed over the Victorian's front door. Mark let him in, then made introductions as Sean Delaney appraised the first floor of the B&B.

Laurel's eyes darted between father and son, his father being a full three inches taller than Mark. He may look imposing, but the former high school math and history teacher was nothing short of a gentle giant. Unless you ticked him off, then look out.

Mark escorted him to the kitchen and made introductions. Laurel offered him a cookie, which he partook of, then he sat on a stool and, wasting no time, walked Laurel through the various options for small business owners like her.

"I get the need for this, but call me old school, or out of it, but whatever happened to people calling or emailing for reservations?"

"I used to feel the same way," Sean said, reassuringly, looking like the biggest man in the room—because he was. "But let me show you a few things."

With his reading glasses perched on the end of his nose, he surfed the web. "There are programs you can download, or services you can sign up for. See this?" He pointed to the screen and Laurel moved in closer. "This is a website reservation group you sign up for and pay a small monthly fee that offers alternative distribution systems, shows availability, and most importantly, gets you greater visibility. See, it even breaks down the price per number for rooms you have to rent. How many do you have?"

"Six." Wrapped up in the moment, Mark jumped in, answering for Laurel. She didn't seem to mind.

"Okay, so for less than twenty bucks a month they can provide all of these services." He leaned back and gave her time and space to read what they offered.

"There are also cloud based reservations software programs, but I kind of like this one."

"So this website reservations program can show my openings on bigger sites, like my local chamber of commerce?"

"Exactly, more exposure."

"You don't have to sign up for this if you don't feel ready," Mark added, wanting to offer Laurel support on whatever decision she made. Laurel looked relieved when she glanced at him.

"So there's no overlapped bookings?"

"Nope," Sean said. "If someone signs up through them it goes automatically to your calendar."

Sean pointed to another section of the computer screen. "See, they offer a free trial, if you want I can sign you up and you can see if this works for you or not. If you don't like it, just cancel."

"Thank you, Mr. Delaney."

"Call me Sean."

"Okay, Sean. If you don't mind, I'm going to think about this, and if you could bookmark this web link for me, I'll know where to go to sign up for the free trial. I can afford a small fee per month, I guess, if it does what it says, and I like the services."

"They've got a good rating, so no problem there." Sean glanced at Laurel, then Mark. Like a gentleman, never pushing a point, Sean nodded and accepted her resistance. "If you decide, any way I can help, just let me know. By the way, you've done a great job with this old house. Looks fantastic."

"Thank you."

Mark liked how Laurel's cheeks flushed the tiniest bit whenever she received a compliment. It made him want to take every opportunity to tell her something nice.

After Dad left, and another half hour with the two of them exploring the various systems available out there, they shut down the laptop. It was the closest they'd been since the spread-tasting incident, and he liked every moment.

"Your dad's so nice. I'm leaning toward his suggestion, too." She showed her gratitude with a hug.

"No harm in trying it out," he said, thinking he had a problem with how much he liked her hugging him.

When she released him, she pushed the plate of cookies at him. "Please take these home for your dad."

When her nearby twins heard what she'd said, they both grabbed another treat, nearly emptying the plate. Soon, Mark left without a single moment completely alone with Laurel. But at least he had all the quick and flirty glances they'd shared before, during and after lunch, and while filming the virtual tours, and that great hug to remember.

As it turned out, between her busy schedule and his hotel projects, those not-so-subtle glances were all he had to hold on to for the rest of the week.

The following Friday morning, Laurel couldn't contain her excitement, and fear. Three local travel agents had responded to her outreach and were coming for a trial stay at Prescott B&B. They'd spend a few hours taking a tour and learning the history of the house, exploring the six guest rooms, testing the beds, reviewing her breakfast menu and sampling the wine and appetizers. Then Saturday morning they'd come back for breakfast.

Mark was working on The Drumcliffe gazebo on

the side yard, the project Peter had helped him with last weekend. Being the first person she wanted to share her news with, she took off across the street.

"Mark! You won't believe this."

He grinned the moment he saw her, and after the cat-and-mouse week they'd spent, with her wondering how to move forward after their romp in the ocean and inaugural kiss, that smile made a huge impact. Her grin was because he happened to be working with his shirt off. Yowza!

"Good news?" He got off his knees and stood, making the display of flesh over muscle nearly blinding.

She had to regather her thoughts, and redirect her line of vision. "Oh. Yes, the best!" She explained the plan for the night, which he was crazy about, even hugged her, which really felt great, and a little naughty considering his being shirtless. She'd missed the scent of warm man skin. Once again having to compose herself, she moved forward with her plea. "The thing is, when they get here, I'll need someone to watch the girls while I give the tour and the open house."

"And Peter isn't available?"

"Peter promised to stay in his room and play video games. If he watches the girls, I can't guarantee a problem won't break out, or that the twins might make a racket or yell at him."

He scrunched up half of his face, and not because the sun was in his eyes. "Are you asking me to babysit?"

Put like that, blunt, it did sound horrible, and completely inappropriate. She cleared her throat, knowing the request was unreasonable, but not having a plan B. "Not, uh, in the traditional se-sense," she stammered. "Just maybe sit with them in their room, keep them quiet for like a half hour, forty-five minutes tops, while I give the tour."

He stood there shirtless, staring at her, looking, maybe, incredulous? "You hadn't thought about this part? When you start having guests? What the kids would do?"

Now she felt like a total fool, but the truth was out. Until she had regular B&B guests, and she could afford to hire a babysitter, her best idea was to make them stay in their rooms and be quiet. But four-and-a-half-year-old twins didn't know the meaning of the word. "I'll work this out better in the future, I promise, but is there any chance you can sit with them at four today?"

He shrugged, noncommittally. "Skip Peter's surf lesson?"

"He's okay with that, I already asked him last night."

Mark had seen Laurel in all kinds of sticky situations over the past two weeks, since the day he'd met her, but he'd never seen her looking desperate before. So he gave her outrageous request—thirty-one-year-old man, not the father, babysitting her daughters—a second thought. And agreed. But only because he really liked her. Really liked her.

At quarter to four, he'd showered and changed clothes and strode across the street. When he hit the porch of the B&B, he could hear Claire's and Gracie's squeals and laughter. Good point about keeping them quiet when the guests arrived. But what about during the Saturday morning breakfast for the guests? Who'd watch them then?

He tapped on the door.

"Is he here?" the girls sang aloud in unison.

"Calm down," Laurel instructed, just before she appeared at the door looking fantastic. Wow. She'd put her hair up, and wore a sky-blue patterned sheath dress that showed off her legs, the matching blue pumps helping highlight those shapely calves. This was a sophisticated side he hadn't seen before, and he really liked it. She was nothing like the girls he used to date. Heck, a woman like her would've never given him a second glance. Maybe that was why he was watching her kids instead of taking her out to dinner? Insecurity wasn't appealing and it was time to change. *Step up, Delaney.*

"Hi," she said, stress and worry ruining her overall appearance.

"You look great."

"Thanks." After a quick sigh of relief, she let him in.

The girls jumped up and down, wearing what looked like frilly fairy outfits, one neon pink, one lime green. "We're gonna have a tea party!"

He wanted to address Laurel's nerves, give her a pep talk or something, but he was being swarmed by the little ones. "You are?"

"No, *we* are!" Claire clarified.

Gracie gave an excited giggle, her fingertips in her mouth.

Mark slowly cast his gaze in Laurel's direction. "We are?"

Her brows came together, making a single quote mark above her nose, as she mouthed, *sorry.*

"Whose idea was this?" he addressed the fairies in a tolerant way.

"Mine!"

"Mine!"

Now they were jumping, and in five minutes Laurel's first-ever guests, local travel agents who could make or break her opening, were set to arrive. "Well, as my grandda always says, in for a penny, in for a pound." He clapped his hands. "Let's do this." Then herded them toward their room.

"I owe you," Laurel said quietly when they hit the hall.

"Oh, yes, you do," he replied, rounding the corner.

She closed the doors, shutting off the family quarters from the rest of the house. Though feeling suddenly trapped, Mark opted to concentrate on several great ideas for how Laurel might pay him back.

"Okay, girls, whenever you go to a tea party, you have to talk quietly." He gulped when he saw the tiny table set and ready to go, with three pip-squeak-sized chairs, one obviously meant for him. Managing to get one bun on it, with his knees nearly up to his chin, he worried the chair might break. But so far so good.

The tea was water, but the cookies were fresh-baked snickerdoodles, so it wasn't all bad. And most important, the girls were following his rule and talking quietly. But how long would that last? If he stayed sitting so low to the ground, would they want to style his hair? Put play makeup on him?

After they finished off the cookies in record time, he got a bright idea.

"Hey, you want to watch me hammer some nails?"

"Yes!" they blurted loudly in unison.

"Shh, shh, shh. Remember the tea party rules," he whispered, and they immediately went quiet. "Okay, follow me."

With his index finger covering his mouth, he took them tiptoeing through the kitchen and out the back door, around the side yard, which had been cleaned up immaculately from the first time he'd seen it, and then headed across the street for the gazebo frame, one twin holding on to each of his hands.

Once on the grass, the girls went directly into play mode and started jumping and dancing around. He picked up a hammer, recovering some of his masculine dignity, and while they frolicked, he began some work.

"Can I try?" Claire asked a few short minutes later, pushing her glasses up her nose.

"Me, too?" Gracie.

So he let them both have a turn. Claire aimed for the nail he held in place with puppy-light taps. When Gracie took her turn, she got serious and wound up like a member of a prison chain gang, coming down hard on the nail head, but hitting Mark's index finger and thumb instead. Mostly his thumb.

"Son of a—" He jumped up, shaking off the pain, biting out the words. His lips came together to form a b, but he hesitated as he glanced at his tiny charges, dressed like frilly fairies, eyes wide like elves. *"—building block!"*

Yeah, Laurel definitely owed him.

"And who might these wee ones be?" Grandda appeared out of nowhere.

Mark pretended nothing was wrong with his hand. "Uh, this is Claire and Gracie, Laurel's daughters."

"She give 'em to you, did she?"

"Just for the evening. Can I help you with anything, Grandda?"

"No," he said, while looking as though he had a dozen more questions. "Just thought I'd be pulling a handle for a pint, wondered if you'd care to join me."

Mark glanced around at the girls twirling in circles to make themselves dizzy, giggling all the way. "Thanks for thinking of me, but I can't."

On the periphery, Mark noticed movement and

turned to see Peter crossing the street with a sour expression. Grandda looked even more interested, so he stuck around.

"Come to help out?" Mark said when Peter joined him at the gazebo frame, suspicious of the reason for his visit.

"No." He pouted and didn't make eye contact.

"Looks like you've been sucking a lemon. Lose your video game?"

"No. Mom said I have to watch the girls in the morning, get them out of the house, when the people come back for breakfast."

"So?"

"I'm supposed to meet someone tomorrow morning."

The girls were cute and fun, and generally easygoing, but, as a grown-up, Mark could appreciate the fact they were wearing fairy outfits. With Peter finally reaching out trying to make new friends, Mark could understand how uncomfortable he might feel, when nothing mattered more than what your peers thought of you.

"I get it, but she needs your help until she gets the business off the ground. And I bet, just in case the person you're meeting tomorrow is a girl from your class, she'd think they're adorable. Why not just buy everyone ice cream instead of fighting it? It might work out in your favor."

Peter poked at a rock with his flip-flop-exposed toe rather than answer, but Mark was almost positive he was onto something with the "girl from your class" guess. He could also understand how a guy might want a first meet with a girl to be just the two of them.

"You two look to be about my little Anna's age," Grandda said, ignoring Peter's sour attitude, and grinning at the bubbly twins.

Then it hit Mark. Anna! Of course, why didn't he think of that? He dug his cell phone out of his jeans pocket and dialed Daniel. "Hey, what's Anna doing tomorrow morning?"

"Well, hello to you, too. I'm at work, don't really know. Let me ask Keela."

"Could you ask her if Claire and Gracie can come to play tomorrow morning, say around nine?"

A minute later, while Peter hung close, waiting for his verdict to come in, Keela came on the phone. "That'd be fine. We can take them all to the park for the morning. I've been meaning to have them over for a playdate anyway. May I ask why *you're* askin'?"

Mark looked Peter in the eyes. "Just trying to help out a friend."

He thought he saw a twitch at the corner of the boy's mouth.

Then he realized how that might sound to Keela, who couldn't see Peter. Now he'd probably get grilled by Daniel about Laurel. "Okay, thanks. Gotta go."

And speaking of Laurel, she was crossing the street in that pretty dress with a victorious grin, as three cars drove off behind her.

"Now you're free to help me on the gazebo tomorrow morning," Mark said to Peter, getting the reaction he'd expected…happy about getting out of babysitting, but frustrated he'd been tricked into helping Mark another Saturday.

If Mark wasn't mistaken, Grandda's interest picked up a notch as Laurel got closer.

"So how'd it go?" Mark asked.

"Terrific!" Her smile spoke a thousand words. He liked how that looked.

On reflex, he hugged her—a congratulatory hug—

soon realizing the huge mistake in front of his grand-father. "That's great."

"They gave me so much positive feedback, I'm reel-ing. Now all I have to do is wow them with my famous peach-stuffed French toast tomorrow morning."

A throat cleared. Loudly. Grandda.

"Oh, hey, Grandda, have you met Laurel Prescott yet?"

"Not yet." He reached out his hand to shake. "'Tis a pleasure." Grandda slid a knowing sideways glance at Mark. Daniel and Keela weren't the only ones he was sure to get grilled by.

"Same here," she said. "I hope you don't mind my entire family being camped out in your yard."

"Not at all. The more the merrier, I always say. Right, Marky, my boy?"

Oh, yeah, Mark would have a dozen questions to an-swer the moment he was alone with his grandfather. But right now, Mark didn't care because he was racking up the IOU notes from Laurel. "So I just solved your prob-lem about tomorrow morning. Or maybe I should say, Peter's problem. The girls have been invited to spend the morning with Keela and Anna at the park."

Laurel's eyes widened as she inhaled. "That's fabu-lous. Thanks so much." She shifted her gaze to her son. "Looks like you're off the hook, Peter."

"Not," Peter grumbled.

"He's going to help me raise the roof on the gazebo tomorrow afternoon."

Laurel shook her head, a twinge of disbelief in her eyes. Yeah, Mark could work wonders when he had to. "You are blowing my mind with your thoughtful-ness. I owe you big-time." She hugged him again and squeezed her arms tight around his back, and his bright idea seemed completely worth it. "Thanks so much."

"As a matter of fact, you do owe me. I was thinking tomorrow night Peter could babysit, since he owes me, too, so I can take you to my favorite seafood place up the road." He hadn't actually been there yet, but something told him the restaurant would indeed become one of his favorites, if present company was included.

Surprise tinted her eyes as her smile widened. "That sounds great."

"On one condition."

She tossed him a "there's more?" glance.

First he noticed Peter had been roped into twirling his sisters by holding them under their arms, so he was sufficiently distracted. Then he glanced back at Laurel. "That you wear that dress and your hair up just like that."

Her face relaxed into a lazy grin. "I think that's doable." Her voice sounded lower. Sexier?

And they were flirting, in front of his nosy grandfather, who, if he knew the man at all, was anything but distracted by the kids' playing. He could also feel his grandfather's stare, the heat gathering on the back of his neck. So Mark turned to look at him, seeing that annoying I-believe-in-selkies twinkle in his eyes. And tried to ignore it.

"Well, I'll be off for a pint now. Nice to meet you, Laurel, Peter, Gracie and Claire." He gave a direct look to Mark. "I'll talk to *you* later."

Not if Mark could avoid it!

It wasn't until Laurel gathered up her kids and headed for home that it hit Mark. *What did I just do?* So caught up in the moment of victory for Laurel, he'd forgotten. He wasn't ready to date yet. To have a normal life again. Was he? The thought of socializing with Laurel for an entire evening made his palms sweat because she was out of his league. They didn't have anything in common beyond his helping her fix things, or his looking after her kids. She'd probably said yes only because he'd put her on the spot. Seriously, what did he have to offer a woman like her? She knew what she wanted for her future, and he was still avoiding his. She'd probably be bored out of her mind having dinner with him. Big mistake asking her to dinner, when he wasn't sure he was ready.

Even if he was thinking about dating and getting involved with a woman again, why pick a sophisticated woman with a family to complicate things, and what could he possibly have to offer her in return? Once she got to know him better, she'd discover how humbly he lived at the family hotel, when she'd been married to a man who'd provided for her and three kids. He couldn't possibly measure up. And probably lose interest. Then how awkward it would be to see her across the street every day.

All the good feelings he'd been enjoying, before insecurity snuck in seemed to swirl tight and settle in his gut as he watched the family walk away, little Gracie turning to smile and wave one last time. If she was looking for security, he wasn't her guy. Nor did he want to be.

He bit his lower lip and went back to work, even though his thumb still throbbed. As he hammered a few more nails, he made a snap decision to not think about dinner out tomorrow with Laurel as a date, that way if things didn't work out, he wouldn't feel as bad. He'd call it payback. She owed him for watching the girls and setting up a playdate so Peter could meet that "someone from school" without dragging his little sisters along.

In case his rationalizing wasn't strong enough yet, he'd also look at it this way: it served in his best interest. Asking Laurel to dinner was convenient, because he'd wanted to eat at The Grilled Sea, a new seafood restaurant in Sandpiper Beach, for the longest time. But he hadn't wanted to go there alone.

So their plans for dinner out were all about calling in a return favor.

Not a date, which he still wasn't ready for. Just payback and convenience.

He'd made the mistake of asking a lady or two out when he'd first come home, and quickly discovered he wasn't ready for casual dating or being social yet. Both evenings had been painfully long and squirm-worthy. So putting that different spin on tomorrow night's plans would take the pressure off. Otherwise, he'd be an anxious wreck for the next twenty-four hours over a date with a woman that interested him. He'd spent enough time being anxious when he'd first been discharged and had to deal with PTSD, and he didn't want to go there again. Things had settled down on that level, but being attracted to Laurel, the thought of just the two of them, made him nervous. Which meant she was special.

Stomething about Laurel made him want to give it a shot again.

Saturday night, still reeling from her successful preview Friday evening and Saturday morning, plus the fact she'd received her very first B&B reservation shortly after, Laurel decided to break one small portion of her promise to Mark. She wanted to wear her hair down. The decision was based on jitters and uncooperative fingers. Truth be told, she was more nervous about her dinner date with Mark than the three mock guests yesterday and this morning combined, and she'd been extremely edgy about that. Couldn't do a thing with her updo.

A date? Was that what this was? Or merely "payback" as Mark had insisted. She hadn't been on a date since college, when she'd met Alan. The significance of Mark's being her first date in nearly sixteen years made her eyes water. He was a nice guy on top of being sexy in a clueless kind of way, and she'd been smiling a lot more since he'd shown up to help her unpack two weeks back. What about the finger lick? OMG, what had she been thinking? She'd just wanted him to try her sandwich dressing, and before she knew it, she'd stuck her finger in his mouth. The zing that'd set off zipped up her arm and shot straight to her lady parts. She couldn't deny she had a secret crush on the sexiest handyman she could ever imagine, or that she wanted to look good for him, but what did that mean? Anxiety streaked through her. Letting herself feel again? Her pulse tapped quicker in her chest.

The B&B was finally opening, and she'd be busier than ever. Her children had to come first, the B&B a close second. Anything else would have to come a distant third. She wouldn't have time to get involved with anyone. With him. *Say it, say his name.* Mark. Her pulse settled down a bit.

She stared into the mirror, checking her freshly applied lipstick after saying his name so quietly, she had to read her own lips. This one date couldn't and wouldn't lead to anything else. He said she owed him for watching her kids, which logically meant she should be buying him dinner.

Maybe that's what she'd do, insist on buying their meal. It would send the message their debt was settled and they could revert to business as usual...once she found a babysitter.

Laurel made a mental note to find a trustworthy teenager, preferably a girl who could enjoy Claire and Gracie, no matter what they wore. Then Mark could be kept at a safe distance and go back to being the handyman at The Drumcliffe. He would be a secret crush she could safely keep and explore for those times when she felt completely alone. Which, with a new business and three kids, was bound to be rare.

The doorbell rang. It turned up the dial on the tiny nerves already jumping around in her stomach. Now a full-out gymnastics routine took place, and she could imagine not being able to get a single bite of dinner down.

Suck it up, buttercup. Regardless of how you've rationalized it, you're on a date!

Laurel rushed to open the door, but Peter had beaten her to it. Mark and her son stood at the entrance casually talking about surfing, from what she could hear.

"Hi," she said, sounding far too breathy to be casual. *Gawd!* Her cheeks went warm.

Mark glanced toward her, and she saw that look again, the one he did a terrible job of concealing, where his eyes lit up with interest. She swallowed against her dry throat. Thank goodness Peter was clueless about such looks yet. At least she hoped so.

"Hi. Ready to eat?" Mark sounded bright, unlike her, relaxed.

Ready to eat? No! "Absolutely." *Switch to Mom mode, keep things business as usual.* "Peter, don't let the girls stay up past their bedtime, and they can have one cookie each, but no more sugar before bedtime, okay?"

"Got it, Mom." He gestured for her to leave.

With the tall, good-looking man? What was wrong with her boy?

Mark smiled wide when she stepped onto the porch. He cocked his head toward the curb, and Grandda sitting behind the steering wheel of a four-seater electric golf cart. What?

"He's dropping us off. I figured after dinner we could walk home. It's not far," Mark quickly added before she had the chance to say a peep.

The guy was full of surprises. Even to the point of putting his hand at the small of her back to guide her down the stairs to their awaiting golf cart. It burned through her dress.

Padraig Delaney offered her a toothy smile, just before she and Mark took the back two seats. "At your service."

"This is different," she said.

"One of the perks of living in a sleepy beach community after summer. No one cares!" he said, smiling at her. "No speeding, Grandda." He didn't bother to move his line of vision.

The long, appreciative stare made her antsy.

"Why ruin all my fun?"

She had to admit she enjoyed his Irish accent, but her smile jolted backward along with her neck when the old man put the pedal to the metal and nearly peeled out from the curb.

Mark grabbed her hand and squeezed. Another highly disturbing gesture, though one she appreciated considering she felt she'd just entered Mr. Toad's Wild Ride.

Due to the transportation, they'd taken the back route, alleys and small side streets, so they entered The Grilled Sea through the back door. The restaurant was small but stylish, and they were seated immediately near a window overlooking the ocean. *So he'd made reservations.* He'd done some planning ahead, another good quality.

"I've walked by this place a dozen times," he said, "—even looked at the menu posted out front, but've never eaten here. My mom keeps her ear to the ground in Sandpiper, and she's only heard good things. I hope you like it."

"I thought you said this was your favorite seafood place?"

"After tonight, I'm pretty sure it will be. Anyway, I hope you like it."

"I'm sure I will." *I'm sitting with a guy with amazing eyes, who's shaved and brushed his rich dark hair that curls just beneath his earlobes. A guy who smells good, and who's wearing a heather-gray Henley shirt and jeans that fit just right.* Why wouldn't she like it here?

After they'd both ordered an appetizer and an adult beverage, she broached the subject. "You said I owed you for yesterday, yet here you are inviting me out to dinner. Shouldn't I be paying?"

He stopped midbite of the recently served shrimp cocktail, his brows crunched down. "What sense would that make?"

"The thing is, it doesn't make sense this way. You can't possibly consider me your reward." Okay, she was fishing for a compliment big-time, but she *was* curious. Was this a date, or just payback?

His brows relaxed, a sly smile creased his lips. He was playing along. "Like I said, if I didn't have you to bring here, I still wouldn't know if the food was good. You're doing me a favor."

Definitely playing along.

"You're that averse to eating alone?"

He took a drink of his beer. "I usually have two choices. Either I eat quick and alone at the hotel restaurant, whatever special Rita, our seventy-year-old chef, made too much of, or with the entire family on Sunday nights in the pub. I thought it would be nice to eat in a restaurant of my choice with you. That's all."

He looked sincere, though she'd had to drag it out of him. His confession, both sad and sweet, humbled her. She took a prim sip of her wine, as her lashes fluttered. "Well, thanks, then. I'm glad to be of service." She almost threw in *anytime* but held back. Why come off desperate? And truth was, soon she wouldn't have a weekend to herself. Hopefully, for her business's sake.

Her tentative smile made his eyes brighten. "So then I guess it's a good thing you're still not off the hook," he said, then gave a half-cocked smile.

"What do you mean?"

"You didn't keep your end of the bargain. You still owe me."

What was he getting at?

He gestured with his fingers near his ear, making a long flip, as in hair.

She reached for hers, wondering if she had something in it.

"You were supposed to wear it up."

Her gaze widened with understanding. "It wasn't cooperating tonight."

"Next time, then."

Another date? "Uh, okay, I'll try to remember that."

They switched to routine conversation after that, though that one threw her for sure. One date she could gloss over, but a second? Her stomach coiled at the thought of a third.

Dinner was served, and despite her tension, they both

enjoyed sea bass and some amazing potato dish, along with locally grown vegetables, as the menu proudly suggested. And fresh sourdough bread that was out of this world. Laurel had to admit, the food was great, with good presentation, but the company looked far, far better.

She'd decided this meal qualified as a date, even to the point of being chaperoned to The Grilled Sea by his grandfather, who she gathered was a big influence in Mark's life. She could tell by their interactions they loved each other deeply, and, having missed her two remaining grandparents' funerals during Alan's illness, she envied Mark and Padraig for that.

Though she struggled with opening the door to someone else, while the abiding love for Alan, the tragedy that claimed his life and the pain of losing him was fresh in her mind—wouldn't it always be?—Laurel made a conscious effort to let go. Alan had wanted her to restart her life in some way by using his second life insurance policy. Surely, he'd thought about what that could mean, starting over, while still a young woman. Though they'd never broached the subject, she was sure he wouldn't want her to be alone the rest of her life. Not that this meal out with Mark had anything to do with the rest of her life. Oh, why was she even thinking like this when raw and jagged feelings still ruled her nights? She wouldn't wish that kind of pain on her worst enemy.

Regardless of the confusion swirling around her mind, she calmed enough to enjoy the delicious food, even indulged in a second glass of wine, which helped the nerves tremendously. Mark insisted they share dessert. Nothing like a carbohydrate coma to relax a girl. Then they took the long way home by walking along the beach. By now she'd happily accepted that Mark could call this whatever he wanted, but she'd consider it their first date. It was probably the wine, but she also looked forward to the next. If she kept the right attitude, they could be a "for now" kind of thing. Something that apparently they both needed, in order to move on with their lives. Definitely the second glass of wine talking.

She slipped off her pumps as they entered the sand. "Just so you know, I have no intention of swimming tonight."

He grinned. "Me, either. Wet and sandy jeans are really uncomfortable."

Without giving it a second thought, she put her arm through his, and he made room for her tucked close to his torso. They walked closer to the water, keeping a respectful distance from the damp sand, but still enjoying the crashing of waves and seaweed-scented air.

"I said it earlier, but you really blew me away when you arranged for Claire and Gracie to play with Anna this morning. They were still talking about it when I was getting ready tonight."

"Anna's had a hard summer, breaking her leg and all, and your girls need to make new friends, right?"

"Absolutely. Oh, and Keela said Anna's cast comes off next week."

"Great news."

She glanced at the sea, beyond the noisy waves, fluorescent whitecaps here and there, yet looking so calm. Power greater than she could fathom, with a whole different world existing below the surface. Feeling suddenly miniscule, it helped to be anchored to Mark. The thought jolted her, but she didn't let go of him. And something else, a sudden desire, prompted her to say more.

"You're very thoughtful, Mark."

He pulled in his chin, crushing down his brows, in denial.

"No, really you are. Even though you used me to eat out tonight."

He laughed lightly.

"Your words, not mine." She smiled challengingly.

"Well, maybe my thoughtfulness was a little manipulating."

"I'm glad."

His brows shot up.

Oh, what the hell, she really wanted to kiss him again. "Yeah, and I'd like to thank you."

She stopped walking, turned toward him and reached for his jaw, enjoying the smooth skin beneath her fingertips. His eyes darkened and his lids looked heavy as she moved closer. After quickly wetting her lower lip with the tip of her tongue, she kissed him in a way she hadn't kissed a man—her husband—since before the twins were born.

Mark couldn't believe his good fortune. The first foray into kissing Laurel seemed like child's play compared with this. With their bodies tight in an embrace, and their mouths locked together, exploring and tasting, tempting and teasing, he was hungry for more and didn't let his thoughts get in the way. As great as licking her finger had been, this was a whole helluva lot better.

His hands wandered her back, and he reached below the waist of that sexy blue dress he'd asked her to wear, to feel through the material and knead her hip and bottom, which was firm and sexy like he knew it would be. Her knee edged between his legs, halfway up his inner thigh, as she nipped his lower lip with her teeth.

Hold on! She was as into him as he was to her, which definitely leveled the playing field. It wasn't just about his finding the woman sexy as hell. Regardless of where he lived, she obviously found something about him appealing enough to kiss him like she really meant it, and right here and now wasn't the time to question why.

Liking the long-term ramifications of taking this next step or not, kissing Laurel Prescott like the world was coming to an end was an extremely excellent thing.

whatever. That was—[?]

Chapter Five

After the hot make-out session on the beach earlier that night, and an equally exciting good-night kiss at her front door, reality blindsided Laurel. She couldn't get involved with anyone yet. She was still getting over losing Alan. Even now a whisper of pain circled her shoulders at the thought of falling for someone again, and how everything good could change in the blink of an eye. No way was she prepared for that, not this soon. Not ever? By the way she felt lying in bed, staring at the ceiling with perspiration lining her upper lip, just from merely considering it, it occurred she might never be ready to open up to someone again. It didn't matter how charming or downright appealing Mark Delaney was. Loss and the pain that followed would never be worth it.

After an ongoing inner conversation between the part of herself that was intrigued by Mark and the other cowering part, afraid to ever open up to such heartache and devastation again, it was Thursday before Laurel asked Mark to help at the B&B. And only then because she had no choice.

"I've lost the power in two of the upstairs guest rooms," she said, showing up at The Drumcliffe workshop and toolshed wringing her hands, panicked over losing the guests she'd booked for that weekend equally as strong as the prospect of looking Mark in the eyes again.

Always glad to see her, he turned off the gas soldering torch and laid the copper pipe down. "Sounds like the fuse box might be overtaxed. Where is it?"

"It's not exactly an emergency. I see you're busy, but as soon as you have a chance?"

"I can do this later." He stepped around the workbench.

He'd been making himself scarce all week, like a coward. What guy in his right mind avoided someone who could twist his socks with a kiss? Evidently, him.

Now here she was, looking great, as usual, even though her pupils were wide with anxiety. It made him think how she might look after making love, and all thoughts after that steamed up his work goggles.

Mark moved the eye protectors up to his forehead, so he could see her better. "Let's go."

When they got to the B&B, she pointed him to the pantry, just off the kitchen, and an antiquated box in great need of updating. "I can replace the couple of blown fuses now, but it will only be a matter of time before it happens again. This thing—" he pointed to the wall box "—is in need of updating."

"Oh, great, another expense. This place is turning into a money pit." Back came the anxious gaze.

He took her by the shoulders. "Calm down. I'm in the hotel business, remember? I know guys who know guys. We'll get this fixed at half the cost."

"You can do that?"

Staring into her eyes, he realized she trusted him, and he felt honored. Another thing that messed with his senses, the fact that he wanted her respect, and respect required him to be more than what he currently was— just a fix-it guy. The most he could do now was impress her by getting a deal on replacing her fuse box. So much less than she deserved—which was an accomplished, financially stable and well-adjusted man, far more fitting—but he powered on with what he knew best.

"My grandfather is a sneaky guy," he said, giving half a smug smile while on the verge of divulging a family secret. "He plays golf, looking like an easy loser, makes bets and wins the game. Takes payback in favors. Just about every businessman in the area owes him something. I'll ask about an electrician, see what we come up with, because electrician is above my handyman grade." Wanting more than anything to continue to impress her, he hated admitting this, but he had to be honest.

She took a deep breath, half of her anxiety seeming to let go. "Okay. Thanks. But what about right now?"

"Like I said, I can replace these burnt-out fuses, no problem, but be careful about turning all the lights on upstairs at once, or using the vacuum in one room with a fan on in another."

Her hand flew to her brow. "I've got guests coming tomorrow! How am I going to handle this? I can't exactly tell them to leave the lights off if they put the TV on. Gah!"

"Let me give Grandda a call."

He made the call, and as predicted his grandfather could call in a favor. In the meantime, with three new fuses in place to keep the house running, for now, he let those previous steamy thoughts take over. He'd been avoiding Laurel for a good reason, because all it took was being in her presence to make him forget how not ready for a relationship he was. Though completely in the present, wanting nothing more than to hold her in his arms again, he got an idea, foolhardy as it was, to take advantage of the moment.

After rushing upstairs to turn off all unnecessary lights, while Mark fixed the fuses, Laurel headed back into the kitchen for a quick drink of water. After, she placed her glass on the counter. The room was completely quiet. Figuring Mark was off getting whatever he needed, she relaxed and wandered toward the pantry to see what he'd been doing. When one step away from the door, a hand reached around the corner and grabbed hers. She squealed as she got pulled into the semidark area. Mark.

"You scared the wits out of me," she said, her heart beating in her ears.

He wore an intent look, a heavy-lidded and sexy gaze. Pulling her near, he put his hands on her waist, bridging the short distance with his face, until their lips met.

She hesitated, knowing it was a mistake to do this, but soon, her arms went over his shoulders and her hands around his neck, holding him close as they kissed the heck out of each other. She could get used to this, which frightened her. A little noise slipped from the back of her throat, which he must have liked, because he pressed his hips closer to hers and kissed deeper. The heady feel of every part of his body along the length of hers made her forget her concerns. Her hands rushed across his muscular deltoids, and around to the back of his hips. She pushed him closer, feeling his obvious reaction to their kisses.

It was dangerous taking their attraction further like this. Yet unable to control herself, she moved over him, letting his solid response send randy love notes straight to her center. Wanting to run with the raw physical draw, she'd put the brakes on emotionally. Go slow, but why not take advantage of their little gift?

Yes, she thought. Yes, yes. Until Mark's cell phone blared "When Irish Eyes Are Smiling." To make matters worse, when Mark answered the obvious tune he'd selected for his grandfather, still wrapped in their tight embrace, Padraig was on FaceTime. Her face was right there along with Mark's, no doubt looking flushed and flustered from the best make-out session she'd had since Saturday night at the beach.

"Any word?" Mark asked, recovering quicker than she had. She zipped out of view of the camera, rather than look at that craggy face and the knowing eyes of Padraig Delaney.

"Ted Wright will be around in an hour. I told him to expect cookies and lemonade."

"Thanks, Grandda."

"Yes, thank you," she said off-camera. "I really appreciate it."

Mark moved the phone to capture her again, and she ducked and pushed his hand away, not wanting the old man to see her kiss-swollen lips.

"You're welcome. Carry on," he said before clicking off.

Laurel looked at Mark, leftover lust lingering in his

gaze. Her breasts were still tight, but the call had defused whatever mojo they'd been working on. Still her eyes remained on those beautiful blues, until she did the only thing she could think to release the thick sexual tension in the tiny pantry. She broke into a laugh, and Mark joined her.

"Whew," she said, jokingly wiping her brow. "Who knows where we would've wound up if he didn't call."

Mark glanced at the long island counter, and some of her lost heat flared up again. He swallowed. "Sorry," he said. "I just can't seem to keep my hands off you."

"Don't you dare apologize." She kissed him one last time, keeping distance between their bodies. "Apparently, I've got some baking to do."

She got down to assembling bowls and cups, flour, sugar, butter, the works, measuring and mixing, and heating the oven. Anything to get her mind off the man driving her crazy in the pantry.

He popped in the new fuses and cleaned up around the box, and a few short minutes later, after checking out the upstairs lights, he kissed her cheek and took off.

Holding a large stainless steel bowl, mixing butter and brown sugar, she stared out the window and let herself imagine what might have happened if they hadn't gotten that damn, but necessary, call.

Then reality kicked in, flooding her with memories of the pain and loss when Alan died, and she thanked her lucky stars nothing had happened with Mark.

Less than a week later, Wednesday midmorning, Mark, still fixated on memories of an exceptionally hot kiss with Laurel, put the finishing touches on the white-shingled roof of the hexagonal-shaped gazebo.

He'd wanted to leave the cedar wood alone with a natural stain, but his mother had her own plan.

"If we want to use this for weddings, it has to be white," Maureen said, her ginger-colored hair lifting with the light breeze.

"But it looks so classy this way," he said, at the top of the ladder.

"You can leave the floor natural wood with a polyurethane stain, but honestly, honey, our whole point of building this was for weddings. And weddings say white."

"Whatever." He'd learned throughout his life, once his mother got an idea in her head, she couldn't be convinced otherwise. "I'll have Peter help me paint it this weekend."

"Thank you." Maureen stopped momentarily as his words sunk in. "You mean that boy?"

"Yeah, the kid I'm giving surf lessons to. It's like payback."

"Sounds fair enough." She lingered, watching him. He could see the battle going on behind her green stare, the dozens of questions she'd like to ask, but had the good sense not to bring up. "Have you thought more about starting surf lessons for our guests?"

"Aren't I doing enough already?" He hated how he'd sounded like a teenager grumbling about chores, but it seemed every day Mom thought up more ways to get him involved in the running of the hotel, and he didn't want to take on anything else.

"I could have sworn you'd offered, that Sunday night at dinner?"

True, he had. In a moment of weakness, when his parents were throwing out ideas for new perks and activities to entice more guests. His new sister-in-law,

Keela, had signed on to give massages, Dan offered to give some talks on the importance of daily exercise, and even Conor thought he could squeeze in an occasional Saturday morning nature hike for guests. What was Mark supposed to do, just sit there and stuff his mouth with pot roast? So he'd thrown out the idea of beginning surf lessons, never expecting his parents to take him up on it. "Did I?" Okay, so he'd play dumb and hope she'd forget the whole thing out of frustration.

"Yes, you most certainly did." She turned in time to see Laurel approaching. "This conversation isn't over."

"Got it. Okay."

It had been nearly a week since he'd stolen more kisses. Things had been going smoothly between them, and their romance had stepped up the more they hung out together. Like they were feeling each other out, sometimes literally, though neither ready for anything full-blown. He'd decided to take his time and enjoy whatever it was they had going on, and Laurel seemed to have the same idea. She was a mom with three kids, and he was a guy who still resisted responsibility. The likelihood of their getting serious was slim, and so far they hadn't crossed any lines. Though they'd come awfully close that day in the kitchen pantry. For now, that was okay. But he'd been feeling almost happy-go-lucky, something he hadn't felt since high school, and Laurel had everything to do with it.

So he kept telling himself there was no pressure on any level between him and Laurel, just lighthearted flirting and kisses. Mind-boggling kisses. Besides, they wouldn't be able to find the privacy even if they wanted to do more. But he wasn't complaining, he'd enjoy what he had, while it lasted. Some days he even thought he'd found a part of himself he'd lost during the war.

Anyway, she deserved a whole lot more than what little he could offer. In fact, he wondered why she hadn't figured that out already.

"Well, hello there," his mother said. Mark could imagine the raised brow by the tone of her voice.

"Hi, Mrs. Delaney," Laurel said with a smile. "I've come to borrow your son for a quick carpentry issue, if you don't mind."

"Hopefully he has some spare time. I've been keeping him awfully busy."

Could she be more obvious? Something told him he'd be giving surf lessons to more than Peter in the near future, too. Mark climbed down the ladder, his tool belt in place, and approached the women, always happy to see Laurel.

"And please, call me Maureen, we're neighbors."

"Thank you… Maureen."

His mother cast her glance from Laurel to Mark, and he was hit with expectations, hers. The subtle pressure took a little of the shine off his upbeat attitude from seeing Laurel. "Hi. What's up?" he said, enjoying the glint of sun in her caramel eyes.

"I swear this old house shifts overnight. I've got a couple of sticky guest closet doors, and I think they either need to be rehung or have some wood shaved off."

"Sounds easy enough." Since Maureen lingered watching them, Mark kept his distance, but he was quick to decide. "Let's go."

Once inside her house, he followed her up the stairs, enjoying the subtle sway of her jeans-clad hips. At the top, before Laurel had the chance to open the first guest room door, he took her hand and tugged her to him, then dropped a kiss on her lips. It'd been a few days since they'd kissed, and he didn't feel like waiting another minute.

Her arms circled his neck and she returned the favor as he walked her against the wall, and leaned in for more. He nuzzled her neck, enjoying the silky warm skin and the fact her hair was in a ponytail, clueing him in this was a workday. Though wanting to linger right there, kissing and cuddling with the woman who had his total interest, he understood necking wasn't the reason she'd come to get him. So after one more thoroughly satisfying kiss, one that would leave her craving more, and him having to adjust himself inside his jeans, he backed off.

"Is this the room?" he asked.

"Yes," she whispered over his ear, her arms still tight around his neck.

He edged back, imagining that answer was to a totally different question. Their gazes met and melded with understanding for an instant, shooting a fine line of adrenaline down his middle.

"I wish we weren't always in a hurry," she said, a sincere and inviting glint in her eyes.

"I wish this house didn't have so many bedrooms. Way too tempting."

That made her smile in a shy way. He touched his forehead to hers, detecting and enjoying the scent of fabric softener on her top. On her, even dryer sheet fragrance was sexy.

"So you gonna let me fix those doors, or are you gonna keep distracting me?"

She inhaled, a slow smile stretching those delicious lips. "You started it."

He let his eyes do the smiling, then reluctantly let her go. Shifting back to business, they went inside where she showed him the sticky closet door in room number one. He opened and closed it, checked the hinges, ran his hand along the top, then dropped to his knees to check out the bottom.

She'd retreated to the room's exit, but he sensed she still watched him.

"You're the distraction," she said quietly, before leaving the room, and setting the hair on the back of his neck on end.

The house had six fancy guest rooms, but the one room he thought of right then was hers, on the first floor, with the antique bed frame, and the half dozen different ways he'd like to see her on it.

Within a minute of reaching his supply shed to retrieve a scribe tool, a belt sander, a hand-sanding block and sawhorses, his mother reappeared.

"The neighborly thing to do would be to invite Laurel and her family over for dinner Sunday night."

"She's been here nearly a month, and now you're thinking of being neighborly?"

"I took her a welcome basket the week she moved in."

"You did?"

"Yes, I did. We've had several conversations. She never told you?"

He scratched the back of his neck. "Well, it never came up, no."

"Daniel, Keela and Anna are coming Sunday for dinner. This would be the perfect time to have Laurel and the kids over."

Not at all sure if he wanted to share Laurel with his family yet, he hesitated. "Would you like me to invite her?"

Getting the last item he needed, he shut the toolshed. "Nope. I'll take care of it." And he headed back across the street.

An hour later, when the girls were home from school and playing in their bedroom, Laurel sat in the kitchen, sorting through her menu list of special breakfast dishes for the weekend guests. A chorizo, egg, shredded potatoes and cheddar cheese casserole caught her attention.

Mark appeared at the door, and her heart tripped on a beat. Could a man look any sexier than when leaning against a door, arms crossed, in a tight T-shirt and with a tool belt strapped on his low-slung jeans? "All done?" She pretended she hadn't noticed a single sexy thing.

"Yeah, they're both fixed. You want to check before I go?" He hiked his thumb over his shoulder, breaking the picture-perfect pose.

"I'm sure they're fine. Thanks." She put the menus on the island counter and stood. "Can I pay you back with dinner tonight? You, me…and the kids?" She batted her lashes.

"Sounds very romantic." He stepped closer, reaching for her hand. Their fingers played touch-and-go, her daughters giggling and squealing down the hall.

"I know." She sensed the longing in his gaze and wondered if he could read her thoughts. Because lately she'd had plenty. Involving just the two of them. But that would require so many arrangements and preparations, there couldn't be any hope of spontaneity, which used to be most of the fun, as she recalled. A long, long time ago.

"Well, I'm never going to turn down an offer to eat with you, so yes." He caught her hand and laced their fingers together, clamping tight, connecting like a bridge between them. "What time?"

"The usual. After you and Peter get back from surfing. He has a lesson today, right?"

"Yup. Mondays, Wednesdays and Fridays."

Claire and Gracie rushed into the kitchen, running under their arms like a London Bridge is falling down game.

"Okay, then. See you later."

"We're hungry!" In unison.

"One second, girls," she said.

Never breaking from his locked-in gaze, he nodded, letting her hand go, the distance between them growing, then, after rubbing both Claire's and Gracie's mop of hair, under their protest, he started to turn to leave. But two steps in, he swiveled back around. "How about having dinner with my family this Sunday? We always get together in the pub, and Mom makes some pretty spectacular meals. I think Anna's going to be there with Keela and Daniel, too."

"You're inviting my kids, too?"

"Yay," the twins chorused.

"It's a family meal."

She stared at him briefly, touched by the invitation. Getting invited to a family meal was a big deal where she came from, and knowing the Delaney family was close-knit, she also knew his asking meant something. "Then my family and I would love to come."

"Yeah, we'd lovey to go over dere," Gracie piped up.

Laurel smothered a smile, trying to stay on task. "May I bring anything?"

"Nope. Just be prepared for chaos." He looked comfortably resigned to being a part of a big and possibly unruly family, and she envied him for that one instant before he turned and left. "See you later," he called out as he hit the front porch.

"Bye!" loudly from the twins.

See you later. The words sounded so normal. Come to think of it, since moving to Sandpiper Beach, things really had normalized, which was saying something for the long-suffering Prescott family. They'd developed a routine that didn't center on their father's illness. The stress that used to hover over them seemed to have dissipated, and in its place, laughter had returned. Even Peter seemed okay now with the move and starting high school, though she had a hunch a girl at school had a lot to do with it. Bottom line, she was becoming part of a community, making friends, and dare she say it, acquiring a boyfriend?

A warm feeling wrapped around her shoulders. She thought of Mark and his *see you later* promise. The man was sweet and sexy and so damn handy! Buying a B&B without any experience in running it had been the craziest idea she'd ever had, but maybe it was also the best idea she'd had since becoming a widow.

If she kept whatever she and Mark had brewing between them in perspective. It couldn't go anywhere. She was a widow, two years in, but still mourning Alan, struggling to care for and raise her children, and Mark's attention was a boost to her flagging ego. She had four years on him, and a world of pain in her résumé.

Though he'd been in the army, he still lived with his family and had the secure job of helping run an established hotel. The way she saw it, he was worry free with few responsibilities. Yet she sensed something deep and painful ran through him, and she could see it in his often-forlorn eyes.

He'd been away, in the service, in the Middle East. They'd only touched on the topic. Maybe that was the key to why a guy like him preferred to play cat-and-mouse romance with her, rather than a host of women who didn't come saddled with kids and obligations. Younger women who'd jump at the chance if he'd only look up and out instead of down. Or in her case, across the street.

It would be interesting to see how he interacted with his family, and maybe Sunday night, if she got the chance, she'd ask him more about his time in the military.

Sunday night, Mom decided to get everyone involved in preparing the meal. Mark had been assigned grilling duties on the hotel patio for the huge salmon fillets she'd purchased from the fish market at the pier earlier that morning. Off to the side he also grilled a few turkey hot dogs for the twins and Peter, in case they weren't seafood lovers.

One of the best parts of fall by the central coast of California was enjoying the excellent "summer" weather after the tourists had all gone home. Early evening, it was still light and warm, and the coastal water was only a few shades darker than the bright blue sky.

He waved the cedar plank smoke away, still managing to get some in his eyes and blinking hard, then looked up to see Peter and the girls crossing the street. Behind them, materializing through the haze like a lovely dream, came Laurel in a sundress.

He blinked again, then smiled, his body sparking to life. When she waved and grinned, all seemed immediately right with the world. Which worried him. Was he ready for what that meant, stepping up his game to be worthy of her attention…and affection?

"Hey," she said, when they'd reached the patio.

"You look great." He wasted no time spilling his thoughts. "Pretty dress."

"Thanks. I bought it, and a couple others, for the days I greet my guests. Figured I needed to look like a proper hostess." She curtsied and gave a light self-deprecating laugh, as though she could only hope to play the part. He knew otherwise. She was born for hosting a fancy guesthouse.

The white with bright flowers patterned sundress had a wide V-neck with simple cap sleeves, a fitting bodice and a semifull skirt falling just below her knees. Sort of like something from an episode of *Mad Men*. She came off sophisticated and all woman, and so out of his league. Yet here he was, staring too long and wishing they were alone.

"How's the fish comin'?" Grandda appeared out of nowhere, wearing a canary-yellow sweater vest over a goldenrod plaid short-sleeved shirt. How could Mark miss him? The eighty-five-year-old stopped short of the grill and let out a long low whistle. "That dress will get you through all the right doors, it will." He slid a sly and loaded-with-meaning glance Mark's way.

Mark ignored it and went back to watching Laurel.

Laurel blushed and smiled. "Thank you." He waited for another curtsy, but it didn't come. *I guess she only does that for me.* The thought revved him up more, and he counted the moments until he could get some personal time with Laurel.

Daisy, his brother Daniel's Labrador mix—the dog he and his brothers shared duties over when they used to all live in the same hotel suite—broke out of a car that had just pulled up and chased away the lingering moment. Good, too, before things could get awkward with overstated compliments from old men and Mark's ogling eyes. The last thing he wanted to do was make Laurel uncomfortable because he was having a hard time controlling himself.

The blondish dog raced toward Peter and the twins, who squealed with glee and chased her around the yard. A friend to all, Daisy romped on the grass and loved it.

"Danny my boy is here!" Grandda announced, switching his attention from Laurel to the midsized power-red car that had just parked on the street at the base of the long yard.

His brother, who'd let Daisy out, and Keela, his wife, soon followed. From Mark's assessment, Keela didn't look pregnant, though she was at least three or more months, since she was due in April. They exchanged friendly waves with him since he was chained to the grill. He glanced at Laurel, who looked as happy as his grandfather to see them. Last, Anna got out with one huge thing missing.

"Look at me!" Anna crooned. Her cast was gone. The one she'd had to wear since early summer, after falling into a slack at the huge sand dunes down the way and breaking her leg while running with Daisy.

The twins stopped playing with the dog when they saw their new friend, then clapped, seeing her without her full leg cast. "Yay!" they sang and danced around. Anna walked gingerly to meet them, one leg noticeably thinner and whiter than the other. When they met up, they all squealed together.

Daniel climbed the slope of the grass, his hand guiding Keela along, looking happier than he'd been since he was a carefree kid. His physical medicine clinic was becoming a success, and he'd met and married Keela after a horrible breakup with another woman, a woman who'd left him heartbroken and lost, and who'd never loved him back. Then he met Keela. Chalk one up for Grandda and his selkie-lore promises. Whatever caused the change, life was good for Daniel, and it showed.

Mark and Daniel shook hands just as a sheriff's sedan pulled up and parked behind Daniel's car at the curb. Conor soon got out in full uniform, looking all business, but when he saw his brothers, his stern face— a look Mark had gotten used to seeing on his younger brother since returning home—broke into a smile. If you could call that nearly pained expression a smile. He always planned his Sunday dinner breaks around the weekly family-meal hour.

"Everything's ready on this end," Mother called from the pub's side door. "How's that salmon coming?"

Mark waved away more cedar plank smoke. "We're good to go," he said, transferring the fish to the huge platter his mother handed him. She noticed Conor and Daniel and Keela and Anna without her cast, and Laurel with the twins and Peter, and left Mark holding the plate, salmon and all. She hugged and greeted each one, her face radiating joy so deep Mark couldn't help but grin along.

A sharp whistle from the same pub door ripped the air. His father Sean stood in the same doorway Maureen had just exited, his head nearly touching the top. "Dinner's ready. Let's go!" he called out, benevolently herding his family inside, then greeting everyone as they passed with a fatherly hug and a deep-hearted smile.

Mark hung back, waiting for Laurel and her kids, escorting them inside.

Sean grinned at Laurel.

"I signed up for that free trial," she said on her way in.

"Great!" He squeezed her arm like they were old friends. After a quick nod, Peter, in usual form, slipped past, when Sean squatted to greet the little girls. It would be their first experience with "dinner" at the family pub. *Oh, boy!*

"I hope you're ready for this," he said to Laurel, knowing there was no way a person could prepare for it.

Her soft hazel-brown eyes crinkled, glistening with the golden autumn sun and happy vibes.

Ready or not, it was time to break bread with the Delaney clan.

After a typical unruly dinner, life still managed to feel good, sweet and filled with possibilities, which put Mark on edge. Until he put his arm around Laurel, who'd managed to stay bubbly throughout the meal, answering questions flying from every corner of the table. Her confident, positive and humble attitude was a huge draw for Mark. And though preferring to be the strong silent kind of guy, she had a way of helping him open up.

He'd laughed along with just about everyone else at Grandda's silly jokes, made eye contact with every person when they spoke, and he'd snuck as many glances at his good-looking date—if that's what he should call it—as possible without getting caught.

He had been caught, though, and not just by Grandda with his knowing stare, or his mother, who returned some sort of hopeful gaze, but Peter, too. The kid had been especially quiet during the meal, and seemed to keep his eye on his mother. Mark wasn't sure how a boy still mourning his father might feel about his mother getting attention from another man. He suspected not good, but it was too late to turn back now. Mark Delaney had a thing for Laurel Prescott, and feeling more like his old self than he had in a long time, he thought he might give whatever they had going on a chance.

Hopefully Peter would understand.

He would also make a point to bring up the subject of *Laurel + Mark* tomorrow afternoon when he gave Peter his surf lesson. Maybe ask Peter for permission to date his mother. He'd planned to butter him up with a surprise—his own board, an old one Mark had been refurbishing in his spare time. He'd removed the wax, fixed the dings, even put on a new, thicker traction pad, and couldn't wait to see Peter's reaction. From the glum expression he'd worn throughout dinner, Peter could use a happy surprise.

The best part about the family pub dinner on Sunday nights was that the hotel restaurant waitstaff cleared the table and cleaned up. After the meal, as everyone meandered toward the family-styled chair groupings in another corner of the pub, he saw Grandda single out Laurel. Not a good thing. But Conor had to get back to work, and he wanted to talk to Mark.

"I was thinking of going to check out the Beacham house tomorrow, and wondered if you wanted to come along."

The Beacham was an old, run-down Gothic-looking house on the cliffs that hadn't been lived in for over a decade. Conor was fixated on it, had wanted to buy and fix it up since he was in high school and dating Shelby. Why? Mark didn't have a clue. But it was the reason a man making a perfectly good salary still lived at his parents' hotel, and life didn't always make sense.

"I've got a surf lesson with Peter at four tomorrow, but after that, I'm good. As long as daylight holds."

"That's what police tactical flashlights are for." Conor nearly cracked a smile. "Talk tomorrow, then."

Off he went, stopping long enough to kiss his mother goodbye and shake his father's and Daniel's hands.

He broke up whatever conversation Grandda was having with Laurel—thank goodness—to give the old man a hug, said goodbye to her, then left.

Mark figured now was as good a time as any to rescue Laurel from the farfetched stories Padraig Delaney was known to tell. He stepped in front of Laurel, reached out his hand and, when Laurel offered hers, entwined his fingers through hers. "If you don't mind, Grandda, I don't want to waste a perfectly beautiful sunset." How could Padraig argue? Then Mark guided her toward the outside pub deck.

Just before they hit the door, he caught Peter with a solemn gaze watching them. Yeah, he'd definitely have a talk with Peter tomorrow afternoon. Because the way things were going with Laurel, he wanted to give the kid fair warning.

A few minutes later, Mark and Laurel stood in a secluded corner facing the ocean, forearms leaning on the wooden deck rails, talking.

"Your grandfather told me an interesting story about you and your brothers."

Oh, no, he didn't! Couldn't the man keep his fanciful thoughts to himself just once? "Really?" He tried to sound nonchalant, even though he had a good idea of which "interesting" story Grandda had told her.

"Uh-huh. About a certain fishing trip the three of you took, and a pod of orca…"

"Oh, let me guess, the one about saving the seal who could turn into a selkie and that now owes each of us a favor?"

"How'd you know?" she teased, a playful glint in her eyes.

"You know he's from Ireland, right?"

She laughed quietly. "So, I guess it's true, then?"

"Touché." Mark sighed. He loved his grandfather with all his heart, but once the old man got a notion into his head, he simply couldn't let it go. Having succeeded in predicting Daniel's finding his wife, all because they'd saved a "selkie," he'd moved on to Mark—the middle brother—and his ideas were nothing short of laughable.

Except here he was with Laurel, a woman he'd met a short month ago, feeling things he hadn't felt since before enlisting in the army…

"What exactly is a selkie?"

"They're folklore characters. Seals at sea who shed their skin to become human on land. That's all Grandda's selkie story has in common with the usual myths, where they marry then return to the sea. He insists the seal we saved will return the favor of saving its life by finding each of us a mate. As I said, that's all his embellishment."

"That's kind of sweet, isn't it? Wanting you all to be happy and in love?"

"Sure he'd like to see us all get married, too, but Conor and I both remind him, in our own time. I think because he's halfway through eighty and getting closer to ninety, he wants to rush us."

"Well, I still think that's sweet, and you're very fortunate to have such a great family."

"They were all on good behavior tonight, except Grandda, of course," he teased.

She tossed a look, not having any of it. "Well, it must be nice to have such a support system."

Which made him wonder. "Isn't your family?"

"Yes, my parents were very supportive during Alan's

trials, but I'm an only child. There were many things I would've liked to talk to a sister about." She went silent for a few moments, staring out to sea. "There was only so much I could dump on my friends, you know?"

He put his arm around her shoulders and tugged her near. "I can't imagine what you must've gone through."

"Nor I you." Her eyes found his and held his gaze. Was she referring to his time in the Middle East, and the PTSD he'd had to deal with since being home? He'd only hinted at it over their dinner out. Had Grandda spilled the beans on that one, too? Or maybe Peter had confided in her about some of their conversations in the ocean during surf lessons. "If you ever feel like talking…"

She'd quickly turned the topic back to him. But it'd been a good afternoon and evening, regardless of Grandda's silly ocean tales, and the last thing he wanted to do was ruin it by bringing up old problems. And lately, the same troubles that'd been plaguing him since the end of his military career seemed to be just that— old concerns. Why dredge them back up now, when the sun was setting bright orange and red on the water? With a beautiful woman by his side.

"Thanks, but right now I'd rather do this." He put another arm around her and pulled her flush to his chest so he could let her know how good she made him feel, with a kiss. A kiss that quickly heated up to equal participation and, from the way her hands dug into his back, equal longing. They took their time exploring, enjoying, fanning the coals that always smoldered between them.

"Hey, Mom, I'm going—" Peter stopped short.

They quickly broke off the kiss and turned toward his voice.

He looked confused, maybe a little upset, but covered it up, like he hadn't seen a thing. "—going home now." His voice sounded different on the last phrase.

"Did you thank Mr. and Mrs. Delaney?" Laurel tried to act like she hadn't just been caught by her son making out with a man. A man who wasn't Peter's father.

"Yeah." The teen did his best to act normal. Sullen. "I've got some homework to do." He averted his eyes.

"Where are your sisters?"

"They're playing with Anna and the dog." He wouldn't look at his mother, just stared at the wood planks on the deck.

"Okay. I'll be home soon."

Mark could tell Laurel, though soundly shook up, tried her best to keep it together. But things had just gone wonky, and he sensed payback would be involved. Making Mark wish he'd broached the subject on his mind—dating Laurel, which, after witnessing their kiss, had to officially and obviously be on Peter's mind, as well—yesterday when he'd taught Peter how to paint the gazebo.

Tossing a cold bucket of water on them couldn't have done a more thorough job of putting out the passion they'd been working up.

"I need to talk to him," she said.

Mark saw the near panic in her eyes as she took off after her son.

"I'll have Keela bring the girls over when they go home."

"Thanks," she said, already down the deck stairs and heading for her house.

Confused and worried, Peter rushed blindly across the street for home, to his room, where he slammed the door. Didn't Mom care about Dad anymore? Would he lose her, too, if she fell in love with Mark?

Anger washed from his head downward, concentrating around his chest. It felt tight and hurt. He'd thought Mark was his friend, but now he wondered if they'd been hanging out together only so Mark could get to his mother.

He wasn't a friend. He was his enemy. No way could he talk to his mother about it, because she'd take Mark's side.

There was a knock at his door. "Leave me alone!"

"I want to talk to you," his mother said.

"I said leave me alone!" He hated that his voice cracked on *alone*. He'd locked his door, knowing she'd want to face him after her betrayal.

But there was only one person he wanted to talk to. His dad. And he was gone.

Chapter Six

Monday, Mark waited for Peter at the regular spot on the beach at four o'clock, but he didn't show. He'd opted not to bring the refurbished surfboard, thinking it might come off as a bribe, and now he was glad he hadn't. After Peter's obvious disapproval of the kiss Sunday night, the last thing Mark wanted to do was make the kid angrier.

He waited a full twenty minutes before texting Peter. Where are you?

Nothing. Yeah, the kid was ticked off all right.

After a half hour of riding waves, Mark headed back to the beach and on to the B&B, ready to face Peter and apologize for any distress he may have caused him. But then what? Quit seeing Laurel? Not gonna happen. He'd just found her, and she'd been a great surprise. Truth was, he didn't want to give her up because her son didn't want his mother to have a life after Dad. Peter needed to understand that, ready or not, life kept moving forward. And his dating Laurel didn't mean anything serious would happen. How could it when he hadn't gotten that far in his personal plans? Their dating also didn't mean Peter's life as he knew it would change.

He arrived at Laurel's as she carried two handled tote bags of groceries from the car.

"Let me help you with that," he said, her smile brightening his mood as he took the next two totes out of the trunk, but it always did. Once inside the kitchen, he placed the bags on the island counter. "Is Peter home?"

"Wasn't he supposed to be with you?"

"He didn't show up for his surf lesson, and didn't respond to my texts."

She stopped unloading canned goods and stared at Mark, obviously stunned. In the next second she dug through her shoulder bag for her cell phone and made a call. "Peter, pick up, it's Mom," she said after a few seconds. "Please pick up?" She huffed, the color beginning to drain from her cheeks, and dialed again. His stomach constricted. She dropped her head back in frustration. "It went right to his messages."

Mark stepped forward, touching her unsteady hand. "At least we know he got your call. When's the last time you saw him?"

"This morning." Her eyes glistened with early tears. "He was angry, wouldn't talk to me last night, but he got up and dressed for school like he always does. Didn't say two words to me at breakfast, though." She sniffed and reached for a tissue on the sink counter. "I dropped him off at school before I took the girls to kindergarten. He barely acknowledged me when he got out, just made a grunt when I said I loved him." Her lower lip quivered. "What if he's run away?"

Mark took her into his arms, but she stiffened instead of relaxed. "Don't jump to conclusions. Maybe he's hanging out with his friends and wants to upset us. He'll probably show up for dinner."

Her brows crashed down with a disapproving expression. "I can't wait that long! I need to know where he is now."

"Listen, today's my brother's day off. He can help us."

Panic widened her eyes. "What if he's run away? Where would he go?"

"If he's run off, Conor and I will find him, I promise."

There was only so far a kid could go on foot. Who knew if he had money for the bus. Would he have the nerve or the wherewithal to head back to Paso Robles on his own? Did he know how to get there, and once he got there, what would he do? He'd never mentioned friends back there.

"What's he wearing today?"

She thought for a second, her eyes brightening. "His father's old T-shirt."

"The Bart Simpson one?"

She nodded.

It was probably a clue that Peter had his dad on his mind after seeing his mother with Mark last night. "Where's your husband buried?"

"He's not. He wanted to be cremated, and we scattered his ashes here in the ocean."

He and Peter had talked about a lot of things while they waited for waves. One of them was the best places to have a complete view of Sandpiper Beach and the ocean. "I'm going to check the pier. I'll call Conor and let him know what's going on." He took off running north to the small fishermen's pier.

Mark had told Peter where his favorite spot was when he needed to think. If his father was buried at sea, it might make sense to want to spend some time thinking about him up there.

He got to the pier and asked around, but none of the regular fishermen had seen him. Then he got an idea, a wild idea, but he didn't have a clue where to start. He also called Conor.

"Got a problem. Peter's gone missing. Can you help?"

Within five minutes, Conor met Mark back at the B&B, where he pulled to the curb in his muscle car and waited for Mark to get in. "I called it in. Does Laurel have a recent picture?"

Mark rushed back to the porch. "We need a picture for the sheriff's station."

"No luck at the pier?"

Mark shook his head.

She rushed inside, then shortly back out to the porch. "Just got his school picture last week." She handed a typically uncomplimentary five-by-seven school photo of Peter to Mark, who rushed it back to the car.

Mark dipped his head to Laurel, who waited anxiously on the porch. "Call me the instant you hear from him."

She nodded, obviously trying to keep it together, while having to hang back with her daughters and pretend everything was okay, so they wouldn't freak out, too.

"I'll take this to the sheriff's station," Conor said. "I'll tell them to get all the details from Laurel,"

"Sounds good. I'll check the beach where the school kids hang out," Mark said, taking some comfort in knowing the department didn't waste time on protocol before considering any kid missing. These days, the sooner they were found, the better the chances no one got hurt, whether the kid took off intentionally or not.

Mark figured it only made sense to check the closest locations before heading up the hillside, so he agreed. "Let's go, then. Meet you back here in fifteen minutes."

Conor drove at breakneck speed up the street, and Mark jogged toward the beach and the area where most of the high school kids congregated. As expected, there was a large group of kids, and Mark spotted the group who'd messed with Peter the first day Mark had met him. He approached the tall guy.

"Have you seen Peter lately? He didn't show up for his surf lesson."

The tall kid curled out his lower lip, thinking, then shook his head. "Not here. Saw him in gym class, though."

"What period was that?"

"Fourth."

Before lunch. That could mean anything. "Any of you guys have classes with Peter Prescott?"

"You mean pee-pee?" one smartass replied with a snicker. "Yeah, I've got art with him."

"What period?" Mark ignored the desire to deck the kid.

"Fifth."

"Was he there?"

"Yeah. He's good at painting. Never misses."

He'd figured out Peter's whereabouts up until two-ish. It was nearly five now, and with the days getting shorter, the sun set between six and six thirty, so he rushed back to the B&B and met up with Conor.

"Let's drive by the school," Conor suggested. "Maybe he's still there."

He gunned the engine, and they made it to the high school in near record time. A few stragglers were still hanging around the red brick administration building. Sandpiper High had less than five hundred students, tiny as far as high schools went, which was to their advantage.

"Any of you know Peter Prescott?" Mark asked.

They looked at each other, and one scrawny girl with long brown hair raised her hand.

"You see him after school?"

"Yeah. He was walkin' toward the beach."

Minimal help, but at least he hadn't headed for the city bus system, and they knew his whereabouts until 3:00 p.m. And Mark hadn't seen a hint of him at the pier or hanging out with the other kids on the beach.

"I'm going to follow my hunch on this," Mark said to Conor. "Let's go to the dunes and catch that trailhead."

"The place we used to go?"

"Yeah, the cliffs. Peter and I talked about that place once. Maybe he's hiding out there. He was wearing his dad's old T-shirt today. They scattered his ashes at sea off the pier, but he wasn't there. The ocean's all he's got left of his dad."

"And the view's awesome from there," Conor added.

"Exactly."

Once they parked and took off toward the sand dunes to find the trail up to the secluded cliffs, Mark explained how Peter had caught him kissing Laurel after dinner last night.

Conor tightened his chin with understanding. "That could be tough. How long's his dad been dead?"

"Around two years, I think."

Conor gave Mark a thoughtful glance. "So you and Laurel?"

"Yeah. I think." Mark kept hiking, gravel sliding under his shoes, feeling odd admitting it to his brother. "Probably not after this, though."

"You can't let a kid keep you from seeing her if there's something going on." For being the fittest man Mark knew, Conor sounded very out of breath as they climbed the steepening trail.

"Laurel would be the one to make that decision." Mark used a boulder to propel himself forward. "And honestly, I'm not sure where it's going with Laurel, just that I like being around her, and I'd like to keep seeing her. Beyond that?"

"Well, that's a start, man."

After today, whatever they had going on was probably finished, anyway.

They'd forgotten how tough the hike to the top of the cliffs were. Conor wondered aloud if Peter was in good enough shape to make it.

"He's skinny, but he's been doing the exercises I said he had to, to learn how to surf, and his leg strength has changed noticeably."

"He's got a hundred less pounds to carry up this hill, too." Conor stopped to catch his breath, then used an ancient bush limb to push off again. "At least we got a good workout today."

Mark hoped all their effort wasn't for naught. "We've got to find him. Laurel will freak out if we don't."

"We'll find him."

"Peter!" Mark yelled as they got close to the top of the cliff trail. Nothing.

"Peter!" Conor called out. "If you're there, answer us, man." Nothing.

Then, "Leave me alone."

Mark glanced at his brother and smiled. "Not gonna happen." They reached the summit, and saw Peter ignoring the wood bench, sitting on a boulder instead, knees up, chin resting on top, looking out to sea. He had to be cold with the kicking-up breeze whipping through that oversize, threadbare T-shirt.

"There you are," Conor said.

Mark didn't say another word, just climbed up next to him on the rock and sat, leaving a safe distance between them. Peter glanced at him, anger flashing in his eyes.

"Like I told you that day, I used to come up here to think." He glanced at his watch: ten to six. The sun would set shortly, and if Peter was cold now, he'd be freezing by then. "I hope you got all your thinking done because we need to climb down before it gets too dark to see."

Conor was already using his cell phone. "Laurel, we found him."

"Your mother's been worried sick," Mark said, doing his best not to sound accusatory. "And you must be hungry. Let's get you home in time for dinner. We can talk later."

The boy didn't budge. Mark heard Conor calling the sheriff's station. He reached for Peter's arm, to help him down, but Peter yanked it away. "Look, I get it, you're pissed that I kissed your mom. We can talk about that, but not here. Let's go."

In true Peter fashion, he continued to stare out to sea, doing a great job of pretending Mark didn't exist.

Mark needed to get real. "It's two to one, man. You gonna go down on your own, or are we gonna carry you? Your choice. Either way, we're taking you home. Now."

With his lower lip curled inward, teeth clamped on top, Peter reluctantly stood. Mark offered his hand again. When Peter took it, his eyes had already welled up with tears. Once they were off the boulder and back on the trail, Mark wanted to hug the kid, which surprised him, but he only patted him on the back, not wanting to push his luck. "We'll talk about this all you want. I promise. But first, let's get you home."

Laurel rushed to the car when Mark brought Peter home. She couldn't help the tears of relief, and didn't care if Peter minded if she hugged him. The twins didn't really understand what was going on, but they knew their brother hadn't come home when he was supposed to. She'd made sure they understood he was in trouble because of it. May as well lay down the rules with them now rather than later, when it might be too late. Like today. She'd never expected Peter to run away.

"Where were you?" Claire asked.

"Are you in trouble?" Gracie also asked.

He didn't answer, ignoring them. Surprisingly, Peter let Laurel hold on to him longer than she expected. Maybe he was shook up, too.

"Please don't ever do that again."

His glance shot downward. There was so much to talk about.

Laurel lifted her line of vision and seized the opportunity. "Conor, could I ask you a big favor?"

"Sure."

"Could you watch the twins while we have a talk?"

"I don't want to talk," Peter groaned.

"Too bad, buddy, we're talking. Now."

Conor went still. Quickly realizing he'd been caught off guard, he shifted his eyes to the little ones. She'd left him no choice, and being a conscientious peace officer, she knew she had him over a barrel. "Uh, I guess so."

"Thanks, man," Mark said standing nearby, obviously relieved.

Claire and Gracie looked up toward the sky to be able to take in all of Conor Delaney. They probably thought he was half giant. They'd met him Sunday night, so he wasn't a total stranger, but Laurel sensed their apprehension, since they hadn't interacted much then. She touched both of their shoulders and bent forward. "Conor is Mark's brother. He's a nice man, and he'll watch you guys for a little bit, okay?"

"Okay," Claire, the leader, said.

"Do you play Legos?" Gracie, the practical, asked.

"Sometimes." No longer resisting the last-minute plan, Conor gave a halfhearted smile and followed them inside.

Laurel guided Peter through the door, aware that Mark followed. "Um, Mark, can you make Peter a sandwich? I'd like to talk to him alone for a minute."

"Sure," Mark said.

"Not hungry," Peter mumbled.

"I'm sure you are." Laurel used her eyes to encourage Mark to step out for a little while. He caught on and followed her lead. "Let's go in here." She led the way to the front sitting room, then closed the pocket doors behind her. Peter reluctantly sat, and she sat beside him.

Instead of starting off scolding him for scaring her to death, as she may have earlier, she held back on her emotions and went for the heart of the matter. "First off—" no point in wasting time "—you've got to know that no one will ever replace your father." She took his chin in her fingers and turned his head so his eyes met hers. "He is your one and only father. I wish you'd had more time with him. God knows, I wish he'd never gotten cancer, but we don't always get our wishes."

Peter must have still been raw from running away and getting caught by the very person he most likely never wanted to see again—the man who'd dared to kiss his mother—because he broke down and cried.

She edged closer to her son and drew him near. "I know you miss him. I do, too. I know it makes you angry that he died. It makes me angry, too."

After a few moments of letting Peter get his feelings out through tears, then offering him a tissue or two, she continued. "It's been two years since Daddy died, Peter. I'm not saying you have to forget him. I'd never do that. We'll both always remember him. But I want you to try to understand that our moving to Sandpiper Beach was to help us all move on." She glanced at him while he blew his nose.

"He's my dad and I'm never going to stop loving him."

"I'll always love him, too."

"Then why are you kissing *him* and going on dates?" Peter protested, pulling away from her hug. She could read his scowl—betrayal. She was a betrayer as far as her son was concerned. She couldn't let him think that because the idea broke her already-broken heart.

"Going on a date isn't the same as what Daddy and I had. But I need friends, too, Peter, just like you do."

"He was supposed to be my friend. Now it feels like he was only nice to me to get to you."

"I don't believe that. You and I met Mark on the same day, and since then we've both gotten to know him better. Wouldn't you agree he's a nice man?"

Reluctantly, Peter nodded, obviously hating where the conversation was going.

"If I like Mark, it doesn't mean he can't be your friend, too."

Peter's angry stare and extra-long sigh made her want to reinforce her original point, because she had a hunch her boy was worried about where he stood in their changing world.

"No one will ever replace your father, or *you*, in here." She pointed to her chest. "We're family. You're my son. I love you more than you can understand."

Things went quiet for a few seconds as Laurel hoped Peter was taking in her declarations. A light tap on the door drew her attention.

Mark opened the pocket doors with a sandwich on a plate in the other hand and a can of soda under his arm. "Okay if I join you guys?"

Peter shot Mark a look that stated he wasn't ready to forgive him for kissing his mother just yet, that maybe he never would. Mark seemed to sense now wasn't such a good time to join in and put the sandwich on the table, then prepared to leave.

"Peter's upset about our dating." Laurel figured Mark deserved an explanation, especially after all he'd done that afternoon and evening searching for her son and bringing him home.

"Peter, I value our friendship—" unfazed by Peter's glower, Mark went on "—and want to keep hanging out, just the two of us. But I like your mother, too. Would it be okay if she and I went out once in a while?"

More silence from Peter, who was definitely not on board with Mom branching out.

"I know you've been through a lot of changes lately, and I thank you for sharing a lot of them with me when we surf," Mark continued. "I don't want to push you, so I'll leave you with your mom for now and we can talk later."

Mark turned to leave. When he got to the doors, he swung around. "I'm glad you're home and safe, Peter. It scares me when my friends go missing." He opened the door.

"Mark?" she said.

He looked back watching Laurel cuddling her skinny son.

"Thank you."

How could he not see the deepest appreciation Laurel could possibly show from far across the room. She'd willed it into him. How grateful she was to him for bringing her son home. Things could have ended up a dozen different ways with Peter's taking off on his own without telling anyone, they both knew it. Surely, his sheriff brother understood.

He nodded solemnly and closed the doors. She offered the turkey and cheese sandwich to Peter and surprisingly, he took half and ate a bite.

"I just want things to be the way they've been, just you and me and the twins," Peter said, his mouth full.

Laurel couldn't let that comment go without a challenge. "Don't I have a say in it? And who says our family unit is going to change just because I go on a date?"

Peter hung his head, looking as though the entire world had just crashed on his shoulders.

"I get that you may feel abandoned by Dad's dying," she said, "Sometimes, I do, too. But get it in your head, I'm not leaving you. You'll be begging me to leave you alone long before I will." She figured a little humor injected into the tension in the room couldn't hurt.

Peter relaxed a tiny bit in Laurel's arms, giving her hope some of the words were sinking in. "You know beyond anything in the world that you're my son and I love you with all my heart."

Peter inhaled a long, ragged breath, and Laurel put her chin on the crown of his head. He'd always be her little boy, even though he was almost as tall as her now. She figured after all he'd been through today, he might want to hear her say it one more time. "I'll never abandon you for anyone else. Please don't ever take off again without telling me where you're going."

"Okay," Peter mumbled, because his mouth was full with another bite of sandwich.

Mark was grateful the kid had made the right choice and come home with him and Conor. He also understood how deeply thankful Laurel was to have her boy home, and that Mark and Conor had brought him. Her sincere thanks was the only payment he needed.

The intense moments had made him thirsty, so he walked to the kitchen to get a drink of water before he left. He heard the girls laughing and making a racket. Then he remembered his brother had pulled bambino duty. The thought made him smile. He tiptoed down the hall to peek a look at how Conor was handling things, but with no intention of taking over. His little brother, who was two inches taller than him, sat cross-legged on the floor, with the twins messily building from mounds of primary-colored click-together blocks.

Seeing his huge brother in that position cracked a smile on his previously grave expression.

He padded back to the kitchen and drank the water. Man, being a parent had to be the toughest job in the world. It was certainly not a job he felt ready for, either firsthand or in a step-in role. He genuinely liked Peter, it was true they were friends, but having the responsibility of being a father figure was a whole different ball game.

Mark had heard enough of Laurel's heartfelt pleas to her son to realize what a great mom she was. How she was nothing like any lady he'd ever been involved with before. And though he was nowhere near ready for anything more than stolen kisses and promising glances, it hit him what a good woman she was. His relationship with Laurel and her kids wasn't for play. It was real, and he better be sure he was ready for it.

That from a guy who didn't even feel ready to take on surfing lessons for guests at the hotel. And he loved surfing!

"Flush, wash and be on your way!" Claire said as the bathroom door closed. Was that for Conor or Gracie?

He gulped down the rest of the water, needing to get out of there but not wanting to get caught by Conor before he left. So he waited until he heard the toilet flush, the water run and the door open and close again. He peeked around the corner again and saw the back of his brother heading into the twins' room. So Claire even bossed big guys around. It made him chuckle inside.

Feeling guilty, he headed down the hall to let Conor know before he left that he was sticking him with the childcare. But he overheard something else first, something he'd never expected to hear in his life.

When we play and make a mess, it's always good to try our best,

To cleeeaaan up.

Conor had taken an old TV jingle and put new words

to it to get the girls to help him clean up the toys. Would wonders never cease? Mark shook his head and smiled, then deciding not to interrupt the little play party, he left for the hotel, because he had a whole lot of thinking to do.

Around eleven, Laurel texted Mark. Feel like talking?

In her usual easygoing way, she'd coaxed him to tell her what was on his mind. *A whole helluva lot!*

After getting chewed out by Conor for abandoning him with the twins, Mark had been sitting on the pub deck thinking thoughts he hadn't expected to think for years yet. About how he might be falling for someone for the first time in…a decade?

He couldn't ignore Laurel's invitation to talk, not after all she'd been through that day. Instead of answering her text, he walked across the street and tapped on her door. When she opened it, it was obvious she'd taken a shower and her hair was still damp. Dressed in pale gray girlie-styled sweats and big fuzzy slippers, she smiled demurely, not saying a word, like she'd been expecting him. As if they belonged together.

When he stepped inside, she hugged him, and he immediately remembered why he'd been thinking about Laurel the way he'd been for the last few hours. She felt right when he held her. Made him want to be around her…all the time.

"You okay?" he asked.

"I needed a hug."

So he hugged her tighter and threw in a neck kiss. "Everyone in bed?"

She nodded. "Want some herbal tea? I just made a pot."

It wasn't his thing, and he didn't want to let go of her, but why not. "Sure."

They strolled to the kitchen, his arm around her shoulders, her arm tucked tight around his waist. She wasn't kidding about having a pot of tea ready. She peeled away from his side and found a small tray, soon putting two of her beautiful bone china English teacups on it, then cream and sugar, and four homemade peanut butter cookies.

"I have an idea," she whispered. "To keep from waking up the kids, I thought we could have tea upstairs."

"Let me carry that for you." He took the tray and let her lead the way to the far end of the second floor. The exact opposite of where her children slept below, he noted. She opened the door to the second-biggest guest room, not the honeymoon suite, but one with ample sitting space, and a gas fireplace that had conveniently already been lit, making the room feel extra cozy. Not to mention the huge bed in the large arched recess. Hmm, she must have been doing some thinking, too?

He set the tray on the coffee table in front of the daintily flower upholstered love seat, then sat.

She stood a couple of feet away, an appreciative look in her eyes. "I owe you a big thank-you for finding my kid."

"Hey, I was glad we found him. All I did was put a few things together and get an idea."

She poured them both some tea, handed him his cup, then sat beside him. "I don't know what I would have done without you today."

He didn't know what he would've done if he hadn't found Peter. "Did he open up more after I left?"

"He told me he trusted you, and got upset when he thought you had used him."

"Damn, that makes me feel horrible."

"I straightened him out. Plus, he believed what you

told him." She took a sip of chamomile tea and stared at him over the cup. "He admits you're a great guy, and I told him that's how I felt, too."

She stopped talking in an obvious *it's your turn* sort of way. He remembered the text and why he'd come over in the first place. "Well, while we're admitting things, I guess I should say, first off, I really do like your son. In fact, I like all of your kids. You've done a great job."

"Thank you. Some days, like today, I'm not so sure."

"Nah, you're a good mother. I can't imagine all you've been through since your girls were born."

Her gaze shifted downward, studying her tea. He could only imagine how hard she'd had it for so many years, and it made those protective feelings he'd been trying to avoid swell up again. "I have to also admit that I, too, really like you." Could he sound stiffer? That was not the way to impress a lady. He needed to make his declaration more personal. He took the teacup from her hand and placed it on the small table to get her full attention, then edged closer to her. "Not to sound like a geeky kid, but that's a big deal for me. Haven't thought about a woman the way I think about you in a long time."

Her gaze lifted ever so slowly, until he captured her stare. "And how is that, Mark, the way you think about me?" Gone was the thoughtful Laurel, in her place the flirty girl he was just getting to know, and especially liked.

He'd played poker enough in the army to know you never gave away your hand. As it stood, he had a lot of crazy mixed-up cards, but he somehow knew if he played them right he might win. One day. If that's what he wanted.

"Besides a lot?" That got a twinge of a smile from her, which always tripped him up.

Could he trust her with his feelings? She seemed to trust him enough to invite him over at this late hour, to take him to a beautifully decorated guest suite, so they could have some privacy. It was damn obvious she trusted him on many levels.

"I think I'm falling for you—" he may just have revealed a card too many "—and to be honest, that's freaking me out."

Her eyes popped open a bit more, and she reached for his face. "I wouldn't want you to freak out about anything on my account." Then she kissed him, and he didn't care if he'd blown his hand or not. "The thing is," she said with a trusting gaze, "I think I'm falling for you, too."

She had his full attention, and the sincerity in those wide, light hazel eyes made her look like a young, delicate-hearted girl. That worried him, yet he was drawn too closely to her in the moment, so he skipped over that "worried" part. Right to his gut reaction.

"Maybe we should test out this liking-each-other theory," she said. It wasn't a question, and it came out breathy and quiet and very, very sexy.

He'd been looking for a sign, or a tell, and she'd just given herself away. Blurted it right out. After a long, thoughtful gaze into the center of his eyes, triggering tiny bolts of lightning along his spine, she glanced toward the elephant in the room. The king-size four-poster bed.

"Did I mention the kids are all asleep?"

Chapter Seven

Mark seemed as shy about getting naked as Laurel felt. Were they ready for this—making love? Her emotions had been on a roller coaster all afternoon, and after all the chaos settled, her one remaining thought had been how special Mark was. He'd taken responsibility for her son's running off, gone after him and brought him home.

She hadn't met such a good man since Alan died—a real man, as her father used to call her husband. She knew better, didn't she? To let her guard down? She had to protect herself for her children's sake. Okay, that was a flat-out excuse, but still partially true. The thing was, Mark possessed the one characteristic she'd always been drawn to. He was trustworthy. Then all those gorgeous "all man" traits came next, which scared the wits out of her. Yet she'd just come this close to begging the man to make love to her. So the question remained, was she ready? All she wanted to do was get lost in his body for a while, to help put the horrors of the day behind her, to forget how lonely she was every day. For that, she was positive she was ready. But more? Not before she cushioned her heart, because she could never go through the torture of losing someone again. Tensing a bit, she worried she was making a mistake to let go with Mark.

He unbuttoned his shirt, then, with that amazing chest on display and those cut abs just beneath, he put a hand on each of her upper arms, with a serious-as-hell expression. "You sure about this?"

No! But her body betrayed her, wanting to be close and comforted, especially after all she'd gone through that afternoon. It had been so long. Couldn't she take this bit of time for herself, just for right now? *Be bold. Go for what you want.* She pulled her top over her head and, in answer to his question about whether or not she was sure about this, whispered, "Yes."

Her reward was a smoldering gaze of appreciation from a man who didn't seem to mind she'd once carried twins and her abs were nonexistent. He moved in, and his warmth enveloped her. And it was exactly where she needed, no, *wanted* to be. With him. Completely.

Tucked safely away in the Gardenia guest room, they kissed and kissed, and he worked her up to near panting. Still, Mark kept his hands strictly above the waist. It gave her pause, and she wondered how long it'd been since he'd been with a woman. Mark would be the only other man she'd ever made love with besides Alan. The thought released a shiver through the heat Mark had done such a great job stoking with his deep kisses and needy caresses. Yet they were still only half-undressed and just halfway to the bed. Besides being the handiest man she'd ever met, he was also a gentleman. *Make it clear that you want him.*

So she stepped things up several notches by reaching between the front of his legs and gently squeezing.

After that he delivered an amazingly ragged kiss, lifted her as she wrapped her thighs around his hips, walked her to the bed, then laid her down. In her excitement, she fought for her breath and let Mark have his way with her neck and breasts. Scattering chills across her shoulders and chest, he explored and kissed the parts bulging above her standard white bra. Her legs remained wrapped around his waist, a deep pulse pounding harder and harder in her core. *Be careful*, an annoying tiny voice far in the back of her mind whispered. She ignored it.

Suddenly needing more to silence her doubts, she cupped his head in her hands and guided his gaze up to hers, first kissing him tenderly on the lips, then reconnecting with those eyes. Silently she communicated, *I'm ready*, at once exciting and frightening her.

With his hair mussed and those heavy-lidded blues knocking her sideways with longing, she could practically hear his reply.

In the next moment, he lifted her again, her legs still wrapped around his hips, pulled back the bedspread and laid her against the supersoft sheets she'd handpicked for guests. Then he removed her bra and lounge-y sweatpants, and peeled down her weekday, nothing-special cotton briefs. Because she didn't have any idea her day would end like this when she'd showered an hour ago. In the next moment, he got rid of his jeans and baby blue boxer briefs.

The sight of Mark Delaney without his shirt or underwear, fully erect, nearly blinded her with desire. The nagging reservations dropped like autumn leaves—she finally and firmly gathered them and tossed them out the window—and the chills ignited in scattershot when he covered her. She felt every part of his tight body. So different from Alan. When Mark rolled over and she wound up on top, his hands cupping her hips snugly against him, sparklers set off beneath every erogenous zone she possessed. As they moved together, slick with heat, powered by passion, she became completely lost in Mark, and the amazing way he made her feel. And how very, *very* lucky she was.

Wednesday afternoon, it was awfully hard to face Peter with memories of Laurel and their Monday love-making night flashing fresh in Mark's mind. But he'd promised another surfing lesson, and because he wanted to build bridges and not tear them down with the kid, he walked Peter to the storage shed with a planned surprise, not caring if the kid saw it as a bribe or not, because it wasn't his motivation.

"First off—" Mark decided to dig right into the conversation they needed to have "—I just want to say I'm not the kind of guy who abandons his friends. And I consider you a friend first, Peter."

Peter found something fascinating with his tire-tread sandals rather than make eye contact.

"Do you believe me?"

"Yes," he said begrudgingly.

"So you've got to understand that if your mother and I like each other, your world isn't coming to an end. That nothing's going to change between you and me. Right?"

"I guess."

"You guess? Is that all you think of me? After all the

time we've spent together, don't you think you can tell if I'm being honest or not?"

Finally Peter glanced up, skipping over Mark's steady gaze and off toward the hotel. "I believe you."

"Good. Now that we've cleared that up, I've got a surprise for you."

Peter's head bobbed quickly back in Mark's direction.

He gave Peter the old surfboard he'd been working on, and his reaction was predictably jazzed. Mark sensed they'd entered a new level of trust and, hopefully, friendship.

To top things off, Peter had his best ride ever that afternoon. They'd hooted and high-fived, and Mark could see new confidence in the kid who'd run off just two short days before.

Thursday, after making love with Laurel a second time just that morning, it was downright awkward stepping in with the twins when Laurel had a meeting with a town historian. Last minute, she'd promised a quick tour of the B&B, and Peter was at the high school library working on a term paper.

Claire and Gracie had a school assignment to gather as many different leaves as they could for an art project the next day. While Laurel gave the B&B tour, Mark took the girls on a walk. They hit the residential area a couple of streets up that was lined with an assortment of trees, including maple. Though the field trip was mostly to get them out from under Laurel's feet, he wanted to do whatever he could to help her build her business.

Because he cared about her? The thought was surprising whenever he had it, but it was true, and he caught a wide smile on his face in a reflection on a parked car window.

Each girl carried a brown paper bag. Gracie piled leaf after leaf in hers, while Claire was more discerning, choosing the biggest or the most colorful. While Claire stood with hands on her hips, making a choice, Gracie put down her bag and found two huge brown and orange maple leaves nearly the size of her head, then ran in circles flapping them in the air.

"I'm pretembering I can fly," she sang.

"She means—" Claire started.

"I got that one, hon. I know what she meant," he said gently with a reassuring smile.

Gracie grinned at him.

Claire pushed her pink glasses up her nose and mumbled "Pretending" anyway.

For different reasons, he wanted to hug both children, which jolted him. Maybe he was getting in way over his head with Laurel and her kids. But he had to admit, standing in the late-afternoon sun, watching them make over leaves like they were the greatest invention on earth, felt kind of good. And he didn't mind—scratch that, liked—he *liked* spending time with the twins. Yikes.

Friday morning, Mark got invited to Laurel's for breakfast. She'd made an incredible egg soufflé, lighter than air, and filled with fresh garden herbs. She planned to serve one for her guests on Saturday morning, and wanted his opinion. They took two bites and made super-satisfied groans to each other, then he fed her a bite and she fed him one. That led to more pleasurable sounds, looking into each other's eyes, and leaving their brains on the back porch, because next thing they knew, they were doing it on the kitchen island.

A half hour later, Laurel had the great idea to try out the modernized, room-enough-for-two bathtub in suite number three. After what they'd done in the kitchen, a bath sounded like a great idea. For fun, Mark picked Laurel up and carried her in his arms up the stairs until halfway up, where he realized he wasn't as strong as he thought.

"Just a second," he said, on the midpoint landing, then hoisted Laurel over his shoulder like a sack of cement and continued up.

She protested but giggled. "I'm not that heavy."

"I know, you're the perfect weight and height and—" He could go on because in his book, she was perfect in every way. But he wasn't sure how she'd feel about him being crazy about her. "—and I'm the one with a problem. I'm not as strong as I like to think."

They'd made it to the top of the stairs. "Which way?" he said, playfully biting her hip, since it was so close to his jaw.

"Ahh!" She giggled more. "Stop that. To the left. Door number two." At least she didn't insist he put her down.

He followed her orders and found his second-favorite room in her B&B. Smaller than the others, but with a skylight that kept the room bright and open, and a bathroom that overlooked the ocean with enough privacy to leave the curtains apart.

He slowed at the foot of the bed. "Want to stop here first?"

She gave an impish glance. "Maybe after the bath?"

"I like the sound of that. Will we have time?" He knew the twins got picked up at noon.

From over his shoulder she checked her watch upside down. "Yes, but you'd better let me down. All the blood is running to my head, and I think with your wicked plans we need to reverse that."

He planted her feet securely on the antique and restored pale blue bathroom tile, then looked at the modern tub taking up nearly a third of the space. He waited for her to get her bearings, made sure she wasn't dizzy, then kissed her bright red face. "I never get tired of kissing you."

She blinked and looked pleased. "We've only been kissing for a few weeks."

"Best few weeks ever." What was wrong with him, acting all crazy about the girl? He could scare her off if he kept this up. Or maybe she liked it.

Instead of chasing her away with his admissions, she settled her palm on his chest. They may not have taken off their clothes in the kitchen, but he'd opened his shirt so he could feel as much of her as possible. Now, the warmth of her hand turned him on as much as if she nibbled his earlobe. But what moved him the most was the way she didn't look directly into his eyes. Instead, she watched her hand slide over his chest and along his side, down to the rim of his jocks. He liked where this was going.

Her lids lifted quickly and she gave a coy smile. His zipper was still down, from their little foray in the kitchen, and as she continued to stare at him, her hand slid beneath the band of his briefs, then around to the back to grab his glute. "Let's get these off you." Seductive, persistent and right to the point. He liked it.

A few simple words, and he sprung to life again. Though in this case her actions spoke louder as she yanked down his jeans and freed him of his underwear.

While the tub got filled, they spent their time wisely, touching, tasting, working each other up for what he was sure would be the best bath of his life.

She directed him into the tub, filled with the perfect temperature of water, then she straddled him. With his head against the cushioned end of a well-planned tub, the view of Laurel's breasts up close and oh so personal, as well as the spectacular ocean over her shoulder, he thought he'd gone to heaven. From the exquisite expression Laurel wore, he was positive he'd brought her along with him.

Soon water was sloshing everywhere, up and over, onto the tile, but they didn't care, because they had a whole lot of other stuff going on. The best lovemaking Mark could ever remember, why? Because he cared about the woman on his lap who took the entire length of him, and gave as much as she took. Tight and deep inside Laurel, bringing her to the brink, was the one place he felt healed and complete. And nothing else mattered.

Several minutes later, after the water settled down, and his heartbeat returned to normal, he held her close to his side and kissed the top of her head. All he wanted to do was hold and protect her. And something more— he wanted to be a man she deserved.

As though she could hear his thoughts, she lifted her face, making close contact with his vision. They didn't say a word to each other, but her nearly fully dilated pupils sent a powerful message. She was as much into him as he was her. Sexually satiated, a tender rush overtook him. He slipped his fingers around the base of her head, his thumb caressing the front of her ear, then drew her near and kissed her with a feeling he could only describe as love pulsing in his heart.

Laurel stopped the kiss, to gaze at him quizzically,

as though she'd felt it, too. As the fine hair on his neck stood on end, her nipples pebbled and gooseflesh covered her chest and shoulders. Something powerful had passed between them. And yeah, whatever it had been, the feeling was mutual.

In silence, they lay in the tub, holding each other, kissing and nuzzling from time to time, until the water cooled. Only one thing bothered him. A drip, drip, dripping. He glanced at the pedestal sink with the antique faucet and saw the source.

"I'll fix that for you," he said.

"I think you could fix everything for me," she whispered against his chest.

The increased and intensifying meetings with Laurel made Saturday morning extra tricky facing Peter. His mother blew Mark's mind, and they couldn't seem to get enough of each other. But the kid had penance to pay, and seeing the gazebo project to the end, as Laurel had put it yesterday morning while naked and tangled up in Mark's body, would help build character.

Yeah, they'd reached the point in their relationship where they talked about all kinds of things after they made love. He hadn't shared so much or so easily with another person of the female persuasion in his entire life. He also got the impression Laurel needed their stream-of-consciousness talks as much as he did. After sex, when they were completely relaxed and intimate with each other, that's when they really opened up.

Mark and Peter touched up the gazebo's white paint, then attached matching bouquet holders on each side of the arched entry. His mother had insisted on it. The morning sun beat down on his shoulders, and he felt alive like he hadn't in several years.

"I brought you some lemonade." His favorite neighbor, Laurel, handed him and Peter each a plastic glass of the best minted lemonade Mark had ever tasted. He knew her guests had to love it, too.

"Thanks," he said, hoping the smoldering gaze he gave Peter's mother went over the kid's head, because, hey, he couldn't help it.

Her shy smile in response was nearly his undoing. Really? He'd seen every inch of her, felt and kissed just about everywhere, too, but right now in front of Peter and the Saturday morning sun, she got shy. He smiled long and happily at her, and she let him look at her the way he wanted.

"You won't believe who I just got off the phone with," she said a few moments later, pride and excitement in her voice.

"The president?" Peter could be witty when he wasn't practicing being a reticent teen, and it always surprised Mark.

He snorted. "Good one."

"*A* president, Mr. Smarty-Pants. Of the historical society." Laurel batted her lashes first at her son, then Mark. If she kept this up, he might have to walk her backward against the fresh paint and kiss her senseless. Because that was what they seemed to do best.

"And?" he said instead.

Her eyes brightened, that enthusiastic expression reminding him of Gracie. "They're adding our B&B to their monthly tours!" One arm shot up like she'd just won the million-dollar lottery, and she looked so damn cute, he wanted to kiss her in the worst way.

"Hey, that's great!" Mark couldn't help himself another moment. He put down his drink and gave her a celebratory hug, swinging her in a circle. And by her reaction, he knew where her twins got their giggles.

"What're we celebrating?" His mother came walking across the lawn, the contagious joy making her smile. Or maybe it was seeing her son laughing and smiling, hugging and twirling a woman like he didn't have a care in the world.

Mark let Laurel explain the good news. Then Maureen hugged her, too. "How wonderful!"

After things settled down, Maureen got a look at the finished gazebo. "Wow, this looks great!" She smiled at Mark and Peter. "You guys did a fantastic job. I can't wait to have our first wedding here." She glanced at Laurel, then clapped her hands. "I have an idea—why don't we all celebrate Laurel's good news tomorrow night. Instead of having dinner in the pub, let's have it out here in the gazebo. We can barbecue. Laurel, bring the kids and we'll picnic outside."

"Sounds great."

But Maureen wasn't finished. Her eyes widened more. "We should work out a wedding package where the couple, who may want a nicer suite than we have to offer, can get married here, by the beautiful sea, then after the reception in The Drumcliffe restaurant, they can walk right across the street to your B&B."

"To start their honeymoon! That's a fabulous idea." Laurel looked amazed and nearly as excited as his mom. "Have you seen my newlywed suite?"

"Not yet."

Laurel slipped her arm through Maureen's and started down the lawn. "Come over and have a look. It's gorgeous and isolated from the other rooms." Laurel smiled at Maureen as they walked arm in arm. "I think you're onto something."

"I know I am."

The sight of Laurel and his mother acting like best friends warmed Mark's chest. She was becoming a part of their little beach community, a part of his family's business and a part of his heart. The thought sat like a cold stone on his chest, yet perspiration appeared above his lip, and the look he shared with Peter could only be described as awkward.

Sunday night Mark stood back, watching Laurel and her kids interacting with his entire family, and, forgetting the hesitation he'd felt the other day, his smile came from deep inside. He'd been asked to grill the chicken, and though they'd planned to eat outside tonight, most of the activity took place farther away on the yard from the built-in patio grill. Still, he watched as Keela and Laurel had an intense conversation about something, probably school-related, while the three little girls played like lifelong friends, chasing Daisy around in circles.

Peter and Sean parked themselves on a picnic bench nearby and discussed The Drumcliffe's and Prescott B&B's websites. Peter's knowledge was impressive. From the look on his father's face, the kid had impressed him, too.

Soon, Mom picked up where she'd left off with Laurel, and announced to the family their big plans for linking their amenities together where wedding packages were concerned. Sean and Peter had a quick follow-up conversation about that, too. How to link the websites together, and how to share photographs of the "wedding" gazebo and the "honeymoon" suite across the street.

He wished he wasn't stuck grilling meat, but enjoyed

seeing Laurel and her kids getting unofficially inducted into the Delaney clan.

Conor came strolling over with a beer in his hand for Mark and a soda for himself, since he was scheduled to work that night. "How're things going between you and Peter?" He lowered his voice to ask, since Dad and Peter were close by.

Mark thanked him for the beer with a nod and took a quick sip. "As good as can be expected. I still don't think he's crazy about my seeing his mom, but he's not complaining. To me at least."

Conor's gaze skipped away to the lady in question across the yard, sitting on a picnic table bench. Currently, Daisy had her front paws on Laurel's knees and was trying her best to lick Laurel's face. She giggled and dodged the inevitable for as long as she could, until the friendly dog's tongue landed smack on her mouth.

"And how're things going with her?" Conor arched his gaze in her direction, rather than be obvious and point at her.

Under his brother's scrutiny, Mark felt his ears heat up. Yeah, he had it bad, and he and Laurel had just started getting to the good stuff. But there was no way he'd admit that to Conor, who'd pester him until he spilled some details. Details that he'd prefer to hoard for himself. "Good, man. Really good." He hoped he'd sounded casual enough.

Conor narrowed one eye. "You dog."

"What?" Suddenly, Mark needed to turn a whole lot of chicken legs and breasts, and wow was he busy.

Then came Grandda. "'Tis a beautiful night. Dinner smells grand. How's the world treatin' my boys?"

"Same old, same old, Grandda," Conor answered first.

Disappointed with Conor's reply, Grandfather threw his attention to Mark. "And you, my boy, need your old grandda to drive you and her—" he tossed his head in the direction that Laurel stood with the other women "—to dinner again?"

It'd been a while since they'd had an official date, mostly because of their schedules and Peter's running away. Mark had been holding off from making waves by taking Laurel out again. Now that his grandfather had mentioned it, the idea was a good one, and he had a special place in mind. "If it would be okay, I might like to borrow the golf cart next time and drive her myself."

"Of course," Padraig said, smiling at Mark, then glancing across the yard to Laurel with her hair blowing in the wind. She wore a sophisticated but simple cream-colored outfit, pants that fit her curves to perfection and a silky top that billowed in the breeze. Even her flats were beige. "She's a good one, Marky."

The heat from the barbecue made Mark's face go red. He fanned the smoke with his hand and tried not to feel the pressure, or let it get in the way of his romance with Laurel.

Dating a woman with children was a challenge, but after the awesome week he'd spent getting to know her in a most intimate way, he thought he might be able to pull it off—getting more and more involved with a lady and her family, and all that went along with it. Which reminded him.

Mark asked Conor to take over for a few minutes, then he approached Peter sitting alone on the nearby bench. Dad had been called into the kitchen by Mom to help with the side dishes, so Mark seized the moment.

He sat beside the teenager. "Thought I'd run something by you."

Peter turned with a questioning glance. "Okay."

"I'd like to ask your mom out to dinner Thursday night. Is that okay with you?"

The boy looked confused followed by thoughtful. "You worried I'll run away again?"

"We're past that, right?"

Peter studied his Vans. "Yeah, I guess so."

Mark had hoped their conversation about moving forward in life since the move had sunk in. But who knew how a teenager thought anymore. It seemed a lifetime ago since Mark had been one.

"Yeah, you guess so, you're over it? Or yeah, you guess it's okay for me to ask your mom out?"

The teen hitched one corner of his mouth and let out a tiny sigh. "You can ask her out," he said begrudgingly.

Peter didn't look at Mark, but Mark thought they'd just cleared a huge hurdle. He gave the kid two firm pats on the shoulder. "Thanks, man. See you at the beach tomorrow at four, right?"

Now Peter glanced at him. "Yeah. I'll be there."

They hadn't even eaten dinner yet, and Mark had already solved one of his problems. Now if he could just get his family to leave him alone.

Later Sunday night, Mark took his grandfather up on his offer to arrange a dinner at a swanky golf club on Thursday night, especially when Grandda offered to watch Laurel's kids. Well, check in on them, anyway, since Peter was perfectly capable of looking out for his sisters. Now all he had to do was ask her. He took out his cell and called.

He and Laurel had been sneaking time together throughout the week. He wasn't being greedy or anything, but he'd been there three times. They used the

stolen hours to strip down and drive each other crazy.
Always pressed for time, before the girls got out of kindergarten, they rarely had a chance to do normal things
like talk. Dinner, just the two of them, at a swanky
golf course clubhouse seemed the perfect way to spend
a Thursday night, since her weekends were usually
booked with B&B guests.

Thursday at 6:00 p.m., he pulled the electric golf cart
to her house, hopped out and whistled his way up the
steps to her door. The thought of spending the evening
with Laurel put him in a terrific mood. He'd borrowed
another shirt from Conor, this one gray, and wore a
new pair of dark dress pants to fit in at the members-
only restaurant. They required jackets, so he'd borrowed
one from Daniel. Grandda had been given an honorary
lifetime membership there for being one of the original
laborers when the golf course had first been designed
back in the 1950s, though the family rarely took advantage of it. *It's about time.*

When Laurel opened the B&B door, dressed like a
sexy dream in a black sheath, with lots of leg showing
and strappy shoes, her hair swept up on her head and
wearing dangling sparkling earrings, his first thought
was to skip dinner and walk her right back inside, preferably to one of the guest suites they hadn't yet tried.

"Wow, you look phenomenal."

She liked the comment, her face brightening and
those sexy lips parting into a smile. "You're looking
pretty hot yourself," she whispered. The kids were in
the next room, and they didn't need to hear the two of
them making over each other. But man, he planned to
revisit the subject the first chance he got.

But her smile soon shifted downward. "Thought I should warn you, Peter's being moody."

"Should I talk to him?"

"I don't think it would do any good. Sometimes he just needs to brood. He told me when he closes his eyes, he can't 'see' his dad anymore. His face looks blurry."

"But you've got pictures all over the house."

"Yeah, I mentioned that. I'll talk more to him later." She looked over his shoulder to the golf cart, and an amused expression followed.

Taking her cue that their conversation about Peter and his sad mood was over, he matched her sudden interest with the golf cart. "In keeping with our dating tradition, I thought we'd take the scenic route."

After grabbing some sort of black-and-gold woven shawl and saying her goodbyes, he helped her into the cart. Then he took time to appreciate how her dress rode up her thighs when she sat. He drove the cart down a deserted beach road to a secret entrance to the exclusive golf course in question. A mid-October evening, it was clear, breezy and cool, with a golden tint making everything look beautiful. Especially his date. He took the time to admire her until her eyes widened and he nearly ran up a curb.

Once at the clubhouse, which seriously hadn't been updated since the sixties—all dark colors and leather upholstery—they ordered a drink at the cozy, traditional-styled bar while waiting for their table. It felt great to have Laurel all to himself, but it took tremendous will-power not to undress her with his eyes.

A small jazz trio played quiet music in the corner. The second song in was an old standard, something easy to dance to. Their table wouldn't be ready for a few more minutes, so, to kill time, he did something he hadn't done in over ten years—he asked a woman to dance. And that woman looked very surprised.

He'd never been a great dancer, but he knew how to move a lady around a floor, and she did a fine job of following him. At least he hadn't smashed her toes or anything awkward like that. Yet. Holding her close, looking down into her dreamy hazel eyes—with that romantic old standard played halfway decently by the trio in the background—he became overcome with Laurel.

"You're beautiful," he said. "I can't believe how lucky I am."

Her lashes lifted slowly, her gaze on his, a tender smile creasing her lips. "I thought I was the lucky one."

That did it, he had to kiss her. Right then. Right there on the clubhouse dance floor, he didn't care who saw them.

Be careful. This could turn into a world of pain. Mark's mouth covered Laurel's. Kissing him was like nothing else in her world these days, tender and teasing, sexy and sweet, all wrapped into one glorious package of a man.

The nearness of Mark always made Laurel skip over the scary part, even though she knew she was in way over her head with this fling or whatever she wanted to rationalize calling it. Way over her head.

A couple of hours later, having shared the Thursday special for two—shrimp appetizers, salad, prime rib, baked potato and seasonal vegetables, and a small chocolate molten something or other for dessert—they arrived back at the B&B. They'd laughed and chatted throughout the meal, and underneath the conversation and good food, there was the constant humming of how good she made him feel.

Laurel was no ordinary date. She was special, in all the right ways. He held her back for one moment before they got out of the cart to kiss her.

"I had a great time," she said, her eyes happy and sincere.

"Me, too. Let's go to a movie next time."

"A grown-up movie? Not animated? Wow, it's been ages."

He sat in the cart, the moonlight shimmering over her hair, and he knew he had it bad, really bad, so he kissed her again.

Waltzing through the door and into the family living quarters, they found the girls asleep in bed and Peter in the TV room still up watching some sort of adventure movie, with Grandda's head resting on the couch as he snored.

"What are you still doing up?" Laurel whispered, though the TV was loud enough to wake Padraig up, if that was going to happen. The man was out.

"I didn't want to wake him up," Peter said, motioning to Padraig.

"That's no excuse. You could have left him there and gone to bed."

"But this is a good movie."

"Too bad, you'll just have to record it and watch the rest tomorrow."

While Laurel and Peter continued their heated whisper conversation, Mark noticed a drawing on the table. It was a perfect likeness of his grandfather—slack-jawed and sleeping. He stepped closer and picked it up. "You draw this?"

Though Peter's brows were pushed down while side-tracked arguing with his mother, he nodded.

"This is really good." Mark remembered the day he and Conor were running around looking for Peter when one of the kids in his fifth-period art class said he never missed, and Peter had once told him art was his favorite subject, but Mark had never had evidence until now.

"Thanks."

Laurel had shared earlier about Peter worrying he couldn't visualize his father in his mind anymore. "Ever think about drawing your father's portrait?"

Peter shot a surprised expression, and Mark worried he'd betrayed Laurel's confidential conversation.

"That's a great idea, Peter," Laurel said, easing Mark's concerns.

"Maybe even try painting a portrait after drawing one," Mark said, sensing he was onto something.

Peter still hadn't said anything, but his crinkled brows at least showed he was thinking about the conversation, so Mark continued.

"You know, my mom's a really good painter. Maybe you two can get together sometime. She's got canvases and paints. The whole works. What do you think?"

Though Peter still held back, Mark saw an inkling of interest. "That'd be cool."

"Great," Laurel broke in. "Now it's way past time for bed. Go."

Peter reluctantly set up the record button for the movie and turned off the TV, then started for the bathroom.

"Peter?" Mark called after him.

"Yeah?"

"Okay if I kiss your mother good-night?"

Silence. Then, "I guess." A resigned tone, but progress.

Mark turned to Laurel with a victorious smile. "I got the okay."

She grinned and stepped into his arms, and he proceeded to kiss her soundly good-night—until Grandda woke up with a snort and a sputter.

The two weeks after Peter had run away were like a schoolgirl's dream. Laurel and Mark quickly figured out they had her house to themselves Monday through Thursday in the mornings when the kids were safely in school, and when she didn't have B&B guests. And they took every advantage. They'd tried out each guest bed in the house, except for the honeymoon suite. For some crazy reason, Laurel considered that room sacred, like it belonged only to people who'd made vows. Especially now that she'd be joining forces with The Drumcliffe and their wedding packages.

They also avoided *her* bed, the one she'd shared with Alan for thirteen years. The thought of making love with Mark in her room, on her bed, even though the mattress had been changed, was still more than she could handle.

Mark brought back the wild, early lovemaking days she'd remembered when she'd first met Alan. She'd also transitioned from letting old thoughts come between her and the moments with Mark, to kissing them goodbye. Literally. All over his gorgeous body. Even when sometimes after he left she'd tremble all over thinking she'd opened up too much with him, that if he walked away tomorrow, she'd already feel pain from losing him. It'd happened that fast, right under her nose.

Afraid or not, it was too late, she'd crossed the line, this guy had gotten to her. The scary part about caring and suffering because of it had already occurred.

In other words, where Mark Delaney was concerned, she was already toast.

Last night, "date night," they'd seen a live-action movie with stars she knew, cussing and mature themes. So grown up. Today, Friday— with nearly a full booking for the third weekend in a row, she and Mark didn't dare mess up a bed. She wore a dress, the style Mark really liked, a fitted sheath, and a simple string of fake pearls. In the upstairs alcove, they stood snug watching through the sunlit window as the ocean rolled in and out. Mark breathed gently over her shoulder, his arms wrapped around her waist.

A storm from up north had caused the waves to swell higher. Curl tighter. The sight invigorated her. She turned in Mark's arms to capture his lips, forcing herself not to ask the dumbest question ever—*what are you thinking?*

Why ruin the moment? Their quiet time, holding each other, the tender act of simply enjoying being together. Trusting they were being honest about whatever it was they had going on. *It is what it is.* Wasn't that the popular phrase?

They'd found a secret, the two of them, like a magic balm for their pain. They could make each other feel good, without getting attached. Or at least that was the lie Laurel told herself as their days as a "couple" went along. She was toast.

"I haven't seen waves like that in years," Mark said, obvious awe in his voice.

"They look scary."

"True, but a real challenge." Things went quiet for a few moments as they continued watching the angry water. "You needed something adjusted?" He snapped out of wherever he'd gone mentally.

"Oh, yes, the honeymoon suite windows are stuck. I didn't realize it until I tried to air the room out yesterday."

"Anyone book it yet?"

"Not yet, but I've got to be prepared."

He offered an understanding smile, and, as always, it stirred up feelings she wasn't even ready to name, let alone examine.

Their biggest challenge, since they'd started having sex, was not to react obviously to each other in front of the kids or his family. Which became harder and harder with each passing day. All he had to do was walk in a room and her core tightened with longing. But her feelings went deeper than that, and that, like the big old scary ocean outside, was what frightened her most.

By Sunday morning, the high surf had made all the newspapers, and people came to the beach in droves to watch the breakers thunder onto the shore. Only the craziest surfers took advantage.

After Laurel's last B&B guest checked out, Mark, Laurel and the kids brought chairs and set up on the beach near the lifeguard station. She'd filled a picnic basket so they could all eat a late lunch together and watch the leftover waves from last week's storm roll in.

"Wow, did you feel that?" Laurel said, munching on an egg salad sandwich.

"Felt like an earthquake." Peter had an eerie look in his gaze, like he might not feel safe sitting this close to the water.

"How come they're so big?" Claire yelled over the noise.

"Yeah!" Gracie.

"There was a big storm somewhere and this is the

aftermath," Mark said, realizing the twins probably didn't understand his explanation. Another whitecap pounded the shore. Fighting an unreasonable desire to hit the water with the other hardcore surfers, Mark stayed put, eating corn chips and the egg salad Laurel had made, enjoying the extra-thick homemade wheat bread. He watched the fearless men on the boards wipe out and get pummeled time and time again, not giving up while getting the snot beat out of them.

"Why aren't you out there?" said a man nearby with a distantly familiar face.

"These little things?" Mark laughed at a mere ten-footer. "I'm waiting for the real swells."

The vague acquaintance laughed with him, but he soon became engrossed in a wave that Mark estimated could be twenty to thirty feet, the first of a swelling set in the distance. His pulse leaped to action. Wow. This was epic, once in a lifetime. He stood for a better view. Ten-plus years ago this would have been a dream come true.

With the promise of more of the same from Poseidon, a lone surfer paddled out, putting himself between the whitecaps and the leftover storm. Mark zeroed in as the surfer waited for the next mega breaker heading his way. Then, with perfect timing, he paddled, caught the wave, and surfed through a large, hollow and thick curl of water.

Mark excitedly tapped Peter on the arm. "Look at that! That guy's riding the tube. Wow. You don't see that around here."

Peter stood and cheered the guy on. When the surfer came out the other side unscathed, Mark and Peter high-fived as if they'd just mastered the curl themselves.

Swept up in the moment, it hit Mark suddenly. He

didn't have time to think things through. But he had to try it. Had to. To be out there, feeling the rush of left-over storm in his own backyard. With a seize-the-day attitude, he took off at a run to the hotel, for his board and some trunks, and ten minutes later, hyped up and ready, he was back.

He saw awe in Peter's eyes and horror in Laurel's.

"You're not thinking of trying that are you?" she said an octave higher than her usual voice range.

"YOLO, Mom!" Peter answered for Mark.

You only live once. Key word being *live*. From what Mark had seen, there'd been plenty of wipeouts, but no one had been seriously injured. Why not go for it? Maybe ride the wave of his lifetime. Outside of meeting Laurel, if this opportunity wasn't evidence of things looking up for him, what else could it be?

"I've got to, babe. Trust me." Yeah, he'd slipped up and called her *babe* in front of the kids, and his plea for trust had fallen on unhearing ears. Laurel had moved from shocked to silent in record time. She'd gone inward and didn't kiss him or wish him luck. So focused on the ocean, he ignored that, too, and amped to the max, took off for the water.

"Epic!" he heard Peter say.

After thirty minutes, several attempts and no luck, Mark saw it. The Wave. Had to be over twenty feet high from trough to crest, and promised to give him that ride of his life. He swam the board out, sat and waited, then set himself up, paddled like crazy, caught the deep face of the wave and took off. He'd never experienced anything like this on his board before. A combination of terror and sheer joy set in.

Everything was going great riding the wall, adrenaline ruled the moment and, like a bucking bronco, the

Herculean power of the Poseidon launched him and his
board off the water and into the air. Which was incredible. Like he could fly. For a moment. Until on landing he buried the nose of his board into the water and
wiped out, face-first.

He'd pearled plenty of times in his surfing career,
but never on a wave with the magnitude of a gulf storm.
Over and over he tumbled under the water, waves
pounding him down, down, down, water rushing up
his nose, stealing his breath. Adrenaline keeping him
alert. Finally, it dropped him on something hard, knocking his head. He opened his eyes to red billows. Fortunately, there weren't sharks in these parts.

As if in slow motion, the wipeout continued, tossing,
battering him, chewing him up and eventually spitting
him out on the shore. He struggled to get his bearings, but somehow made it to his feet, having no clue
where he or his board was, and not really caring about
the board. Then he felt two sets of hands under both
of his elbows.

"You okay, man?" one of the lifeguards asked.

Shaken to the core, but not about to let the world
know, he fudged. "Yeah, wow, what a ride."

Laurel's heart, like that wave, rose from chest to
throat to toes. The sight of Mark getting knocked off his
board, going under for what seemed like forever, then
showing up on the shore with his head bleeding was
her undoing. Seeing him need help, struggle to stand,
spiked her rapidly beating heart down to her stomach.
She thought she might hurl or pass out, so she sat before she could fall. The overworked lifeguards didn't
need two patients.

Peter ran toward Mark, the girls clustered near her.

She had to keep it together for their sake, but she could barely stand. She'd slipped up and fallen for him, hard. She'd ignored the warnings and overlooked the fear, and when she'd tried to be honest with herself, to admit that she'd gotten too involved with him, too soon, she'd brushed it off. Now she paid the price of caring.

Her pulse felt like a machine gun in her neck and chest. Thank God, he was okay. And she wanted to kill him for putting her and the kids through this reckless stunt. Did he not give a damn about her or them?

Walking like a zombie, she followed the crowd, because she had to know he was okay.

His stupid, stupid risk-taking had outed her. Her feelings. Behind her smiles and feigned confidence, she was still very much afraid of what life did to people. She cared for Mark, which she was in no way ready to grapple with. It was too soon after Alan. Now, Mark's rash actions had forced her to face her feelings and fears head-on, before she'd processed who they were together and what they were doing. Her carefree fling had turned into a nightmare right before her eyes. She'd been such a liar to herself.

She glanced ahead at the man lying on the sand, the guy she'd just been forced to admit she loved, thanks to his thoughtlessness. He could have broken his neck out there! Right in front of the kids. Did he even think about that?

They'd all been through enough loss for a lifetime.

On shaky legs, she approached the spot where the lifeguards were tending to his head wound and checking out the rest of his body. Seeing him on the sand—getting butterfly strips applied to the gash above his eyebrow—the pain she'd suffered by losing Alan came rushing back. Panic set in. Feeling scared to death, because she'd dared to open her heart again, she let anger take charge. She knew she could never survive losing anyone she loved, ever again.

And he'd risked his life for fun!

What'd that say about how he'd handle her love?

"He's okay, just some cuts and bruises," one of the lifeguards said, seeing Laurel and her apparent ashen color.

"It's a badge of honor, babe," Mark said, sounding giddy or maybe punchy from the beating he'd just taken.

A hazy red wall circled her. She was so angry she couldn't say a word.

Peter and the girls ran up, the spectacle too hard to resist.

"I'm fine, I'm fine," he answered their questions, sat up to prove it, looking disoriented or dizzy. Laughing. A lunatic. He had to be.

How could she fall for someone who didn't care if he lived or died?

She stood there, hands on her hips, so wrapped up in fear and anger, she was unable to show an ounce of compassion or relief. The damage had been done. Her nervous system had reverted to overload. Her worst memories ever.

His grandfather and mother jogged across the sand. Laurel barely noticed until Padraig spoke. "Are you okay, lad?"

"Mark, what were you thinking?" Maureen scolded.

Her old nemesis had returned. Fear. Now close to a panic attack, she fought the primal sound fighting its way from deep in her belly to her throat. But lost. A wail escaped her lips. She shook her head. The sound quickly turned to a scream.

Mark jumped to his feet and grabbed her. She fought

him. He'd made her like this, he couldn't touch her. From the periphery, she saw her little girls and Peter recoiling. Not because of Mark's accident, but because of her reaction to it. Like the night their father died. She'd lost control, and Mark had to fight her flailing arms before he could wrap his around her and hold her tight and stationary.

She groaned and cried, completely out of control, her nose running as much as her eyes. Unwavering, and so much stronger, he forced her still.

"I'm okay. I'm okay. You're okay. It's going to be okay," he chanted over and over, for what seemed like minutes, until she quit fighting. Whether from exhaustion or his calming effect, she settled down. He'd forced her to.

"Is she okay?" Maureen asked, concern obvious. "Let's have her sit down. Bring her here."

Mark escorted Laurel, shaken to the point of rubber-band legs, to the beach chair. He nearly had to carry her the last few steps. She thudded into the chair and buried her face in her trembling hands. Nowhere near ready to face Mark, or anyone else, she stayed that way for what seemed like minutes. Humiliated on so many levels.

"You shocked her, that's what you did, son," Padraig said, stating the obvious. "What she needs is some good Irish whiskey." The words trailed away as he headed off.

The thought of anything going in her mouth made her gag. Mark stayed by her side rubbing her back, as she shivered and dry-heaved, until finally her body began to put itself back together again. It was then she noticed she was surrounded by a crowd of onlookers. More humiliation. She'd made a spectacle of herself, had probably embarrassed her kids beyond repair.

All because she'd let herself do something she had no business ever doing again—caring for Mark.

Obligation weighed as heavy on her shoulders as the stares from the lookie-loos. She struggled to make her mouth move. "I'm sorry I ruined things," she pleaded to her kids, who stood silent with fearful expressions on their faces.

Grandda was back with whiskey, and she took a swallow, letting it burn down her throat and esophagus. She coughed. Couldn't help it.

The crowd lost interest once she'd quit screaming and yelling, and had already disbursed. Mark was still at her side, stroking her arm, concern so prominent in those blue eyes, she couldn't bear to look at him. She took another swallow of Padraig's magic elixir and began to feel warm and lighter, the nerves letting go of their choke hold. She closed her eyes and drifted, as images of the day Alan died, and the deepest pain she'd ever known, replayed.

Mark had released her demons. She'd fooled herself into thinking this, whatever she had with Mark, was different, or was easier. But losing someone she loved had left a scar so deep it would never heal. Today had forced her to face the fact she'd never be normal in a relationship again.

A minute later, "I'm sorry I ruined things," she whispered, her eyes remaining closed, accepting she couldn't do this again. Fall for someone. Ever.

Laurel's extreme reaction to his accident freaked Mark out. She'd acted like he'd tried to kill himself in front of her and the children. Which, when he thought clearly about his impulse to surf the wild waves, came pretty close to the description. Bonehead! But she'd always seemed so together under pressure. So calm about dealing with life. He'd assumed being a widow at such an early age had taught her how to roll with the punches.

He ran fingers through his wet and sandy hair. He'd messed up. Made a bad decision. And Laurel had completely lost it.

"If anyone ruined the day, it was me, babe. I take full responsibility."

She didn't open her eyes. Nor did she relax.

"Peter? Don't ever think about showing off for a girl," he said, trying to lighten the mood, but failing miserably. "That's what I just did for—" He stopped himself from saying "for your mother," realizing it might open a whole other can of worms—dating was one thing, but the fact they'd become emotionally involved, well, baby steps. Especially after insisting to Peter that they were friends just like he and Peter were friends. So he made an immediate edit to his sentence "—you guys, and look where it got me. Your mother's a nervous wreck on account of me." He turned his attention back to the shattered woman next to him in the beach chair, then dropped to his knees. "I am so, so sorry, Laurel."

His mother had taken off and now came back with a cool compress, placing it on Laurel's forehead. "This might help, dear," she cooed.

Laurel whimpered in reply, while his mother patted Laurel's hand and fussed with a few stray strands of hair around her face.

He felt useless…because the damage had already been done. He couldn't take it back. He'd been careless, and she'd paid.

Having seen her meltdown, and how devastating it was to her kids, Mark was overcome with guilt. On top of the aches and pains, not to mention the humongous headache he had, his stomach roiled. A premonition that he'd done something irreparable sent a deep chill through him.

Laurel shook her head, opened her eyes and sat up, looking like her usual self.

"You okay?" he whispered.

She nodded. "I'm fine. Sorry."

"You don't have anything to be sorry about. This is all on me."

She tried to get up, but needed Mark's help. "Peter," she said, "can you get the picnic basket and, girls, help him gather the plates and food?"

Was she back on track or faking it? Mark knew her well enough to suspect she'd forced herself into mommy mode because she had no other choice. Because of him. Once again, his stomach went sour at the thought of what he'd put her through.

The group walked her back home, his mother and grandfather taking off across the street when they reached the B&B and deposited the beach chairs on the lawn. He guided her up the walkway to the steps. She stopped at the door. "I think I'm going to lie down, if you don't mind," she said, her eyes never finding his.

"You need me to watch the kids?"

"I'll do it," Peter broke in, as though sensing his mother needed time alone. Away from Mark. And making it obvious they were a family and he was the outsider.

"If you need anything, call me, okay?" He said it to Peter, but meant it for Laurel's ears. "I'll be here in a flash."

"Is my mommy okay-oh?" Gracie asked, her voice trembling, as her lower lip quivered.

Mark knelt to answer. "She's shook up. It's my fault. You take good care of her, okay?"

"We will," Claire said, sounding far more confident than her sister.

Some teenager Mark didn't know ran up the walkway. "Sir? They think they found your surfboard."

With that, and a heavy heart, and one hell of a throbbing headache, he left Laurel and her children to themselves, and took off to find a surfboard he'd just as soon never see again. And after that, he needed a bottle of aspirin.

Sometime around seven, Laurel, feeling half human again, had showered and eaten—if two bites counted for a meal—and had gotten the kids settled in. The twins watched an animated movie, and Peter was content playing a video game. Still shaken to the core, but back in control, she texted Mark: Can we talk?

She'd spent a lot of time thinking about what she wanted to say while in the shower, almost running out the hot water heater. Then more before she took a nap.

No sooner had the message been sent than she got his reply: Be right there.

She wished she had another jigger of Padraig's whiskey to give her the confidence to say what needed to be said. Mark was a wonderful man, but today he'd reminded her of the most important lesson of her life.

He tapped on her door, and though she didn't feel anywhere near ready, she opened it and let the man she'd regretted letting her barriers down for come in. With her insides zigzagging to her toes, she led the way to the living room. Now all she had to do was explain it to him. That after tonight she couldn't go on seeing him.

Chapter Eight

Dread threaded through every capillary as Mark sat on the small sofa in the B&B living room. Laurel had made sure there was one cushion between them, which ramped up his regret. He'd pulled one of the dumbest things in his life that afternoon, thinking he could surf the mother of all waves. Nearly got himself killed, too. After the new territory they'd entered the last couple of weeks, he couldn't blame her for being pissed.

"I'm sorry, Laurel. I swear I'll never be that reckless again." He hoped to preempt her.

"It's not that easy. I wish it were." She stared out the window.

Mark followed her line of vision and noticed one of the letters on The Drumcliffe sign had gone out— HOT L—and made a mental note to fix it. How had that slipped by him? Because he'd been too busy falling for Laurel? And why couldn't making up for a stupid stunt be as easy as fixing a broken bulb in order to get back on track with her?

"I've lost so much," she said, absorbed in thought. "Then this afternoon, I could've lost you." It was a statement devoid of feelings, as though after her beachside meltdown, she didn't have any left.

He moved closer, tugged her to his side. "But you didn't."

"That's not the point." When she finally looked at him, there was such sadness in her eyes, all he wanted to do was erase it. Some way, somehow. "In that moment, I *had* lost you. It brought back every horrible memory of watching my husband die. Of seeing my kids suffer along with Alan. Of thinking I'd never be able to live without him. But this time it was you."

Now having an inkling of what he'd set off by being selfish and inconsiderate, the previous dread turned into remorse so deep it sank into his lungs, making it hard to breathe. How horrible of a person was he? "I never meant—"

"It's not the point." She flashed a frustrated glance. "My reaction is. I've still got a huge hole inside me." She shook her head. "I'm not ready—"

He wasn't ready to hear what she might say next, so he intervened. "I'm messed up, too, and I'm not any readier than you are for whatever it is we've discovered. It's just, I thought we were good for each other. I hoped we were helping each other. I thought so, anyway."

Her eyes glistened. "You made me want to move on. I let my guard down and let you in. Then today everything came crashing down when you went under that wave. I realized I'd only put a bandage over my pain. I'm not healed. I can't love again." Tears brimmed and slipped over her cheeks. The sight of her angst stabbed deep in his chest. "I can't love because I can't bear to lose anyone else, and until there is some sort of guarantee that won't happen—" her wet, defeated gaze split his heart "—I can't take the chance."

There was no way he could argue with her logic, after all she'd been through, but feeling adequate or not, he needed to try. Because she'd just as much as said she loved him.

"Laurel, I lost so many people during my tours in the Middle East, I lost count. I know it's not like losing a spouse, but I promised myself I wouldn't forget even one of them. Carrying around that burden kept me from living. That's the guy you met in the beginning. Then you came along and I forgot things when I was with you. I felt light again, smiled, started to enjoy life again. You've helped me in so many ways, I can't begin to explain."

Her brows softened, but he could still see resolve in those eyes. "My letting my guard down with you put me in a horrible place today."

"I was hoping maybe I'd helped you some, too."

"I thought you had. But today I found out I'm not ready to care about anyone else yet. The threat, or fear, or whatever you want to call it, of loss is still too real for me. It's too great for me to overcome. I can't do that again. I can't put my kids through it."

He understood her point. *But I didn't die.* He may as well have, because he'd seen firsthand how she'd suffered from the chance he might've. If he had a better handle on what it was they had going on, maybe he could fight back. But he was as confused and new at this as she was. Until he had a better understanding of what he wanted in life, and where a relationship would fit in, she didn't deserve his inflicting irresponsibility and selfishness on her on a whim. She deserved more. Better. Even so, something made him take one last stab at making things right.

"There's no guarantee for anything in life. The only way to avoid loss is to never feel. To hide out. Be a by-stander. I thought that was what I wanted until I met you. So now I'm asking, is that what you want? For the rest of your life?"

A long, strained silence ensued. He was hell bound to leave without an answer. Until recently, he'd been the master of passivity, but Laurel had helped him want to change. Not that he had, but at least he wanted to. He'd hoped he'd done the same for her. Thought maybe he had.

She stared straight ahead, not trying to engage with him. "I can't do it, Mark, I'm sorry. I'm not ready."

Evidently, he hadn't done the same for her.

"My grandfather always talks about the silver lining after our struggles and troubles. Will you at least consider that?"

That drew a quick, rye laugh. "I've fallen for the silver lining bit before, after Alan's remission. I believed it would last. Knew it would, because it had to. We had three kids. I'd believed with all my heart that our nightmares were over—only to find two years later that he'd relapsed."

"I can only imagine what you've been through, all of you."

There was no arguing the point. If she wasn't ready to live, he couldn't force her—that was another thing he knew firsthand. So he did the only thing he could. He stood and, respecting her wishes, prepared to leave the best surprise he'd found in years. The beautiful B&B

lady, who happened to live across the street. "I'm sorry about today, but I understand your decision."

Before he closed the front door, he thought he heard her crying. Torn between running back and comforting her or leaving because she'd asked him to, he honored her request.

Mark walked into his room and found Conor home, sitting on the couch watching sports news.

"You got a minute to talk?"

Inquisitive blue eyes flashed from the TV screen to his. "Sure, what's up?"

"Besides the fact I blew the best thing I've ever had today?" Mark had been changing since getting involved with Laurel, and this was further proof. Instead of shutting down or going off by himself to brood, he was glad his brother was around to talk to. "Did you hear about it?"

"I was working. Does it have anything to do with that bandage on your head?"

"Yeah, I thought I was still a kid and decided to try surfing those crazy waves today. Almost got myself killed. Right in front of Laurel and the kids."

"That's not good."

"Nope. And it didn't go over well. Evidently, I put her in shock, and now she doesn't want to see me anymore."

"You've got it bad for her, don't you?"

"Man, I didn't think I had it in me anymore, but I do. I want to be with her. But I don't have anything to offer, and now she's kicked me to the curb, so what does it matter?"

"Quit shortchanging yourself."

"Dude, I'm a fix-it guy, a handyman."

"Who could run a hotel if he wanted to."

Mark plopped on the adjacent couch and faced Conor, who clicked off the TV. "That's the thing, I didn't think I wanted to. I didn't want the pressure or to have to make decisions. But lately I keep getting ideas about how to do things better, more efficiently around here. I don't dare say anything to Dad or Mom because they'd just encourage it."

"You've always been an organizer."

"What?"

"You started the surf club in high school. And remember when we were kids and you talked Daniel and me into convincing Mom and Dad to take us to Hawaii? You got all those travel brochures and wrote up a presentation for us to give. You covered every angle, and they bought it."

Mark smiled remembering the confident kid he'd been back then. "That was a great vacation, too."

Conor laughed. "It was, and it would never have happened if you hadn't come up with ways for all of us to save money for it. That trip was because of you, brother."

A crazy image of his grandfather wearing a colorful Hawaiian shirt with equally loud golf shorts made him laugh, too. Just as quickly, he remembered how he'd been a platoon leader in the army because of his organizational skills, and how one of his decisions had put his unit in peril. How they'd taken fire for it and lost people. His decision had cost lives.

As if reading his mind, Conor leaned forward, an earnest expression in his gaze. "I know you went through some shit in that sandbox over there, man, and you came home changed. But lately you've started acting like your old self again, and I'm glad. I missed you.

You're not meant to hide out doing chores for the hotel. You've got what it takes to run this place."

He didn't want to hear it, but he also couldn't deny that lately all kinds of ideas had been popping into his head about The Drumcliffe. Being with Laurel and seeing all of the fine touches she put into her B&B had inspired plans of his own.

"What if I fail?"

"Dude, this place has been around so long, it could run itself. All you have to do is try. I think you're ready for it. And maybe it's because of Laurel, or maybe it's because you've finally gotten tired of being a slacker. That really never suited you, man. The point is, whatever the reason, it's time. Step up. You can do it."

Mark wished he had one-tenth the confidence in himself Conor had for him. "I'll think about it."

He'd meant to boo-hoo on Conor's shoulder about Laurel breaking up with him, but something had taken over their conversation and sent it in a completely different direction.

Maybe every messed-up and confusing thing that had happened today right up to this talk with his brother had happened for a reason. Maybe it was time to step up. For himself. For his parents. For Laurel...if she ever gave him a chance again.

By now his head was spinning and he couldn't bear to think of one more thing, so he thanked his brother for the talk, excused himself and went to bed.

Sunday night, a week later, the family dinner may have been more subdued than usual, but Mark had been doing a lot of soul searching and planned a surprise for his parents. He knew he looked as bad as he felt, having stayed awake nearly every night that week, thinking.

Once he told them his conclusion, they might assume he was off his nut, too.

Part of the reason he didn't have a comeback with Laurel that night was because he still didn't know where he was going. Until now he'd been holding out for some reason to take off, to escape the responsibility of the future of the family hotel. But over the past week, after seeing what he'd blown with Laurel, wanting it back more than anything in the world, something changed. He was ready to step up for the family, take on some real responsibility, prove he was a man who could be trusted.

"Mom and Dad, I just wanted you to know I'm ready for you guys to start transitioning to your retirement."

He thought his mother might fall off her chair, and for the first time in ages, he spotted a flash of pride in his father's eyes. "Any way you want to work this, we're on board, son," his father said.

"You can have as much on-the-job training as you need," his mother added. "We can start as soon as you'd like."

"Okay, then. Let's sit down with the reservation software and hotel budget a couple hours every morning starting tomorrow, and for however long it takes until I get the hang of it." That might help keep his mind off the way he'd been spending the best mornings of his life for the last few weeks with Laurel, too.

Nothing short of surprise brought a broad grin to his father's face. "You're on. For as long as you need."

"Well, that's the best news I've heard since the boys in green beat Scotland in 2015!" Grandda announced with glee.

Then they all shook on it, and Mark realized he'd officially changed. Whether Laurel wanted to be in his life right now or not, she'd helped him get here. Never one for being an optimist, he held on to the hope that Laurel might see how he'd impacted her outlook on life, too. Hopefully it would be enough to keep the door open between them, just enough.

Mark didn't let the breakup with Laurel keep him from Peter's surf lessons, either. Each Monday and Wednesday at 4:00 p.m. since the breakup, he met him at the beach, surprised that Laurel still let Peter come. At least she trusted him with something.

"Mom's been really sad," Peter said, while they waited in the water for a wave decent enough to ride.

It'd been two weeks. "The way to help her is to be there for her. Do stuff without her having to ask. Offer to watch the twins while she does the weekend brunches. You know, things like that."

"I don't understand why she got so mad at you."

"I was stupid. Listen, one day you'll have a girl you like break up with you for something stupid you've done. It's inevitable."

"Why?"

"We guys can't help it."

Peter laughed, and it helped lighten Mark's mood, but only for the moment.

"You said that you were friends with my mom like you were friends with me," Peter said, earnest as hell. "I knew that wasn't true."

They stared at each other, Mark seeing a kid who needed his "friend" to be straight with him.

"I'll be honest, I like your mother in a whole different way. Have from the beginning. That's also something you'll figure out real soon for yourself."

Things went quiet, and they watched for a wave with possibilities. The moments stretched on.

"Hey, how would you like a part-time job helping with surfing lessons for hotel guests? It wouldn't necessarily be regular work, it would depend on whether people signed up for it or not. You could be my assistant. What do you think?"

"You want me to help you?"

"You're the perfect choice. You're my friend and you can give the beginner perspective on things. I thought you might want to earn a little cash, in case there's a girl you'd like to buy ice cream for or take to the movies. You in?"

Peter's amazed expression said it all. "Sure."

"Okay, then. I'll let you know over the next few weeks what we set up."

"Okay. Oh, and just so you know, I'm not naive like you think. After I thought about it for a while, I was glad you liked my mom *that way*," Peter finally said.

Surprised, Mark gave the kid a skeptical stare. "Really?"

"I could tell she liked you a lot. You made her happy. I liked seeing her happy."

Peter's simple comments meant the world to Mark because it gave proof that he'd made Laurel happy, before he'd made his ridiculous mistake. "Except now I've made her really sad and angry."

"Yeah."

The facts were the facts. Even a fourteen-year-old could see that.

Needing a change in topic, Mark glanced over his shoulder and saw that wave with possibilities. Nothing huge, but completely adequate for Peter's novice abilities. "Let's take this one."

Peter saw the swell rising and flashed Mark an elated grin. "Let's do this!"

Later, when they walked home together, each with a board under his arm, Mark patted Peter on the shoulder when they parted ways. The kid smiled. "I'm gonna tell my mom you said hello."

It was Mark's turn to grin. "You do that," he said, heading off to his hotel room, thinking it couldn't hurt to have Laurel's son on his side.

A week later, on the first-ever Historical Society house tour, Sunday afternoon, there was a mishap at the Prescott B&B. Along with the leftover storm waves a couple of weeks back came damper weather. A second-floor door stuck so hard, Laurel had to use her shoulder and hip to shove it open. Not the impression she'd hoped to make.

"As you may know, this is part of dealing with a hundred-and-fifty-year-old house. It's always a good idea to have a handyman on staff." Which made her think about Mark for the thousandth time since she'd sent him out of her life. Not in his fix-it-guy mode, no, but for the great guy he was. The one who made her feel again. After that, she struggled to keep her train of thought.

During the rest of the tour, several other minor but annoying issues made themselves known. A chandelier flickered on and off, one particularly squeaky floorboard every single guest managed to walk over, a constant leak in the antique pedestal sink faucet of suite number three, the very one Mark had promised to fix the day they'd tried out the bathtub. Her face flushed with that memory. What couple would want to listen to that all night on a lovers' getaway?

Her mind went directly to Mark again. If they'd ever had a chance to spend the night together, they certainly wouldn't use it to sleep. But if they happened to be in that room, he would know exactly how to fix the offense. She liked that he was practical in one respect and impractical on the personal side, and sexy as hell. But more, too. Tender. Kind. Patient with her kids. Peter's self-esteem had doubled since getting surf lessons and learning how to build stuff and paint things, as Peter himself described what he'd learned from their new neighbor. And living with Peter had been easier lately, with him brooding less and drawing more. She'd even caught him playing Candy Land with the girls the other night while she checked in a couple and gave them a quick tour of the B&B. The girls had also learned to pipe down whenever she got a phone call on the reservation line, thanks to Peter giving them the high sign—a finger over the lips as he coerced them down the hall. The kid was stepping up and taking some responsibility since working for Mark.

For the last two weeks, she'd felt lost at sea, tossed by the waves, helpless, alone. Why? Because she'd banished Mark from her life. Because she was afraid. Afraid of feeling. Afraid of losing. That was no way to live. What about the silver lining? It had to exist.

She'd taken back some control in her life by buying the B&B and getting her business up and running. She'd enrolled her kids in new schools, and other than the running-away incident with Peter, she'd kept them safe and fed. The twins seemed ridiculously happy with their new bedroom and with going to school, and their new best friend, Anna. They'd be five soon. Growing up fast.

Peter was working on being less glum and his anger management had improved so much, a huge part of it due to hanging out with Mark. He even seemed to be making friends his own age. Along with developing an unlikely friendship with Maureen Delaney, over their mutual love of drawing and her giving Peter painting lessons with the special portrait of his father in progress. Again, thanks to Mark.

Laurel took a load of bedding to the laundry chute at the end of the second-floor hall, went to the next guest room, stripped the beds and repeated the walk to the chute. When the sheets and towels were all removed, she took the stairs down to the laundry room just off the kitchen to start the wash. On the way, she passed a window and caught sight of Mark. She stopped and watched as he directed a gardener where to trim some bushes and trees. It occurred to her that he used to do that himself, but she hadn't seen him out and around the hotel like she used to.

After Mark finished talking with the gardener, he went inside the hotel office, and only then did Laurel notice he was dressed nicer than usual, like when he'd taken her on their dates. It made her wonder what might be going on with him. It also created a pang of regret and pain in her stomach.

She'd broken up with him because of what she'd been through with Alan. That wasn't exactly fair.

It was time for Laurel to change. To quit letting fear and loss rule her world. Of course, it would be scary to open up to love and loss again, and yes, it wasn't just about her anymore. Not like when she'd first met Alan, and had only herself to think about. She had children to consider now. Children who'd all been through as much loss as she had, who'd experienced more sadness than any kid should have to already. Yet the girls were blossoming and Peter was coping better than he ever had since he'd lost his dad.

If life was all about moving forward, where was she? Stuck in a rut. Part of her couldn't believe she'd ever have to go through the kind of pain and loss she already had ever again. Life should be only a smooth ride from here on out, right? But the other part couldn't let go of the old helpless freefall into widowhood, the part that fought for her husband's life to the very end, then couldn't believe he was gone and would never see his children grow up. That part had ached so deeply for Alan, had grieved to the point of numbness, that it'd become a habit. Along with fear of ever going through that again.

So the question was, did she want to let those sad old habits control the rest of her life, or should she give the "smooth ride" theory a shot?

She shoved as much laundry as she could into the washer and set the controls, then went to the kitchen to figure out what to have for lunch.

She hadn't moved here expecting to meet a man, yet practically the very day she'd arrived, he'd dropped into her life to help. To make things better, and to slowly but steadily pry open her heart again. Maybe Padraig Delaney, with his silly selkie theory, had the right idea. Maybe they were meant to meet each other and fall in love. Because that was the real problem, a much greater issue than his making a stupid decision to ride a wave and possibly break his neck. Nope. The trouble was her fear of loving again. With Mark, she'd started to feel unmistakably like the young girl who'd met and fallen head over heels for Alan. Who'd walked on air when he'd told her he loved her. She and Mark may have been working up to that point, but she'd nipped it in the bud. She'd hid behind a self-righteous decision that she couldn't trust him because he'd made a huge mistake, potentially risking his life. Yet she'd asked him to stand on ladders and crawl onto her roof to fix things with little concern, when he could have gotten injured just as easily at her B&B. She'd trusted him to be careful. Then, at the beach, he wasn't.

Was it fair to punish him, when he'd obviously learned his lesson and had the forehead scar to prove it? In punishing him, she was also punishing herself, and the kids. They all missed him. Sure Peter still surfed with him, but they'd all gotten used to Mark having dinner with them a few times a week. And she'd gotten used to a heck of a lot more.

After a quick sandwich and glass of lemonade, she went back to her chores. Finishing the laundry, cleaning the guest suites.

It was crazy how hard it had become to clean the upstairs suites. To put fresh linen on the beds she'd made love on with Mark. The reminders made her body ache for him, but her pride kept him away.

She thought about the man she'd just seen delegating work instead of doing it himself, then dressed for success, heading inside for who knew what.

Mark seemed so right for her *and* the kids. Her fear had shut him out, and she'd missed him so much for the past two weeks, she could barely take it. Well, maybe it was her turn to learn a lesson and make some changes.

Yet it wasn't that easy anymore. She had to consider her babies.

She walked back down the stairs to Gracie and Claire's room, opened the door, then went across the hall to Peter's, knocked and did the same.

"We need to have a family meeting," she said standing in the middle. "Be in the kitchen in ten minutes. Girls, that gives you both time to use the potty, and

Peter, put on some clothes. Preferably ones that don't smell."

Then she went to the kitchen to pour everyone a glass of lemonade, and to figure out the best way to explain her problem of the heart to her kids.

She also set out a plate of cookies to butter them up.

Ten minutes later, with all eyes on her, Laurel leaned her elbows and forearms on the kitchen island, took a swig of lemonade and went for broke.

"So you've all noticed that Mark doesn't come around here anymore."

"Why not?" Gracie asked.

"I'm gonna get to that. When he got hurt that day at the beach and I was all upset, I asked him to stay away." She took a peanut butter cookie and nibbled a tasteless bite. "And now I miss him."

"I miss him, too." Gracie seemed all into the family meeting, sitting on her stool, looking serious.

"Me, too." Claire pushed her glasses up her nose, then took a second cookie.

"So my question is, if I asked him to come back, and he wasn't mad at me and wanted to hang out with all of us again, would that be okay with you guys? Would it be okay for Mark to be involved in our lives in maybe a more permanent way? That is, if he wants to."

"Yes!" Gracie was first to chime in. "What does perm-ma-mint mean?"

Close. It occurred to Laurel that since the district speech therapist had been working with Gracie for an hour once a week, that her language had improved.

"Forever and ever," Claire, said, snatching another bite and sitting straighter.

How did Claire know that? Both her girls were growing up.

Also, put like that, the thought gave Laurel pause. A mild wave of fear trickled through her, but nothing she couldn't handle. "Well, that's kind of right, I guess. So is that a yes from you, too?"

Claire nodded while making crunching sounds.

So far Peter either abstained or was thinking. She'd wait a few seconds more to see what he thought and how he felt about it. Because, if Peter didn't want Mark around, she'd have some extra discussions to conduct, with him alone. Maybe he wanted Mark to himself, as his friend, and she'd have to help him see and understand the bigger picture. Her children and their feelings would always come first, but there were also times, like now with Mark, where life should be negotiated.

She drank some lemonade and remembered a magazine article she'd happened to read recently, waiting in line at the market, about divorced women starting new relationships. It had emphasized that a woman's personal life and dating shouldn't be put up for a vote. It was personal business, and the woman deserved a life of her own. But that was just a magazine article, and she was a widow, not divorced, and these were her kids. All she had in the world.

"And you, Peter?"

"Mark's my friend, Mom. I see him all the time."

Yup, just what she'd expected. Peter wanted to keep Mark to himself. Okay. That changed things.

"And he seems sad about your telling him to stay away," Peter went on. "And you seem miserable." He took a long draw on his lemonade. "So if it makes both of you happy, I say yes."

When did Peter become so observant and philosophical? She suppressed a smile and the desire to hug him, but let the pride ripple through her for a second or two. Her son was growing up.

"I think it's pretty obvious I've been stuck in a rut, and I'm not sure how to go about it—you know, inviting him back."

"Make him cookies!" Gracie was on her game.

"The chocolate ones," Claire added.

"You're the one who sent him away," Peter said, on his third peanut butter cookie. "And because he's a cool guy and respects you, he's stayed away."

Clearly, she did not know this young man. "Do you know that for a fact?"

"I know him. He's a good guy. So it's up to you to invite him back." Peter glanced around the kitchen, toward the family dining table. "Have him over for dinner, with all of us. Then we'll all go to our rooms so you can talk to him alone."

Why hadn't she thought of that? "Well, that's certainly a good suggestion. I'm just a little nervous about falling on my face in front of you kids, if he wants nothing more to do with me."

"He *loves* you," Gracie piped up again.

"How do you know?" Laurel was fascinated with the girl's blossoming right before her eyes.

"When he sees you, he looks like Daisy when she sees Anna," Claire clarified.

"And Daisy *licks* Anna's face all the time." Gracie got the giggles, and Claire joined in.

Face licking? She'd thought they'd been discreet. How much had her daughters seen of her and Mark kissing? Her cheeks went warm, but she loved how the family meeting was going so far.

Truth was, she couldn't be a good example to her son and daughters if she let fear rule her life by cowering and not going after what she wanted. She'd wanted to make them proud with the B&B, and it hadn't been easy. But Mark was different. He was a person, not a building. She wanted a relationship with him, and that took two people to agree. It was a risk to ask him back into her life, and he may not want to come back.

"So now that you have our support, how are you going to bring him back?" Peter asked, leaning in, looking more like a junior lawyer than her previous temperamental son.

She wanted to burst into tears thinking that one day they'd all be grown and leave…and she'd be alone. Is that what she wanted for her life, to give it all to the kids and forget about herself?

"Good question, Peter." It seemed like it was now her duty to go after what she wanted, as an example for her children. She was an adult, right? So why did she still need backup? She finished her cookie and took another drink of lemonade, deep in thought.

"Okay, here's my plan…"

Chapter Nine

Sunday morning, Mark took a good long look in the mirror while he shaved. He'd quit walking around with a two-day growth since he was stepping up to more responsibility with the hotel. May as well look the part, even if he didn't feel it yet.

Before, with Laurel and the kids, life was chaotic. Now, on his own, it was merely a challenge. But he was willing to power through, to learn the ins and outs of the business. His parents deserved their retirement. As he shaved, he thought about the day Peter asked him to show him how. The kid still had peach fuzz, but they'd borrowed one of Laurel's disposable blades and he'd given Peter a lesson with shaving cream and all.

He'd felt a lot more alive when he was involved in Laurel's hectic life. Something else occurred to him—he wanted that back. He wanted her most of all. Yeah, he'd scared Laurel with his surfing stunt, and she couldn't handle it. Remembering what she'd been through, losing a husband to cancer, with three children to look after, he completely understood her reasoning. But at this point, two years later, was she using that as an excuse? Maybe the real fear was about opening her heart to someone new. But was he the guy? The right guy for her?

He tilted his chin up and shaved his neck, then used a warm face cloth to wash away the excess shaving cream. Maybe she'd given him a huge clue without realizing it? She must care about him or she wouldn't have gotten so upset when he'd gotten hurt that day. The question was, did she care about him in the same way he'd finally admitted he did for her?

He'd taken the first step in changing his position in life, being willing to take on running the hotel and becoming responsible for the business. Wasn't it time he went after what he wanted in his personal life, too? All he had to do was figure out how to convince Laurel that they had a good thing going on, and they should stick with it. Who knew what they might have together?

He looked at himself in the mirror again, looked hard and swallowed slowly. It was time to admit it— he wanted her *and* her three kids. The whole package. That was the kicker. And it scared him. He couldn't just find a woman and tiptoe back into getting involved over time. No, he had to go and pick one with a family. But he'd never done things the easy way.

He wiped his entire face with the cloth, realizing he'd do whatever it took to convince her he was the right guy. When the cloth came down, he smiled in the mirror. Decision made.

"You can quit admiring yourself for now," Grandda

said, appearing from thin air. "We've got a big problem in the boiler room."

Shifting gears from hotelier with an agenda back to fix-it guy, he threw on his T-shirt. Forced to push back his plans to confront Laurel, Mark rushed out the door after his grandfather, heading for the basement.

Laurel gathered all her existing nerves, the long list of needed repairs Peter had suggested she use as the excuse to confront Mark in one hand, and her backup in the other hand. The twins. Gracie was linked between her and Claire. Because, how could Mark resist her adorable girls? She'd also worn the sundress he especially liked the night Peter caught them kissing on the deck of the pub for added effect. With that and a batch of butterflies winging around her insides, they headed for The Drumcliffe.

Entering the lobby of the hotel, she spotted Maureen behind the check-in desk. When she looked up, she immediately smiled. "Hi! What can I do for you?"

"I'm looking for Mark."

"We want to talk to him," Claire said, businesslike and so grown up.

"We *need* him." Gracie went a bit further, and Laurel gently squeezed her fingers. "Ouch." She looked at her sister, who'd evidently done the same, but probably harder.

Embracing the importance of the situation—everyone seemed to know about the breakup—Maureen gave a serious nod to the little ones. "He's in the basement fixing a pipe. We sprung a leak this morning."

"Oh, maybe this isn't such a good time—" After all it took to work up the nerve to come over, Laurel was struck by disappointment. She'd been handed a chance to postpone facing Mark. But she really did want to get this over with, to admit she'd overreacted and wanted a second chance. Hopefully he still did, too. Since she'd made up her mind, every second before facing him seemed like an hour.

"No, I'm sure he'd like to see you. Take that elevator—" she pointed down the hall to the end "—to the basement, then turn right to the boiler room. He should be there."

Today was the day, no squirming out of it. The butterflies were running out of space inside.

A couple of minutes later they followed the noise and found the boiler room, peeked around the door and saw Mark. Now her breathing needed prompting. *Take a breath, blow it out.* He was wearing goggles, using an air hammer and some kind of tool to cut an old, corroded-looking pipe above the water drum. Grandda looked on. A blaring machine-gun-like sound made the girls cover their ears, and didn't help Laurel's hammering heart a bit. It was hot like a sauna in the close quarters, but she couldn't back down now. She had the girls stand behind her skirt as they stood near the exit, in case there was any danger of stuff flying, and waited to be noticed. Which Grandda did immediately.

"We're almost done here," he yelled, as if he was working just as hard as Mark. Then when the racket had ended with the metal cut made, he tapped Mark on the shoulder. "You've got company," he yelled, even though the sound had diminished.

Mark turned, obviously surprised by Laurel and the girls in the hotel boiler room. "Hey, is everything all right?" he said, dropping the tools and standing from his squat, while removing the protective glasses.

The spotlight was on her, and she couldn't even swallow. How could she talk? By sheer willpower. "Actually, no, everything isn't all right. But you look busy—" she could feel it coming…the cave "—so I'll come back later."

"We're halfway done here, but I can take a quick break. What do you need?"

She'd memorized a short speech on the way over, and, ready or not, now was the time to use it. Because it would never get easier to say what she needed to. "I'm here because I need you," she said as her lips betrayed her by trembling, as did her hand holding the list. Dang thing was shaking so much, she wadded it up and hid it behind her back.

He stared her down, while processing what she'd said. "You need me." He repeated her loaded words as if he hadn't heard her right.

There was no hiding now, and her backup team was staring at her, waiting for their mother to fix things. She nodded, feeling excruciatingly awkward.

"What's that?" He stared in the direction of the hand she'd just tried to hide.

"A list."

He motioned for her to hand him the paper.

She did, though she couldn't will her hand to stop shaking. "It's a list of all the little things that need repair since you haven't been coming around."

"Oh." He looked disappointed. "So when you said you 'needed' me, you meant in the fix-it way." He glanced at Claire and Gracie and smiled.

"Hi," Gracie said.

"Hi, kiddos."

Laurel wanted to explain that she needed him in a hundred different ways, too, but now wasn't ideal, near a boiler room with Grandda hanging around, so she kept quiet. Kicking herself for backing down.

When he took the list, their fingers touched, and the reaction was so intense, Laurel almost jumped back. He unwadded it and glanced over the words, keeping a business-only expression in place. "I've got to finish this and clean up, but I'll come over as soon as I can."

She still felt him, where they'd touched, like a lingering low-level electrical shock. She'd missed his touch more than she thought.

"Okay. Thanks. We'll go home, then, and—" she glanced at her flats because it was easier than getting caught up in his steady gaze "—wait." Did she have to sound so desperate on the "wait" part? "Take your time."

This wasn't life or death, it just felt like it.

He was onto her, she could tell by that sweet expression and understanding smile. "Give me about an hour."

Gah, an hour would be equal to eternity.

Mark watched Laurel and the girls leave, Gracie turning back and giving him a wave. Claire walking tall and proud like her mother. A sensation that could only be described as love overpowered him. She'd come here, list in hand, admitting that she needed him. He'd seen the evidence of her fear in the tremble of her lip and the shaky paper. It hadn't been easy. He didn't doubt for one instant that she wasn't sincere. Why else would she bring her girls?

Maybe Peter wasn't around to watch them? Even so, they were witnesses to their mother needing help.

She looked as beautiful as ever, and it was all he could do not to take her in his arms. Who cares who saw? But he wanted to do this right, this making-up and moving-forward business. He was filthy with plumber's grease and dirty water, and he needed to finish the hotel project before he could move on to the most important job in the world. Winning Laurel back.

His plan was to clean up, look his best. Make sure she knew how much he'd missed her, then state his case about "them" being right for each other. Not just right, either. Perfect. They were perfect for each other and if she needed evidence, he'd make a list for her, too.

He'd seen the questions in her eyes, like he was torturing her by not dropping what he was doing and running after her. He understood how hard this had to be for her. Hell, he'd nearly dropped the air hammer when he'd seen her. But he wanted things to be right when he told her how he felt, and from the looks of her anxious expression and trembling hands, she had something more than a to-do list on her mind, too.

Mark showed up at Laurel's an hour to the minute later. He'd showered and changed into a clean pair of jeans and one of his newer T-shirts. She answered the door, quieter than usual, but with a thoughtful smile on her face. How he'd missed those hazel eyes with their golden flecks and hints of green, and those bee-stung lips, which he noticed bore a light shade of lipstick. She wore some kind of loose black lounge pants and a thin purple fleece pullover.

"Get the problem fixed?"

He'd missed hearing her voice, too.

"Yeah, had to replace one of the old boiler tubes above the water drum. Was only the second time I'd done it, so Grandda was talking me through it. The hotel seriously needs a plumbing update, but until business picks up, we'll just have to keep fixing and patching." This mundane stuff was so not what he wanted to be talking about, but he couldn't just dive into the topic of the rest of their lives.

"I hear you on the business-picking-up part." Her nervous hands, wringing and unwringing fingers, were her tell. He tried to ignore them. "I'm going to have to open up Thursday nights if I want to break even. It's a good thing I have Alan's other life insurance policy as backup."

Small talk was going to rule the day, unless he took charge. First, though, he had to figure out what Laurel needed, really needed, from him. He didn't want to go the whole "we're meant to be together" bit if all she actually wanted was a few small repairs to her B&B. How embarrassing that'd be, but he figured he owed her that much for the emotional distress he'd put her through.

He produced the seriously creased list from his back pocket, deciding to go all business. "So, I see from the list you have some tricky lighting issues, a leaky faucet." He paused to catch those caramel eyes flitting around his body and finally landing on his face. "This wouldn't happen to be *the* leaky faucet I noticed a couple weeks ago, would it?"

That halted her for an instant. "That would be the one." A mild flush on her cheeks let him know she, too, remembered what'd gone on in that bathroom before he'd noticed the leak.

So this was how it was going to work. He'd actually have to do some repairs before he could have "the" conversation he really wanted. "Since plumbing seems to be the theme of the day, I'll start there." He carried his toolbox past Laurel, and couldn't help but notice how uptight she seemed as he passed. Was she afraid he was going to grab her or something? That was the last thing he wanted to do to her, make her nervous. He decided he'd get right to work and give her a chance to get used to him being there. Then maybe she'd calm down and relax enough to talk. Because talk they would, before he left today.

Surprisingly, she followed him up the stairs to suite number three's bathroom, and though she didn't talk, she hovered around him while he got set up and went to work. He had to admit her nervous energy was amusing as she flitted about pretending to be busy in the adjacent guest room. She picked this up, moved that, smoothed out the duvet, all while keeping close watch over him. He had excellent peripheral vision. Was she searching for the best way to say what was really on her mind? She was the one who'd come to him. There had to be a reason.

At some point, when he was concentrating on the job at hand, Laurel left, and later, he was just cleaning up around the faucet on the pedestal sink when she reappeared with lemonade and a plate of chocolate cookies. Always a good sign. He couldn't hide his smile, or the direct question that just popped into his head. "Where're the kids?"

With a sly smile, like the Pied Piper, she led him out of the bathroom and into the hall to the window seat. She set the drink and cookies on the small antique table there, then sat. Slowly, she lifted her shapely brows, a cue for Mark to take a seat, too. Which he did, right next to her. Now he could smell that fresh-out-of-the-shower, flowery lotion she used. Yeah, he'd missed that, too. Big-time.

"Peter offered to take the girls to see the new animated movie," she said, after he'd taken his place on the cushion she'd patted. Then she shrugged. "Will wonders never cease?"

"My grandda always says small miracles are all around. I guess we can count that as one." Then he wondered if there might be any more miracles scheduled for his day where Laurel was concerned. Instead of taking a cookie, he took her hand, thinking the time had come to take the risk. "Did you miss me?" He dipped his head, looking out under his brows and sporting half a smile—his way of acting direct but shy. He hoped she liked it.

Her gaze locked on to his. *Do you want the truth?* those eyes seemed to challenge.

Yes. He. Did. He wanted the truth, and nothing but. He was tired of beating around the bush about their feelings.

"For two whole weeks."

"You did?" You mean he wasn't the only one? A warm, simmering sensation in his chest helped relax his shoulders and boost his outlook. A small miracle?

She slowly nodded, never taking her eyes off him. "I fought with myself, too, because I still wanted to wring your neck for being so reckless. Then I realized my anger was based on lo—caring for you."

They held hands and stared at each other, and Mark wanted to think she'd corrected herself from saying *love*. But caring about someone enough to get that furious had to border on love, didn't it? Whether she said it or not. Because that's how he felt about her. He *loved* her. There was no other way to explain his feelings.

There was something else he needed to know, too. "Have you forgiven me?" He waited a beat, and since she didn't jump right in, he prodded. "Since you came *all the way* over to the hotel with this list? Or do you really just want my fix-it expertise?" he teased, hoping she'd be honest in return.

"I haven't forgiven you, because I'm still working on

forgiving myself for melting down in front of you and my kids and God only knows who else."

"My mother, grandfather…"

She covered her face in shame. "Oh, don't remind me."

His hand flew to her shoulder to comfort her. "It was my fault."

She peeked between her fingers. "You scared the crap out of me."

The leftover fear he saw in her expression made the protective part of him go nuts. All he wanted to do was take her in his arms and promise anything she wanted him to. But this was their chance to lay it all out there, to tell each other how they felt about each other, and decide what to do about it. He couldn't let anything get in the way of that.

"I'm sorry," he said. "You know I am."

"Can you forgive me?"

"For caring about me? Hell, no. That was the first time I realized you might have some feelings for me. Until then I thought we just had a lopsided thing going on where I was falling hard, and you were living in the moment."

His comment seemed to startle her. She narrowed her eyes in disbelief. "I thought you were the one living in the moment and I was the one falling."

Sweet music to his ears. "Now we're getting somewhere, babe. What else haven't you been telling me?" He tugged her to his side, and she rested her head on his shoulder. It felt so great and right to be near her again.

"We had a family meeting about you."

He lifted his chin from the top of her head. "You did? This is really getting good." All that time he'd been moping around they'd held family meetings with him as the topic?

"The kids and I decided we needed you back in our lives."

"The kids and you."

"Uh-huh. Peter said since I'd sent you away, you were being a gentleman, and it was up to me to go to you."

"That Peter is a smart kid."

"Claire and Gracie said I should bring you cookies."

He laughed. "Also smart kids. So I guess I should take one, then." He reached for the freshly baked chocolate cookies and ate one in two bites. Delicious as always, but maybe more so now, with Laurel at his side, and their world opening back up.

She laughed lightly. "The girls also said something in regards to us, and likening it to how Daisy loves Anna and licks her face a lot. I wonder how many times they caught us kissing."

"We did give them a lot of opportunities." He grinned then screwed up his face as it occurred to him. "They thought I was licking you?"

"They're still four, honey."

He especially liked her calling him *honey*.

She went tense again, he felt it in her shoulders. "I'm still not sure I can handle being in a relationship," she continued. "Family meeting or not."

"Who can? But sitting around and waiting for something bad to happen is a waste of time, don't you think?"

"If you put it like that, yes. But I have history, remember?"

"No doubt." He kissed her temple and smoothed her hair. He felt her relax a little. "Look, I can't promise to never get hurt again, or not ever get sick, life is too unpredictable for that. I *can* promise not to take unnecessary risks. But I could be the most cautious guy in the world and step into the street and get hit by a car.

The thing is, we can't control life any more than who we fall in love with." He held her tighter. She'd hinted enough about how she felt about him. Maybe he should tell it straight up, about his feelings. "And speaking of that, I *can* promise one more thing." He sat straight, held her by the shoulders so he could look her in the eyes again. "Because I've given this two full weeks of thought and made changes to my life to prove it. I can promise to love you. Already do. That won't change, whether you love me back or not. It's out of my hands. Too late, babe, I love you. So there."

"I need to catch my breath." Doe-eyed and murmuring, she reached for his face, running her fingers down his cheeks. "I came to ask you back into my life today, because I missed you so, so much. We all did. You're such a good man. Every day I panicked thinking I'd lost you, yet not having the guts to name what I felt." She kissed him softly. "That's another thing I love about you, you don't beat around the bush." Her brows shot up. "You love me? Really?"

"Want me to prove it?"

Her face flushed, her eyes fully dilated. "Yes," she whispered.

He reached for her, then led her back to guest room number three, where he'd just fixed the leaky faucet. They may have tested out the bathtub that day, but they'd never made it to the bed.

"How long is that movie supposed to last?"

Mark hovered above Laurel, ready to enter her. As always, when they made love, he'd worked her into a frenzy by giving every part of her body his utmost attention. He'd already proved beyond a doubt that he loved her. Hell, he'd said the words. Deep in the moment, she wanted him more than anything, but another urgent need made her stop him short of entry. Her hands cupped his face, forcing his wildly sex-charged eyes to delve into hers. His obvious desire jolted through her center, making it hard to speak. But she had to. She hadn't told him yet, and he deserved to know how she felt.

"I love you," she whispered, her body covering with goose bumps as she did.

His smoldering bedroom stare softened with love. They studied each other, isolating the special moment for a time. There was no doubt the feeling was mutual. "You know I love you, too," he said, then with a thrust, they came together. She swore as he moved inside her, it felt different, everything was different, and better than ever. Soon overcome with sensations and reactions thanks to the man she loved, she didn't have any thoughts at all.

Chapter Ten

After Mark and Laurel had finished a lovemaking session hot enough to grill steaks, and topped it off with a long and satisfying shower, Laurel's kids came home. It was a little after four, and she and Mark had started a real barbecue. It occurred to her that they were a couple, whether she was ready for it or not. How could she deny the best thing that'd walked into her life since Alan?

"Burgers coming up," Mark said, as the twins rushed him and hugged his legs.

"We missed you." Gracie was the first to say it, while gazing up at him adoringly. Laurel felt so full of love she didn't know what to do. So she stood and let the goodness run over her, head to toe, and basked in the sweet feeling.

Even Peter's eyes lit up when he saw Mark at the grill, tossing burgers and drinking a canned soda. "Good going, Mom. I guess our plan worked."

She put an arm around her son. "Your plan. You're the man, Peter." They playfully high-fived, and Mark noticed, a smile slanting across his gorgeous face.

"Have you learned how to grill a burger yet, Peter?"

Peter flashed Laurel a help-me glance, but she suspected it was obligatory for being a teenager. She also hoped he not only didn't mind, but looked forward to learning all he could from Mark. If she played it right, maybe he'd get a lifetime of that fatherly attention. Peter leaped down the back porch steps to join his mentor by the fancy grill. "Is this gonna impress girls?"

"Ever met a teenage girl who didn't like hamburgers?"

"Awesome." Her son grinned, and it melted her heart. Though she did worry a little about his wanting to impress girls.

Laurel went back to the kitchen to whip up a salad and check on the sweet potato fries baking in the oven. The golden moment of having her kids *like* the man she'd fallen in love with, after all they'd been through losing their dad, put a grin on her face that started deep inside. After all the years of pain, fear and sadness, they all needed this normal kind of life. For however long it lasted with Mark, she'd decided to give their relationship 100 percent of her effort and attention, because Mark deserved so much. Her mind drifted to earlier that afternoon.

Two weeks later, record waves once again hit the shores all along the central coast. Sandpiper Beach was making history, this time, due to a hurricane down south. Mark, Laurel and the kids couldn't resist taking their beach chairs and setting up for another crazy show. Sweaters on, they watched along with the other lookie-

loos on the crowded beach, while the usual suspects—
wild and fearless surfers—took on the record-breaking
waves.

After his brush with death last month, he wasn't the
least bit tempted to try one out, nor was he envious of
those crazy surfers getting tossed around and battered
by the sea. Still, he and Peter watched with awe as the
surfers seemed brave in battle with the monster waves.

If anyone should be envied it was him. He was a guy
who a few short months ago was as lost as a soul could
be, no plans, no future, no idea how to change his life.
Now he sat with the prettiest gal on the beach and a
ready-made family. A little piece of heaven right there
in Sandpiper Beach.

He'd changed into a guy with potential. Putting the
past behind—though he'd never forget his tours in the
Middle East, or his friends and fellow soldiers who'd
fought so valiantly alongside him, and those who'd been
taken out by IEDs—no, he'd never forget, but he was
finally ready to move on, to quit letting old nightmares
keep him down or hold him back. Today, those memories seemed from a lifetime ago, and he preferred the
here and now. Especially with Laurel in his life. She,
like his parents and brothers, had seen his potential
long before he had. Some days he wondered where he'd
be if he hadn't met and fallen in love with her. Good
thing she'd gotten the crazy idea to buy that old house
and open a B&B.

Surprisingly, he'd enjoyed learning the ins and outs
of the hotel business, and was thankful to his parents for
being patient with him. For the first time in over a year,
he was confident in his knowledge and business sensi-
bilities. Some days he felt ready to take on the world.
With Laurel by his side, why not, he could do anything.

He and Laurel had many conversations about how to grow their businesses, and had come up with some great plans. He'd built the perfect place for weddings, as his mother had the foresight about the gazebo on the large side yard, and Laurel had the ideal honeymoon suite. All the couple had to do was walk across the street. Putting their efforts together, they'd come up with a wedding package approved by his mother, and they'd already booked the first ceremony.

From his seat on the beach, Mark's world, like those wild and crazy waves, was filled with possibilities. His eyes flew open as far in the distance the wave of the century swelled. Everyone saw it and waited, even the kids. So moved by the greatness of Mother Nature, one particular thought came to mind: now was the time. Why not? He looked at Laurel. Like the sandwich that day at her house, her secret sauce still drove him nuts. Always would.

"I have a crazy idea," he said, grinning.

Disbelief widened her eyes, lifted her brows and turned her beautiful smile upside down. "Oh, no, you are not!"

"Oh, yes, I am." He beamed and stood, getting her full attention, though not necessarily in a good way, then dropped to a knee in front of her. "Laurel." He took her hand. "Give me the rest of your life, and I'll prove how much I love you, every single day. Will you marry me?"

That humongous wave must have crashed onto the shore because he could swear the earth moved, and people screamed in awe and clapped behind them. It wasn't because he'd just asked the woman he loved to marry him, that much he knew. All Mark saw was Laurel, with the most amazing expression on her face. A mixture of surprise and love so deep his heart nearly melted.

When the journalists wrote about the record-breaking phenomenon from the sea today, Mark would remember only one thing, which turned out to be far, far greater. His special moment didn't crash onto the shore, or make so much noise everything else got blotted out. His little miracle was a small sound that couldn't even be heard. Fortunately, he could read her lips.

Laurel said yes.

Sunday dinner at the Delaney Pub was crowded and noisy as usual and overflowing with great food, but most importantly, filled with love. Mark had never felt greater in his life. Laurel had said yes to his proposal earlier that afternoon, and now it was time to share their special news with his family.

He waited until everyone was halfway through dinner, when mouths were full and conversations had ebbed. Then he tapped his water glass with his butter knife. *Ting, ting, ting.*

"I have an announcement to make."

Curious eyes rose from around the table, none more so than Grandda's. The room went quiet as forks and cutlery went still. Eyes settled on Mark, and not surprisingly, passing over Laurel first, for a hint. Laurel looking beautiful as always, her hair shining under the pub lights, her eyes bright and dancing with their secret. She smiled demurely and looked to Mark, who sat beside her.

"I've asked Laurel to marry me, and she said yes."

Grandda's palm slammed into the table, in a good way. "I knew it!" He jumped to his feet and danced a little jig. Maureen's hands flew to her cheeks, and Sean grinned until his eyes nearly closed, shaking his head in a will-wonders-ever-cease kind of way. Mark had stepped up to taking over the hotel, hadn't he? Why should his father be surprised about this next step?

Daniel, being recently married himself, was the first to come around the table and slap his brother on the back. "So happy for you." Mark stood so they could hug.

Immediately, they all broke out of their seats, having a total hug fest, everyone hugging everyone else. Congratulations flying left and right.

It had taken a near miracle to keep the proposal private, but thanks to the distraction of a monumental wave, he and Laurel had pulled it off. He'd proposed, she'd said yes, they kissed and the kids thought they were just doing what they always did. Oblivious to the love-you-forever looks walking back to her house, her children didn't have a clue that their world had just changed forever.

Once they were all home, he and Laurel sat the kids in the front parlor and told them their plans. The twins acted like they'd just seen Santa. Peter chewed his lips and sat quietly for a few seconds, then, seeming more like an old man than a teenager said, "I hope you'll be very happy."

Laurel dropped to her knees and hugged her boy until they both cried. "I am happy," she'd said.

"I know, Mom, I can tell."

Then everyone cried and clapped, and the twins jumped up and down until Peter told them to stop it.

In the celebratory chaos, someone tugged on Mark's hand. He looked down. Little Gracie. "Does this mean you'll be my daddy or my pretember daddy?" Evidently, it had taken this long for the question to occur to her.

He bent to meet her face-to-face. "I hope you'll call me Daddy. I want to be."

Peter jumped in. "Dude, are you gonna be like my friend or my father now?" He'd saved up his question, too.

Mark threw an arm around Peter's shoulders. "I hope to be both. Is that okay?"

After giving it some thought, Peter nodded. Mark knew a longer conversation was needed about his role as a step-in dad and that would require Laurel by his side. Together they'd explain to all three of the Prescott kids exactly who he was—a man who loved them with all of his heart—and how he could never replace their real father. He wouldn't ever try to do that. While keeping their father's memory alive, he'd promise to be there for them every day, and they could count on that. But that would have to wait.

Claire pushed her glasses up her nose, standing behind her brother. Mark pulled her closer. "You're okay about me marrying your mom, right?"

"Can I be a flower girl? And wear a princess dress?"

This one never ceased to surprise him. "I don't see why not."

She beamed and threw her arms around his neck. "I'm gonna call you Daddy."

Mark had thought the best part about proposing had happened on the beach when Laurel had said yes. Just now, though, breaking the news to his family and seeing their joy, and then fine-tuning what it all meant with his future kids, came a very close second. But something still nagged at Mark.

Though Conor looked genuinely happy for Mark, he remained on the other side of the table. He'd been instrumental in Mark's regaining his confidence after his breakup from Laurel, but due to Conor's busy schedule, he hadn't been in on all the plans Mark had made. Last Conor knew, Mark was just trying to put the pieces of his life back together by taking on more responsibility with the hotel. The proposal had never been discussed.

Finally, Conor reached across the table to shake Mark's hand. "Congratulations, man. I'm happy for you." There was honest-to-goodness goodwill behind the gesture. Mark felt his sincerity.

"I didn't know I was going to propose to Laurel until I did."

"That's the guy I remember. You were always fearless." Conor's smile widened, and they hugged. His kid brother had remembered all kinds of things Mark had forgotten about himself.

He hoped Conor would find his lucky break, too. He worked hard and kept his nose clean. Plus he still wanted to buy the old Beacham house. Lord only knew what for. He was the kind of guy who needed a special lady who could understand his job, and the way he kept his heart protected since Shelby had broken it. His own special girl had to be out there. Somewhere.

Grandda bear-hugged Mark, breaking his thoughts. "Oh, my boy. Was I right? Huh?"

"Yes, Grandda, you were right. Laurel is a great girl and she's the one for me."

"You know why, don't you." It wasn't a question.

Oh, Lord, there it was, *the look*. And the story behind that look. His engagement to Laurel, in his grandfather's mind, would forever be compliments of a selkie—the seal he and his brothers had saved from orcas eight months back. There would be no arguing the point of fantasy versus reality. So Mark simply accepted it. Yeah, it was the selkie.

Fortunately, Padraig Delaney's attention had now shifted from Mark...to Conor. Poor Conor. Grandda walked to the other side of the long table and cupped the youngest Delaney brother's shoulder. With all the ruckus with Maureen, Keela and Laurel's hugging, laughing and making plans, and the little girls' jumping up and down about getting to wear princess dresses at the wedding, Mark didn't have to hear what his grandfather said to Conor. From across the table Mark read Grandda's lips, then saw Conor's brows shoot halfway up his forehead.

"Lad, you're next," Himself said with complete confidence.

* * * * *

MILLS & BOON

Coming next month

RESCUING THE ROYAL RUNAWAY BRIDE
Ally Blake

"Look," Will said, stopping to clear his throat. "I'm heading towards court so I can give you a lift if you're heading in that direction. Or drop you...wherever it is you are going." On foot. Through muddy countryside. In what had probably been some pretty fancy shoes, considering the party dress that went with them. From what he had seen there was nothing for miles bar the village behind him, and the palace some distance ahead. "Were you heading to the wedding, then?"

It was a simple enough question, but the girl looked as if she'd been slapped. Laughter gone, colour gone, dark tears suddenly wobbled precariously in the corners of her eyes.

She recovered quickly, dashing a finger under each eye, sniffing and taking a careful step back. "No. No, thanks. I'm... I'll be fine. You go ahead. Thank you, though."

With that she lifted her dress, turned her back on him and picked her way across the road, slipping a little, tripping on her skirt more.

If the woman wanted to make her own way, dressed and shod as she was, then who was he to argue? He almost convinced himself too. Then he caught the moment she glanced towards the palace, hidden some-where on the other side of the trees, and decidedly changed tack so that she was heading in the absolute opposite direction.

And, like the snick of a well-oiled combination lock, everything suddenly clicked into place.

The dress with its layers of pink lace, voluminous skirt and hints of rose-gold thread throughout.

The pink train—was that what they called it?—was trailing in the mud behind her.

Will's gaze dropped to her left hand clenched around a handful of skirt. A humungous pink rock the size of a thumbnail in a thin rose-gold band glinted thereupon.

He'd ribbed Hugo enough through school when the guy had been forced to wear the sash of his country at formal events: pink and rose-gold—the colours of the Vallemontian banner.

Only one woman in the country would be wearing a gown in those colours today.

If Will wasn't mistaken, he'd nearly run down one Mercedes Gray Leonine.

Who—instead of spending her last moments as a single woman laughing with her bridesmaids and hugging her family before heading off to marry the estimable Prince Alessandro Hugo Giordano and become a princess of Vallemont—was making a desperate, muddy, shoeless run for the hills.

Perfect.

Continue reading
RESCUING THE ROYAL RUNAWAY BRIDE
Ally Blake

Available next month
www.millsandboon.co.uk

LET'S TALK
Romance

For exclusive extracts, competitions
and special offers, find us online:

f facebook.com/millsandboon

◎ @millsandboonuk

𝕏 @millsandboon

Or get in touch on 0844 844 1351*

For all the latest titles coming soon, visit
millsandboon.co.uk/nextmonth

Want even more
ROMANCE?

Join our bookclub today!

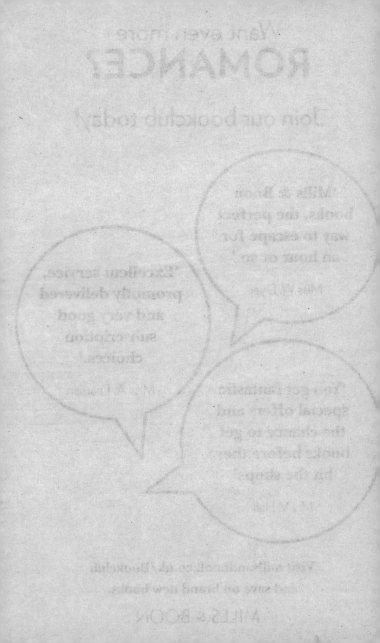